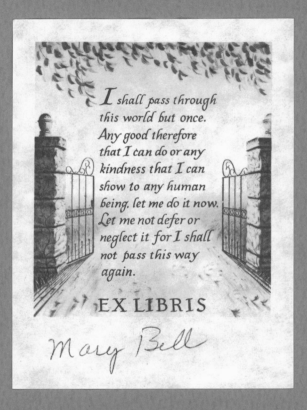

I shall pass through this world but once. Any good therefore that I can do or any kindness that I can show to any human being, let me do it now. Let me not defer or neglect it for I shall not pass this way again.

EX LIBRIS

Mary Bell

Books by Celestine Sibley:

THE MALIGNANT HEART
PEACHTREE STREET, U.S.A.
CHRISTMAS IN GEORGIA
A PLACE CALLED SWEET APPLE
SWEET APPLE GARDENING BOOK
ESPECIALLY AT CHRISTMAS
MOTHERS ARE ALWAYS SPECIAL
DEAR STORE
DAY BY DAY
SMALL BLESSINGS

Jincey

CELESTINE SIBLEY

SIMON AND SCHUSTER · NEW YORK

LIBRARY OF CONGRESS CATALOGING IN PUBLICATION DATA
SIBLEY, CELESTINE.
JINCEY.
I. TITLE.
PZ4.S5635JI   [PS3569.I25]   813'.5'4   78-26168
ISBN 0-671-22603-7

For my mother

Part One

JINCEY LAY face down on the sand beneath the palmettos and tried to cry without hollering so Sugar John wouldn't find her. The ball he had thrown, which wasn't a real ball but a rock with rags around it, had hit her back of the ear and it sure-god raised a whelp.

She caressed the knot back of her ear with the heel of her hand. It was a big one and swelling fast. She thought fleetingly of telling Aunt Scam on Sugar John but there was no use in that. Aunt Scam was Sugar John's mama and she never faulted him for anything. She wasn't anything to Jincey except a lady-to-stay-with.

She thought of her own mama and her throat hurt and one of the tears which had been puddling around her eyes slid off the end of her nose and fell into the white sand. Instead of soaking in as it rightly should it collected fine grains of sand to itself and rolled a minute in a little hollow like a glass bead before dissolving.

Jincey poked at it with interest and tried to squeeze out another tear to see if it would do the same.

Somewhere back toward the house she could hear Sugar John calling her. She ducked her head and closed her eyes against the hot white light of the sun on the sand. Even under the palmettos the sun burned through her thin cotton dress and her head hurt something fierce.

The shade of the house would have felt good, she thought, but Sugar John and Aunt Scam would be there to laugh at her for letting herself get hit on the head. It was a game, hail-over, that they were playing. She was on one side of the house and Sugar John was on the other and he threw the ball over the house, yelling, "Hail over-r! Hail . . . watchit it come OVER!" The idea was to catch the ball and run around the house and tag Sugar John with it. Only Jincey never caught the ball. Mostly she tried not to get hit with it, if it came over.

Since they had been here at this house on Santa Rosa Sound Sugar John couldn't always get the ball over the house. Twice he had thrown it through the window glass and many times through the window screens. It was the clubfooted lady's house and a bigger one than the cabin where Aunt Scam and Uncle Fox and Sugar John lived when Jincey first came to stay with them. They had come to live with the clubfooted lady and keep her company after her son and his wife were murdered.

Jincey had heard all about that and reviewed it in her mind, trying to sort out the parts she didn't understand. The clubfooted lady's son had been 'way yonder to fight a war and had married a frog. Jincey sure didn't understand that but she accepted it as something that might go with the clubfooted lady, who was so different in many ways. She was a Yankee and she talked funny and lived funny too in a high-ceilinged red painted house with screen wire all around the front gallery and over all the windows. She sure was scared of mosquitoes, the clubfooted lady was, but Aunt Scam said she'd rather be mosquito bit than to have to spit her snuff through that scrinch wire.

That was another thing, the clubfooted lady didn't dip snuff and every evening when she sat on the front gallery and had Jincey brush her hair she fussed about Aunt Scam spotting up the screen with snuff spit. She did her fussing to Jincey though and not to Aunt Scam because she was afraid Aunt Scam and Uncle Fox might move off and leave her all to herself in that big house on the Sound and not another soul in sight and the blood where the murderers came and shot her son and his frog wife still dark on the boards of the gallery.

Jincey felt sorry for the clubfooted lady but she got tired of brushing her hair, old rancid gray stuff that made her hands feel sticky and her stomach chancy.

She blew her own straight sorrel-colored bangs out of her eyes, wriggled deeper into the sand and slept.

When Jincey awakened it was to the sound of croaking and for a minute she thought it might be the frog wife of the clubfooted lady's son coming back to haunt them. She lay still, stiff and waiting, and the sound came again.

It wasn't a croak but a boat whistle, the whistle of the *Naomi Louise,* the big sternwheeler that went up the Sound in the evening and back in the morning, sometimes leaving off mail and freight at the stand built out in the deep water in front of the house. Jincey turned over on her side and saw the *Naomi Louise* was stopped at the stand now and somebody was climbing down the little rope ladder from the deck.

She sat up and watched.

Uncle Fox and Sugar John were already down at the beach pushing off in the skiff. Nobody had ever gotten off the boat at the stand since they had been living with the clubfooted lady. Mail and freight were seldom. Excitement grabbed Jincey and lifted her to her feet.

Somebody was coming coming coming. She started running toward the beach.

When her feet hit the water she stopped and, holding a hand to screen her eyes against the sun, she stood watching.

There was a person on the stand all right. And the captain of the *Naomi Louise,* seeing that Uncle Fox had heard his whistle and was in his skiff pulling for the stand, had the paddlewheel turning and the mail boat moving off. Jincey could see the figure on the stand more clearly now.

Blue. A blue *dress?*

Suddenly Jincey knew and the knowing caused her breath to stop in her narrow chest and stay there packed down and hard.

Mama.

If she didn't look again at the stand, if she turned and walked away, it would be Mama. She squeezed her eyes shut tight and backed away from the water and turned and walked up the beach in the direction the *Naomi Louise* had gone. The boat with her old stern wheel turning, whipping up a white wake behind her, was something to keep her eyes on while she willed it to be Mama.

It took Uncle Fox and Sugar John a time to get to the stand. Jincey heard the bow of the skiff strike a piling and then their voices, a woman's mingled with them. She kept her back turned and looked stolidly after the *Naomi Louise,* putting her feet down carefully in the wet sand at the water's edge.

After a long time she heard the oars dipping water. The skiff was coming back.

She stopped.

Just ahead some myrtle and palmettos came down to the water in a little point. If she got beyond that they couldn't see her and they might not call her back. Sand flies swarmed over her legs and went up under her dress. She slapped at them and shook herself, standing on first one leg and then the other. The oarlocks creaked and the old skiff wallowed through the blue water of the Sound, closer and closer to the shore.

Jincey noticed she was breathing again and wished she hadn't been. It might of helped if she'd held her breath. To hold your breath and not look was her only formula for magic.

Then she heard her name spoken, first softly and then in a loud and joyful whoop.

"Jincey! Is that my little young 'un standing on one leg like a old crane? Jincey, honey!"

Jincey spun around and started running. She heard the skiff bottom scrape the sand and Mama was running, too, her arms outstretched.

Jincey only left Mama to live with Aunt Scam and them because she had to. It was in the agreement Mama and Papa made when they parted that they would go halvers on Jincey.

They were living in the house on Intendencia Street in Pensacola when Mama swept Papa out. Jincey should have known it was coming and part of her did but the other part wanted Mama and Papa to be together and to have a house that didn't change all the time. So she did whatever she could think to do to keep them from parting.

The trouble was that Mama pure-tee couldn't stand laziness and Papa was about the laziest man in the world. He didn't have a job and he wouldn't look for one on account of it made his legs hurt. Once when he had been very young Papa had cut crossties for the railroads in the river swamp and wading in the water had caused his legs to break out with sores that wouldn't go away. That had learnt Papa a lesson about trying to work.

Mama got a job as a saleslady in a jewstore up on the square and went to work every day leaving Papa and Jincey to batch for themselves. It had been kind of nice having Papa stay around the house. He made Jincey a board seat in the fig tree in the backyard and sometimes she would sit high up in the tree and he would lie on his back in the shade on the ground and they would sing songs like "You Gotta See Mama Every Night" and "My Country 'Tis of Thee."

Sometimes Papa whittled, turning any piece of wood he found into fragrant white shavings which Jincey collected and played with. If they were long ones she could hang them over her ears and pretend they were golden curls. Sometimes they walked over to the city dump and looked for things. The dump smelled something fierce because people in Pensacola liked a lot of fish and shrimp and oysters and when the hot sun hit an old fish head it was enough to give Jincey's stomach the jump-and-runs. But Papa didn't mind. He would take a stick and poke at a fish head and tell Jincey it had been a mackerel or a flounder or a mullet. She shouldn't take on over the smell of rot, Papa said, because it happened to everybody and everything sooner or later and it was just one of the Lord's mysterious ways of handling things.

"All are of the dust and all turn to dust again," Papa said.

And Jincey, recognizing it as one of Papa's Bible sayings, said promptly, "Saith the Lord."

"Saith the psalmist," Papa corrected her, but he smiled when he did it because he didn't want her to feel bad about guessing wrong again.

One of the things Jincey tried to do to smooth things between Papa and Mama was to let Papa do this Bible talking to her so he would hold back on it around Mama. Jincey kind of liked Bible talk, even if she didn't understand most of it, but Mama would grit her teeth and leave the room when Papa started speaking scripture. If she didn't leave the room she would say one of the words she wouldn't let Jincey say, like "Puke!"

Mama didn't even like the things they brought home from the dump. They stunk, she said, and she would put them back in the garbage. But she did let Jincey keep a blue granite cup that was perfectly good except for a little crazed place in the enamel on the inside. The crack was kind of star shaped and a good place for filth to collect, Mama said, but Jincey loved it so much Mama boiled the cup on the stove in soapy water for a long time and that seemed to make her feel better about it. She would let Jincey drink milk and water out of it and would smile to see her gulping it down fast so she could glimpse the cracked star in the bottom.

Mama didn't smile much when they lived on Intendencia Street. Standing on her feet all day in the jewstore was causing her insides to fall down in her, Papa said, and if you put that with the way she drove herself to wash and iron their clothes and scrub the floors and sweep the yard and plant flowers and cook their food you had a sweet cream woman about to clabber.

Papa explained that to Jincey one day when they sat on the front steps waiting for Mama to come home. The way Mama dug the weeds out of the yard and planted flowers was vanity-vanity, he said, because weeds was as much God's doings as flowers. And he aimed a stream of tobacco juice at a four o'clock by the steps.

Mama didn't see her flowers wet down with brown spit when she come home, it was too dark. But when she got up the next morning and went back in the kitchen to fix their breakfast she saw that Papa had peed in a vase during the night and that did clabber her.

Papa was asleep in his clothes on a cot in the kitchen. He didn't like to strip and expose his nakedness and Mama wouldn't let him sleep on her clean sheets in the front room so he was on his cot by the stove when Mama saw her rose-painted vase some of her kinfolks had given her was full of pee.

"You sorry, no-'count good-for-nothing!" Mama said in a low mean voice. "Too lazy to get up and piss out the door!"

She slammed the vase against Papa's head and it broke, pouring pee all over him. Then she grabbed the broom and started beating on him. Papa was a big man, the tallest and broadest Jincey had ever seen, and it took him a time to get his long arms and legs to moving and to stand up.

He didn't hit Mama back or anything. He just towered above her and stood wiping the pee off his head with his hands and waiting for Mama to stop hitting him.

"You're a damned fool, that's what you are," Mama said between clenched teeth. "Get out of here *now* and don't you ever come back!"

And she swept him out of the kitchen and into the backyard with the broom like he was a shovel full of trash.

Somehow he got his cap as he left and put it on his head and then he stopped outside the window and looked in at Jincey sadly.

"He who calls his neighbor a fool shall be cast in hell's fire," he said.

Jincey worried some about Mama and hell's fire but not as much as she worried about where Papa would go and what he would do for a place to live and rations to eat. Mama would know how to beat out a fire but Papa wasn't much of a hand at managing.

She didn't say anything to Mama about her worries because Mama was busier than ever after Papa left. She had to take Jincey to work with her and it meant washing and starching and ironing dresses and rolling Jincey's hair up on kid curlers every night because Mama was determined that her young'un would look good to the other salesladies at the jewstore.

Jincey couldn't stay in the store but there was a park right across Palafox Street from it and she could play there and Mama could look out and see her and wave at her now and then. Sometimes she would have a nickel to give Jincey so she could go three doors down the street by herself to Kress's and buy a celluloid duck to float in the fountain in the park and at noontime Mama would come out and bring their lunch and they would sit in the shade on one of the iron benches and eat it.

Jincey liked those days in the park. The sun was hot but the fountain made a pretty sound and under the magnolia tree the ground was greenish with moss and cool. Jincey pretended it was her house and played there until the walkingstick man, who came every day and sat on one of the benches, started talking to her.

He was a smiley man and he said he liked little girls and to come and sit beside him. He smelled flowerdy and he gave her some of the purple plums he had in a paper sack and when she asked him why he always walked with a stick he said one of his legs got shot in the war.

Jincey would have liked to know which was the shot leg and maybe see it but trousers covered both and she couldn't tell by looking. So she didn't ask but sat quietly by the man, swinging her legs and answering his questions about where her mama and papa were. Papa was gone and Mama was at work, Jincey said, and he told her he had a nice room near the park and he would be glad to have her come and visit him and see some of the play-pretties that he kept for his friends to enjoy.

"Have you ever seen any ice skates?" he asked and Jincey shook her head. She knew about sidewalk skates because she had wanted some for Christmas when some of the big children on Intendencia Street got them but she didn't know about ice skates.

The walkingstick man talked then about far-off places where water like that in the fountain and even in the bay would turn hard and shining like silver from the cold and children put on skates that had wings on them and soared across it like birds flying or white-sailed schooners riding the wind.

It sounded so fine Jincey wanted to go right away and see the ice skates and the walkingstick man smiled and squeezed her arm with his fingers and stood up to go.

But she didn't get to see the skates after all and she never came to spend the day in the park any more. Mama was watching from the store as she started to walk away with the man and she came running across the street and grabbed Jincey by the hand and pulled her away.

For a long time Jincey felt bad that she didn't get to see the ice skates but years later when she did see some she was disappointed. They didn't have wings on them at all nor even rollers but some skinny blades that she couldn't even stand up on.

Mama told her the man in the park was a Stranger and she

shouldn't talk to Strangers or go off with them anywhere because sometimes they hurt you. After that Jincey stayed at home all day in the house on Intendencia Street while Mama worked.

It got lonesome sometimes without Papa and one time Jincey asked Mama where she reckoned he'd gone.

"Putting up on his kinfolk somewhere," Mama said shortly. "He's got a plenty of them and they won't turn him off because he's 'Little Howie.' "

Mama spoke mockingly and made a face when she said "Little Howie." It was maybe a funny name for a man taller and wider than most doorways but Jincey could understand it. Papa's kin-folks started calling him that before he had grown out of being littler than his father, Big Howie.

Cold weather was coming on and Mama worried about Jincey staying by herself. It was dangerous for her to keep a fire in the grate in the front room and they both knew she wasn't going to stay in bed under the cover all day the way Papa sometimes did.

"I'll think of something," Mama said and Jincey knew she would. It was what Mama always said when they didn't know what to do next about something. And pretty soon she did think of something.

Not long after that a pair of old Strangers, a man and a woman, came to the house one day and told Jincey her papa had sent them to get her. They were in the front room looking around when Jincey came indoors from sweeping off the back steps.

"We're like your papa's kin, been knowing him all his life," the old woman said. "We come to git you to stay a spell with us. Won't you like that?"

Jincey eyed them carefully, her green-flecked eyes peering out from beneath a ragged fringe of rusty bangs.

"Might," she said cautiously.

"Well, hep me git your clothes together," the woman said. "We got a boat to ketch."

Jincey looked down at the old lady's black shoes, which were dusty up to where the high tops lapped over her black cotton stockings. She kept looking at the shoes and edging toward the door and when she was in reach of it she grabbed the knob, pulled it open and tore off running toward Palafox Street, the jewstore and Mama.

The day was chilly but she was dripping with sweat and panting hard when she rounded a corner and saw Mama coming toward her.

"Jincey! Jincey!" Mama cried, running to meet her. "What in the world's the matter?"

"Two old Strangers, Mama!" Jincey gasped. "Two dusty old Strangers are trying to git me!"

By now Jincey was sobbing and Mama grabbed her and knelt down on the sidewalk and held her in her arms.

"Don't, honey, don't," she begged. "Nobody's going to hurt my young'un. They're practically your kinfolks. Aunt Escambia and Uncle Fox. Been knowing your papa since he was born, near neighbors to his folks. They're good people and your papa wants you to go over on the bay and stay with them a while so he can see you. It's the only way he'll agree to leave us alone, Jincey, if we go halvers on you."

Mama looked about to cry herself and Jincey couldn't stand that. She buried her face in Mama's shoulder and tried to swallow her sobs.

The old Strangers came walking up then, looking red-faced and upset, and Mama smiled up at them.

"She didn't know," she said, hugging Jincey. "I told her to be careful about strangers and she didn't know you. I should of made you wait till I could get off work and go with you to tell her about going to your house."

"Pewter, you ought to be paddled on the stern," the old man grumbled, reaching out a hand to Jincey and looking more good-humored than he sounded.

Mama pulled Jincey closer and gave him a quick look out of her bright brown eyes.

" 'Pewter,' as you call her, gets paddled on the stern by me and nobody else, Fox," she said. "She's a good child, a minding child, and you won't have any trouble from her if she goes home with you. But nobody's going to hit my young'un except me. Is that straight?"

The old man looked embarrassed and withdrew his hand. The old woman shifted her snuff stick to the other side of her mouth, spat into the gutter and said briskly, "Now Della, all young'uns need the peach switch now and then. We put it to our own and you'd not want us to be sparing it and spiling Jincey, would you?"

Mama smiled. "I know you would mean well, Scam," she said. "But *nobody hits Jincey* excepting me. Now if you don't want to take on looking after a child you can't spank that's all right. I'll thank you for your offer but Jincey'll stay right here. Give the word to Howie when you get back to the bay."

Mama stood up and smoothed her dress and touched her hair and reached for Jincey's hand. Jincey looked at her and swallowed hard. Mama . . . oh, Mama . . . she thought. And her throat ached with love.

Papa had been at the dock to meet them when the little launch brought Aunt Scam and Uncle Fox and Jincey to Swenson's Landing. Long before the boat docked Jincey could see his tall frame leaning against a big mossy oak tree at the edge of the water or hunkered down in the shade at its base. Whittling, she thought, and was glad Mama couldn't see him.

"If he'd only make something!" Della used to rage. The uselessness of Papa's turning sticks into shavings which weren't good for anything except to make a mess drove her wild.

But Jincey was glad that he was there on the point of land where the dark trees grew down to the water's edge and nothing else in the little cluster of store buildings and dock and boats was familiar except him. He threw down the stick and folded up his knife and put it in his pocket and walked out on the wharf to meet them as the boatman killed the engine and let the launch ease in to the landing. The man threw the line to Papa and Jincey was relieved to see that he caught it and looped it around a post.

The boatman said he was much obliged to Papa but Papa didn't answer him. He was stooping down and reaching his long arms to lift Jincey out of the boat and on to the wharf.

He smiled at her shyly as he set her down.

"I'm glad you come," he said briefly and turned to help Uncle Fox with the suitcase Mama had packed Jincey's things in.

A gangling boy sucking Dime Brand sweet condensed milk through a hole in the can came out of the store at the end of the wharf and Aunt Scam told Jincey that there was the youngest of her six boys, Sugar John. He had brought the oxcart to meet them, she said, and they'd be home and eating supper in no time at all.

The boy didn't speak to Jincey but when the grown folks weren't looking he rolled his eyes back in his head and let his tongue hang out the corner of his mouth in a way that made Jincey uneasy that he might be having a fit. He was a white-faced boy with pale eyes and the strings of hair that stuck out from under his knitted cap were dirty white too.

An old hound, liver spotted and sad faced, was lying under the oxcart when they got there.

"This here's Wink," Aunt Scam said. "Something put out one of his eyes when he was a puppy so we named him that. He ain't much use to hunt but he's a right good ketch dog."

"Good to ketch a biscuit," Uncle Fox said and Papa laughed politely.

They couldn't all ride in the oxcart because Charlie, the bull yearling, wasn't very big and the two-wheeled cart itself tilted backwards and creaked and groaned and lurched over the rutted sandy road like a wounded animal being dragged along. Aunt Scam and Jincey started out in it with the tallow-faced boy driving and Papa and Uncle Fox walked along behind. They went past a row of houses facing the bay and a white church with red and blue trimmings around its windows and doors. There was a graveyard next to the church and Jincey could see some of the graves were covered with pretty shells and one of them, a very small grave, had a china doll leaning up against the wooden cross at its head.

The road turned inward away from the bay after a little while and Aunt Scam took that as a signal to get out and walk.

"When you are in sight of the settlemint womenfolks ride,"

she said to Jincey, "but now we can get out and walk. Pull off your shoes, young'un, and let your toes take air."

Aunt Scam pulled off her own dusty high-topped shoes and stockings and carefully removed her hat and set it on Jincey's suitcase in the wagon. Bareheaded and barefoot, Aunt Scam looked younger and right dauncy, Jincey thought, and she smiled at her and took the hand Aunt Scam offered her to get out of the wagon.

The menfolks climbed in and Aunt Scam and Jincey took a wagon rut each and followed along behind. The evening was cool and the dust in the road was powdery and fine and felt like silk between her bare toes. Live oak trees grew close to the road and last year's leaves, which had fallen during the summer, mixed with the sand looking brown and polished as beetle wings.

Papa, hunched over in the cart, looked back at Jincey and smiled. He still wore the blue serge cap he had put on the morning Mama swept him out of the house and something about the pointed bill over his eyes put Jincey in mind of a young boy. His mouth, even smiling, quirked down at the corners like he might cry. Suddenly Jincey wanted to do something for him. She walked faster to get close to the wagon and leaned toward him and said softly, "Your legs hurting you, Papa?"

He nodded. "Some. But they'll ease up now that I'm riding."

Jincey meant to walk all the way so Papa could ride but the trip to Aunt Scam and Uncle Fox's was longer than she knew and night came on and after a time Papa got out and lifted her back into the cart. She tried to sit up straight but she felt her head bobble and finally she scrunched down beside her suitcase and slept.

A terrible quavering, chilling screech jerked Jincey awake. She opened her eyes to darkness and the lurching of the cart and the cry came again, beginning low like the mournful howl of a hound dog and rising and trembling in the darkness like the scream of a hurting woman.

For a minute Jincey couldn't remember where she was and fear held her stiff and still. A gritty corner of her suitcase jabbed her in the cheek and she remembered and sat up.

"Now see what you done, Sugar John," Aunt Scam said. "You woke Jincey."

The boy on the wagon seat laughed and a gargling noise started low in his throat and the awful piercing wail rose up and quivered in the air again.

"Don't let it scare you, honey," Papa said and Jincey saw he was walking close behind the cart with Uncle Fox. "It's just John's way of letting them at home know we're coming."

"Ain't done it!" the boy said promptly. "I'm scaring off painters. Big ole painter lives in the river swamp, comes up at night and gits in that hickory tree. One time I passed here and he purt' near jumped on me and Charlie."

"Painter bite you, John, he'd go off snaggle toothed," Papa said.

"Damn right," the boy agreed smugly.

"Painter claw you to death before he'd taste your meat," Uncle Fox put in.

Jincey shivered and wished for Mama. Whatever a painter was —and she sure didn't know—she'd feel safer about it if Mama was in the wagon. She peered anxiously into the dark branches of the trees arching over the road but nothing stirred there and in a little while the trees gave way to open sky and they rounded a turn and entered a lane leading between two open fields.

There was a light at the end of the lane.

"Well, Howie, there's pore-do," Aunt Scam said cheerfully. "I reckon you all will be glad to see some vittles. I know I will. Ain't et a bite since we left home before day this morning. Hellfire's cooked, ain't she, Sugar?"

"Shore, she's cooked," Sugar John said, adding on the little giggle Jincey had begun to notice went with anything the boy said.

The house was two houses, a black boxy shape showing no light, connected to a log cabin by a little bridge. Light from a kerosene lamp made the door to the cabin a soft yellow patch of brightness and Jincey, feeling stiff-legged from sleep and grainy with dust from the road, rubbed her eyes and allowed herself to be hoisted from the wagon and led in.

Warmth from a big black iron stove reached out into the room

22

and Jincey walked toward it, not seeing the woman in the rocking chair in the shadows at first. Aunt Scam bustled ahead, hanging her hat on a peg next to a string of dried peppers on the log wall, rattling stovelids and poking up the fire and talking. The woman in the rocking chair was her sister, she told Jincey as if the woman couldn't hear or wasn't there.

"Her name is Ellighfair," she said. "Ain't that pretty? Our Mama had a hand for names. Master woman ever I saw. I was the first one born when they got here from the old country and she named me Escambia County Florida because that was where they landed. I reckon she would of named the next one Santa Rosa County Florida for where we settled but she was homesick by that time and named her Ellighfair for somebody across the water. It ain't easy remembered and somebody called her hellfire and that took. You can call her Aunt Hellfire."

Jincey peered shyly at the tall thin woman who sat in the rocking chair, moving it rapidly back and forth and smiling at her with a steady unwavering smile. She had pale yellow hair in a braid over her head and white bony hands clasping the arms of the chair. Suddenly she stopped rocking and held them out to Jincey.

"God love hit!" she cried in a high sweet voice. "A baby child no bigger than a washing of soap. Come here, come to me!"

Confused, Jincey turned to look behind her for Papa. He was standing in the doorway and he smiled.

"Go ahead, she won't hurt you," he said.

"I ain't no baby," Jincey started to say, looking up into the woman's face with its wide deep blue eyes fixed on her with fearful brightness and intensity.

"Aw, she's loony," put in Sugar John snickering. "She calls everybody a baby child since her little wood's colt died."

"Shut your mouth, John!" Aunt Scam yelled and the woman in the chair burst into tears and ran from the kitchen out into the darkness.

"Now see what you done," Uncle Fox put in wearily. "For the love of the Lord, let's have some peace in this house. You all wash up and we'll get at the vittles, Howie."

Papa took Jincey by the hand and led her out on the gallery

where there was enough light from the open door to see a water-shelf and a bucket and a dipper. He poured water into the tin washbasin for Jincey and handed her a bar of lye soap and she lathered her hands and splashed cold water on her face. Out in the darkness somewhere she heard the sound of somebody crying. As she dried her face on the sour-smelling flour sack hanging from a nail by the shelf she asked Papa if it was Aunt Hellfire.

Papa was busy washing his own face and hands but he always answered Jincey sooner or later.

"I expect so," he said. "Hellfire does a heap of crying. She sinned and her sins have found her out."

"I declare," said Jincey in a tone she borrowed from Mama and felt sounded grownup, without understanding what Papa was talking about or really caring in the darkness and strangeness of this place.

When Papa talked of sin it was always scary. Nothing good come of sinning but it didn't seem right to have a little horse die just because a lady sinned.

"I'm sorry her colt died," she offered as she handed Papa the drying sack.

Papa stopped drying his face and looked at her a moment. "It wasn't . . ." he started and then he stopped. "A wood's colt, honey, is . . ." He hesitated again and then he put down the sack and took Jincey by the shoulders. "Don't say anything about it. Don't let the words pass your lips. As long as you stay in this house never say a word about a wood's colt. Promise."

"All right, Papa," said Jincey, awed by Papa's manner. "I won't even talk about horses at all if you think it makes that lady feel sorry."

Papa sighed and took her hand and led her back into the kitchen. Aunt Scam had moved the lamp from a shelf by the stove to the middle of the long oilcloth-covered table where there were plates turned face down over wooden handled knives and forks. She directed Jincey and Papa to sit on the bench next to the wall and she poured Jincey a glass of milk still warm from the cow.

Aunt Hellfire was not back from crying but she had cooked

biscuits and fried smoked meat and there was a bowl of stewed dried peaches in the middle of the table. Jincey ate hungrily, liking the way the crisp salty meat with the rind on it tasted with the sweet peaches and the warm milk.

When she felt full she leaned her head against Papa and looked drowsily about the room. The yellow light of the lamp made black streaks of shadows along the long walls but where it fell on the side of a log she could see a lot of things—a turkey wing fan and cow's horns carved to make blowing horns, long guns and an intricately carved walking stick, more peppers and bunches of other dried plants. The grown folks talked and sopped up the juice from the peaches with their biscuits and Jincey never knew when she fell asleep.

Jincey woke up the next morning on a pallet made of quilts on the floor of the front room of what Aunt Scam called the living house, to separate it from the log kitchen which she called the cook room. Papa had slept beside her but he was up and gone and Aunt Scam said he went a-looking for work. He would be back, bringing her a pretty and Jincey was to make herself at home.

Nobody else was in the kitchen when she went in for breakfast, her face feeling tight and stingy from a washing at the water-shelf. She ate biscuits and fried meat again and drank warm milk and Aunt Scam showed her how to wash her plate and cup in the big gray granite dishpan on the stove and turn them back down on the table for the next meal.

Jincey had slept in her dress, one of the good ones Mama had made her for Sunday, and she worried that she should have changed it. She mentioned it to Aunt Scam and the old woman looked at the trimming on the collar and the little flowers Mama had embroidered in the corner and she laughed.

"Change, I reckon!" she said. "I ain't no hand to wash and arn. Never have been. While you're at this stay-place, Jincey, you can wear a frock a week and keep it as clean as you know how. That's the way I raised my own young'uns and it's a good enough way."

"Mama says . . ." Jincey began, thinking how Mama made her

bathe herself and put on clean clothes every afternoon, even if she was in the house by herself.

"Mama says . . . Mama says . . ." Aunt Scam mocked. "I got a idy what Della says. She is a proud woman, always has been. That's where her and your papa differed."

"Mama's *good!*" Jincey cried heatedly and Aunt Scam laughed again.

"Good and proud, I'll say," she said. "I recollect how when she married your pa and come to the bay to live she painted the house where your grandpa lived, inside and out. Put up wallpaper and made scrim curtings for every winder and flowers everywhere . . . even had 'em setting in the fireplace in the summertime."

"I wish I could see that house," said Jincey wistfully. "Mama said I was borned there."

"You was," said Aunt Scam. "When you come into the world I went over to see you first thing. Picked a bunch of red flowers I found blooming along the road and carried them to you. Young'uns like red and I vow you smiled at them flowers even though you was less than a week old."

Jincey looked at Aunt Scam with new interest. She had known her as a little baby and brought her flowers. It made the old woman seem closer and nice.

"But you can't see much of the house," Aunt Scam went on, "because they ain't much of it left. Hurricane got it the fall after your pa sold it. Blowed off all but one room. Last folks to live in it picked up and pulled out. It ain't the house it was when your grandpa lived and your ma come and started ordering off from the catalogue and fixing up."

Aunt Scam went to the open kitchen door to spit snuff, which was filling her mouth and making her talk sound gurgly. She was barefoot and wearing a shapeless dress that hit her ankles and was the brownish color of the Railroad Mills staining the wrinkles from her mouth to her chin.

"Come on and change your dress," she said. "I got to go look for Hellfire and you can come with me."

Jincey's clothes Mama packed were still in the suitcase and they mostly stayed there. Aunt Scam looked at the dresses with

27

the lace-trimmed bertha collars and the little drawers that buttoned to underbodies and snorted. Her stubby brown hands fingered the hair ribbons gently but she packed them all back and pulled out a gingham every-day dress that Mama made and gave it to Jincey to put on.

"It's got bloomers to match," Jincey said.

"Bloomers?" Aunt Scam looked puzzled and then she laughed. "You mean drawers? Child, ain't a bit of use in wearing them around here. Just makes more washing for me. Till cold weather comes you best wear one thing at a time."

At first Jincey felt funny going about without drawers and an underbody and for a time she worried when her dress got dirty and she couldn't change it. But after a while she got used to the free way her body felt with no buttons or elastic or underbody straps to bind it. The dirt rubbed into her gingham dresses, gradually dimming their colors and blending into the dark checks so that everything she wore came to be the same color. She was glad to skip the daily pain of having a topknot of her hair scooped up and combed and plaited and tied with a big butterfly bow of ribbon the way Mama did it, checks for everyday and pinks and blues and yellows for Sunday. Only there were no Sundays at Aunt Scam's. Her hair hung down and for a time she brushed it herself every morning with the little blue painted hairbrush Mama bought her one time. But as the days passed she began to forget and nobody reminded her.

Aunt Scam spent a lot of time riding her mare, Beck, around the woods. She had no saddle but she would fold a corn sack and put it on Beck's back and leap astride as easily as one of her sons did. Jincey learned to climb up behind Aunt Scam and they rode to round up the two milk cows that grazed freely in the woods or to the little grove across the field to look for Aunt Hellfire.

Sometimes Aunt Hellfire lived with them and cooked and cleaned up the house and sometimes she would be missing for days. When she didn't come back Aunt Scam would put the bridle and the corn sack on Beck and they'd ride over to the little house and tell her to come back. Sometimes she would be sitting on the steps and she would smile and wave at them and follow

Beck home. But sometimes the door would be locked and she wouldn't answer and Aunt Scam would go get a jar of milk and a piece of cornbread and leave it on a tin plate by the door for her.

There was no furniture in the little house but Aunt Hellfire had scooped up oak leaves and filled a couple of corn sacks to make her a bed and she had a square meat can on the shelf on the porch containing a single periwinkle plant. She watered it regularly and moved it in the house when the cold nights came and frost was in the air. Aunt Scam said Aunt Hellfire was plumb foolish over flowers and once had planted a yardful at their house, making circle and diamond-shaped flowerbeds all over the yard and hauling up creek sand to whiten the places between. But Sugar John had turned the hogs in and they had rooted them all up.

"He like to busted laughing," Aunt Scam said fondly, "but Hellfire don't understand young'uns, being what you might call a old maid. She cut up a right smart and didn't come back from her old house for a week."

Jincey didn't see why Aunt Hellfire couldn't stay at the little house in the woods since she loved it so much but Aunt Scam said she didn't have a living or a man to farm for her and she had to share what Uncle Fox made for them all.

The house was all she owned, left to her by their daddy. Once her and her intended, a Swede boy from over at the landing, had planned to get married and live there but he went to the war and got killed.

"I'd give her a shoat and six hens and a rooster," Aunt Scam said, "and she was sewing and fixing up stuff to start off. But then she got the word that Brock was dead. She's been what you might call off-and-on ever since."

Jincey liked Aunt Hellfire and sometimes when Aunt Scam and Uncle Fox and Sugar John left home to go a-fishing or to spend the day with one of their married boys she and the pale yellow-haired woman played together. Once Aunt Hellfire cooked syrup and they had a candy pull and once she made Jincey a rag doll with shoe button eyes. Best of all was the playhouse they marked off on the ground under the chinaberry tree. Aunt Hellfire took a gallberry brush-broom and showed Jincey how to sweep the place clean of leaves and sticks and then they took a hoehandle and drew walls and partitions with spaces for doors and windows. They drove stobs in the ground to make shelves and tables to hold the bits of broken crockery dishes and they fashioned a center table for the front room. Aunt Hellfire said they ought to have flowers on the center table and they went into the woods and looked but the frost had killed everything. In the end they picked some gray rabbit tobacco, which Aunt Hellfire said was as pretty as a flower anyhow, and put it in a blue Vicks salve bottle and set it on the table.

Sugar John had to hitch up Charlie, the ox, and go to school some and it was a long time before he noticed the playhouse and tore it up. He had a long whip he was learning to crack and he made a game of standing on the back gallery and twirling the whip around and knocking down the little shelves and tables and sweeping the Vicks salve jar and the rabbit tobacco and all the pretend dishes to the ground.

Jincey started to cry when she saw it happen but Aunt Hellfire took her by the hand and they ran off to the woods and hid in a huckleberry thicket. They sat on the ground under the bushes and Aunt Hellfire picked wiregrass and plaited Jincey a little finger ring and a bracelet just big enough for her wrist.

After that they sometimes played in Aunt Hellfire's house. They cut broomsedge and bound the stems together with strings to make a handle and swept the little house clean every time they went. There was a pump in the yard and they watered the periwinkle and sometimes filled a bucket and scrubbed the kitchen floor.

"Pretend your name is Gayly and you're my little girl," Aunt Hellfire would say.

But Jincey thought it was silly to be a little girl if you were pretending. You might as well be a grownup lady. So as often as she could she would beat Aunt Hellfire to starting the game by saying, "Pretend I'm Miz Jones and I come to see you," or "Pretend you're Miz Smith and you come to see me."

Even then Aunt Hellfire called her Gayly most of the time when they were by themselves.

Papa didn't come to see Jincey every week. He said he was doing some carpentry work for a man and he was aiming to buy back the land of his daddy's that he had sold with the half blowed-down house on it and fix it up so him and Jincey and maybe Mama too could live in it again.

Once he took Jincey to see the house. It was a long walk from Aunt Scam's, all the way back to the bay where the boat that brought her from Pensacola had docked and then past the church and the other houses and down the beach by itself. Although it was fall-time it was a warm, sunny day and Papa let Jincey heist her skirt and wade in the water on the way to the house. She knew the house when she saw it because what there was left of it was painted white and there was a rose blooming in the yard.

"Mama's doings, ain't it Papa?" she said, smoothing the white painted wall with her hand and smiling at the single shattery pink rose bloom in a sheltered corner by the gallery.

Papa squinted at the lopsided shell of a house, its front door ajar and creaking in the wind, most of itself spread over the yard in a tangle of rotting boards.

"People said your Mama made it the prettiest house on the bay," he said. "Of course, it was a right big house when me and her married and come here to live with your grandpa. Six rooms and a big front gallery and a boardwalk leading down to the wharf and your grandpa's store. In them days the bay was busy with schooners and barges hauling off timber and turpentine and my pa was a big man. He had a grocery and drygoods store and the post office, even."

He looked out to the line of rotting, barnacle-encrusted pilings straggling out into the water, sighed and sat down on the step and took out his pocketknife, reaching absently for a fragment of board at his feet.

"It was that old hurricane," Jincey began but Papa shook his head and sighed again.

"It was me and the hurricane and I reckon the times," he said. "They cut off all the timber and turpentined out the woods and then your grandpa died and running the store and the post office by myself was more'n I could manage. I lost the post office first and then the store and then the house and the land."

Through the broken window glass Jincey could see the blue-sprigged wallpaper Mama had ordered from Sears Roebuck and pasted there. It looked so much like Mama she wanted to go inside and lean her cheek against it and cry. Instead she decided to try to chirk Papa up.

"We'll get it back, Papa," she said. "You'll make carpenter money and I'll help you. Let's gather up the boards now so we'll have them ready to put back."

Papa smiled and put up his knife and for a long time they worked in the sun, picking up the boards and stacking them on the lee side of the house. Then Papa brought a sack of oysters he had left at the edge of the water where the tide would keep them damp and showed Jincey how to eat them. The biggest oyster shell made her a plate and Papa mixed ketchup and pepper sauce in it and showed her how to dip the oysters in it as he opened their shells and handed them to her on the blade of his knife. Jincey didn't like the first one much but Papa had tonged them out of East Bay himself and he was proud of them so she ate enough to where the taste began to be good.

The sun had slipped out of sight behind the marsh grass and the cypress trees when they started back to Aunt Scam's. Jincey ran back to look in the house once more and to let her eyes rest on the fine stack of boards they had accumulated. If they nailed them all back it would be a big house again and maybe Mama would come and they could all be together.

She stopped at the step and looked at the pink rose.

"Could I pick it and take it with me, Papa?" she asked.

Papa looked surprised and then stern.

"No," he said. "It don't belong to us. That would be stealing. You know the Bible says Thou shalt not steal."

They never went to the house again and after a while Jincey stopped thinking about it.

Winter came and with it some cold and rainy days stuck in between the hot and bright ones. The first chilly weather they had a cane grinding and a syrup making and so many people came from around about to help it was like a party. Jincey drank the cool sweet cane juice as it poured from the mill old Beck made go round and round until she was almost sick at her stomach. And then she stood by the big vat where it was cooking into syrup and scooped the white sticky scum off with a length of cane peeling and ate it.

The warm south wind from the Gulf of Mexico switched to the north and blew cold and they killed hogs. Jincey hid under the bed and held her hands over her ears while Uncle Fox and Sugar John and some of the older boys went to the hog pen with the axe and knocked the hogs in the head.

When the squealing stopped she came out and watched them dip the hogs in the boiling water in the big pot in the yard and scrape the hair off them. And when they hung them up by their feet from a board laid across some trees she stood and watched as the men slit them down the middle and all the hog insides spilled out into a tub. Sugar John got the pig bladders to play with and he blew them up and tied strings around them and bounced them into the air, taunting Jincey that she didn't have any.

Aunt Hellfire had her head tied up in a rag to protect it from the grease and smoke and she worked hard helping with the meat, washing chittlings and grinding sausage and standing over the wash pot boiling the fat to make lard and cracklings, which would be used all winter to flavor their cornbread. But she took time to smile at Jincey and to comfort her that she didn't get one of the pig bladders.

"They had three," she said wistfully. "You could have had one."

But Jincey didn't really care. The bladders were greasy and had streaks of blood on them even after Sugar John had washed them under the pump. They didn't seem to Jincey to be anything like as fine as the red gas balloon Mama had bought her once.

Papa quit carpentering and looked for some other kind of work so he didn't have time to come and see Jincey very often. Once he came and said he had heard from Mama and she was having an operation so Jincey could stay a while longer. Mama herself sent boxes often—dresses she had made for Jincey, a coat and once a little red pocketbook with two dimes in it. If she wrote letters Jincey didn't know because Aunt Scam and Uncle

Fox couldn't read for sure and Sugar John, for all his going to the one-room school over on the bay, hadn't got past the primer.

The new clothes were put in the suitcase under the bed with the others Jincey had brought with her but never worn. Aunt Scam said there was no use in it. But once Mama sent a little butterfly pin with shiny enameled wings that changed color when you turned it in the light and Jincey thought she would die if she couldn't wear that.

"Pride! Pride!" chided Aunt Scam. "You are just like your ma. Silks and satuns, paint and flowers! Go ahead, decorate yourself if you've a mind to—but you'll just lose it, see if you don't."

For a long time Jincey wore the butterfly on the collar of her dresses, changing it every week when she changed dresses. And then she forgot to take it off her dirty dress one week and it got in the washtub with the lye soap and boiling water and never was the same again. Jincey grieved over the drab little butterfly with its rusty pin and wings turned a dull soap gray and finally she put it in a matchbox and buried it under a peach tree in the orchard.

The orchard was Jincey's favorite place to play when she was by herself. She collected peach seeds and pretended they were cows and horses and people and, remembering the graves at the cemetery at the landing, she sometimes buried them, mounding the dirt over them to make graves. That was when she got to worrying about Mama dying and being buried in the ground. She asked Aunt Scam if it would happen and Aunt Scam laughed and said, "It shore will, young'un, to your ma and all the rest of us someday."

Jincey couldn't speak of it again but the fear was there like a rock in her chest and sometimes in the middle of playing or helping around the house she would think of it and misery and pain would wash over her. Mama a prisoner in the ground . . . Mama gone.

Jincey never did know if Christmas came that year. Nobody said anything about it. She remembered hanging up her stocking in the house on Intendencia Street and she asked if Christmas would come here but the answer they gave her wasn't clear and she forgot about it. Uncle Fox did go over to the bay and bring back some apples and oranges and a box from Mama had a little celluloid doll in it. Jincey thought it might be Christmas but she wasn't sure and she didn't like to ask.

They cleared up new ground that winter, cutting down bushes and trees and burning stumps. Uncle Fox ploughed up the land, and the women and Jincey followed the plough picking up big clods of wiregrass, shaking the dirt off them and throwing the grass over the fence. When spring came they would plant it to corn and beans, Uncle Fox said, but they never did.

The weather was just warming up when Sugar John lassoed Aunt Hellfire with his whip and broke her neck. It was the worst kind of accident, Aunt Scam said, a pure accident and Sugar John didn't go to do it.

He was riding Beck through the yard where Aunt Hellfire was hanging out clothes and he looped his long whip around her neck and gave a yell that caused Beck to jerk and run, yanking Aunt Hellfire after them. She fell backwards, a wet pair of overalls in her hands, and John, laughing loudly, dragged her across the yard before he thought to drop the whip and stop Beck.

Aunt Hellfire didn't stir again. She lay on the ground with her eyes open, her hands still on the galluses of the overalls.

Aunt Scam cried some and Uncle Fox got a peach switch out of the orchard and whipped Sugar John and people from around about came and laid Aunt Hellfire's body out on a door set across two sawhorses. Papa came and helped Uncle Fox build a box to put Aunt Hellfire in and the next day they buried her beside a little grave at the edge of the woods.

No preacher was handy so Papa said some scripture and some of the women sang "Nearer My God to Thee." Jincey, watching them shoveling the dirt on the new box, started shivering and jerking with cold and the rock in her chest stirred and heaved. She didn't cry. Aunt Scam screeched and hollered some and told Jincey she should do the same, it would heal the sorrow.

Two days later Jincey remembered Aunt Hellfire's periwinkle plant and wanted to go and get it but she was afraid to visit the dead woman's house by herself. She asked Sugar John to go with her and he turned white and spit out the corner of his mouth and yelled, "Hell damn no!"

After some days Aunt Scam put the bridle and the sack on Beck and she and Jincey rode over to the little house across the field. The periwinkle plant was on the steps where Aunt Hellfire put it to catch the sun, but it was dead.

Spring was slow in coming. It rained a lot and the days were chilly and Aunt Scam and Uncle Fox sat around the kitchen stove or the fireplace in the front room a lot, not talking or doing anything.

Uncle Fox had been one to sing, even when he was ploughing but especially when he was nooning on the gallery. After he ate his dinner he would lay on the floor with his head propped against the wall and sing church songs about sinners at sea. "Throw Out the Life Line" and "Let the Lower Lights Be Burning" were his favorites.

But after Aunt Hellfire died he didn't sing much at all and Aunt Scam didn't talk. Sugar John didn't go to school any more either. Jincey thought the teacher might have asked his mama and papa to keep him at home because she walked over from her boarding house three miles away to see them one evening. Jincey didn't hear what was said but after that Sugar John stayed around the place. He taught Jincey how to bend a pine sapling down and hang on to it and ride it back up and they played at riding trees for days and days.

Sugar John didn't play rough with Jincey or even get tired of the game until Uncle Fox had to mark pigs' ears. He took a sharp knife and cut some notches in the pigs' ears so people would know they were his when they wandered in the swamp. John held the pigs for his pa and watched how he did it and later he took his pocketknife and cut a notch in the ear of Wink, the dog.

Uncle Fox whipped him for that but Aunt Scam didn't seem to be much interested one way or another. When Wink walked in the house and dropped blood on the floor she didn't try to drive him out or even wash up the blood. Sometimes Jincey would take a dipper of water and the broom and wash up the blood spots but sometimes she would let them stay till flies covered them and they dried.

About that time Uncle Fox went to the landing one day and

came back with the word about the clubfooted Yankee woman that lived over on the Sound, how her son and his frog wife had been murdered and she needed somebody to come and stay with her and do for her. It was a way to go but when they got there they would have a good house to live in and rations furnished and fishing would be plentiful.

Aunt Scam said they might as well and after Uncle Fox had come back from going to see the clubfooted lady she started packing up. They filled the wagon and the oxcart with jugs of syrup, a crock of dried peaches and jars of blackberries and huckleberries and what meat was left over in the smokehouse, wrapping quilts around everything to keep it from rolling around the wagon and getting dusty. They dug the rest of their sweet potatoes from the bank in the field and sacked up the black-eyed peas that had been drying in the barn loft and took Aunt Scam's trunk and Jincey's suitcase and put them in the wagons to sit on.

Uncle Fox crated up the hens and tied them on the oxcart and they hitched the two milk cows on to the back of the wagon, pulled the door to and left.

Uncle Fox worried some about leaving his pigs in the woods but Aunt Scam said they would have plenty to eat with summer about there and he could come back and get them in the fall-time when they had fattened on acorns and pine mast.

Jincey worried that Papa wouldn't know where she was and Sugar John grinned at her and said that was right, nobody would ever find her where she was going.

For a minute she had faltered.

"I'll stay here and wait," she said. "Mama'll come maybe . . ."

"Aw, no, Pewter," Uncle Fox said gruffly. "You coming with us. We've left plenty of word."

"Where?" said Jincey frantically, looking at the lonesome, shut-doored house. You couldn't say words and leave them in an empty house!

"Shut your mouth, child, and git in the wagon," Aunt Scam said.

Jincey started to cry but Uncle Fox took her by the shoulders and shook her gently and told her the word he left was with people, his grown sons and their wives and the storekeeper at Swenson's Landing and the postmaster and the men that ran the boats.

"I reckon everybody in creation must know by now that Fox Thorson and his crew are running off to Saint Rose Sound," he said. "The word is left, all right."

Jincey climbed in the wagon behind Uncle Fox and Aunt Scam, taking a seat on her suitcase, and in the end it turned out fine. She had no more than got used to being there on the water in the clubfooted lady's big red painted house than here was Mama.

Mama had on a blue dress and white shoes and stockings and a broad-brimmed hat with flowers on it and she knelt right down in the sand and hugged Jincey and kissed her and shook her and hugged her some more, laughing and crying all together.

Jincey was laughing and crying, too, and breathless from hugging Mama back and all she could say was, "Mama, you smell good!"

"Do I, Jincey?" Mama said, holding her off and looking at her. "I try to. But you, honey . . ." Mama's laughter was no longer shaky but strong . . . "you smell like a dead fish!"

Jincey ducked her head in embarrassment and Mama put a finger under her chin and tilted her face up and brushed her lips across Jincey's forehead. "You taste like salt and sand and you've been crying!"

Suddenly the pain was back in the knot behind her ear and anger at Sugar John and a feeling of abuse came rushing back and Jincey started to tell Mama all about it. But Mama looked over her shoulder to where Uncle Fox and Sugar John stood, holding her suitcase and waiting by the water's edge, and she gave Jincey a look out of her dark eyes that Jincey knew from a long time back meant, "Be quiet. Shut up."

"Wait," Mama whispered. "Tell me later." Then in a louder voice she said, "Come on. Let's get to the house and see Aunt Scam."

Later in the day after Mama had changed to a pale yellow

everyday dress and some low-heeled white canvas shoes and they sat on the front gallery rocking, Aunt Scam asked her how long she was going to stay.

"Just tonight, Escambia," she said. "I have to catch the down boat in the morning. I just came to check on my young'un and bring her a few clothes."

"She's a-doing fine if I do say so myself as shouldn't," Aunt Scam said, "and she's got wearing clothes she ain't ever had on yet."

"Howie been keeping her supplied, I reckon," Mama said dryly.

Aunt Scam looked vaguely surprised.

"I don't reckon he thought of it," she said. "I was speaking of the ones you sent."

"But that was before I went to the hospital for my operation," Mama said. "I haven't been able to send any since. She must have outgrown what she had."

Aunt Scam laughed heartily.

"We ain't even looked to find out!" she said it like it was a big joke on them all.

Mama bit her lip and looked at Jincey.

"Let's take a walk down the beach," she said. "You can show me where you go in bathing and all the pretty places to play."

"I'll go with you!" Sugar John put in eagerly. "You want to see where the stinger I got off a old stingaree killed a tree?"

"Oooh!" cried Mama, shivering. "It did? I sure want to see that, Sugar!"

Jincey didn't really care if Sugar John went with them. She was so proud to have Mama there and if Mama wanted to see where the stingaree's tail killed a tree she was glad somebody could show her.

Mama put on a big show of being interested and kept John galloping ahead pointing out things but all the time she talked in a low voice to Jincey.

"I'm going to take you with me tomorrow," she said. "But you mustn't say a word about it—not a word, you promise? It could be they wouldn't care but then they might try to stop me and

I'll not have that. I'll ask them to let you ride out to the stand with me and when the boat comes I'll push you on ahead of me and it'll be too late for them to get you back."

"Oh, Mama!" Jincey cried, big-eyed and solemn. "I'm so proud ... I missed you so bad!"

"We won't be separated again, not if the Lord is with me and my head is hot," Mama said fervently, and then in a loud tone to Sugar John, "Show me the stinger again! How did you ever get it in that tree?"

"Drove it with a hammer, hell damn it!" said Sugar John happily. "In less than a week the poison dreened down into the tree and look ... !"

He pointed to the top of the little pine and sure enough it was brown and its needles were falling.

"You're the smartest thing I ever heard of!" Mama cried to John, rolling her eyes and making a funny face at Jincey. "You reckon you could find another stingaree and show me just how you did it?"

Sugar John ran for the crab net and set to wading in the water, searching the sandy bottom joyfully.

Mama turned to Jincey.

"What clothes you have that you can wear we'll pack in my suitcase tonight," she said. "Whatever they let you wear around here you can keep on to go to the stand in the morning so they won't get suspicious."

Jincey was thinking what Mama had said about not being separated again and she said hesitantly, "Mama, do you mean we ain't going halvers with Papa on me any more?"

Jincey's hand absently caressed the knot back of her ear and Mama laid her cool fingers on the red lump beside Jincey's.

"Not if I can help it," she said fiercely. "The dirty-necked, do-nothing crackers ain't fit to bell a buzzard, much less raise a child!"

Later that evening when the sun went down and supper was over Jincey hurried to wash the dishes so she could sit on the front gallery with the grownups. Aunt Scam made Sugar John help her, although he never had before, and he started bragging again about the stingaree and how he was going to catch lots of them and maybe kill all the pine trees on the clubfooted lady's land.

"You can hep me if you want to," he told Jincey and for a long moment Jincey wanted to tell him she wouldn't be there. The knowledge that she was going with Mama was so big in her she felt like she might have swallowed a pig bladder that was making her puff up and float with happiness.

She looked at his tallow face with the tufts of white hair beginning to come out on his chin and the gimpy way half his face smiled and she thought maybe he hadn't gone to hit her on the head any more than he meant to kill Aunt Hellfire. She'd tell him it was a secret and make him promise not to tell.

But then John poured boiling water in the dishpan while her hands were still in it washing a plate and she had to snatch her hands out and hold them under the pump to cool them and she didn't tell him after all.

On the porch Mama was talking to Aunt Scam and Uncle Fox and the clubfooted lady about her operation. She had to stay in the hospital and then she couldn't work for a long time, she said.

The clubfooted lady had an operation once and she told about it in her high Yankee voice that sounded like she was holding her nose and they all listened and made "I declare" sounds. When she finished she asked Jincey to brush her hair and Mama smiled at Jincey like that was the very thing to do. So while dark came on and Uncle Fox built smudge fires out of rags and sulphur and set them around the edge of the gallery to drive the mosquitoes away Jincey brushed and the clubfooted lady dozed and pretty soon Mama and Aunt Scam and Uncle Fox forgot them and talked about other things.

"Della," Aunt Scam said, "me and Fox always have hoped you'd see your way clear to gittin' back with Little Howie. You and him ain't got any right to live asunder. You made a promise to the Lord. Your union was blessed with Jincey and you could have other young'uns. They'd bring you closer together."

Mama laughed shortly.

"I'm as close to Little Howie as I can stand to be. Escambia, don't you remember anything at all? Don't you remember I *had* another baby, a sweet little boy baby, that starved to death?"

Mama's voice was low but so full of fury and pain Jincey stopped brushing and drew closer. Uncle Fox shifted in his chair and said, "Now Della . . ." But Mama went on like she couldn't stop.

"As long as Howie's father lived we had a good home and plenty at it. Young'uns would have had a chance. When Grandpa died Howie couldn't get off his lazy do-nothing long enough to hang on to what we was left, much less add to it! Why, many's the morning he lay up in the bed and slept till the mail boat was blowing and I'd have to run and get the mail bag and rush out on the wharf and hand it to Cap'n Lovel myself, me pregnant with Woodrow at the time. They took the post office away from us and then the store closed and then, after Woodrow was born, Howie sold the house and the land. We went to live near Milltown because he thought he could get work there.

"Work!" she laughed harshly. "He was always looking, looking, looking—never finding. He was gone to look for work when Woodrow got sick. There wasn't any food in the house. I made up the last flour into biscuits and flour gravy and fed him and Jincey that. But it wasn't enough. The little fellow weakened every day.

"Finally I took him on my hip and got Jincey by the hand and walked them down the railroad track and across the trestle to the store. We owed them a bill but my baby was sick. I asked them if we could have a few more rations on credit and the man said, 'No, ma'am, I'm sorry. I'd like to accommodate you, Miss Della, but Little Howie ain't good for it.' I turned to go and the baby saw some red apples and he held out his little hand and smiled at them and said, 'Ap, ma, ap.' "

Della's voice broke and for a moment she was silent. When she spoke again her voice was low and full of grief.

"I was ashamed and I slapped his hand and jerked him away from the apples and we walked back across the trestle to that lonesome little shack. That night Woodrow died.

"Somebody went and got Howie. Our nigger neighbors—Lord, they was good!—they kept Jincey for me and fed her and we brought the baby back to Swenson's Landing to bury him. The wind was blowing and the water was rough and the little casket with his body in it kept slipping and sliding about the stern of Cap'n Lovel's boat."

Jincey was crouched by the rocker where Mama sat, her hand holding tight to the hem of the yellow dress.

"Git back with Little Howie, you say Scam?" Mama's voice dropped as she asked the question and she laughed a little. "I'd see him in hell first!"

"Now, Della," began Uncle Fox, "you ought not talk like that."

"No," agreed Aunt Scam, "there ain't no call for you to use bad words and blame Little Howie for what he didn't go to do."

"Bad words don't worry me like bad actions," Mama said and sighed.

"But there ain't any use going over what's past," she said in a minute. "Besides, I reckon it's bedtime. I'll be gittin' a early start in the morning."

Mama took Jincey's hand in hers and pulled her to her feet. "Come on, young'un. Time to wash," she said.

Jincey felt numb with Mama's pain and she moved stiff-leggedly across the gallery trying to think of something to say to comfort her. Finally she said, "I washed my feet, Mama. Right after supper."

Mama looked down at her and smiled. "Don't tell nobody, honey, but we're going to wash you all over. I saw a foot tub on the back gallery and I filled it full of water before the sun went down. It'll be warm enough, I think, and if it's not, cold water will get you cleaner than you are."

They had a room and a bed to themselves. (The clubfooted lady's house had a lot of rooms and beds.) And after she got the foot tub of water Mama shut the door and made Jincey take off her dirty dress and stand in the water.

"Where are your drawers, Jincey?" she asked.

"I don't wear 'em," Jincey said. "Aunt Scam said it made too much washing. But I don't need 'em. The weather is warm."

"Weather or no weather, you'll wear drawers!" Mama said firmly, taking sweet smelling soap and a new wash rag out of her suitcase and beginning to make a lather on Jincey's neck and back.

"Always remember, Jincey, that the difference between being

poor and being poor trash is that trash won't take trouble to wash themselves and their clothes, to wear drawers and clean dresses. We're not trash and we're not going to act like it."

"Aunt Scam . . ." Jincey began tentatively but Mama, frowning at the dirt in her creases, made a face and said promptly, "Trash. Po' white trash, if I ever saw any."

Jincey's body felt lighter and somehow different when Mama finished scrubbing her and washed the soap off with cool water and powdered her all over. She had a new nightgown in her suitcase for Jincey and she slipped it over her head and stood a minute, her hands in Jincey's hair.

"Lordy, Lordy," she murmured, "it feels and smells like seaweed! But never mind, go to bed."

After Jincey was in the bed Mama sat a while going over the things in the suitcase by the lamplight. Now and then she clucked her tongue and made sounds of disgust. The sight of clothes she had made that Jincey outgrew without ever wearing made her mad and finally she stuffed them all back in the suitcase and pushed it under the bed.

When Mama had washed herself and plaited her long brown hair into two pigtails she got in bed beside Jincey and Jincey curved her legs around Mama's seat and put an arm in the little hollow made by Mama's waist. The pig bladder where her heart was puffed up with a sadness and a happiness so big she didn't dare to go to sleep. For a long time after Mama slept Jincey lay awake, trying to hold her breath so nothing would happen to change anything.

The next morning after breakfast Uncle Fox and Sugar John got the oars and Mama's suitcase and headed for the beach and Mama asked Aunt Scam if it would be all right if Jincey went along to see her off.

"Well, I don't know," Aunt Scam began doubtfully. "What if she was to fall overboard? That there's deep water out there."

"You're right to be careful," Mama said. "I want you to know I'm obliged to you for taking such good care of my child. But I would like for her to ride out with me. You'll sit still in the boat, won't you Jincey?"

"Yes, ma'am, oh yes ma'am!" cried Jincey hopping up and down on the gallery.

Aunt Scam laughed. "Well, your ma put a clean dress on you and I reckon you're bound to go. Go ahead."

Mama had put a clean dress on Jincey, against her own plan, because she said the week-old one was a filthy rag and it made her gag to think of having Jincey get on the *Naomi Louise* in it.

Jincey sat close beside Mama in the bow of the boat and nobody talked because of the noise the oars made dipping water and the rush to get to the stand before the *Naomi Louise* got there. She was in sight way up the sound and her old stern wheel was pushing her closer fast. Mama took out a white handkerchief and waved it when she stepped up on the stand and pretty soon the boat slowed up and swung in beside the stand.

Uncle Fox lifted Mama's suitcase up to somebody on the deck and then he held the rope ladder so Mama could take a hold and climb up. Instead, she leaned over as if to kiss Jincey goodbye and then quickly picked her up and handed her to the man on the deck. Then grabbing the ladder with both hands, she ran up it herself. Somebody closed the railing and the *Naomi Louise* began to move.

Breathing fast, Mama grasped Jincey by the shoulder and cried, "Wave goodbye, honey! Tell 'em thank you for a nice time!"

Uncle Fox stood stock still on the stand and Sugar John sat in the rowboat, which was now wallowing from side to side in the wake of the *Naomi Louise*. Both of them stared up openmouthed.

"Goodbye, Fox, goodbye!" called Mama, laughing.

And dumbly Uncle Fox lifted his hand and let his fingers flutter in a wave that even to Jincey looked helpless and childlike.

There were dressed up ladies sitting on the deck of the *Naomi Louise* and Mama bowed and smiled to them as she pushed Jincey into the big room with a lot of windows and one long narrow bench that wrapped around the whole wall. Nobody else was in there and Mama put down her suitcase and opened it and brought out a new dress for Jincey.

"It's the prettiest thing, Mama!" Jincey began but Mama,

glancing toward the door to the deck and the ladies who sat there, gave Jincey a shut-up look.

"You've had dresses before," she said in a low tone. "Don't carry on like it's new." She looked at the dress critically. It was creamy cloth, full-skirted with bunches of red cherries and green leaves appliquéd around its hem.

"Too long," mumbled Mama, "I'll hem it up later. We'll get you some sandals in Pensacola and see what we can do about your hair. Right now we'd better stay in here out of sight in case the boat stops somewhere else and somebody your papa knows gets on."

"Are we hiding, Mama?" Jincey asked, not really caring because the crisp feeling of the new cloth across her shoulders and against her legs was all she could think about just then.

"Umm," said Mama absently, looking out the window at the shoreline and little boats at docks. "I just don't want to be slowed up, that's all. We're going far off. I think."

Jincey hadn't thought ahead about where they'd go. She might have figured that they would go back to the house on Intendencia Street and things would be the way they were before she went to live with Aunt Scam and Uncle Fox. But she didn't think about it. She was busy feeling the pleasurable movement of the boat under her and looking at the shiny woodwork and the mirrors in the big room and standing on her knees on the window seat and watching the paddlewheel turn.

The dock in Pensacola was scorching hot and splintery to her feet and she walked on tiptoe, taking long steps to touch the boards as little as possible.

Mama had the suitcase and it was heavy and they couldn't walk fast so they stopped at the very first store that sold shoes and bought Jincey some socks and brown barefoot sandals with holes punched in the toes in a flower shape. Mama asked if she could leave the suitcase there and they went upstairs in a big building to a beauty parlor. A lady with hair in deep scallopy waves like bean rows on the curve of a hill put Jincey in a chair and tied a cloth around her neck and started cutting her hair.

"I want you to wash it, too," Mama said, "and do something about the color, if you can. When she was a baby she was a goldenhaired blonde. Now she's a greenette, if that's what you call somebody with green hair and green eyes."

The lady laughed and got a bottle of peroxide and when she was done Jincey's hair gleamed yellow gold like lemon drops. Her bangs were cut short and straight once more and the crown of her head ached under a tight little plait with a bow of cherry-colored ribbon on it.

"Now you look like my little girl again," Mama said approvingly, counting out the money to the lady.

They didn't go to Intendencia Street but caught a streetcar and rode a long time and got off at a house that had a red-striped barber pole and a sign with a big hand on it in front.

Mama said it was the home of a friend of hers, Madame Zillah, a lady who told fortunes and also cut hair. They were going to get Mama's trunk she left there and visit her until time to catch the train for their trip.

Madame Zillah, whose real name was Bessie Johnson, greeted them with hoarse whoops of pleasure. She was an old lady with cushions of fat on her like bed pillows and she had snow white hair which just exactly matched the hair on six poodles which swarmed after her barking.

"Della, dolling!" she yelled to Mama over the noise. "I knew you were coming! I read the cards this morning and there it was plain as the stars in the sky—my dear friend Della and a bee-yutiful little goldenhaired girl! Come in, come in!"

She put her arms around Jincey and crushed her to the starched blue gingham cushion of her front.

Jincey wriggled to get away and looked to Mama for help. Mama gave her a be-nice look and said, "Bessie, this is Jincey."

"Jincey, Jincey, Jincey!" sang the lady. "What a sweet, funny little name! Is it really Virginia? Or Genevieve?"

Mama's brown eyes considered for a second and Jincey could see her decide.

"Jeannette," she said.

It was the first Jincey had heard of such a name and she looked at Mama inquiringly and Mama looked back, smiling brightly.

Madame Zillah led the way through the barbershop to her quarters in the back. They stayed all afternoon. Mama made

Jincey take off her dress to keep it clean and play in her drawers and underbody. She played with the poodle dogs under the dining table while the lady and Mama talked and drank coffee. Twice Madame Zillah had to go to the front room and cut hair and shave men customers. She left the door open and Jincey and Mama, who lay on the sofa in a borrowed kimono, keeping her dress clean too, could hear her laughing and talking.

In between customers she made fresh coffee and poured Jincey milk and gave her a cinnamon roll and told Mama's fortune in a lot of different ways. She shuffled cards and spread them out, saying over and over, 'To your house . . . to your heart . . . to what's sure to come true!"

Then she would peer at them fixedly and let out little squeaks. "Money . . . oh, you're going to be well-fixed, Della! Let me see, there's a man . . . a light-complected man with blue eyes and he's going to fall in love with you!"

"Pooh, you said that about Philip Harrison," Mama said.

"Well, didn't he?" demanded Madame Zillah. "Didn't he ask you to marry him?"

Mama sighed. "Yes, I reckon. But you remember how it was. He took me to see the house his mother left him on North Hill and it was the finest place, Bessie. I loved it. In my mind I had moved in and was hanging curtains."

"Yes, dolling, but the cards didn't promise he would want a child," put in Madame Zillah.

"No," said Mama. "I sure wish they'd said something though. I wouldn't have wasted all that time and hope on him."

She glanced at Jincey who promptly turned her attention to the littlest poodle dog.

"He was showing me the upstairs and he said, 'This will be our room.' It was the big front room looking out on trees and the park beyond and it was so pretty. There was a smaller room next to it and I said, 'This can be Jincey's room.' You should have seen his face, Bessie. He said, 'Jincey? Your little girl? I thought she was going to stay with her father!' I said, 'Why did you think I'd marry you except to get a home for my child?' And I walked straight down the steps and out the front door. He didn't come after me or try to stop me either."

48

"Della, dolling, you're a fool!" cried Madame Zillah. "You should have married the man and then sprung the child on him." Mama sighed.

"No. No, I don't think so. That would be tricking him. And how do I know he'd be good to her?"

"Well," said Madame Zillah, chuckling hoarsely, "that's water over the damn dam, as the saying goes. Let's get back to this fair man. I love a light-complected man. You can trust 'em and they usually like children. Have you noticed that? And don't worry about tricking a man. That's what the Lord gave you a pretty face for."

"Pretty!" snorted Mama. "I'm pretty ugly and pretty apt to stay that way."

Madame Zillah stopped shuffling the cards and looked at Mama's face.

"The trouble with you, dolling," she said, "is that you're so young you think this year's style in beauty is all there is. Golden curls and blue eyes and pink cheeks, huh? Your dark hair and eyes are distinguished and your figure is nice—tall but trim. You're pale but I've got something that will take care of that."

She pulled herself out of the chair and waddled off, coming back with a bottle of stuff she called "Magnolia Balm." She spent a while smoothing it on Mama's face and Mama looked in the mirror a lot and laughed happily and wet her forefinger and ran it over the dark silky line of her eyebrows, making them stand out even more in her newly pinky-white face.

"See?" said Madame Zillah. "You don't have to be sallow. Now a little rouge and lipstick . . ."

"Oh, no!" Mama protested, laughing. "I don't want to look like a fallen woman."

"Foot," said Madame Zillah. "That's your trouble, dolling. You're so iron-willed looking. You don't have to *fall* to look soft enough that a man might think you could be *pushed.*"

"Go ahead," said Mama, tilting her cheek so Madame Zillah could pat pink into it and holding her straight colorless lips steady for the rosy lip salve. When she looked back in the mirror she seemed pleased at her reflection but she sighed and lifted her eyes to Madame Zillah's face which was above hers in the mirror.

"Bessie, where will I go? What will I do? I can't stay in Pensacola and have Howie coming and going and taking Jincey off to
stay with that dirty-necked, do-nothing tribe. I've got to have
something better for her. Being sick and helpless in the hospital
—a charity hospital, for pity's sake!—convinced me I've got to
make a move of some kind."

"How much money have you got?" Madame Zillah asked.

"Almost fifty dollars," said Mama. "It was all I could save,
clerking in the drygoods store by day and cashiering at the drugstore by night. I spent some of that to get Jincey some shoes and
get her hair cut and fixed. I had to. She looked so stringy-headed
and awful. And the boat trip cost a couple of dollars."

Madame Zillah looked thoughtful.

"Let's ask the Ouija board," she said.

They brought out a little three-legged thing shaped like a
smoothing iron and Mama held her hand on it and thought hard
on her question. Both women were quiet and Jincey got tired
and moved to a swing on the little porch back of some thick
green vines and let it rock her gently to and fro until the dark
shade and the hot sunlight beyond it blurred together and she
fell asleep.

When she awoke Mama had her dress back on and was shaking her.

"Come on, Jincey, we're going!" she whispered excitedly. "The
dray's coming for the trunk and we're going to get on the train
and go to *Mobile!*"

"Where's that?" mumbled Jincey sleepily.

"Oh, it's a big town a long old ways off and you're going to
love it," Mama said, repeating the name like it was the prettiest
thing she ever heard: "Mobile, Alabama!"

THE TRIP to Mobile took a long time, most of it spent between trains at the Flomaton depot up the road from Pensacola. Jincey was tired and would have leaned her head up against Mama and gone back to sleep when they got that far but Della couldn't sit still. She had to move about and she took Jincey by the hand and pulled her after her.

"Come see, childee!" she whispered. "There's a pretty little garden with a fishpond and fountain. Let's look at the flowers."

They walked up and down the paths in the little station garden and Mama pointed out flowers and told Jincey their names and said someday they would have a house with flowers like that in the yard.

It reminded Jincey of something.

"I saw your old house where you used to live," she said, "and the rose you planted."

"Is it still there?" Della asked, looking pleased for a minute and then her face turned and she moved away and looked at the goldfish in the water.

Jincey followed her and took her hand.

"Mama?" she said anxiously.

"I was a fool to try so hard," Della said, "and I reckon I keep on being a fool. But I don't know what you can do but try."

She smiled down at Jincey and said, "Let's eat our supper now out here in the garden. I was going to save it till we got to

Mobile. Madame Zillah packed us such a nice lunch! But this is such a pretty place. You ought to always eat in the prettiest place you can find."

It was dark night when they got to Mobile. The railroad station was a busy place inside and even busier outside where taxi drivers and Negro draymen with horses and wagons called out to Mama, "Ride, miss? Taxi, miss? Haul your trunk, ma'am?"

Mama talked with one, asking about rooming houses, and finally he loaded the trunk on his wagon and Jincey and Della climbed on the seat beside him and they rode through the streets where great clusters of lights hanging from posts fought the darkness which was trapped and held in the black twisting branches of big live oak trees lining the sidewalk.

The house where they stopped was a tall narrow one with a front gallery and an iron fence around it. A big yellow cat sat on the gatepost, but when Della and Jincey walked toward him he switched his tail and jumped off and disappeared into the shrubbery. Mama rang the doorbell and somewhere back of the frosted glass in the big front door a light went on and pretty soon a tall redheaded woman came and let them in and showed them a room upstairs. It was one of the littlest rooms Jincey ever saw, just the butt end of the hall with a window looking out on the street and a little iron bed almost filling it. There was a mirror on the wall with a shelf under it but no room for a dresser or a wardrobe—just hooks on the door for hanging clothes.

The drayman toiled up the stairs with Mama's trunk and Jincey's suitcase and they had to stand in the hall so there'd be room for him to put their things down.

"Tight squeeze, ain't it?" the redheaded woman said sociably.

Della looked tired.

"You got a bigger room you said?"

"Sure have," answered the woman. "Five dollars a week."

"We'll stay here for the time being," Mama said.

"You could leave your trunk out in the hall, I reckon," the woman offered.

Della shook her head. "We'll keep it with us."

When the drayman had taken his money and gone and the

landlady had taken hers and followed him back down the stairs Della closed the door and took off her hat and stood a minute looking at the room and Jincey standing in the little sliver of space between the foot of the bed and the corner.

She started laughing.

"Oh, childee!" she cried. "You look like a coon in a trap. Come out of there and let's spread out!"

She flopped across the trunk on her stomach and started rotating her arms in the air like she was swimming and Jincey, laughing too, ran and climbed on her back and flapped her arms about.

They were red-faced and giggling when Jincey finally slid off Mama's back on to the bed and Della pushed herself up and started undressing.

"I'll say 'leave your trunk out in the hall,'" Della mimicked the landlady. "We don't intend to have pilferers going through our things, do we, honey? Besides, we need it for flying."

Jincey hadn't thought they were flying but she had no doubt that they could if Mama put her mind to it. She went to sleep thinking about sticking great swoopy white feathered bird wings on the trunk and soaring out the window and all over Mobile, Alabama, in it.

Some time during the night Jincey awakened to find the electric light on and Mama squatting on the trunk in her nightgown hitting the bed with a shoe.

"Mama?" Jincey said, sitting up.

"Chinches," Della said grimly. "This place is working alive with them!"

Jincey sighed and burrowed her head back into the pillow. Bedbugs were Mama's old enemy. Everybody had a few in the crevices of their mattresses and in the chinks and cracks of their walls and nobody took on about them like Mama did. She fought them with kerosene and sulphur and scalding water and all manner of insect powders. She thought you could keep from having bedbugs if you tried and Jincey reckoned that someday Mama would win out over them. But not now, she thought sleepily, scratching some red lumps they had raised on her legs.

In all the days they were at the redheaded lady's house on St. Joseph Street Jincey never remembered Mama sleeping. The little single bed had a sink in the middle of its mattress and when Mama and Jincey tried to sleep they rolled together and Mama would get hot with Jincey against her and get up and sit by the window hoping for a breeze. Or the bedbugs would be bad and Mama would spend the night on the trunk turning the light off so the bedbugs would come out of hiding and then switching it on in a hurry and hitting out at them with a shoe as all the bugs ran for cover.

The air of the room was hot and smelled of squshed chinches, which Jincey didn't think was a bad smell but Mama did.

"Never mind, young'un," Mama would say. "We won't be in this old place long. Tomorrow maybe I'll get a job."

It was the days that Jincey hated. After they had been there a while the landlady, Mrs. Oakley, offered to let Jincey stay with her while Della looked for work.

"You can play with Buster, my tomcat," Mrs. Oakley said, "and help me water my porch plants."

Jincey tried to but she couldn't bear to do anything but sit on the steps and look up the street where Mama went. Mama said she was coming back and Mrs. Oakley said she was coming back and Jincey didn't cry and run after her like she wanted to. But she knew way down in herself that Mama was gone and she would never see her again and all her insides stopped running like a broken clock and were still and waiting.

"Come and eat some butter beans and corn with me," Mrs. Oakley would say, but Jincey couldn't. She knew she couldn't chew and swallow. She could barely shake her head for "no."

"Come play on the back porch where it's cool," Mrs. Oakley would say. "The sun's on the front and it's not near time for your Mama to come back."

Jincey would shake her head and cling to the porch bannister. She didn't think or even plan what she would do when it got dark and Mama wasn't there. She just waited with everything in her broken and still.

The sight of Della coming down the street would set everything inside her moving again and Jincey would jump up and run to meet her, laughing and crying.

"I vow I believe your child ain't right up here," Mrs. Oakley told Della, tapping herself on the temple.

Mama's eyes snapped and she grabbed Jincey's hand and held it hard.

"You better wish you had one as 'right' as this one!" she said. "I'm much obliged to you for looking after her but I won't ask it of you any more."

"Aw, now don't get mad," said Mrs. Oakley. "Jincey ain't a bit of trouble. Just the opposite. She sits out there like somebody in a trance—a plumb grieving statue. Won't eat or talk or anything."

Della looked down at Jincey and Jincey ducked her head and swallowed hard.

"Never mind," Della said. "I'll think of something."

That night they sat on the bed and Mama brushed Jincey's hair and talked about it.

"You know, don't you, that I've got to get work so we can have a place to live and food to eat?" Della asked.

"But we got bread and milk," Jincey said, pointing to a bottle of milk keeping cool in a pan of water in the corner.

Della nodded grimly.

"That's the last I'm going to be able to buy. I've got fifty cents left after I pay another week's rent. There's a tent works where they might put me on tomorrow but I'll have to leave you to go see about it and if I get to work I'll have to stay all day."

Mama sounded so worried Jincey wanted to make her feel better.

"I could go with you," she offered.

Della stopped brushing her hair and looked at Jincey with her lips tucked in firm and mad.

"Bossmen don't want workers that bring children with them. They'll think you'll get in the way or I won't work hard if I have you to see after. You got to help me by staying here and acting like somebody with good sense!"

Jincey didn't see how it would help if Mama left and never came back and although she wouldn't say it for fear of making it true, the knowing was there. One day Mama would go and

Jincey would never see her again. She could feel the dread seeping into her through her skin and paralyzing her insides. She wanted to cry and hang on to Mama and somehow keep it night so Mama would be there.

Della felt the skinny little body quiver and she took Jincey by the shoulders and turned her so she could look her in the face.

"Jincey, listen to me," she said. "There'll be times, lots of them, when I have to go and you have to stay. And there'll be times when you have to go and I have to stay. But we'll never really leave each other. We'll come back from wherever we are. Why, honey . . ." Her voice gentled and she laughed softly, "Don't you know Mama would swim through hell's-fire to get to you?"

It reminded Jincey suddenly of Papa. He spoke a lot of hell's-fire but the way he talked it seemed to Jincey like the garbage fires in the dump in Pensacola, mostly smoulder and smell and kind of interesting with things around to pick up and look at. But when Mama spoke of swimming through hell's-fire Jincey could see the flames rolling over her and lapping at her like the waters of Santa Rosa Sound. She shivered and clung to Mama's arm and said tentatively, "Papa said . . ."

"Never mind about Old Sorry Sorelegs!" said Della, putting Jincey aside and standing up. "I wouldn't give you the rapping of my finger for what he said or what he did. Now tomorrow while I see about work at the tent works I want you to clean up this room. I'll unlock the trunk and you can go through our things in there and straighten them up."

And that was how Jincey came to spend the time Mama was away playing in the trunk. After she had spread up the bed and hung up Mama's nightgown and straightened her comb and brush on the shelf under the mirror she would open the trunk and take the things out of the tray one by one and line them up on the bed and look at them.

There were two albums full of pictures that it took a long time to look at. Some of them were of Jincey herself—a tinted one that she looked at over and over again because of the shape of her head. She was a little young 'un in the picture, wearing white rompers and white high-topped shoes and she stood in a big chair with her hand on the arm, looking cleaned up and red-lipped the way Mama liked. Only her hair was not in golden ringlets the way Mama always said. It seemed smooth and straight except for a sprangledy something like a rooster's tail sprouting out of the top. Once she asked Mama about it and Della was tired and said she didn't know what Jincey was talking about and to please help her get a pan of water to soak her feet because her corns were killing her.

Later in the cool of the evening when they sat by the window with the light off to keep from attracting mosquitoes and looked at people passing on St. Joseph Street Della suddenly started laughing.

"Childee," she said, giggling softly. "I know what that sprangledy rooster tail is. That's not you. That's the back of the chair! It was carved in the shape of a pineapple."

The next day when Jincey looked at the picture again she tried to see a carved wooden pineapple shape but she didn't know what a pineapple looked like and it still appeared to be the top of her head to her. And sometimes when she was much older she would pat the top of her head to be sure it was not sprangling out like a rooster tail.

Next to the pictures, Jincey liked the things in a big candy box that had a pretty lady's picture and a pink satin ribbon on the cover. The box smelled chocolatey from candy long since eaten and there was a special rich smell about all the things that were kept in it—a little lavalier with a green stone in it and a fine chain black with tarnish, a folding ivory fan that once belonged to Mama's grandma, a soft gray furry rabbit foot with real toenails and a chain for wearing it and a big greenish bean that smelled wonderful and foreign. The bean and the rabbit foot were for luck, Mama said. Somebody had given them to her at a fair once. She didn't think enough of them to carry them around with her but she thought too much of them to throw them away. Jincey didn't like to touch the rabbit foot but she made herself pick it up and give it a place in the lineup of the others on the bed because it seemed little and lonesome if it was left by itself in the box.

The bottom of the trunk held mostly clothes and Jincey didn't bother to take them out. But there were two things that she liked to see, wrapped up in blue paper. One was a yellowed square of muslin with an owl embroidered on it in red and the other was a shirtwaist with tucks and crocheted lace on it. Mama made those things when she was a little girl living with her grandma and Jincey liked to hear about it.

"I was seven years old, not much bigger than you," Della would say, "and Grandma decided it was time for me to learn to do fancywork. She drew that owl off on the cloth and got me started. It was the first thing I ever made."

"The blouse," Jincey would prompt her.

"Oh, you know about the blouse!" Della would say, half amused and half impatient. "It was the last thing Grandma ever helped me with. I was a big girl and needed something to wear to school closing. Grandma made me a blue skirt and we worked together on that shirtwaist, tucking the front and whipping on the lace. Some day when we get a place of our own I'll show you how to sew and you can make things for yourself."

"Why was it the last thing Grandma ever helped you with?" Jincey would ask, fingering the soft yellowed goods.

"I didn't stay at Grandma's house any more," Della would say and then shortly, "Jincey, stop picking! I've told you about these things a hundred times. If you don't stop picking at me you can stay out of the trunk!"

That was a threat Jincey couldn't stand. The trunk and the things it held made the long, hot days when Mama was out job-hunting bearable. They were assurance somehow that Mama would come back and as she sorted the little possessions and lined them up on the bed the gaping pain of Mama's awayness eased. Mama had never been separated from her trunk and the things in it, even when she was separated from Jincey. She would come back.

A job for Della didn't seem to exist. She walked everywhere she could think of and when she came back to the room in the late afternoon she looked tired and worried and her feet were so sore she would limp up the stairs. Jincey always hurried to get a pan of cool water so Mama could ease her feet into it and she would squat beside it and dip the water with her hands and let it run over Mama's swollen ankles.

One day as she brought the water to cool Della's feet Mrs. Oakley came and stood at the door talking. Della started to pull off her stockings and Jincey saw that they were new black ones with a lacy design up the side of her legs.

"Mama!" she said delightedly, "you got new stockings!"

Della flashed her a black look so full of anger Jincey's hands shook and she sloshed water on Della's shoes.

"I say 'new'!" Della said scornfully. "I've had these forever!"

Bewildered, Jincey squatted on the floor by the pan and looked again at the stockings. They were new and so pretty.

When Mrs. Oakley went back downstairs Della turned to Jincey furiously.

"Don't ever say anything I have is new!" she cried. "I had to have some stockings and I used part of the rent money to get them. You go telling that old witch I bought stockings when I can't pay the rent and she'll throw us out on the street! Just keep your mouth shut and . . ." Her eye fell on the ribboned candy box Jincey had not put back in the trunk. ". . . and *leave my things alone!*"

Della took her feet out of the pan, stood up and, grabbing the candy box, she raised the trunk lid and threw it in, slamming the lid after it.

Jincey huddled on the floor in a knot of misery, trying not to cry. Suddenly she couldn't hold it back. Her mouth wobbled and her eyes filled up and her shoulders jerked with sobs.

Della was down on her knees beside her lifting her up in her arms.

"Oh, Jincey . . . poor Jincey!" she said softly. "I'm sorry, honey."

And then Jincey knew Mama was crying too, quiet crying that was more terrible than anger. Jincey burrowed her face in Della's neck and gulped hard.

"Mama, don't!" she pleaded. "I won't say nothing more. I won't play with your things. Please, Mama . . ."

"Never mind," Della said after a while, fumbling for her

handkerchief and wiping her eyes. "It wasn't anything you did. I just had a cry coming. When I get worried I get mean to you. You're a good childee. But . . ." She whammed Jincey on the seat with her hand and said firmly, "Don't go around talking about me getting new things, even if it's true."

They had bread and milk for their supper, the last of both, and when Della had washed out some of their clothes in the bathroom and hung them on the back gallery to dry they sat a while feeling a little breeze spring up and stir around in the wet drawers and princess slips on the line.

Mrs. Oakley's cat came up the steep back steps and Jincey picked him up and held him in her lap, leaning contentedly against Mama's chair and stroking him.

The backyard was crowded with trees and little bushes and smelled of figs ripening and crumbling old city houses that crowded it in on four sides.

"I saw a pretty place today," Della said after a while. "It was a big house with a yard full of swings and slides and a lot of children lived there. I thought about it for you, Jincey."

Jincey let the cat go and reached for the hem of Della's skirt.

"You might like to go there and stay a little while till I can find us a place. I saw a lot of little girls like you in the yard and I thought you'd enjoy being where you'd have somebody to play with."

"And sleep there?" Jincey put in uneasily.

"Oh, yes," said Della. "You'd probably have a room with a roommate. You know, another little girl who would be your best chum."

Jincey thought about it and said nothing but her hold on Della's skirt tightened.

"It wouldn't be for long," Della went on. "I'd come and see you every week and then when we could get us a place I'd come and get you."

Jincey wanted to cry but she was afraid that would make Mama cry too and when Mama cried it was scary. She gulped and said nothing.

"You don't have to go if you don't want to," Della said, "but

I know you'll like it. Good rations and friends and maybe even some school."

Jincey liked the sound of school. She had been wanting to go to school for a long time.

Long after the mosquitoes came winging in from Mobile Bay and they went inside to bed Jincey lay awake thinking about the new place with a best chum and school.

The next day Della didn't go work hunting but dressed Jincey and herself up and they caught a streetcar and went out Dauphin Street to the big house where all the children lived. It was a pretty place—a big creamy house with clusters of iron grapes hanging off its front gallery like black lace and a high iron fence around. A lot of children were playing in the yard when Della and Jincey unlatched the gate and went in, but they all stopped and came and stood by the walk, watchful and silent, as the visitors went toward the door.

One little girl, smaller than the others, rushed through the group and ran up to Della and wrapped her arms around her legs.

"Ma-ma?" she said, hanging on so hard Della stumbled and had to stop.

"Bless your heart, I'm not your mama," she said, stooping over to pat the little girl. "But I'd like to be. You're mighty pretty."

She did have curly hair, which Mama liked, but it wasn't yellow, Jincey was deciding, when an older stringy-haired girl came and grabbed the baby's arm impatiently.

"Come on, Maybelle," she said. "That ain't our mama." And then apologetically to Della, "She thinks every lady that comes is our mama. She ain't but two and a half. Say," she added, looking at Jincey, "you bringing your girl to the orphan's home?"

"I don't know," Della said hesitantly. "I'm thinking about it. Is it nice here?"

"Oh, it's tol'able," the old-faced child shrugged. "If you can't do no better. Want me to show you around?"

Della looked uncertain.

"Shouldn't we go to the office first?"

"Shoot, naw," said the child. "Miz Sims is laying down with

61

one of her migreen headaches this time of day. Come on, I'll show you."

Hefting Maybelle up on her bony hip she led the way toward the house. The other children turned back to the swings and seesaws.

Her name was Bonnie, she told them chattily. "And what might your'n be?"

Della told her and out of the corner of her mouth instructed Jincey, "Say 'Pleased to meet you.' "

Jincey gaped in surprise and mumbled something and Bonnie received it airily.

"Likewise, I'm sure," she said.

Jincey thought it was the finest lineup of words she had ever heard. Likewise I'm sure . . . likewise I'm sure. She said it over and over to herself as she followed Bonnie and Mama through the big upstairs rooms where iron beds were set up row on row almost touching with all their mattresses stripped and flopped over the foot to air. The floors were scrubbed yellow and the whole place smelled of soap and pee. Jincey wondered which bed would be hers and if Bonnie could be her best chum. Bonnie took them back downstairs to the front room and showed it off with pride. She said she would call Mrs. Sims in just a minute.

"We don't git to come in here," she said, "unless our mama comes or something. It's kept nice."

Della stood in the middle of the room resting her hands on a square table covered with a crocheted cloth. She looked tired and Jincey tried to cheer her up by pointing out a big colored picture over the black iron mantel.

It showed a man in a nightgown in swimming. Only he had stopped swimming and was groping to get a hand-hold on a rock.

"He sure-god can tread water," Jincey said admiringly. "He ain't even got his hair wet!"

"Hush, Jincey," Della hissed and Bonnie said severely, "That there's a *religious* picture. Rock of Ages Cleft for Me . . . you know, like's in the song."

She screwed up her face, shifted Maybelle to her other hip and looked at Della and Jincey thoughtfully.

"You Baptist or Catholic?" she asked suddenly.

"Why?" asked Della.

"Cause this here's a Baptist orphan's home. If you was to be a Catholic there's another place, run by sisters and fathers and the Pope of Rome."

Della looked relieved and grabbed Jincey's hand.

"Well, thank you for telling us, Bonnie," she said. "We're Catholic so I reckon we'll go. We're much obliged to you for showing us around and sorry to put you to the trouble. Come on, Jincey."

When they had said goodbye to Bonnie and Maybelle and were halfway down the walk Jincey said, "Mama, what's a Catholic?"

"Hush up," said Della. "I just said that to get out. I wouldn't leave a dog in that place!"

Jincey skipped on the way back to town, partly to keep up with Della and partly from happiness that she didn't have to stay at the orphan's home.

They walked because Della didn't have enough money for carfare to get them back to Mrs. Oakley's. After a while they came to a little park with iron benches and an iron statue of somebody with long hair and a nightgown like the man in the picture.

"Look, Mama!" cried Jincey. "That picture man!"

Della read the words printed on a metal sign and laughed.

"Nope. This is a Catholic fellow," she said. "Father Ryan, the children's priest."

She mopped her face with her handkerchief and sat down suddenly on one of the iron benches

"You all right, Mama?" Jincey asked anxiously.

"Tired and hungry, that's all," Della said. "We'll rest here and look at Father Ryan."

While they sat two Negro women pushing baby carriages and holding the hands of walking-size children came to the next bench under the same tree. They spread mosquito nets over the carriages to keep the flies off the sleeping babies and the walking children ran to the statue and started climbing over it. Jincey wanted to play with them but she held back, edging closer to Mama until she said sharply, "Go on, Jincey. Stop hovering me. It's too hot."

The Negro women laughed and one of them said, "She be shy, that's all. Go put your hand in the priest's hand, lil' girl. He be's cool and smooth this time of day. He like chillun."

"Go on," said Della, giving her a push and smiling at the Negro women.

Jincey went up the little flight of steps to the metal figure and looked timidly in the man's face. He held a little book in one hand and she touched that first and then she curled her fingers around his. The little children stopped their climbing and stared at her a moment and then they started yelling, "Look at me! Watch this!" and swinging from his arms.

Jincey tried to do the same but her legs were longer than theirs and she had to scrooch up to get them off the ground and pretty soon she gave it up and went and sat on the bench by Mama, who had been talking to the Negro women.

"Us brought a little lunch," one of them said. "Just ham and cold biscuits and some teacakes for the chillun. Won't you all have some wid us?"

She reached into a bag and brought out a fringed cloth and held it out toward them. Jincey could smell the cold biscuit and the ham and her stomach writhed in a spasm of wanting it.

She looked at Della and Della smiled.

"Go on, honey, if you want one. She's offering it to you. Take it and say thank you."

Jincey took the nearest biscuit. It was small and brown and crisp on the outside and soft in the middle and the ham tasted sweet and cool. She was chewing the second bite when she remembered Mama was hungry too.

"Here, Mama," she said, holding it out. "You eat some."

"Oh, no thank you!" said Della and she laughed her polite in-company laugh.

"Yes, ma'am, have one wid us," invited the Negro woman, unfolding the fringed cloth again.

"You *said* you was hungry," urged Jincey.

"No!" cried Della sharply. "No such thing! Come on, Jincey, we got to be going!"

Jincey stuffed the rest of the biscuit and ham in her mouth and got to her feet and followed Della.

"Mama, you *said* . . ." she began.

"Jincey, if you don't shut up I'm gon' whip you!" Della muttered between clenched teeth. "You want every nigger nursemaid in Mobile to know what a pass I've come to? Haven't you got any pride?"

The next day Della sent the telegram to her relations back in Florida. She took Jincey with her to the telegraph office but she didn't explain about the telegram until late in the afternoon when one came back. Then she held it in her hand and read it and her face crumpled up and she hugged Jincey and hid her face in her hair so people in the telegraph office wouldn't notice she was crying.

"You're going to Epoch," she whispered. "You're going to Epoch!"

And then to people back of the counter: "My cousin and my aunts have invited my little girl to come and visit them."

"Are you coming too?" Jincey asked.

Della's eyes were bright and her cheeks, paler than usual lately, reflected the pink of the shirtwaist she wore. She shook her head at Jincey and said loud enough for the telegraph people to hear, "Not right away, honey. Mama's got to finish transacting a little business in Mobile first. But I'll be to get you, never fear."

"Am I going by myself, Mama?" Jincey asked fearfully.

Della stuffed the return telegram in her pocketbook along with ten dollars that came with it, and took Jincey's hand.

"You're going in care of the conductor," she said importantly. "That's the way lots of little girls travel. I'll fix you a lunch and if you get thirsty there's a water cooler at the end of the coach. Paper cups cost a penny apiece, but you won't have to worry about that. I'll let you take the punch cup out of my trunk. How's that?"

It gave Jincey something to think about all the way back to their room. On the way Della stopped and took out the ten dollars and bought more bread and milk for their supper and, just to celebrate, a lemon pie as yellow as the very lemons it was made from and piled high with egg whites that came up in peaks and dips that were gold-freckled with a drop of brownish syrup rolling tantalizingly in a valley. They sat on the bed and ate every bit of it and then Della gave Jincey an all-over bath and washed her hair and rolled it up on rags to dry.

She took out Jincey's clothes and went over them, replacing buttons and fixing hems and as she sewed she talked about Epoch and the people there.

"Jincey, you'll love it," she said. "You'll be in the house where I was a little girl. Aunt Sweetie may let you sleep in my old room. And eat . . . Lordy, Lordy, the rations!"

Della rolled her eyes comically but Jincey, full of lemon pie on top of milk and bread, didn't much want to hear about food. Her stomach felt chancey the whole time she was kneeling in the bathtub getting her head soaped.

"When I was coming up at Aunt Sweetie's every Sunday morning she would be up early cooking for a house full of company. Always fried chicken for breakfast and whipped up a buttercake to go with it. All the milk and butter you can put away—from their own cows. You won't be hungry while you're visiting my kin."

She bit a thread and sat a minute, rubbing her cheek with her thimble and staring into space.

"You may be other things," she said after a time, "but not hungry."

"Mama, where will you be?" Jincey asked over a knotted ache that had settled in her chest.

"Right here until I can do better," Della said briskly. Her eyes rested on Jincey's face beneath the knobs of hair looking under the white tie-rags like a dozen sore toes.

"Don't look so downhearted," she said, leaning forward and tapping Jincey's forehead with her thimble. "I know you feel bad that we're going to be separated and I do, too, but I can't help it. If there was a thing in God's world I could do about it I'd never let you go. But Jincey, we was down to nothing—no bread, no milk, no money to pay the rent, no job. I swallowed my pride and wired Titter, blessed old Titter. She's the one who wired us back a ticket for you and ten dollars to carry me a while and she hasn't got much. She's half on their charity herself."

"I wish you could go too," Jincey said.

"Well, now shut up about it," Della said, pulling the suitcase out from under the bed and beginning to pack it. "No use running the thing in the ground. I can't go. You can. So that's the way we got to work it for the time being. Besides, I want you to know my people. Like as not, Aunt Sweetie's house will be stuffed with them."

Then she tried to fix in Jincey's mind the names of her kin—Aunt Sweetie's husband, Uncle Ditmore, who worked for the railroad for years and then died, leaving them a living, if not well fixed; Aunt Sweetie's sisters, Aunt Ruby Pearl, who was permanent since her Ma died, and Aunt Jessie, a widow with no stay-place of her own but married children she could visit if she had to.

"They the blood-kin's," Della explained. "Then there's Aunt Elvie who's black and no real kin but she lives there too and helps out what little she can. One of Aunt Sweetie's boys, my Cousin Hugh, threw a firecracker at her and blew off her right arm at the elbow when I was a little girl."

"A nigger?" Jincey wanted to be sure.

"Don't use that word," Della said sharply. "Aunt Elvie is colored but no use making a to-do about it. I grew up sleeping in the room with her and many's the cold night when I'd get scared and creep in the bed with her. She was good to me and she'll be good to you."

Della talked so unaccustomedly steady and fast that night and the next morning that Jincey didn't get to think much about not wanting to go. Almost before she knew it they were back at the railroad depot, Della carrying her suitcase and Jincey, her hair standing out curly and clean beneath a bow of ribbon to match her navy blue "traveling dress," carrying a banana and a bread and butter and sugar sandwich for her lunch and the little World's Fair cup to drink train water from.

It was night when Jincey got to Epoch. She was asleep on the green plush seat and the conductor woke her up and pulled her suitcase from the rack overhead and she heard the whistle blowing and felt the train slowing to a stop. She followed the conductor down the aisle and stood watching the darkness rushing by for a minute before the train stopped and the conductor swung down and lifted her to the ground. For a minute she thought she was all alone in the night and she stood rubbing her eyes sleepily and wanting to crawl back on the train when she heard running footsteps and a woman calling her name.

"Jincey! Jincey! Here we are!" called a woman. And then to the conductor who had swung back on the step, "I'm her mother's cousin, Latitia Rhodes. We're late because we got the car stuck in the sand."

And then she hugged Jincey to her and the conductor yelled "All aboar-rd!" and the train was moving off taking its lights with it.

When it was gone Jincey saw a car with headlights glowing a little distance away and she felt herself being walked toward it. A man standing beside it took her suitcase and a big girl stared at her curiously from the back seat.

"You just climb back here with your Cousin Rose and we'll be home pretty soon and you can go to bed," the woman said.

Jincey hadn't ridden in a car before that she could remember but she thought she would have liked it if it hadn't gone so fast in the night that she was thrown about on the back seat, once against her Cousin Rose who said in a loud voice, "Quit that!"

"Now, Rose . . ." said the woman in a pleading tone.

"I can't help it, Mama," said the girl. "She's hitting me."

"Well, she didn't go to do it," said the man. "It's this road. When we get on the new gravel road it'll be smoother."

Jincey huddled in her corner of the seat and stared at the dark face of the big girl beside her.

Wherever you go, she thought bleakly, you always got to put up with somebody's sorry young'uns. Mama hadn't even told her she had this Cousin Rose and here she was, a pure-tee pain.

The road ran along another railroad and Jincey wondered why she hadn't stayed on the train until she got to Epoch. It would have been better than having to tough out a car ride with Rose. She was to learn later that only two passenger trains a day passed through Epoch and most travelers got on and off the trains that passed five miles away.

After what seemed like a long time the car drew up and stopped in front of a little store building where the light of a single kerosene lamp could be seen shining through the window.

"Git out, girls," Aunt Titter said.

The man took the suitcase and set it inside the door and Aunt Titter called after him, "I thank you, Horace. Until you're better paid."

"Why don't you kiss him?" asked Rose, giggling.

"Rose!" Aunt Titter whispered, shocked. "You hush up and git in the house."

The store room was only dimly lit and Aunt Titter stopped and turned up the wick in the kerosene lamp so they could see to make their way along a counter and shelves to a door in the back leading to a big room with two beds and a wood cookstove in it.

Jincey stood uncertainly and looked around her while the woman lit a lamp and Rose flopped on one of the beds.

"Is this where Mama used to live?" Jincey asked.

"Lord, no, child," said the woman, smiling at her. "This is where me and Rose live and you're going to stay all night with us. First thing in the morning we'll walk you up to Ma's—your Aunt Sweetie's. That's where me and your mama was girls together."

In the light of the lamp Jincey got her first good look at her mama's cousins. Aunt Titter was a tall, thin, freckled woman with reddish hair piled into a knot on top of her head and fluffed out around her bony, big-toothed face. Her daughter Rose was a stocky black-browed girl, twelve going on thirteen, with dark brown hair pulled back from her face with a barrette and hanging down her back in six fat curls.

Rose had taken a nightgown out of the wardrobe in the corner and was yawning and undressing. She felt Jincey's eyes on her and she turned angrily.

"She's watching me strip, Mama!" she cried. "Make her quit!"

"Now, Rose," said Aunt Titter soothingly. "Jincey's just a little girl and it won't hurt a bit for her to see you undress. After all, we all three gon' sleep in the same room. You can git back of the door or go in the store if you want to change privately."

"I will," said Rose haughtily, taking her gown with her into the dark store. "I'm *developing*."

Aunt Titter smiled forgivingly after her and included Jincey in the smile. "She's getting her breasts," she explained softly. "Makes her shy."

Jincey hadn't thought Rose was shy, just mean, but she smiled back at Aunt Titter, who had put her suitcase on the oilcloth-covered kitchen table and was hunting for her nightgown.

"Such sweet little dresses," she murmured. "Just like Della—all that sewing and embroidery to have things nice. You got a fine mother, Jincey. I reckon you know."

"Yes'm," said Jincey, pleased. And then to her own surprise, to win this new cousin's favor, she said something she had never put in words before. "I like Mama a lot better than my trifling no'count Papa."

"Oh no, Jincey!" whispered Aunt Titter in pain. "You must never, never say a word against your father. Howie's . . . well, *different*, say. But you have to love him because he's blood kin and you have to honor him because he's your father."

"Mama says . . ." began Jincey defensively.

Aunt Titter smiled and left off sorting through Jincey's suitcase to cup her hands around Jincey's head, resting her wrists on her shoulders and looking into her face.

"Honey, I know what your Mama says. She's like my ma and all the aunts—harsh to judge. You got to watch that they don't make you mean and fault-finding. It's *unbecoming*, that's what it is. A little girl . . . well, anybody, Jincey . . . has to remember to be kind and patient and always think the best of other people, especially their own flesh and blood."

Aunt Titter, Jincey decided, sounded a little bit like Papa without the scripture reciting. She really was sorry she had bad-mouthed Papa and she didn't know how she had come to do it. She bobbed her head meekly and said, "Yes'm," and Aunt Titter kissed her on the forehead and turned to pick up her nightgown and hand it to her.

More than once in all the time she stayed at Epoch Jincey was to see in Aunt Titter a favor to Papa. Everybody, especially Rose, picked on Aunt Titter and sometimes she left the room crying and sometimes she bit her lip and smiled shakily and tried to apologize. Jincey later decided why. Aunt Titter was divorced and it looked like when you got divorced you weren't worth the rapping of anybody's finger and everything was against you—no man to work for you so you had to be beholding to your kin for help. Aunt Titter had had to get money from her folks to start the little grocery store she ran. And there was the disgrace of it. Jincey wasn't sure what disgrace was but it must have been pretty bad from the way Aunt Sweetie and the other aunts talked and Jincey sure-god hoped. Mama, whatever she did, wouldn't get a divorce.

But that was later, after she had been in Epoch what seemed like a long time and after she had made the acquaintance of the rest of Mama's kin.

The first morning she was in Epoch Aunt Titter got her up early and told her to wash and put on one of her best everyday dresses and they would get to Aunt Sweetie's in time for breakfast and before Rose woke up. Aunt Titter seemed to hate to disturb Rose and Jincey could already see why. Even in sleep the square, dark-browed face looked angry and disapproving.

Jincey put on her blue-checked gingham dress with the red rickrack on the collar and the bloomers to match and Aunt Titter folded her nightgown and put it in the suitcase and closed it and picked it up and led the way out the back door through a gone-to-seed vegetable garden and past the privy by the back fence. A sandy street with half a dozen houses facing one another from little picket-fenced yards led to Aunt Sweetie's house two blocks away. In the midst of the rash of new small houses Aunt Sweetie's stood out big and gray—an old-time farmhouse with giant water oak trees planted in a row across the front and a cluster of out-buildings around it. There was a big gallery across the front full of flowerboxes and pots and high-backed rockers and an L-shaped gallery across the back with more rockers and a well and water-shelf. Chinaberry trees shaded the backyard and a wash bench where six big tubs were turned down.

Aunt Titter took the way through the backyard and Jincey

suddenly saw an old lady squatted on the ground trying to get a fire going under two big black iron pots.

"Aunt Jessie?" Aunt Titter said timidly. "Good morning to you. Is Ma around?"

"Well, good day to 'Is Ma around?'" said the old woman mockingly. "What you reckon, she's gone to Dothan? She ain't ever anything but *around*. In the cookroom quarreling—like always."

"Yes'm," Aunt Titter said meekly. "Well . . . I brought Della's Jincey. Say hello to your Aunt Jessie, honey."

The old lady looked up, her eyes bright and dark and darting beneath the brim of a starched sunbonnet.

"Pleased to meet you, I'm sure," she muttered sourly, looking from Jincey to Aunt Titter. "Della's played the fool agin, I reckon, and your ma's got to take a hold."

"Oh, no'm," said Aunt Titter, laughing falsely. "Della's work hunting and Jincey's just come to give us all a chance to know her. After all, she's our kin."

"Kin's what we need," snorted the old woman, poking at the sickly little blaze under the biggest iron pot with a pine splinter. "Hungry kin."

Aunt Titter said nothing but squeezed Jincey's hand and drew her along toward the back gallery. As they reached the steps the back door opened and another old woman, who looked at a glance almost exactly like the first, stuck her sunbonneted head out.

"Lord help us, here's Latitia with another mouth to feed!" she called over her shoulder to somebody in the room behind her. And then to Jincey, "Howdy, Miss Pied."

"This here's Jincey, Ma," said Aunt Titter nervously. "Jincey, this my ma and your Aunt Sweetie."

"I say, 'Jincey'!" The old woman mimicked Aunt Titter's tone in a high prissy voice. "What kind of fool name is that Della's put on her? Pied's more like it. Look how pieded her face is with all them freckles. Looks like a old cow spit bran in her face!"

Jincey clutched at Aunt Titter's hand and drew back into the shelter of her long black skirt. But help came from the room behind Aunt Sweetie. The door opened wider and a black woman with her head tied up in a snow white cloth squeezed by Aunt Sweetie.

"Shame on you, ole Miss," she said sternly. "Whatever name Della put on her child is bound to fit her better'n 'Sweetie' do you. If you be's sweet, Lord have mercy on them that be's sour! Come here, child, come to Elvie!"

Kneeling, she held her arms out and slowly, pushed along by Aunt Titter, Jincey walked into them. It was only after the colored woman had hugged her hard and held her off to look at her that she saw that one of the dark arms was a nubbin, off at the elbow.

"This is Aunt Elvie," Aunt Titter started to say, but the Negro woman interrupted.

"She know me," she chuckled. "My baby Della done told her 'bout me being the colored, 'flicted aunt, ain't she, child? How is your ma? Did she send Elvie a present?"

"Present, I say 'present'!" snorted Aunt Sweetie. "Nobody ever sends presents to this house!"

"Hush yo' mouth now, Sweet," Aunt Elvie said in a low, shaming tone. "A little child be's the best present this old place can have. Della send us what's the most precious thing she got. And us gon' love her and make her feel at home, ain't us?"

The black face waited, stern and unsmiling.

"Ain't us?" she repeated.

"Aw, hush up, Elvie," Aunt Sweetie said crossly, turning back to the kitchen. "Come help me put breakfast on the table. Jincey must be starved because I know her Aunt Latitia ain't even built a fire in the cookstove this time of day."

Aunt Titter smiled and looked relieved.

"No, Ma, I knew we'd get better rations at your table."

Aunt Sweetie rattled pot lids and banged at the door of the big iron wood stove, poking more wood into the firebox. Aunt Elvie gave Jincey another hug and went to help her. Aunt Titter went ahead of Jincey toting the suitcase through the dining room and down a little hall into a big front room where there were two double beds standing high and puffy under crocheted spreads.

"You got one more aunt to go," she told Jincey. "Aunt Ruby Pearl, Ma's oldest sister."

"And the purtiest!" said a voice from the floor and Jincey, startled, looked down to see another old lady—like the others except smaller and more shriveled—sitting cross-legged by the hearth with a big clock beside her and its works spread out on a tin tray.

"Come here, young'un," said the old lady to Jincey. "See if you can find a little screw about the size of a grain of sand. You got good eyes, ain't you?"

"Yes'm," said Jincey, kneeling down. In a second in a crack in the scrubbed yellow boards of the floor she saw a gleam and she used her fingernail to lift out a minute brass screw. She extended it to the old lady, who wet a finger in her mouth and lifted it from Jincey's finger on the dampness.

"Good girl," said the old lady. "Now with your eyes and my sense working together it won't take us long to git this old Joe ticking again."

"Aunt Ruby Pearl," began Aunt Titter timidly, "this here is Jincey, Della's . . ."

"I *know* it, Titter!" said the old lady impatiently. "Go put her suitcase in the back room. She's got her ma's old bed next to Elvie. Now young 'un, hand me that balance wheel."

Aunt Titter went away and Jincey squatted beside Aunt Ruby Pearl and the clock's insides and pretty soon forgot the strangeness of the place and her mama's kin in trying to guess what in the bewildering array of tiny parts the old lady was talking about and hand it to her when she directed.

It was later, after she had been sitting at the big round table in the dining room long enough to eat a bait of grits and sausage and fried eggs and hot biscuits dripping with fig preserves, that Jincey began to see the differences in the aunts. She was going to be able to tell them apart after all, she decided. They all had mighty wrinkled faces and turned-down mouths but when they took off their bonnets you could see the difference. Aunt Sweetie was the youngest and she had her own teeth and blue eyes and gray hair that curled when it came loose from the knot on top of her head. Aunt Jessie had slick brown hair with only a little gray in it and one of her eyes sometimes slipped off to one side like it was loose and uninterested in what the other one was looking at. Her cheeks were pink, maybe from being outdoors starting the washing. Aunt Ruby Pearl's face was like seamy shoe leather, dry and brownish with deep runnels and rivulets running from her mouth to her chin, a mouth full of glittering false teeth and the blackest, straightest hair Jincey had ever seen worn in a thin little plait like a buggy whip around her head.

Aunt Ruby Pearl, Jincey was to learn later, took a heap of interest in that black hair, brushing it a hundred strokes each night, greasing it well with White Rose ointment and never, never washing it. When she had it loose from its plait brushing it she talked of how when she was a gal it was so long and thick she could sit on it. But age had thinned it and drawed it up and now all it had left to it was its blackness.

Missing Mama was an ache in Jincey's bones that never went away but never engulfed her either, mostly because she didn't have time to herself for grieving or loneliness. Everybody at Aunt Sweetie's house worked constantly, getting up early in the morning to begin by lamplight and staying at it past lamplighting time at the other end of the day. There was almost always a fire in the big wood stove in the kitchen and something cooking and Jincey, helping out, found herself thinking about food and either eating or waiting to eat all day long.

Aunt Sweetie and Aunt Elvie spent most of their time in the kitchen and the smells drew Jincey there in spite of the sure knowledge that Aunt Sweetie would grumble at her, give her things to do and find fault with the way she did them. If she was lucky Aunt Elvie would hand her a teacake or something hot and tasty on a saucer and hurry out to the back steps to eat it out of Aunt Sweetie's notice.

Aunt Sweetie complained loudly about the mouths she had to feed and how hard it was to stretch the railroad pension Uncle Ditmore died and left her but she seemed to want everybody to eat and cooked things she knew they especially liked. The little pantry room off the kitchen with its high window was cool and dim and smelled of pickles and sauerkraut and ginger cakes. No matter what time of day the notion for something to eat hit her Jincey knew she could find victuals there—a piece of leftover potato pie or a bowl of clabber turning for the next day's churning. It was the first time she ever lived where food was always handy and her thin, pointed face began to round out shinily where it had been flat and dull. Her underbodies grew tight across the chest and her drawers bound her around the waist. Aunt Titter brought unbleached muslin out of her store and the aunts boiled it in lye soap water and dried it in the sun to whiten it and made her new ones.

Sewing went on in Aunt Sweetie's house all the time. When any of the aunts sat down to catch a breeze on the front gallery she had a mending basket in her lap or squares she was piecing for a quilt in a box beside her. All except Aunt Ruby Pearl. She almost always had a clock all to pieces and worked to get it back together, sitting cross-legged on the floor like a child. The work on the big mantel clock went pretty fast because the pieces were bigger and then Aunt Ruby Pearl decided to repaint its scarred, battered old face with flowers and Roman numerals. After the new face had dried and the clock was ticking away on the fireboard in the front room somebody noticed Aunt Ruby Pearl had put the numbers on backwards. She said it didn't matter, telling time was like reading music, you didn't have to know music to be able to tell from the spaces where to put your voice. You could tell from the spaces on the clock what time it was without paying any attention to the numbers. Besides, if you had to be sure, you could wait for the clock to strike.

Up in the loft room, which was reached by a steep little stairway that ran from the room Jincey shared with Aunt Elvie, a quilt always hung from the rafters in a big frame, ready for the old women to put on their glasses and their thimbles and take the tiny stitches in it that held top and back together over a layer of cotton. In summer it was too hot to work up there but now fall was coming and here were long rainy afternoons when all four of the old women and occasionally a neighbor gathered in the loft room, lit little kerosene lamps and quilted and talked till suppertime.

Aunt Sweetie didn't want Jincey in the way but Aunt Ruby Pearl kept her handy for needle-threading and they finally taught her to quilt.

"She's a gal young'un, Sweetie," Aunt Ruby Pearl insisted. "You want her to grow up ignorant and kivverless? If we don't larn her to quilt, who's to do it?"

"Not Miss Fine Lady Della, I know that," Aunt Sweetie said.

"Mama will!" put in Jincey heatedly. "Mama will learn me to quilt! Don't you talk like that about Mama!"

All the aunts laughed, including Aunt Sweetie, who said, "Whoa, there, Miss Priss! Git off your high horse and run downstairs and look in the machine drawer and git that little thimble with the flowers on it. My Ma give it to me and I'm going to let you use it."

Aunt Elvie, following her to poke up the kitchen fire and put on the coffeepot, whispered, "Take good care of it, baby, and maybe Old Miss give it to you. She love her lil' thimble but her fingers be too swole from hard work to fit it any more. Mus' be right for you."

The little silver thimble with an enameled border of flowers was right for Jincey and at first she was so busy admiring the way it looked on her middle finger under the lamplight that she didn't pay enough attention to the quilting. Then Aunt Sweetie rapped her on the head with the thimble she was wearing and sharply brought her back to the job at hand. Poking a small needle through two layers of cloth and one of cotton was hard enough but following the faint lines chalked onto the quilt top with stitches small enough to satisfy the aunts was practically impossible. Jincey stood on a stool to reach the quilt and doggedly worked her needle in and out of the small bright patches that made a design of stars and flowers. But it was many a day before Aunt Sweetie would let her stitches stay.

"Rip it out, Elvie," the old woman would say. "She quilts like a fieldhand with a hoe in her hand instead of a needle. Best she'll ever do is kivver quilting."

Jincey didn't understand what was so bad about kivver quilting. Wasn't that what they were trying to do, make something to cover them from the cold in the winter nights ahead? She didn't ask Aunt Sweetie but Aunt Jessie, the fastest and best needlewoman among them, explained it to her one day.

Quilts put together every whichaway and quilted in plain big shells with long running stitches were warm enough to sleep under and, if kept clean and aired in winter and stored away in summer with deer tongue leaves between them, were good enough for most folks. But their ma had been a *fine* quilter who put thought and love into her work. She made up her own patchwork patterns and pieced designs and quilted with such care that you couldn't see her stitches at all—only the sculptured shape of petals and leaves and hearts and triangles that she worked over and through the pattern. With a ma like that to larn them quilting it would shame them all to settle for plain kivver.

"Will I ever be able to do it?" Jincey asked hopelessly.

Aunt Jessie took one of her hands in hers and turned it over, looked at it carefully and sighed.

"You mighty big-handed," she said. "I expect there's a high strain of white trash in you."

"I wear my drawers and wash myself every day," Jincey pointed out, remembering what Mama had said.

"Well, I reckon!" said Aunt Jessie, as if she had never heard of anybody going drawerless and unwashed. "That don't signify. You *born* somebody or you ain't. I reckon with Howie's blood in you and some of old Prince's you ain't got much chance to be anything but trash."

"Who's old Prince?" Jincey asked.

But Aunt Jessie was tired of the subject and didn't answer her.

Jincey didn't worry much about being trash but she thought of it from time to time. It was a kind of mystery disease, she decided, and some folks were born with it like Miss Lutie Shepherd, who lived across the street, was born deaf and dumb. Then some folks caught it like Papa caught sore legs working in the swamp.

The aunts said Rose was trash. She had taken to reading and every time any of them went to the store for anything there would be Rose laying on a bed in the back room reading. She didn't speak to them and they didn't speak to her but when they got home they talked about it.

"I wish you'd seen that sorry thing laying up there on her do-nothing with a book in her face," Aunt Jessie would say to the others. And they would click their tongues and slap their thighs in a way that meant did-you-ever surprise and disgust.

"She gits around—*if* she gits around—like dead lice are falling off her!" put in Aunt Ruby Pearl.

"Blood will tell," Aunt Sweetie would say darkly.

Aunt Elvie, who felt sorry for just about everybody but espe-cially anybody the aunts were down on, always took up for Rose.

"Why you be so hard on that lil' young'un?" she would ask Aunt Sweetie. "She your own grandchild, your own blood ebbing and flowing in her. Poor Titter don't even bring her to this house no more, you all so mean to her."

"Good riddance!" Aunt Sweetie would say sharply and leave the room.

Jincey thought it was good riddance, too. Rose pinched her or kicked her every time she caught her at the store and accused her of things she never did, like sneaking drinks out of the drink box in the store. Jincey had never even tasted a cold drink and she looked at Aunt Titter in hurt and astonishment, waiting for her to tell Rose it wasn't so. But Aunt Titter liked to believe Rose and all she said was, "It's all right. I don't care. It's all right."

"But I *didn't,* Aunt Titter!" Jincey protested. "It's a lie."

"Jincey, don't use such language," Aunt Titter said. "It's all right if you drank a Nehi. A five-cent drink won't break me. But ask first next time."

"I didn't . . . I didn't . . . I didn't!" Jincey cried and ran out the back door and toward the refuge of Aunt Elvie's one strong black arm and the nubbin that would pat her gently on the back and move across her forehead with a little dabbing motion that wasn't like Mama's hand smoothing her but was cool and comforting anyhow.

"Trouble, trouble, quit troublin' this child!" Aunt Elvie would croon, holding her and rocking her back and forth.

Most nights Jincey was so tired when she got on her cot she went right to sleep. But sometimes she would get to thinking about Mama and a lost and lonely ache would take possession of her and she couldn't sleep. Aunt Elvie would come out of a big snore snorting and hacking and somehow know that Jincey was awake and reach down from the big bed and pat her. On such nights Jincey would do like Mama did before her and climb into bed with Aunt Elvie, pushing her arms and legs and chest up against the big soft body in the old gray outing gown.

About the time cold weather came school started and Jincey started with it. There was a big two-story frame building across town that Rose and all the older children went to. But the young ones gathered in the empty store building by the A. & St. A.B. railroad tracks close to Aunt Titter's store. Jincey's clothes were all too short and too tight and the aunts got out the catalogue to look at dresses for her.

There was a dress with grapes on it that Jincey hoped they would order. She looked at it often and wished for it but when she mentioned it they all clicked their tongues and hit their sides with their hands.

"I'll say 'order'!" cried Aunt Sweetie. "You must think you've fell among the rich and well-to-do. We're looking at the pictures to git the idy for frocks to *make*, not buy."

Jincey still hoped for grapes but there were none. The dresses the aunts made were serviceable gingham, cut big and long to allow her to grow to them.

One day a package came from Mama with a coat in it—a beautiful green coat with a fur-like collar. They opened it in the dining room and Jincey was so happy she clutched it to her and started dancing up and down. Aunt Ruby Pearl and Aunt Jessie, catching some of her excitement, started clapping their hands and prancing around the table with her and even Aunt Sweetie, coming in from outdoors, cut a fancy step or two when she saw the goings-on.

When they showed her the coat she stopped and looked at it carefully, fingering the collar and turning it inside out to look at the lining and the label in the neck.

"Wonder where Della stole this?" she asked.

Jincey stopped stock still and looked at her. "Stole?" she whispered.

"You know she stole it," Aunt Sweetie said calmly, putting the coat back on the table. "She'll end up back of bars yet."

The old fear that Mama would die and be buried in the ground rose up in Jincey in a new form. Mama locked up in jail, never to come out again. Once more Jincey felt everything in her stop like a broken clock. She couldn't move or speak and she didn't want to look at the new coat. Pretty soon Aunt Ruby Pearl took it and hung it in the wardrobe in the front room, where they could all look at it from time to time and show it to Aunt Titter and anybody else who came. Jincey didn't look at it if she could help it and she tried to get out of wearing it, even when the weather turned bitter cold. The aunts put this down to a desire to save the coat for good and didn't push her.

Jincey needed some new shoes bad but Mama didn't send those and finally the aunts rooted around in the wardrobe and found a pair of Aunt Ruby Pearl's that were green with mould but their soles were sound and when they put blacking on them they looked fine enough to all the aunts.

Jincey hated them. Although Aunt Ruby Pearl had the smallest feet of any of the aunts the shoes were still so big on Jincey the toes turned up and they laced so high the tops hit her knees.

"Do I have to wear 'em?" she appealed to Aunt Elvie.

Aunt Elvie nodded. "They be's good shoes, baby. New-bought ones would cost cash money and it ain't right to expect old Miss to spend it. She got enough with all us here on her."

"All our hungry mouths to feed," Jincey said soberly.

She started toward school in the shoes but with every step she took she hated them worse. Maybe Aunt Titter would save her from them, she thought, and limped into the store, glad that Rose was gone and Aunt Titter was alone.

But it was too much to expect Aunt Titter to go against the aunts. She looked sympathetic and offered to put some more polish on the shoes but she said Jincey had to wear them. Jincey drooped toward the door and Aunt Titter called her back and gave her a piece of orange gumdrop candy but Jincey didn't care much about it. The shoes plagued her so bad she couldn't taste the candy, even letting it lay long on her tongue.

The morning was so cold there was a crust of ice on the puddles in the road and Jincey took some kind of pleasure in treading on it in the hateful shoes. By the time she got to the store building school had taken in and the shoes were soaked through. It was necessary now to take them off, she decided, and hunkered down by one of the tall brick pillars that held up the store building, she unlaced the shoes and hid them back of the pillar.

When she walked into the school barefoot the teacher, Miss Edna Mae Edwards, stopped whatever she was reading and said loudly, "*Where* are your shoes?"

Jincey tossed her head in Rose's don't-care way and said lightly, "Oh, I'm not cold!"

Miss Edna Mae went by Aunt Titter's store that afternoon and although Jincey retrieved the shoes from under the store building and carried them back to Aunt Sweetie's with her, she never had to wear them again. They took her across the tracks to a drygoods store bigger than Aunt Titter's and bought her some low-quartered oxfords with blunt toes that fit her and didn't turn up at all.

School wasn't the way Jincey had thought it was going to be with a lot of learning going on. She thought after a day or two she would get the hang of reading and writing but Miss Edna Mae had too many children huddled around the heater in the store building to fool around much with learning them things. She kept them singing a lot. "O Beautiful for Spacious Skies" was one of her favorites and "Darling Nellie Gray." When the weather was rainy or cold she would sometimes make them soup in a pot on the heater and keep them in at big recess and read them a story out of a book. When she got to the best part she always stopped and closed the book and smiled and told the children to be at school the next day and find out what happened.

It kept Jincey willingly plodding back every day but she sometimes thought if it wasn't for the book she'd a sight rather stay home and help the aunts. They had washing and ironing and cooking and scrubbing and yard-sweeping and wood-gathering going on all the time. And when they rested they quilted or sewed or sat by the fire in the front room shelling peanuts for seed to be planted in a field Aunt Sweetie owned out in the country in the spring. Everybody, including Jincey, had to shell a measure of peanuts every day and sometimes after the aunts went to bed Aunt Elvie sat up with her and helped her finish her portion.

One night the thought came to Jincey that Aunt Elvie might be a better teacher than Miss Edna Mae and she could stay with her.

"Aunt Elvie," she said, "will you learn me to read and write?"

"Lord honey, I'd be larnin' you something I don't know myself!" the old woman said, laughing a little. "You be's a school scholar. They'll larn you."

"I been there two weeks and I ain't learned nothing yet," Jincey said. "I believe I'll ask Aunt Ruby Pearl how to do it."

"You let yo' aunts alone," Aunt Elvie said firmly. "Don't pester them about books. They already larnin' you plenty. Why, old Miss done said she gon' start you to knitting and crocheting mos' any day now."

Jincey dreaded that and didn't say any more about reading and writing for two or three days for fear of setting Aunt Sweetie off on more needlework. But when Saturday came and she knew there'd be two days when she would have to miss the reading of the story at school she was so disgusted at the delay that she broached the subject to Aunt Sweetie. If she could learn reading and writing at home, she said, she wouldn't have to waste time going to school.

"I'd be more help to you," she said, teetering on a stool by the cook table in the kitchen and watching Aunt Sweetie pour fresh ground coffee into the cloth sack, which would go into the gray granite pot of boiling water on the stove. "I could finish that book myself right here."

Aunt Sweetie snorted and turned her back on Jincey to rattle things on the stove.

"You want to help, git at it," she said. "Git that bucket and lye soap and take some scalding water out there and scrub the privy."

"Now?" said Jincey, surprised. They scrubbed the privy every Saturday morning but never before breakfast like this.

Aunt Sweetie turned on her furiously, the kettle of boiling water in her hand.

"Don't you hell hack me about reading!" she yelled. "Git that bucket and go scour that shithouse!"

Jincey turned over the stool getting off and hurrying from the kitchen. Her face burned and her hands trembled as she took the scrub bucket off its nail on the back porch. She felt stunned and surprised by Aunt Sweetie's outburst. Once at the privy, out of sight and sound of the house, she commenced to cry.

Tears poured down her cheeks as she sifted white sand on the seat with its two big holes and one little one, sloshed lye water on it and scrubbed with the cornshuck mop. So intent was she on mopping and crying she didn't see Aunt Titter come in the back gate nor hear her until she was standing beside her.

"What ails you, Jincey?" Aunt Titter asked. "Why you crying?"

"I want my Mama!" cried Jincey.

Aunt Titter took the mop out of her hand and finished scrubbing the floor of the privy.

"I know," she said. "You bound to. But tell me what ails you now."

Jincey wiped her eyes on her sleeve and, snuffling and catching her breath, she told about Aunt Sweetie and the reading.

Aunt Titter put the mop back in the bucket and put her arm around Jincey.

"I'll tell you a secret, Sugar," she said. "And you mustn't tell a soul because it would hurt their feelings too bad. But Ma and Aunt Jessie and Aunt Ruby Pearl can't read themselves. They are ashamed of it because they are smart and could have learned it when they was young but they didn't have a chance. They grew up in Georgy, where school wasn't too handy anyhow and they had a Pa who made them work in the fields all the time. What little they know about figgering and how to sign their name

Grandma taught them but she had to do it unbeknownst to old Prince."

"Who is old Prince?" Jincey asked, forgetting her own troubles.

"That's what they call their Pa," Aunt Titter said, nodding toward the house. "They hated him and they never called him Father."

"You said . . ." Jincey began, remembering what Aunt Titter had told her about honoring your father and mother and not bad-mouthing your blood kin.

Aunt Titter nodded and looked sad.

"I reckon I had a bait of folks hating," she said. "Our family is full of it. I hoped for something better for you and Rose."

Suddenly she smiled. "Rose . . . Rose could learn you to read, Jincey! She's a first-rate reader. Don't say nothing to Ma and the others but come down to the store after dinner and maybe Rose'll start you off. I'll tell 'em I want you to help me a while."

Jincey dreaded a session with Rose. As much as she wanted to read it would be better to stay with the aunts and learn crocheting than to put up with Rose's meanness. But after the dinner dishes were washed and the yard was swept bare of leaves and twigs for Sunday she put on a clean dress and went the two blocks to the store. Rose greeted her grumpily but she had some of her old school books piled on the cook table in the back room and the chairs pulled up to it like in school.

She started Jincey off on the ABC's and when Jincey faltered or made a mistake she whacked her on the head with a ruler. After three pretty bad whacks Jincey slammed the book on the table and got up.

"You can keep your reading to yourself, my lady!" she said, unconsciously imitating Aunt Sweetie. "I'll just wait on Miss Edna Mae. She's slow but she don't hit her scholars."

"Aw, sit down," Rose said, surprisingly. "I ain't gon' hit you no more. Say the alphabet right this time and I'll read you a story."

It was the first of many sessions with Rose. Jincey couldn't make heads or tails of the printing on the page but she could rattle off the ABC's like the words of a singing game, right every time. Rose seemed to enjoy the lessons and always ended up laying on the bed and reading Jincey a story from one of the love magazines she kept hidden under her mattress. Jincey didn't like to tell her but she didn't think love was as interesting as what Freddie and Flossie did in the Bobbsey Twins book Miss Edna Mae was reading.

Rose let her take a primer home with her one afternoon and Jincey never knew how it happened, whether it was Rose's doing or Miss Edna Mae's, but suddenly she could read. She was sitting on the front steps because in winter the aunts stayed mostly toward the back of the house and she didn't want them to see her wasting time with a book. The sun had gone from the sky but there was still light enough to see and she leafed through the book, studying the pictures for the hundredth time. Suddenly the words beneath them came to life. She knew them and she knew what they said.

"Mamma loves baby," she read aloud. "Baby loves mamma."

And then, louder and breathlessly, over again.

"Mamma loves baby. Baby loves mamma."

The third time she whooped the words so loud a dog passing beyond the gate began to bark.

Clutching the open book to her chest, Jincey jumped off the steps and started running around the fence. The dog, catching some of her excitement, ran along the other side of the fence with her, yapping frantically. Darkness was creeping up from the earth but the sky was a clear silver with a new moon, bright and polished as a breast pin, riding in it.

"I can read, I can read!" Jincey whispered to the moon and ran faster, ducking under bushes by the back of the house and brushing the chimney as she rounded the corner. The moon was following her like a good yard dog. No matter how fast she went or how many turns she took the moon was right along beside her. She laughed aloud with pure happiness.

About the third time she went running by the kitchen window Aunt Sweetie saw her.

"Lord have mercy!" she cried to Aunt Elvie. "The young'un's possessed! You reckon she's been dog-bit and's having a running fit?"

Aunt Elvie stepped out in the yard and stopped Jincey the

next time she came flying by, throwing her apron over her head and pulling her toward her.

Jincey, still holding the book, laughed and fell against the old woman, all out of breath.

"I can read, Aunt Elvie, I can read!" she said when she could speak.

"Shh!" the old woman started to say, looking toward the kitchen door where Aunt Sweetie stood, but it was no use, Aunt Sweetie had heard. She came out on the steps and said brusquely, "Let's see. Let's hear you."

Jincey held the book in front of her and chanted, "Mamma loves baby. Baby loves mamma."

Aunt Sweetie exchanged a look with Aunt Elvie.

"That's tol'able," she said. "Come into the stove and let's hear the rest of it."

There was more and Jincey could read it and all the aunts sat in the kitchen and listened. They didn't stop her to correct her. They listened like it was the best story they ever heard.

After that Jincey liked school better because Miss Edna Mae let her bring home a book every night—and most nights all the aunts, even Aunt Sweetie, would sit in the kitchen after supper and listen to her read.

When a letter came Aunt Titter always brought it from the post office and everybody stopped what they were doing and gathered around and listened to the reading of it. Aunt Jessie got the most letters from her married children who lived in that part of Florida they all called "down south." She talked about going down to spend the cold months with Lou and Ed but either Aunt Sweetie had a quilt in or it was hog-killing time and they'd need her help so she put off leaving. The most mail Aunt Sweetie got was a railroad pension check each month, and Aunt Ruby Pearl didn't get anything.

Mama's letters were few and far between and then one day Aunt Titter brought a fat one from the post office and they all stopped what they were doing and listened to the reading of it. After Jincey had went off to Epoch on the train, Della wrote, she looked for work for many days and had no luck until one day she stopped at a street crossing and a policeman blew his whistle at her. She looked at him and would you all believe it, he turned out to be Tee Walton, an old friend from the days when Uncle Ditmore was alive and railroading and they all lived in Waycross, Georgia.

Aunt Titter interrupted the reading to look up and the aunts were all clicking their tongues and slapping their thighs in amazement at such news. Tee Walton 'way over there in Alabama!

"Does it say there Ina was with him?" asked Aunt Ruby Pearl.

Aunt Titter read on: "He took me home with him and Ina just would have it that I move in with them. They rent out rooms and when one is vacant they are going to let me have it. Tee got me work in the overall factory and I hope soon to save up money for Jincey's fare here. Ina has offered to look after her for me. Right now I am sleeping on their davenport and I am fearful it would crowd them if I brought Jincey here before the other room is vacant."

She signed off with love to them all and a lot of X's at the bottom, which meant kisses for Jincey. Jincey went back to finish gathering eggs so happy she stood a long time feeling each egg's warmth and smoothness before she put it in the basket and not even minding the smell of the chicken house.

Jincey never knew for sure how they came to have the party. One chilly afternoon she was bringing in a basket of splinters for morning fire-starting and Aunt Sweetie met her at the front door and asked her if she would like to have a party.

"What's a party?" Jincey asked uneasily.

"It's people and frolicking and playing games and having refreshments," said Aunt Sweetie. "I'll go stir up a cake and you run down to the store and tell Aunt Titter to give you fifty cents' worth of candy. Then you can go invite everybody."

Jincey put the basket of fat pine by the hearth and stood looking at Aunt Sweetie helplessly. She didn't know what a party was or how to invite.

Aunt Sweetie was in a good humor and she explained. Jincey

was to go to this house and that and tell the children and young folks there that she was having a party at first dark and they were bid to come.

Aunt Jessie would build a fire in the yard and Aunt Ruby Pearl would walk over to Mrs. Suggs's and ask her simple-minded daughter, Asia, to come and help out. Asia was thirty-five years old and silly in the head but a real good hand with games.

Jincey suddenly thought of Willie Mae, the little girl who shared her desk at school. She lived a short distance down the railroad track but Jincey never got to play with her except at recess at school. She would ask her first.

"Where you going?" Aunt Sweetie called out after her as she started.

"To invite Willie Mae Diamond," Jincey said, pleased that she had caught the hang of inviting.

Aunt Sweetie snorted. "A Diamond, I say! You'll do nothing of the kind, madam. Diamonds are the scum of the earth and I won't have them in my house."

"But you said . . ." Jincey began.

"I'll tell you who to invite," Aunt Sweetie said briskly and she rattled off a list of the neighbors who had children. "Now git along while I make the cake."

Aunt Titter weighed up a big sack of hard candy for Jincey and said she would be along to the party later but Rose had a sore throat and couldn't play out in the night air.

"That ain't all I got," said Rose mysteriously. "I'm unwell."

"Hush, Rose," said Aunt Titter hastily. "Jincey is too young to know about that."

It sounded important, being unwell, but Jincey didn't have time to think about it then. She had inviting to do and she went off down the street at a gallop.

Later Jincey stood in the shadows and watched the party. She was the only girl there. The neighbors Aunt Sweetie had listed for her had yielded up twelve boys.

Asia Suggs, a moon-faced woman who laughed a lot, noticed the lack of girls when she got the ring games going. For King William Was King James's Son you needed girls. It sounded silly when you come to the part about "Salute your bride and kiss her sweet" to have only boys. The aunts filled in. At least the white aunts did. Aunt Elvie stayed in the kitchen parching peanuts and setting out the other refreshments. But Aunt Sweetie and Aunt Jessie and Aunt Ruby Pearl, old as they were, joined hands with the boys in the ring games and danced around the fire singing "Skip to My Lou" and "A Tisket a Tasket."

None of the boys chose Jincey and she was glad. She would have died if anybody had taken her by the hand and drawn her out into the firelight in the middle of the circle.

Asia Suggs noticed her once and did what she was doing to all the shy ones. She poked her in the stomach and yelled, "Go to laughing!"

Jincey fled to the kitchen and Aunt Elvie. Aunt Titter had come in the back way and was drinking a cup of coffee and eating a piece of cake by the kitchen stove.

"Are you having a good time at your party?" she asked Jincey.

"Yes'm," said Jincey.

"Well, why ain't you out there playing?" Aunt Elvie asked.

"I don't know how," Jincey admitted. "I reckon I ain't much of a hand for parties."

"Why did Ma decide to give her a party?" Aunt Titter asked Aunt Elvie.

"You know yo' ma," chuckled Elvie. "She wanted a frolic for herself. If it be's a jug in the house she have a frolic for grown folks. No jug, a chillun party."

Aunt Titter laughed and said she'd have to git Horace to try and find them some whiskey for Christmas, law or no law.

The party lasted until the boys started playing hide-and-go-seek and hiding in the barn and climbing up in the live oak trees. Then the aunts called them into the dining room for the refreshments and sent them home.

A long time after the last of them had gone the old women sat around the fireplace in the front room and talked and laughed. Jincey went off to bed with Aunt Elvie but she could hear them and pretty soon Aunt Ruby Pearl got her fiddle down off the top shelf of the wardrobe and started sawing out a tune and Jincey could hear the chairs being moved back and the shuffle of

Aunt Sweetie's and Aunt Jessie's feet as they do-say-doed around the fire.

The aunts didn't go to church every Sunday but they sent Jincey to the Baptist Sunday School and she was about to be an angel on the Christmas program when Della wrote that she was sending money for her fare to Mobile the very next payday. Aunt Jessie had cut her out a white outing nightgown for an angel suit to wear at the church so she just went on and finished it for Jincey to sleep in, hurrying to get at the traveling dress they all agreed she should have.

Jincey went with them to buy the goods. Mr. Hinson's mercantile store and post office across the tracks was open late every night till Christmas and Jincey and Aunt Sweetie and Aunt Ruby Pearl and Aunt Jessie bundled up after supper and walked over there in the darkness to trade. A lot of people had gathered around the big heater in the center of the store and clustered about the counters beneath the swinging kerosene lamps. Jincey would have liked to linger at the front of the store and look at the dolls, which were lined up on the shelves all the way to the ceiling. But Aunt Sweetie walked straight to the back of the store where the bolts of cloth were stacked up and the others followed her.

They looked at all the goods there, smelling it and holding it up to the light and rubbing it between their fingers and talking together in low voices. Once Aunt Ruby Pearl asked Jincey what she liked best and she was trying to decide between red velvet and blue taffeta when Aunt Sweetie told the clerk they would take the brown serge and four yards of red braid to go with it.

Jincey looked at the brown serge and her heart sank. It was pure-tee ugly. She tugged at Aunt Ruby Pearl's skirt and made a face.

"Be glad you gittin' a dress at all," Aunt Ruby Pearl said. "Brown serge is warm and serviceable and suitable for wearing on the train."

Aunt Jessie had just finished making the dress—big enough for Jincey to grow to, with the hem halfway between her knees and her ankles—when Mama's letter with the train ticket came.

"Well, my lady," Aunt Sweetie said, packing her suitcase, "you'll be leaving us but you'll turn up again like a bad penny. They always do."

"No'm," said Jincey happily. "I'm gon' stay with Mama forever. I ain't ever coming back."

Aunt Sweetie laughed shortly. "That's what they all say when they leave. But then they always come back like old cats, dragging a kitten or two with them. Your Ma and your Aunt Latitia left and I said joy go with them and a bottle of moss, if they never come back 'twould be no loss. But you see what happened, don't you?"

Jincey didn't see exactly and she was saved from hearing Aunt Sweetie line it out for her by Aunt Elvie calling them to breakfast. Because it was her last day there they let her have a cup of coffee with her breakfast and Aunt Jessie said she would read the grounds for her. The cup had to be turned down to dreen on the edges of two saucers and when it was dry past dripping Aunt Jessie had Jincey turn it slowly in her hands and then she put on her glasses and took it in her hands and peered into it.

"I see a safe journey for you, young'un, and a happy home."

"Thank the Lord," breathed Aunt Elvie from the stove. They turned and looked at her and she said it again, "Thank you, thank you, blessed Jesus, if you reserves one of yo' happy homes for this child."

They were all quiet for a minute—so quiet they heard the mantel clock with the backwards face strike and it was time to leave for the train.

Jincey had been awake and fixing up for Mama a long time when the conductor came through calling, "Mo-bile! Mo-bile next stop!" She had noticed that hair that stayed plaited all the time like the topknot on which she wore ribbons was crimped into hills and valleys like waves when you undid it. Since Mama was such a fool about curly hair she was going to surprise her by unplaiting hers and letting it hang down over the short straight sides and the bangs. She didn't have a comb or a brush but she could see her reflection in the window and she looked pretty curly-headed all right.

Next she put on her coat, which was still practically new and must not have been stolen after all because Mama was not in jail but was going to be there at the station to meet her. She was glad she had kept it nice because Mama was a big hand to take care of your clothes.

The skirt of the new brown serge traveling dress hung below the hem of the coat about a foot and Jincey thought about hitching it up and tucking it under the elastic of her drawers but she couldn't decide about that. It felt scratchy next to her skin and besides there was a chance that Aunt Jessie was right when she said *long* was the only sensible way to make any dress.

Jincey's face felt dirty from train dust and coal smoke and she did what she knew Mama would have done, wet the corner of her handkerchief in her mouth and scrubbed at the dirty-feeling parts.

Then the conductor came by and took her suitcase from the rack overhead and presently the train had stopped and Jincey, waiting for the step to be put down, saw Mama's face right in front of her.

She was gathering herself to jump into Mama's arms when she felt the conductor's hand on her shoulder.

"Wait, Sister," he said. "You'll hurt yourself or your mama in your hurry. Now then ..." And he lifted her down and Mama was there to grab her and hug her and kiss her and kneel down in the middle of all the people hurrying off the train and hug her again and hold her off and look at her.

After a minute Jincey noticed a man and a woman standing close by, smiling at her and Mama. The man had on a policeman's uniform.

Della looked up at them, half laughing, half crying, and said, "Well, Ina, Tee ... here she is, my Jincey! And, Lord, she's bigger'n a mule."

They started walking home to Aunt Ina's house, with Uncle Tee carrying Jincey's suitcase and Mama holding on to Jincey's hand and swinging it gaily back and forth. But on the way Mama saw a barbershop still open and she stopped them.

"You all go on ahead," she said to Aunt Ina and Uncle Tee. "I just can't stand Jincey's hair another minute. I'm gon' git it cut this night!"

Jincey watched in the mirror while the man thinned and trimmed the wavy plait hair and scooped it back into a topknot for her ribbon. The hair underneath was as straight as it ever had been and Jincey felt bad at the way her surprise for Mama had turned out.

Aunt Ina and Uncle Tee had a house in the south part of town that had once belonged to a rich old maid. The neighborhood went down and some of the big houses on the street became rooming houses and the rich old maid moved to her summer house at Point Clear and let the roomers and comers and goers have her house. Aunt Ina and Uncle Tee put up their iron bed in the front parlor and on the other side of some big sliding doors that opened into a back parlor they put up another iron bed and added a table and a kerosene stove and called it a light housekeeping room and rented it out. There were other rooms to rent upstairs but Della and Jincey were lucky enough to get the big room downstairs, which had long windows like doors opening out on to a side porch, and Aunt Ina and Uncle Tee close by in case Jincey got scared when Mama wasn't there.

A coal fire burned in the grate in Aunt Ina's room and they sat there until bedtime. Mama sent Jincey upstairs to wash in the big cold bathroom and when she was dressed in her new white angel nightgown she sat on the floor in front of the fire and listened to Mama and Aunt Ina talk.

"Lord, they meant well, Ina, but please look!" Mama was saying, holding up Jincey's dresses Aunt Jessie had made her.

Aunt Ina burst out laughing and Mama laughed with her.

"Honey, did you wear these things?" Mama asked and Jincey said, "Yes'm," and laughed, too, although she wasn't sure why.

"What did they think of you at school?" Della asked.

Jincey didn't know what they thought. She didn't remember noticing what the other girls at school wore but she had a feeling their clothes weren't much different from hers. Everything too long and too full—to grow to—and dark so it wouldn't show dirt. She thought of Aunt Ruby Pearl's shoes and, knowing that she would get sympathy from Mama and probably Aunt Ina too by telling it, she told it.

"And you went to school in that cold barefooted?" Mama cried. "Oh, poor baby! Now, Ina, you know they didn't have to do that —sending a little girl off to school in an old woman's high-topped shoes!"

"They could afforded better, I know," Aunt Ina said. "They used to be well fixed."

"Oh, I reckon they don't have much money now that Uncle Dit is dead," Della said, sighing. "There's always so many there . . ."

"Hungry mouths to feed," Jincey put in.

Mama's brown eyes met Jincey's and she made a face.

"They told you that, too, huh?"

"Yes, ma'am," said Jincey. "All the time."

"Oh, I know it. Don't I know it." Mama sighed. "You know, that's why I married Howie, Ina. I never would have driven my ducks to *that* market if I hadn't waked up early one morning and heard Aunt Sweetie talking to Uncle Dit. She was getting him off to work and she said, 'I'm sorry you have to push yourself so hard. If you didn't have so many of my parasite kinfolks laying up here waiting to be fed you could take it easy.' That very day I wrote to Howie to meet me in Pensacola and I'd marry him.''

While she talked Mama was ripping the seams out of Jincey's brown serge traveling dress.

"Are you tearing it up, Mama?" Jincey asked, pleased at the idea.

"Now, missy!" said Mama laughing. "You know I'm not tearing up good cloth. I'm going to make it over and you're going to wear it to Sunday school day after tomorrow. And I'll work over your school dresses so they'll look stylish, too. Stand up and let me measure."

That night when they were in bed and Jincey had wrapped herself around Mama's back for warmth and was half asleep Della said, "Honey, they was good to you, wasn't they?"

"Yes'm, I reckon," Jincey said, "but I don't love 'em and I don't want to go back."

Even as she said it she wondered if it was true. She thought of Aunt Elvie with a pang and then of Aunt Jessie sewing for her and Aunt Ruby Pearl sitting cross-legged on the floor working on her clocks and she thought she might love them some. But not Aunt Sweetie. Aunt Sweetie was the mean one. She could hate her.

But the next morning when they finished unpacking her suitcase they found a tiny box containing a bed of cotton and nestling in it was the flower-ringed thimble Aunt Sweetie loved.

"She must have liked you to give you this," Mama said, holding the thimble on her finger and looking at it. "It was my Grandma's —your Great-Grandma's. We'll put it away in the trunk and when you're a grown lady and big enough to take care of it you'll have it."

Jincey found out for sure that Mama didn't steal her new green coat. She bought it at the Askin-Marine Credit Clothier store and a collector came every Saturday to get fifty cents she owed on it. Sometimes Mama wouldn't have the fifty cents left after she had paid Aunt Ina five dollars for their room rent and bought some groceries. Then she dreaded to see the man and would vow she was going to hide in the closet under the stairs until he had gone. But she never did.

"He'd just come back later," she told Aunt Ina. "Poor devil, I reckon he's got it tough, too, having to walk all over town nagging poor folks for a measly little twenty-five or fifty cents a week."

So Mama would go out to meet the collector and offer him a cup of coffee and whatever she had left in the way of money— twenty-five cents or fifteen, if that was all there was. He was a tired man with hurting feet and he would sit a while in Aunt Ina's big dining room and talk to them. Sometimes he would fuss at Della a little about how she could manage her money better if she would only try. Pay at the overall factory was sure to be a living wage, he said.

"Little you know about it," Della scoffed. "I been sewing all my life and I can't put one seam in them overalls that they don't make me rip out. My boss lady is a hussy and the foreman's fooling around with her so he lets her throw bundle after bundle back on us. You don't git paid if your bundle don't suit them. I made seven dollars last week."

The collector sighed and got up to go.

"Maybe you ought not buy expensive clothes for your daughter," he said gloomily.

"*Expensive?*" cried Della. "I reckon it is when I git through paying you all interest and carrying charges on a $12.95 coat! But what would you do, send your little girl to school cold?"

The man sighed again and said he would come back next Saturday and she should have a dollar for him then.

Christmas came and Jincey hung one of her long plaid socks by the fireplace in Aunt Ina's room. Coal was twenty-five cents a bucket and most nights she and Mama wouldn't have a fire in their room but would warm by Aunt Ina's and Uncle Tee's. Uncle Tee, being a policeman, got paid regular and they lived it up, Mama said enviously.

Jincey awakened early and wanted to run and see what Santa Claus had left in her stocking but Mama wouldn't let her get up until she heard Uncle Tee raking the ashes out of the grate and building the fire. Then Jincey pushed the big sliding doors apart and hurried into the front room.

Her sock had been replaced with a long black cotton stocking and it was lumpy and distended with riches—a doll, a little painted tin tea set, nuts, an orange, an apple and a Hershey bar!

Jincey was so happy she stood on the cold tile of the hearth a long time just looking at the stocking hanging there and gently fingering the black cotton and the lumpy shapes of the wonders within it.

Mama came out of their room, smiling to watch her going through her things and later they both got back under the cover to keep warm while Mama rested and Jincey lined up her tea set on a pillow and nestled her doll down in a little hollow next to Mama.

There was something about the doll that made Jincey wonder. It was a Kewpie doll like people won at the fair and kept on their mantels in crepe-paper dresses but it wasn't exactly new and it didn't wear a crepe paper dress but a long white baby dress and a little crocheted cap on its head with ribbon rosettes over the ears. The dress was feather-stitched in pink around the neck and the hem, just like Mama feather-stitched some of her clothes and Jincey wondered if Santa Claus had gone to that trouble or if it was Mama again.

Something kept her from asking and when it turned out they didn't have anything much to eat she was glad she didn't raise any questions about the doll. Mama took it hard that they didn't have a lot of rations in the room on Christmas Day. Aunt Ina and Uncle Tee went off to a policeman's barbecue somewhere and Della stayed in bed most of the day. A little boy had come around a few days before giving out sample packages of a new cereal called Grape Nuts and they ate that, for breakfast and dinner and again for supper. It suited Jincey very well. She was too caught up in playing with her doll and her tea set to care but it made Mama mad.

"Some day ... *some* day ..." she would mutter and bust the oil stove a lick because it wouldn't burn properly and heat up a cup of coffee for her and a cup of hot-water tea for Jincey to drink out of her little tin cups.

Not long after Christmas Della got a job sewing at night and Jincey didn't see much of her. She went to the big brick school down the street and when she came home she played around hers and Mama's room or sat with Aunt Ina by her fire. Aunt Ina was a great one for sitting. She made up hers and Uncle Tee's bed first thing and that was about all she did. Uncle Tee had been a cook in the Army and he was a sight handier in the kitchen than she was. They had a washwoman to come and get their dirty clothes and take them off and bring them back all clean and starched and ironed, and except for a little sweeping and dish-washing, Aunt Ina didn't do much. She didn't bake cakes or sew or quilt or do any of the things that kept the aunts in Epoch busy all the time. She did like to go out to the sidewalk when the vegetable man came by every day and talk with the other women and spend a long time picking out tomatoes and collards.

The vegetable man had an old truck with scales swinging from the back and boxes and hampers of greens and fruit tilted so they showed from the sides. He drove slowly and Jincey liked to hear him ring a bell and sing out:

"All you little young'uns playing in the sand,
Run tell your mama here's the vegetable man!
Veggie, Veggie, Veggie, Vegetable man!"

After Aunt Ina got the vegetables and cooked them Uncle Tee almost always found fault with the way they tasted and tried over and over again to tell her how to boil the meat first and then put the vegetables in the seasoned water with it.

"If you don't like the way I cook, cook it yourself," Aunt Ina would say cheerfully and later send Jincey to Mr. Bostwick's store (Staple and Fancy Groceries) to get a jar of Seafoam sandwich spread, which they would eat with a spoon after Uncle Tee was gone.

Della's job was sewing on the Mardi Gras queen's dress. The lady who made the dress the queen would wear at the carnival in February had got behind on her work and advertised for seamstresses to help her. Della saw the ad in the *Mobile Register* and went and got the job, which was mostly sewing shiny beads on white satin for hours and hours. She left the overall factory every afternoon and caught the streetcar out Government Street and stayed until midnight.

One night when they were finishing up the dress Della stayed so late the streetcars had stopped running and a man, kin of the Mardi Gras queen, had brought her home in his car.

The next afternoon, the dress being finished, Mama didn't go to the night sewing job but came straight home from the overall factory. She had been paid and she stopped on the way and bought stew meat and lemon pie for their supper. She cooked supper on the gas stove in Aunt Ina's kitchen and served it to them all in the dining room, laughing and making jokes and sending Jincey down to Mr. Bostwick's store for French bread to dip in the stew.

"You can pay him our bill while you're there," she said, giving Jincey a five-dollar bill.

"Be sure and wait for the 'nappe," Aunt Ina called after her.

"Oh, I don't know, Ina," Mama said. "I don't want her waiting and hinting around for something free."

"Silly!" said Aunt Ina. "She's entitled. Any time you pay up a bill a grocer's going to give a lagniappe. If he don't, trade somewhere else."

Mr. Bostwick, who had never given Jincey the rapping of his finger before when she went in for bread or milk, smiled at her when she gave him the five-dollar bill and said, "Mama wants to pay you what we owe you."

"Fine, fine!" said Mr. Bostwick, taking out all but a few pennies. "Now let's see, what you want for a 'nappe. Bananas?"

Jincey shook her head. Uncle Tee brought bananas from the fruit dock where they gave you the overripe ones free. They had a spate of bananas.

"Tea cakes?" asked Mr. Bostwick.

Jincey was tempted but not sold.

"Raisins?" said Mr. Bostwick, holding up a bunch of dark pur-plish dried raisins on a stem.

Jincey's stomach, turning over inside her, told her it was the perfect 'nappe. She nodded in an ecstasy of expectation. The raisins were dry and seedy but Jincey liked them and was glad when Mama and Aunt Ina, after a quick sample, told her to keep them.

It was a poor enough 'nappe, Aunt Ina said, for practically a five-dollar paid-up grocery bill. Dusty raisins. But Jincey sat on an old leather settee in the bay window of the dining room and ate them carefully, one raisin at a time, holding each one in her mouth until it stopped being dry and dusty and puffed up and sweetened. The taste of the raisins and the sound of Mama laughing and talking and cooking something good for supper filled her with a deep content.

Now and then Jincey listened to the talk. The man who brought Della home in his car the night before was a cousin of the Mardi Gras queen. He had brought the queen for a fitting and taken her home and come back for Della. They had stopped at a restaurant on Royal Street for a cup of coffee and he had insisted on buying Mama one of those little crab omelets that come in a bun like a sandwich.

"He was the nicest kind," Mama said. "And he asked if he might come and call on me some time."

"Not married?" Aunt Ina asked.

"Not married," Della said with satisfaction. "Can you believe it? Good-looking, too. You'd think one of those society girls would have grabbed him by now. Practically thirty years old."

"Hmm, old bachelor," Aunt Ina said. "Well, you watch him. He might just want to play around a little before he settles down with one of them debutantes."

"Anyway, he's light-complected," said Della. "And that's what Bessie Johnson saw in my future when she read the cards—a light-complected man."

A few nights later on a Saturday a light-complected man did come and Della was in a flurry getting ready. On Saturday morning she washed her hair and sat in the sun on the sheltered side of the house in the backyard drying it. While it hung down on her shoulders in a red-brown tide she buffed her nails and rubbed rosewater and glycerine into her hands. She had a new dress, a yellow-checked housedress with wide sleeves and flowers embroidered on the pockets.

"I was a fool to spend two dollars for this frock," she told Aunt Ina. "A bungalow apron I could run up on the machine for seventy-five cents. But I had to have something to put on. I just hope the Askin-Marine man realizes it's only a cheap bungalow apron and Mr. Hinkel thinks it's a party frock."

Mr. Hinkel didn't say anything about Mama having on a party dress. He didn't say much of anything that they could understand, him being a seaman just off a German boat. He sat on the davenport in the front hall with Mama and after a while he gave Jincey two quarters, opening her hand and putting them in and closing her fingers over them.

"You can run to Mr. Bostwick's store and get you a Eskimo pie," Della said, smiling. And then, excusing herself to Mr. Hinkel, she followed Jincey to the back hall.

"Get bread and milk!" she whispered. "A big loaf and two quarts!"

Jincey opened her hand and looked at the two quarters and clamped it shut again. It was a lot of money, she decided sadly, and Eskimo pies weren't very lasting. If she hurried through the alley she could get to Mr. Bostwick's before he closed.

When she got back Mama and Mr. Hinkel had gone and Aunt Ina told her to get a bowl and fix herself some bread and milk for her supper if she wanted to and go on to bed.

Mr. Hinkel didn't come back again and Mama told Aunt Ina he was going to see one of the younger women at the overall factory.

"Scared of a woman with a child, huh?" Aunt Ina asked.

"Maybe," said Mama thoughtfully. And then, making a long, slack-jawed face, she did a funny imitation of Mr. Hinkel, putting in a lot of "Ja, ja's" and "Goot, goot's."

"She's welcome to him, I'm sure," she summed up, tossing her head.

The Mardi Gras queen's cousin did come to call. He rang the

doorbell one night and asked Aunt Ina if "Miss Della" was at home. Mama hurried to pin up her hair and put on her shoes and on the way to the front door she told Jincey to take her doll and tea set and go play in Aunt Ina's kitchen.

"You want me to hide, Mama?" Jincey asked, pleased by the idea. "I could sneak under the bed and be as quiet as a tumblebug."

"Hush about tumblebugs," Mama said absently.

And then she came back and hugged Jincey and smiled at her. "Just stay out of sight, honey, and we'll see what happens."

The man's name was Mr. Barton McPherson and what happened was he came to see Mama almost every Saturday night. He had a car with a canary-bird whistle that trilled when he turned in from Government Street and Mama would start rushing about, patting her hair and powdering her face and telling Jincey to run hide.

Mardi Gras came and Mr. McPherson, who lived in the country, made a special trip into town to see his cousin crowned.

"He asked me to go, Ina!" Della said happily. "Can you believe it? He wanted to take *me!*"

"You going?" asked Aunt Ina.

"You know I'm not," Della said bitterly. "What would I wear? How would I act among them society people? Poor as pig shit all my life, I don't know *nothing!* I told him I already had a engagement."

"Ha!" Aunt Ina hooted at the word. "But I reckon it ain't too bad a idy to let him think he's not the only tarpon in the Gulf. Just don't do it too often."

Della sighed. "He acted like his feelings was hurt a little but it may have been just a act."

That night there was masking in Bienville Square and Mama got the idea that they should all dress up and go. Jincey could black her face and wear one of Aunt Ina's housedresses with a pillow tied around her waist and go as an old colored washwoman. What with the parades and all the goings on downtown Uncle Tee had policing to do and Aunt Ina and Mama didn't have any trouble figuring out costumes for themselves. Aunt Ina could wear her own Ku Klux Klan robe and Mama would wear Uncle Tee's.

They giggled a lot when they were dressing and Jincey capered about them in a state of high excitement, but when they put on the tall peaked hoods with masks that blotted out their faces, except for dark eye holes, she shivered a little in near fear. Later they moved slowly down the street toward the square and other children squealed and ran. Then Jincey, feeling brave and very proud, walked up and took Mama's hand.

A band played in the bandstand in Bienville Square and all around the great iron fountain men and women and children in costumes and masks danced and cut the fool. There would be prizes later for the best costumes and Jincey felt sure Mama and Aunt Ina would win something. There were a lot of children better costumed than she was in on-purpose clown and gypsy suits and even one little boy dressed in a red devil outfit with horns and a pitchfork. Sailors from the ships in port mingled with the maskers, and once when the band played a fox-trot both Mama and Aunt Ina started moving with the music like they wanted somebody to ask them to dance. Nobody did, not realizing they were women, probably, and finally they started dancing together.

When the parade started, frolicking in the park stopped and everybody rushed to the curb to see the floats go by, pulled by mules and lighted by pinkish torches carried by Negro men. Men in tights and spangled suits and masks danced about on the floats, throwing candy to the children on the curb and slicing the air with long colored paper streamers which they sent shooting out from coiled rolls in their hands. Children screamed and scrambled to catch the candy and the serpentines and grown people clapped their hands and yelled to the dancers on the floats, calling some of them by name despite the masks.

Della grabbed Jincey and lifted her up so she could see better and then she almost dropped her.

"Ina!" she hissed. "There he is—Mr. McPherson! Let's go. I don't want him to see me."

Directly across Dauphin Street from them a tall man in a dark suit and a gray felt hat stood alone, a little away from the curb-side crowd, watching the parade.

"Silly!" giggled Aunt Ina. "You think he'll recognize you in that rig?"

Della laughed too. "I forgot." And then after a minute she added, "He looks like he's alone. Wonder why he's not out with his royal kinfolks?"

Aunt Ina wondered, too, and Jincey could tell they had lost interest in the parade and were busy looking at Mr. McPherson. But she watched every bit of it, and pranced up and down and squealed with the other children when the all-Negro Excelsior Band struck up right in front of them.

Later Jincey heard Della cautioning Aunt Ina not to say anything to Mr. McPherson, if he came back, about them masking in the square.

"His kind of folks don't git out on the street and frolic around with niggers and trash," she said. "They go to the balls and the private parties. In their evening dresses. Oh, Ina, you should see some of them clothes!"

"Well, I noticed he was out on the street watching the parade by himself," Aunt Ina pointed out. "Not on the reviewing stand in front of the Athlestan Club with the upper crust."

"That's so," Mama said thoughtfully. "He looked kind of lone-some, didn't he?"

Aunt Ina said she would hold her tongue around Mr. McPher-son if Della and Jincey wouldn't say anything to Uncle Tee about them going to the square in the Ku Klux robes.

"He'd think it was a desecration," she said. "You know how sacred he thinks this regalia is. I got a good mind to wash and iron these outfits before he sees them."

But being lazy, she didn't. Uncle Tee did it himself, not want-ing the Negro washwoman to know he and Aunt Ina were Kluxers. But he had a hard time understanding why the robes were so dirty around the tail, when they had only been wearing them to go marching into country churches recruiting members on Sunday nights.

Mr. McPherson did come back, almost every Saturday night. Mama would listen for the canary-bird whistle singing at the corner and her dark eyes would light up and she would kiss Jincey hurriedly and run to the front door.

One night when Jincey had been drooping around the house a couple of days with a bad cold Mama felt her forehead before she left and told her to run and get in bed.

"I feel all right," Jincey protested. "I just ain't got nothing to do."

"Oh, foot to that!" Mama said impatiently. "You can get one of my *Delineators* and cut out paper dolls."

Magazines with pictures of pretty clothes in them were a vice with Della. They cost a quarter, which she could not afford, but almost every month she bought one or borrowed one from somebody at the overall factory, to spend long moments reading the stories and poring over the pictures of dresses for ideas to make over something she had or a skirt or old coat that somebody gave her for Jincey. She liked to keep every magazine she got, but lately she had been going out so often she didn't have much time to spend with them and she had started letting Jincey cut out the paper dolls.

It had been a big treat at first but now Jincey was tired of being indoors and tired of paper dolls. She was still hanging around the front hall trying to decide what to do when she heard Della's rapid footsteps coming back across the front gallery. Before she could get to the door it opened and Della rushed in, smiling.

"Run wash your face and git your coat, honey. Mr. McPherson is going to take you for a little ride!"

Jincey couldn't believe it. A ride—a car ride!

She ran to get her coat and Della followed her with a wet washrag and a hairbrush.

"Now, listen, Jincey," she said in a low, serious voice, *"Don't call me Mama!* It's very important. *Don't call me Mama!* If you have to call me anything, call me 'Aunt Della.' You understand? It's serious, Jincey, 'Aunt Della'—not Mama."

"Why?" Jincey faltered. "Ain't you my Mama? Can't I call you that?"

"Of course I'm your mama!" Della said impatiently. "It's a kind of game—a trick we're playing on Mr. McPherson. He thinks you're my dead sister's child. I'll tell you about it later. We haven't got time now. But another thing, when you git out of the car you must say thank you to Mr. McPherson for taking you for the ride. Can you remember that? Say, 'Thank you, Mr. McPherson, I enjoyed the ride.' "

The double instructions weighed on Jincey so heavily the leaping delight of automobile-riding was diluted considerably. She followed Della to the car, which was waiting at the curb and the man standing beside it.

"Barton, this is my little niece, Jincey," Mama said and nudged Jincey to hold out her hand.

"How do you do, young lady." Mr. McPherson said, taking her hand in a hard grip and pumping it up and down. "I'm mighty pleased to meet you. Miss Della has been telling me about you. You want to ride in the back or sit up front with us and blow the canary whistle?"

Jincey's face lit up. "The whistle!" she cried.

"No, Jincey, not now," Mama said. "Maybe later. You sit in the back now."

Jincey didn't pay much attention to Mr. McPherson, car-riding through the night-lit streets was so much fun. She was afraid he was going to turn back at every corner and she would put her weight on the side against such a turn. They stopped at a drugstore and Mr. McPherson went in to get them drinks.

"Young lady, could you put away a chocolate ice-cream soda?" he asked Jincey, but before she could answer Mama spoke up. "We'll both take root beers," she said.

"Mama, I want what he said—the chocolate ice-cream something," Jincey said when he had gone in the store.

"Hush," said Della. "It costs fifteen cents. When you're out with somebody who is going to pay always order the cheapest thing. A man thinks you're extravagant if you order a fifteen-cent drink. Root beer is five cents. And don't forget, say 'Thank you.' "

It reminded Jincey once more of what she had to say when she got home and for the rest of the time she was very still, thinking about it and saying the words in her head. Thank you, Mr. McPherson, I enjoyed the ride.

Just before they got to their street Mr. McPherson pulled over to the curb and turned around and held out his arms to Jincey. "Come on, young lady, ride up front and blow the whistle."

Mama made a face at him but it was a pleased, indulgent face and Jincey, avoiding Mr. McPherson's hands, was quick to scramble over the high-backed front seat. A cord attached to the steering wheel and running down under the hood of the car blew the whistle and Jincey yanked on it delightedly half a dozen times before they reached the house. She was so absorbed in the pretty sound, the bird-like fluting from under the hood, that she forgot to worry about, "Thank you, Mr. McPherson . . ." until they stopped at the door.

Then the chore fell heavily on her mind and her mouth once more. Mr. McPherson jumped out of the car and lifted her over the door and he was smiling and telling her how glad he was to have met her. She waited numbly with her head ducked for him to finish, conscious of Mama's eyes on her. When he paused she choked and mumbled the first "Thank you" but the rest of the speech died on her tongue. She swallowed and looked miserably at Mama whose face showed up plain and disgusted under the street light.

"Thank you . . ." Jincey tried again.

"You're very welcome," said Mr. McPherson solemnly, holding her hand and shaking it again.

"Run on in the house and git in bed," Della said. "I'll be in a little later."

Jincey went to sleep worrying about how mad Mama was going to be in the morning. But Della was so cheerful before she went to work that Jincey thought she had forgotten the messed-up thank-you speech. It was only when she was tying the sash on Jincey's made-over school dress that she mentioned it.

"I want to tell you about saying thank you to people," she said. "It's something you've got to remember, especially with men. When they do something for you it makes them feel good to know you appreciated it. Now last night Mr. McPherson was driving clear out Cedar Point Road when I told him you hadn't been feeling good and acted a little blue when I left. He turned right around and come back and went to the trouble to buy you a drink and let you blow the canary whistle. Don't you think he deserved to know you were thankful?"

"Yes'm," said Jincey. "Next time . . ."

"If there *is* a next time," Della said. But Jincey could tell from the forgiving way she smiled that she was pretty sure there'd be another chance to thank Mr. McPherson.

Aunt Ina and Uncle Tee were worried about the front room upstairs that wouldn't stay rented.

"Comers and goers," Uncle Tee growled. "And it's worth seven dollars a week if it's worth a dime."

"I think I could rent it to Cora and Mabel," Aunt Ina said. "They mentioned getting out of where they are."

"Whores?" Uncle Tee said. "I'm a officer of the law and I won't have whores consorting and carrying on in my house!"

"Aw, Tee," pleaded Aunt Ina, "They wouldn't do their business here. It would be kind of a home for them—a place to be when they wanted to rest. You know."

Uncle Tee said no, and that would be the end of that. But Cora and Mabel, who lived in a big three-story house with iron lace on the upstairs and downstairs galleries on St. Louis Street, kept coming by in the afternoons and talking wistfully about having a little place of their own. Aunt Ina sent Jincey to show them the vacant room upstairs and Jincey could tell they liked it. Cora, who was plump and had curly red hair cut short so it frizzed all around her face, looked at the three-burner oil stove in the corner by the front window and sighed.

"A place to cook, Mabel, look. Lord, God, I'd love a place to be able to fry fish or cook pork chops once in a while. Working like we do is all right if you just had a little home cooking now and then."

Mabel was thin and dark with slick black hair cut in a bang like Jincey's, except no plait for a hair ribbon.

"Let's beg Mrs. Walton to rent it to us," she said. "When we got tired we could stay off work and Edna couldn't make us take on any jobs we didn't want."

Jincey asked if they did piecework like Mama and Cora

laughed in a hoarse, sweet voice and hugged Jincey and said it was like Mama's work in a way but different.

"Yeah," said Mabel. "We work in a factory and we do piece-work but it ain't the overall factory, thank God. I know some-thing about that. It's where I started to work when I first come to this town."

Aunt Ina told them she'd like mighty well to have them rent that room but they'd have to ask Uncle Tee. They waited around until he came home and were so friendly and jolly with him he was laughing and talking to them before he knew it. At first he told them no about the room. And then he told them he'd think about it.

"I know what you're thinking, Tee," Cora said. "But we won't bring no disgrace on your house. Try and see."

A few days later they were back when Uncle Tee got home, and Cora had been fooling around the kitchen cooking. While Aunt Ina and Mabel sat and rocked and talked Cora had fried two chickens and was whipping up potatoes with hot milk and butter when Uncle Tee walked in.

"Tee, I hope you don't mind," she said. "I git so lonesome for home cooking. Sit down and let me git you a plate!"

Uncle Tee said he had been dreading to start supper and the chicken smelled mighty good. He ate a bait of that and then some pudding Cora made out of some bananas from the stem of overripe ones on the back gallery.

"What did you put in this?" he asked, taking a second portion.

"It's a new receipt and easy, easy," Cora said happily.

"Ina, taste it," Uncle Tee urged. "Why don't you get the re-ceipt and make it for us some time?"

"You ain't talking to me," Aunt Ina said. "I ain't taking on any extra cooking. Get the receipt yourself if you want it."

"Would you give it to me?" Uncle Tee asked humbly.

"Sure," Cora said. "But better still, let me fix it for you any time you want it."

That was how Cora and Mabel got to rent the room upstairs. Every Sunday Cora made a banana pudding for Uncle Tee. Once or twice he tried to make it himself, using her receipt, but it wasn't as good and finally he told her to go on and move in upstairs.

All of them liked being at home better with Cora and Mabel there. There was always a smell of good cooking floating in the front hall when Cora was off work and at home and Mabel was always sewing on something and ready to sit and talk with Mama and Aunt Ina.

When Easter came Jincey was going to be in a program at the Baptist Sunday School, where she went with Uncle Tee each week, and she needed a new dress.

"I know just what I'll make for her," Della told Mabel. "I saw one in Gayfer's window—a yellow organdy with ruffles from the waist to the hem. Let's walk up there after supper and I'll draw a picture of it and copy it, if I can get the goods on payday."

"You don't want me to walk down the street with you, especially at night," said Mabel, laughing. "Go by yourself and I'll see you tomorrow."

"Aw foot," Mama said, but she laughed, too, and agreed, taking Jincey with her to look at the dress.

The store was closed but the window was brightly lighted and Della stood a long time with a pencil and a piece of paper drawing the yellow dress and counting its many ruffles.

"Oh, you'll be the prettiest childee!" she crowed to Jincey. "I'll get the ruffles picoted in black at the store and with yellow socks and black patent-leather slippers . . . um, um. Maybe Mr. McPherson will take you out with us on that Sunday afternoon!"

When payday came Della put off paying the man from Askin-Marine's and went straight to a jewstore on upper Dauphin Street where they put bolts of cloth on the sidewalk and searched and searched until she found just the right shade of yellow organdy. They spread the goods out on Aunt Ina's dining-room table and, while Cora made meatballs and spaghetti for supper for all of them, Mabel and Della drew threads through the goods so the ruffles would cut smooth and straight.

"I'll leave them off for you to be picoted tomorrow," Mabel offered. "It won't take more than a day or two."

Mabel left off the ruffles and then picked them up, paying for them herself and bringing them home all neatly edged with a tiny black scalloping made by Gayfer's machine.

"Mabel, you're the best thing!" Della said. "Can you wait till payday for your money?"

"Oh, sure," said Mabel easily. "Any payday you're not strapped will do. I just have to make a payment on Mama's furnitoor is all."

Della sewed on the yellow dress every night and made Jincey practice a new thank-you speech.

"Thank you for a nice time, Mr. McPherson. I enjoyed myself very much."

Over and over she said it and as the dress grew she perfected it. All Mama had to say in a certain tone was, "Scree-eech! Here we are at home, young lady!"

And Jincey, giggling, would pretend to climb out of a car and hold out her hand for shaking and rattle off the speech: "Thank you for a nice time, Mr. McPherson. I enjoyed myself very much."

The Saturday before Easter Mama got paid at noon and came home crying.

"That hussy. That no-good hussy!" she raged, throwing her hat and pocketbook on Aunt Ina's bed. "You know what was in my envelope this week? Eight measly dollars! She threw every bundle I've done since Wednesday right back at me, and even though I did them over I didn't get credit for them!"

"Did you talk to the boss?" Aunt Ina asked.

"You mighty right I did," Della said. "But he was in a hurry and told me to wait till Monday. *Monday!* And tomorrow Easter!"

"Well, now," said Aunt Ina soothingly. "We can wait on your room rent. That'll give you enough for the grocery bill and Askin-Marine."

"But I wanted to buy Jincey some shoes!" cried Della. "I wanted something to wear myself. Going out on Easter with Barton McPherson in what I've been wearing to work all winter! Look at my shoes."

She held up a foot to show a hole in the sole.

Mabel and Cora, hearing the commotion, came down the stairs and got Mama to tell it over again.

"That's the way they do you," said Mabel. "That's why I took up whoring." And seeing Jincey listening, she grimaced. "I mean my *work*."

"If I can get Barton McPherson to marry me they can eat their damned overalls," declared Della, sliding the door open to their room.

The yellow dress was hanging on a hanger on the wall and Della took it down and turned it this way and that, looking at it.

"Mama, it's the prettiest thing..." Jincey began.

"Sure," said Della bitterly. "It's pretty all right, and it'll look like hell with scuffed brown oxfords and long plaid stockings."

"Della," said Cora from the door. "I know what we'll do. I can make up a yellow dye and we'll cut off a pair of Mabel's silk stockings and dye them to match Jincey's dress. If I had the money I'd loan it to you but you know I have to help out at home."

"I have the money for some black slippers for Jincey and why don't you try on a pair of mine?" Mabel put in. "Weatherby Furnitoor Company can't get to Mississippi and repossess Mama's furnitoor before next week and by then we can pay them. Come on, young'un, Mabel's gon' buy you some shoes!"

Before they left for the store Mabel brought a pair of her pumps with bows on the toes down for Mama to try. They were practically brand-new, but Mabel said she didn't give shoes much wear and for Della to go on and keep them if she could wear them.

She could just get them on and they hurt so bad she couldn't take more than a few steps in them.

"Oh, if I just had little feet!" sighed Della collapsing in a chair. "Why was I born so big-footed and common?"

"Hush," said Cora, "and let me think. There's a way to stretch shoes with beans if I can just remember it."

Jincey and Mabel left for Dauphin Street and gave three dollars for a pair of patent-leather slippers so thin and light, after her winter oxfords, that Jincey practically danced home in them.

"You let her wear them out of the store?" Della said when they walked in the kitchen, but she smiled. "It's all right. I reckon I would have too. The young'un don't git much that's new."

Jincey's shoes didn't get much more attention because everybody was so busy with Cora's receipt for stretching Mabel's tight shoes with beans. They soaked a potful of dried Yankee beans in water until they began to swell and then they poured the water off them and put them in the shoes, still wet and swelling.

"Leave them all night," Cora directed before she went to work. "By morning they will have the shoes pushed out enough for you to be comfortable in them."

The next day the shoes were soaked through and not much bigger but Mama put them on anyhow and she and Aunt Ina went to church with Uncle Tee and Jincey. Skipping along between them in her patent leathers with her ruffles sticking out yellow and crisp, Jincey thought she must be the most dressed-up person in the world.

Her part in the program wasn't much. She marched in with the rest of the Sunday school children and blended her voice with theirs when they sang "Up from the Grave He Arose!" She could see Mama and Aunt Ina sitting back in the middle of the church and Mama looked proud—of her dress, not her singing, she knew —but she was happy anyhow.

Mabel and Cora were up when Mr. McPherson came to get Della and Jincey to take them on a picnic after church and they came out on the upstairs gallery to get a look at Jincey in her finery.

Jincey waved goodbye to them and Mr. McPherson looked up and saw them standing there in their cotton crepe kimonos, looking sleepy and tumble-haired from just having crawled out of bed.

"Who's that?" he asked Della in a low voice.

"The Misses Taylor and Wooten from Lucedale, Mississippi," Della said primly. "I think they are schoolteachers but I don't know them very well."

"I'll tell you something about them when I get a chance," he said, glancing at Jincey.

Jincey was leaning forward and looking at Mama in surprise, ready to correct her. Mabel and Cora weren't schoolteachers but piecework whores, Mama knew that. Not know them very well . . . why, Mabel's shoes were even then drying on Mama's feet!

Della threw her a dark, shut-up look and Jincey leaned back.

Thank you for a nice time, Mr. McPherson, she practiced in her head. And then the other lesson: Not "Mama" but "Aunt Della." Because Mr. McPherson might not want to marry a woman with a child.

Mr. McPherson stopped at the Battle House coffee shop to pick up a picnic basket the cook in there had packed for them and the minute he was out of hearing, Della turned to Jincey.

"You got to help me, Jincey," she said softly. "I can't stand that overall factory much longer. If I was married to a nice man like him I could stay home with you and we could have clothes and things. Be good, Jincey, be extra good."

Jincey thought hard about being good and then she began to have such a fine time she forgot about it. Mr. McPherson came out of the Battle House whistling and when he put the picnic basket on the back seat beside Jincey he looked at her new dress for the first time and let out another kind of whistle—long and low and admiring.

"Who is this dressed-up young lady we have with us?" he asked Della. "Introduce me."

"Jincey!" cried Jincey delightedly, jumping up and down. "Jincey, Jincey, Jincey!"

"Whoa, wait a minute!" he said, rumpling her bangs with his big hand. "Jincey is an ugly freckle-faced little girl. Now this young lady..."

"See, I'm ugly!" Jincey said urgently, pushing her face closer. "See my freckles!"

Mr. McPherson threw back his head and laughed, showing all his strong white teeth.

"Miss Jincey, you won't do!" he said. But Jincey knew he meant she would do, that he liked her very much.

He got in the seat beside Mama and he smiled at her and told her she looked pretty, too, and what was her name? And after a while they were driving along the bay shore and Mr. McPherson started singing and Mama sang along with him and Jincey thought it was the prettiest sound she had ever heard.

Mr. McPherson looked at Jincey in the mirror and winked at her and on the next song he said, "Come on, Ugly, you can sing too."

Jincey didn't know the song but she joined in on the chorus, and then Mr. McPherson asked her what songs she knew best and she said, "Up from the Grave He Arose" and "My Country 'Tis of Thee."

"Two of my favorites," said Mr. McPherson. "Let's try part singing."

And he tried to teach Jincey to carry the melody while he did the tenor and Mama did the alto. Jincey came out sounding funny but Mr. McPherson didn't seem to know it. He said they made a great trio and he was going to see if he could get them booked at the Lyric Theater and maybe a few churches.

"Nigger churches," Della suggested. But Mr. McPherson laughed and said not hardly, the way the colored folks he knew could sing.

They put their picnic lunch down under some trees on a bluff overlooking Mobile Bay and Della let Jincey take off her shoes and socks and walk down to the beach and look for shells. She was coming back, climbing slowly in the soft sand when she heard Mama crying.

"Mama . . . ?" she faltered, beginning to run. And then she remembered. "I mean . . . Aunt . . . what's the matter?"

"Nothing, Jincey," Mama said. "Go play."

And then to Mr. McPherson: "Barton, what am I going to do? I can't live in the house with bad women!"

"Well, maybe I shouldn't have told you," Mr. McPherson said. "But I thought you would want to know. I've seen those two operating on the street at night and I'm almost certain they belong in a house down on St. Louis Street."

"Imagine, women like that moving in among respectable people!" Della sounded very disgusted. "And me trying to make a home for a little orphaned girl."

She sighed. "I don't know . . . I don't know where to turn."

"I know one way you could turn," Mr. McPherson said.

Jincey drew closer, wanting to hear, but Della gave her a dark look which said be quiet, go away, and she went a little distance where acorns had fallen from the big oak tree and she started picking them up for cups and saucers.

She could almost hear what Mr. McPherson and Mama were

saying but if she shut out the sound of their voices by singing maybe something good would happen. Maybe Mr. McPherson would marry them.

"Up from the grave He arose!" Jincey sang to herself. "With a mighty triumph o'er His foes!"

Later when the sun was going down and a breeze from the bay was stirring around in the gray moss in the live oak trees around them, they ate the Battle House fried chicken and sandwiches and chocolate cake and Mama and Mr. McPherson looked at each other and smiled a lot. And after a while they packed up the picnic things and sat watching the light on the water and Mama's hand was in Mr. McPherson's and her head was on his shoulder. Jincey, playing back of the steering wheel in the car, pretending to drive it, felt full of food and peace.

Thank you for a nice time, Mr. McPherson, she practiced, I enjoyed myself very much.

The speech went off without a bobble that night and Mr. McPherson was so taken with it he stood a long time shaking Jincey's hand and smiling down at her with his white teeth making a light in his face and some of his fair hair hanging down on his forehead where the wind had blown it.

"It was my pleasure, young lady," he said.

"Ugly," Jincey offered daringly.

He laughed aloud. "That's right. Ugly. Goodnight, Miss Ugly!"

Jincey ran into the house, her heart racing, and the first person she saw was Aunt Ina, sitting and rocking by the cold fireplace.

"I think . . ." she gasped ". . . I think Mr. McPherson is going to marry us!"

"Is that right?" Aunt Ina perked up. "Come here and tell me how you know."

At that moment Mama came in and Aunt Ina said, "Is it true, Della? Jincey says you've hooked him."

Mama was smiling and pink-faced from the day outdoors and some of her hair had escaped from its knot and hung around her face in fluffy little wisps, making her look young.

"That's not the way to put it—hooked him," she said, giving Jincey a look. "But, yes, he did ask me."

Uncle Tee spoke up from the bed where he had been dozing over the Sunday *Register*.

"How about the divorce from Howie? You're not forgetting that you ain't free to marry anybody yet?"

Della's face fell. It was still pink but the smile was gone and the pinch of worry and trouble was back, tightening her lips and dulling the shine in her eyes. She even brushed the soft hair back from her face and pulled out some hairpins and stuck them back in to hold it tighter.

"I had forgotten," she said tiredly. "Lord, God, Tee, I *had* forgotten."

She turned toward their room.

"Come on, Jincey," she said. "Let's get to bed. I'll think of something."

They were having a play about a little old Indian boy named Hiawatha at school and Jincey was supposed to have a dress made out of a corn sack and some beads to wear. The smartest boy in the class, named Barry, was going to be Hiawatha and a girl named Elizabeth Adams who had long pigtails was going to be Minnehaha, a Indian maid. All the rest were plain no-name Indians who just had to dress up and romp around toward the end of the reciting. All the parents were invited but Jincey didn't say anything to Della about it because she knew she couldn't stay off from the overall factory for a bunch of put-on Indians.

At the last she didn't mention the corn-sack dress, either. Mama was too worried about not being divorced from Papa to mess around with beads and corn-sack dresses. She would have asked Aunt Ina but Aunt Ina wasn't the kind of lady who did anything about anything, and ever since she heard that Mabel and Cora were bad women she hadn't spent much time with them.

Della talked to them as much as ever though. They heard about the worry over the divorce and Cora said if Della had her wits about her she would get Mr. McPherson to hire a lawyer to get the divorce and pay for the whole thing himself.

"He'd do it just to get you," she told Mama.

"Huh!" snorted Della. "You don't know. He wouldn't have me at all if he thought I was a divorced woman. You don't know what they're like in that family. Genteel, honey. Presbyterian. He thinks divorce is a sin and anybody who'd marry a divorced woman would be living in sin."

Cora and Mabel laughed at that and Jincey thought they were laughing at Mr. McPherson and it made her mad.

"Mr. McPherson is not a Presby . . . whatchamacallit!" she said furiously. "He's nice."

They all laughed at her and Mama told her to run, play and stay out of grown folks' conversation. But she didn't go far because she was worried. It looked like they might not get to marry Mr. McPherson after all.

Mabel asked Della why she didn't write Papa and tell him to get a divorce since she was supporting Jincey and he wasn't.

"And have him show up here and try to ruin the whole thing? Or take Jincey back to East Bay with him? Not on your tintype! He don't know where we are and if I can help it he won't find out."

Worry was heavy on them all. Only Aunt Ina was cheerful and Jincey could see why. Aunt Ina had herself a pretty good husband and didn't have to go to the overall factory every day or to the whorehouse every night. Her shoes never wore out because she didn't spend much time on her feet and every payday just about Uncle Tee would bring her a new hat. She didn't even have to worry about a corn-sack dress because she didn't have any children.

The corn-sack dress and the beads worried Jincey almost as much as the divorce. Other children in her class kept showing up with sacks their mamas had cut arm and neck holes in and fringed around the bottom and they spent art time drawing pictures on them with crayons.

When Miss Parker asked Jincey where her sack was she always said, "My mama's going to get it for me tomorrow."

It was as good an answer as she could think of and it kept Miss Parker quiet until the last day before the play. Then she really got on to Jincey about the sack.

"You can't be in the play if you don't have a costume," she said. "I don't understand why you're the only child in the class who hasn't made any effort to get one. Ask your mother to come and see me in the morning and maybe we can rig up something together."

Jincey thought she might mention the sack that night, but Della was so tired she went right to bed when she got home from the overall factory. Jincey drank milk and ate the last of the bananas for supper and fooled around in the yard until dark, making bracelets out of the coral vine, which was just coming into bloom on the porch.

The next morning she started to school but when she was a block away her feet began to drag. She lingered behind a hedge that ran along side a big old house that had a little naked-boy fountain in the yard. It was a dry fountain now, but you could see from green streaks on it where the water had once run out of the mouth of a big fish the boy held in his arms. It was really something to look at, Jincey decided, and she drew closer and sat on the rim of the dry pool until she heard the school bell ring.

She was still sitting there when a little tin wagon came creaking along on the other side of the hedge and pretty soon, through the gaps in the green leaves, she saw the wagon was pulled by an old woman dressed in black.

Catching a glimpse of her the old woman stopped and poked her head through the hedge.

"What meanness you up to now?" she demanded in a high, cracked voice. "What you fooling around in Miz Stanton's yard for? You some of her kin?"

Jincey fumbled for an answer but the old woman didn't wait for it.

"You want bananas, come on," she said. "New boat in at the fruit dock and they giving 'em away. Come on."

Jincey slid off the fountain rim and followed her. She was accustomed to minding grown people, especially dusty old ladies, and besides, it was something to do until the Indian mess was over at school.

She didn't know the old woman's name but they had a fine day. They pulled the wagon through alleys and along back streets to the railroad docks where men were taking big stems of bananas off a boat and loading them into railroad cars. The sun was warm and the breeze from the bay had a good salty smell that offset the sweetish smell of rotting bananas. The black, cindery ground in front of the railroad cars was littered with bananas too ripe to ship, and a lot of Negro women and children were already there picking them up.

When the old lady saw them she started running, pulling the bouncing and jerking wagon so fast it threatened to fall apart.

"Git! Git!" she cried. "Go 'way from here! These is white folks' bananas!"

"Aw, kiss my ass!" said a little black boy, turning his rump toward them and slapping it.

"Hush yo' mouth, Junior," one of the women said. "You know dat ain't no way to talk. Come on, white folks, they be's plenty for us all. We hep you load yo' wagon."

They all worked along together until the old lady's wagon was filled and then the women filled the sacks they had brought.

Above them in the railroad car and on a ramp leading up to the car big black men swung the great green-gold stems around and made a kind of music to work by.

"Debt I owe, Lord, debt I owe," they sang. "I ain' gonna pay no debt I owe, I ain' gonna pay no debt I owe, I ain't gonna pay no debt I owe! Debt I owe in Jewstown sto', I ain't gonna pay no debt I owe! Oh, Mister Watchman, don't watch me, I ain't gonna pay no debt I owe. Watch that nigger behind the tree, I ain' gonna pay no debt I owe!"

At the end of every line when they got a bunch of bananas in place they went "Hunnnh!"

Jincey would have liked to stay and listen but one of the Negro women said, "You all got any fish? If you be's fish hongry they giving away mullet at the fish wharf."

"Come on!" said the old lady.

They made a big parade, Jincey and the old lady and all the Negro women and children, but there was enough mullet for everybody. A man on the boat said they weren't taking any more at the fish market and mullet wasn't a fish to keep so they could help themselves.

He was frying some over a charcoal bucket on the deck of his boat and it smelled so good Jincey's stomach growled and she figured it must be long past noon recess at school. Somewhere along the way she had lost the brown paper bag with her sandwich in it and usually she didn't much care. On days when Aunt Ina fixed her lunch she was glad if one of the boys in the class stole it from the cloakroom, as often happened. When the Seafoam sandwich spread ran out Aunt Ina was likely to put anything between bread—sliced onions or butter and sugar and once, a raw, cold wienie.

Today she would have welcomed even one of Aunt Ina's lunches, especially when the man on the boat lifted a brown, crisp piece of fish out of the skillet, slapped it between two slices of bread, and started eating it there in front of them all.

The sight didn't make the old lady hungry but it reminded her that her son, who was locked up in jail, might be hungry.

"Come on, girl," she said. "Let's go fetch Frank some bananas."

Together they pulled the loaded, fish- and banana-smelling wagon toward the police station downtown. It was a red brick building with a wide hallway through it, and the old woman directed Jincey to lift the back of the wagon while she pulled the front and they got it up the steps and were pulling it through the hall when a policeman asked them what they were up to.

"Bringing my boy something to eat," said the old lady.

The policeman looked at their load of raw fish and bananas and laughed, but he stood aside so they could pull it on to the little office at the end of the hall.

"Look out, Tee," he called. "Here comes a package for Frank Donleavy!"

Uncle Tee came out of the office with a wad of keys in his hand and then he saw Jincey and he yelled.

"What on earth are you doing here, child? Why ain't you in school?"

"Nev'mind that," said the old lady. "She is assisting me now. Officer, I want to put this food in the very hands of my boy Frank. I don't want anybody else to have it."

"Aw, Miz Donleavy," said Uncle Tee. "You know Frank is too

full of canned heat to eat bananas. It'd kill him. You better go on home and fry your fish before they spoil. Save some for Frank when he gets out."

"Officer!" cried the old lady, her voice going high and cracked. "I got a right!"

"Yeah," said Uncle Tee. "And it looks like I got a charge of kidnapping against you. What do you mean taking this child off?"

The old lady looked at Jincey as if she had never seen her before.

"Git!" she yelled. "Go 'way and stop bothering me! I won't have you follering me!"

Jincey looked at her in astonishment. She didn't know how to go home. She had no idea where home was. She looked at Uncle Tee and he was putting on his policeman's coat. He turned his keys over to another man and took Jincey by the hand.

"Come on, Sis," he said. "I think you got a frailing coming to you. Miz Donleavy can stay around here mouthing and stinking the rest of the day but I bet folks at home are worried about you."

Aunt Ina wasn't worried. She hadn't thought to notice the time and see that school was out and Jincey hadn't come in. But when Della came home and heard about it she was more upset than Jincey had ever seen her.

"You better give her a whipping," Uncle Tee suggested, and Della sighed and agreed.

Jincey went with her to get a limb off a little peach tree in the backyard and then stood still while Della flapped it against her legs. It didn't hurt much but Jincey cried because Mama was crying.

Later they lay across the bed together, snuffling away the last of the tears, and Mama put her arm around Jincey.

"Honey, how could you do it?" she asked. "Going off with that poor crazy old woman and laying out of school? Don't you know you'll have the truant officer coming to git me? Why did you *want* to stay out of school? I thought you loved it."

Jincey told her about the corn-sack dress and Della's eyes filled with tears again and she sat up on the bed and scooped Jincey into her lap and rocked her back and forth.

"Oh, Lord, Lord, Lord!" she sighed. "What *am* I going to do?"

It was about a week after that that Mama came home on Sunday night and told them she and Mr. McPherson had been to Pascagoula, Mississippi, and got married.

Part Two

ALL THE WOMEN in the house knew good news when they heard it and they swarmed around Della, hugging her and laughing and saying happy things. Aunt Ina even got up out of her rocking chair and put on the coffeepot and set out the rest of the dinner-time banana pudding for them all to have a little feast.

"But where's the groom, Della?" demanded Cora. "This is your wedding night, hon! Where's he at?"

Della glanced at Jincey as she answered. "Gone back to the mill to make arrangements. He lives up over the commissary in a room next to his uncle's. He's going to git us a house in the morning and I'm going out tomorrow and start fixing up."

"No more overall factory," said Mabel with satisfaction.

"Not as long as my head is hot," Della agreed fervently.

Jincey stood as close to Della as she could, holding a fold of her skirt and searching her face anxiously. It was good news that they had married Mr. McPherson, she knew that. Mama had said it was for both of them but there might be a hitch in it. There might be something that would cause Mama to go and Jincey to stay.

Della rumpled Jincey's hair absently as she told Aunt Ina and Mabel and Cora how they had gone to a Justice of the Peace in Pascagoula and he was out somewhere to an all-day sing with dinner on the ground. She had thought that they might leave and

127

maybe come back another time, if Barton was still of a mind to marry her, but he wouldn't budge. He parked his car in the shade of a tree in front of the Justice of the Peace's house and they had sat there all afternoon. He talked a long time about the life he had lived and the sins he had committed and he asked Della to do the same.

"I bet his sins was black as tar," put in Cora in her hoarse voice. "Something like catching a fish out of season."

Mama nodded, smiling. "He gambled some in the Army but swore off when he come home. He had a car wreck once that killed a nigger woman and a mule, but they was traveling without a lantern and it wasn't his fault. He took it hard—still does—and sends some money every month to the woman's children."

"The Lor-rd!" murmured Mabel, impressed.

"What about your sins, Della?" put in Aunt Ina. "Did you tell him the truth about Jincey and her daddy?"

"That I didn't!" said Della, tossing her head. "I told him I had a mean disposition and I'm bad to burn biscuits."

They all laughed, Jincey, too, because she knew Mama made fine biscuits and anything else she put her hand to. It was the first she had heard of Mama's mean disposition and she was thinking about that when Uncle Tee came home from directing Sunday traffic to Monroe Park. He had taken off his gun and was getting ready to put it away on the top shelf of the wardrobe as Jincey and the women came in from the kitchen.

"Tee!" cried Aunt Ina. "Della's done it. She's married McPherson!"

Uncle Tee stopped, his gun and holster in his hands.

He looked at Mama, his mouth ajar. He swallowed and turned to the wardrobe and he turned again like a man who couldn't remember what he had been doing and didn't know what to do next.

"Della," he said finally. "You'll go to jail."

"Foot to jail," said Della lightly. "I'll go to Bayou Bien and be Mrs. Barton McPherson and nobody will ever know to come a-looking for me there."

"Sis, you better go to bed," Uncle Tee said to Jincey. "I want to talk to your mama."

"Come on, Jincey," said Mabel. "We'll take a good bath. I've got some bath salts to put in the water and I'll scrub your back. You want to be clean and sweet-smelling when you move to your new home."

Della smoothed Jincey's bangs and said carefully, "She won't be going tomorrow. If I can leave her with you all a while. Barton wants a few days to ourselves and I want to git the place fixed up a little."

"Della!" cried Uncle Tee harshly. "Della, listen to me!"

Jincey followed Mabel upstairs, dragging her feet and straining to hear what was being said in Aunt Ina's room. Her heart was so heavy it rested in her stomach, which ached like a rising. She had thought marrying Mr. McPherson would be so fine and now Mama was going off somewhere—to jail or a place called Bye-o Bean, leaving her behind.

Later back in hers and Mama's bed she listened and then tried not to listen to what was being said on the other side of the big sliding doors. She was clean and sweet-smelling all right and wearing one of Mabel's silk nightgowns hitched up on the shoulders, but she didn't feel good about it. Uncle Tee was shouting at Mama.

"You're a bigamist, Della, that's what you are! Don't you know that's a felony? They can lock you up for twenty years. Why couldn't you wait and git a divorce and do this thing right?"

"Oh, Tee," sighed Della. "What's the use of talking any more? You never tried to raise a young'un by working in a overall factory. I don't reckon you've ever been hungry yourself, much less had to call on your kin for charity for a child."

"She's right, Tee," Aunt Ina said. "She had to grab McPherson while the grabbing was good. He wouldn't have hung around waiting, maybe, and if Della had filed suit for divorce he might of found out about it."

"He's going to find out anyhow," said Uncle Tee positively. "He's going to find out she's a bigamist and he's a accessory to the fact."

"Whatever that is," giggled Aunt Ina, unimpressed.

"Tee," Della said desperately, "who's going to tell him? You're not, you know you're not. Howie ain't got sense enough to bell a buzzard, much less to put the law after me for bigamy. It'd mean he had to git up in the morning," she added scornfully.

"Remember," Uncle Tee said ponderously, "I'm a officer of the law. I got a duty."

"Foot to that!" cried Della in exasperation. "Go catch a murderer! I ain't hurting a soul in this world. I'm helping myself and my young'un and what's the law got to say about that?"

"He won't tell, Della," Aunt Ina said. "I promise you that. Tee ain't mean."

Uncle Tee tried to reason with them. He spoke of his sworn duty and living outside the law and then he talked of Barton McPherson's part in it. A good man, he said, enticed by a heedless woman into breaking the laws of God and of man. What would Barton McPherson think of her when the sheriff come up with a warrant and handcuffs, Uncle Tee wanted to know.

Jincey pulled the cover up to her chin and lay very still staring at the ceiling. A wind blew, making shadows of the sweet olive tree at the corner of the house dance overhead. Somewhere out in the bay a boat sounded a lonesome whistle.

Jincey didn't know when Della came to bed and when she woke up the next morning Della was gone.

Aunt Ina said she was to go on to school as usual and not worry about a thing because her mama had gone to Bayou Bien to git their new home ready for them. But Jincey did worry the whole long week. She went listlessly to school and dragged her feet coming back home, knowing that Della wouldn't be there then or later.

Once a storm blew up and she worried that Della might be in it and hurt. In hurricane season roofs blew down on people and trees fell on them. She said something about it to Aunt Ina who laughed.

"Quit your fretting, old woman," she said. "This ain't the hurricane season. Spring storms never hurt a soul. You're the biggest old woman I ever seen about worrying."

Jincey didn't tell her she was worried about Della going to jail. That was a worry too big and too deep to speak of. She pushed it back and tried not to think about it. But sometimes it would rise up in her and she couldn't eat the food Aunt Ina set before her or sleep at night. Cora and Mabel weren't there much that week. There was a U.S. Navy destroyer in port and the sailors gave the whorehouse such a good run of business they didn't feel like they ought to leave and come home.

One afternoon Jincey felt especially bad when she walked home from school. The sun hurt her eyes and the raw wienie Aunt Ina had put in her lunch made her so sick at her stomach she stopped and vomited back of the azalea bush in somebody's yard. When she walked into the house she went straight to the tumbled bed she had crawled out of that morning and fell across it. Aunt Ina looked in on her but the vegetable man's bell was ringing and women up and down the street were answering his "Veggie, veggie, vegetable man" cry. So Aunt Ina grabbed her pocketbook and went out to join them.

When Jincey woke up Cora was sitting on the side of the bed with a hand on her forehead.

"Burning hot," she said over her shoulder to Aunt Ina. "She's coming down with something. Git me a pan of water."

Cora undressed her and sponged her off with cool water and powdered her and put a clean nightgown on her and smoothed the bed to put her back in it. Jincey's throat was sore and her eyes hurt and she started to cry.

"Now, Sugar," said Cora, patting her. "Mustn't cry, mustn't ever cry. Be a big girl and Cora'll hold you and rock you a spell. And before you know it your mama'll be here to git you."

Jincey tried to snuffle back the tears and Cora lifted her up in her arms like she was a little baby and sat in the rocking chair and held her and rocked her and sang.

"I ain't . . . no baby," Jincey started to say once, but Cora's plump body next to her and her arms around her felt so good she snuggled down and closed her eyes.

"Go to sleepy, little baby," Cora sang in her hoarse voice. "When you wake I'll buy you a cake and all the pretty little horses . . ."

During the night Jincey woke up and stirred and Cora, sleeping beside her, stirred too and felt her forehead.

"Burning hot," she said again, and went and got Jincey some cool water to drink and a wet washrag to hold against her hot face.

The next morning Jincey was covered with red bumps and Cora, sitting up in bed, laughed aloud.

"The chicken pox!" she cried. "I shoulda knowed. Lord, how you fergit! You'll begin to feel better now, Honey. Now that you're broke out the worst is over. When your mama gits here you ought to be as good as new."

Aunt Ina and Uncle Tee came and stood by the bed and looked at Jincey and Uncle Tee sighed heavily.

"Pore McPherson," he said. "A bigamist wife and a poxy young'un. He didn't know what he was gittin' into."

It was Sunday morning when Jincey woke up to find Della sitting on the side of the bed.

"Mama!" she yelped.

"Sh-h!" whispered Della. " 'Aunt Della' it is now, and from now on. Don't ever forget. Our happy home depends on it, honey."

She leaned over and hugged Jincey, poxes and all.

"I'm gon' git you some breakfast now and then we'll pack up and head out."

She hurried off toward the kitchen and Jincey got out of the bed and went upstairs to the bathroom. When she finished in there she looked out the window and saw Mr. McPherson lying half under his car in the driveway. He had on some long brown coveralls and the sun shone on his fair hair, which stood up in twigs over his head from being rumpled under the car. He hit something with a wrench and squinted against the sun and then he saw Jincey at the window.

"Young lady!" he called and pushed himself all the way out from under the car and sat up. "Come out where I can see you."

Jincey walked out on the upstairs gallery and stood shyly looking down at him. He saw the scabby places on her face and he stopped smiling.

"Aw, now," he said sympathetically. "Chicken pox. I'm sorry, Jincey. Does it hurt much?"

Jincey shook her head and said nothing.

"You feel bad?"

Again Jincey shook her head.

He smiled his wide white smile. "That's good then. You won't have to wait a day longer to come with us to the mill. Come on down here where I can look at you."

Jincey ran down the steps and out on the side porch and then, overcome with shyness, she clutched a post with both hands and swung herself behind it. Barton McPherson, now standing in the yard, wiped grease off his hands with a rag and reached up and took one of Jincey's hands.

"Old Ugly," he said gently. "You're my little girl now. You're coming to live with us in the country. Did you know that?"

Jincey bobbed her head.

"You can call me 'Uncle Bart' because I'm your aunt's husband. I hope you'll be happy where I live because you sure are as welcome as the flowers in May."

Jincey stopped ducking around the post and stood still, one hand quiet in Mr. McPherson's big hand. Welcome as the flowers in May, she said in her head, welcome as the flowers in May. It was the first time she knew that what came out of a person's mouth could be pretty. She didn't know what poetry was then and later, when she learned, she never found anything that could match "welcome as the flowers in May."

Standing there feeling the scaling paint of the porch under her bare feet and squinting into the sun, she couldn't think of anything to say.

Barton McPherson closed his big hand over her hand, shook it and let it go, and Mama called them to breakfast.

The sun had set and dusk was settling on the swamps and dark pinelands when the little Ford, with Della's trunk and Jincey lurching around together on the back seat, turned off the gravel road into a narrow sand road winding among the pine trees.

"This is the home road, young lady," Uncle Bart called back to Jincey. "Three miles to go. I used to walk it to school when I was a young feller and you'll be walking it, too, one of these days."

133

Della turned around and smiled at Jincey and reached for her hand.

The woods came close to the sandy ruts and the scent of pine needles warmed by the hot spring sunshine enveloped Jincey. They came to a long bridge with no bannisters and far beneath them Jincey could see coffee-colored water moving slowly over white sand.

"Um-m, something smells pretty," Della said.

"Bay blossoms," Uncle Bart said, slowing down. "See."

He pointed to little gray-green trees with their feet near the water and their tops near the floor of the bridge and Jincey saw they were loaded with smudges of white.

"Oh, Bart, I want one!" cried Della.

"Do you, sweetheart?" the man asked, smiling at her. He stopped the car and shut off the engine. "You wait right here."

"No," said Della, "I'm coming with you. You might fall off the bridge."

Bart pulled her close and kissed her. "You'll hang your heels in the cracks in the bridge," he objected softly.

"No, I won't," said Della. "I'm taking off my shoes and stockings."

Jincey leaned out the side of the car giggling and watching them. Mama sat on the edge of the bridge swinging her bare feet and legs and reaching out her arms toward the green tree Uncle Bart was pulling toward them. They were laughing and Jincey, watching, felt happiness flowing from them and washing over her. Barefoot and with her skirt tucked up and her hair coming loose from its pins, Della looked like a young girl.

In a little while they were back, leaning together and laughing softly as they walked toward the car. Della's arms were full of bay branches and with them she brought into the car a fragrance Jincey was to remember the rest of her life as the very smell of home and deep content. The sharp, spicy scent of the oval gray leaves, the magnolia-like sweetness of the little white flowers, would forever evoke the night she came home to Bayou Bien and Barton's Mill.

There were other smells which became a part of it. The sharp smell of rosin dripping out of the slashed faces of the pine trees, the powdery dust of the road, the sweetish scent of sawdust burning in the slab pit at the end of a long snake-like lumber run, which the sawmill thrust out along the creek bank, the smell of kerosene lamps and fresh-scrubbed pine floors and the faintly acrid smell of a new puppy.

Dusk was falling fast and the stacks of boards in the lumberyard were shadowy hulks when Uncle Bart stopped the car again. Back from the road at the edge of the lumberyard a lamp was burning through the open doorway of a little house and a man and a boy were working over a mosquito smudge fire in the front yard. When they heard the car the boy raced around the house and in a little while was back, followed by two girls, the smallest of them stumbling under the weight of an armful of fat, sleepy puppy.

"These are the Bates children, Jincey," Della explained before they reached the car. "I met them and their folks last week. They are our nearest white neighbors."

"They've got something for you," Uncle Bart added. "Howdy, Old Pa, Miss Eva," he called to the man in the yard and the woman who had come out on the front gallery, as he climbed out of the car and went to meet the children.

"Zack, Virgie, Lula," he named them. "Come meet my little girl, Jincey."

The smallest girl was plump with long brown curls to her shoulders and she stared at Jincey shyly over the head of the heavy puppy.

"Here," she said, holding him out to Jincey. "We been keeping him for you."

"Tell her his name, Virgie," Uncle Bart directed.

Virgie turned shy but the two older ones said it for her: "Welcome Jincey."

Jincey took a deep breath and let it out slowly.

"Oh, let me . . . oh, can I have him?" she faltered, looking at Della.

"Sure you can," Della said. "Uncle Bart got the Bates children to pick him out of the litter and put your name on him two weeks ago when he knew you'd be coming here to live. What do you say?"

All the thank-you speeches she had learned painfully and slowly went spinning through Jincey's head and she would have babbled them out together if she hadn't been so overcome by the moment and the gift. A puppy . . . *her* puppy. She choked out something that passed for thank you and then she was half over the door of the car holding out her arms.

"He's had his supper," Lula, the older girl, put in. "Be careful he don't wet on you."

Della and Uncle Bart thanked them and said they'd be coming to visit and to play but Jincey was so wrapped up in the wonder of the soft little body, the sleepy little face in her arms, that she no longer saw the children or much else that they passed. It was the first pet that she had ever owned.

The road led through dark rectangles of stacked lumber, across a creek and past the big two-story commissary and office building. It climbed past a barn and a lot where the warm smell of animals was heavy on the twilight air, across another little bridge and up a slight hill where there were no longer pine trees but big oaks planted in rows on either side. Uncle Bart pulled up under one big tree and stopped the car and Jincey saw the house for the first time.

"Home, women," Uncle Bart said, yawning and stretching and reaching out to pull Della close to him. "That sounds mighty good to me, does it to you?"

"You don't know how good," Della said in a low voice, leaning her head against his shoulder for a minute. Then she lifted it and said briskly, "Hop out, young'un, you're home. Let's go in."

Bart walked ahead and lighted a kerosene lamp in every room. The yellow light flowered against red pine walls and made circles of brightness on scrubbed pine floors. There were four rooms lined up two by two with a kitchen and little back gallery at one end and a long narrow front gallery across the other end. Bart found a wooden box and made a bed for the puppy on the back gallery and Jincey squatted beside it, patting him, until Della called her.

"Come wash your face and hands," she said. "I'll give you something to eat and then you've got to get in bed. You can see everything tomorrow."

Jincey, drowsy from the trip and bemused by the wonder of the puppy, fumbled through washing her face and hands in the enameled pan Della put before her and allowed herself to be led to a canvas deck chair in the corner of the dining room. Della brought her a slice of raisin bread and butter and a glass of buttermilk. It was the first time she had tasted raisin bread and she savoured it, holding it in her mouth a long time to get the full taste of the sweet raisins and the dark cinnamon. It seemed at one with the golden lamplight and the feeling of homecoming.

When she had finished eating Della tucked her in a cot in the little back bedroom with a door open to the bigger front room where she and Uncle Bart would sleep. When she was under the light cover Uncle Bart came and stood with his arm around Della and looked down at her.

"My wife, my home, my little freckle-faced gal," he said. "I'm a lucky fellow."

The sweet imperative sound of the six o'clock whistle calling men to work awakened Jincey. The sun was up but it was still so young and tender the fingers of light it sent through the green of the big trees around the house were baby-soft and pale. Jincey lay still and looked and listened. It was a little room, all doors, one by the little brick chimney leading to the kitchen, one behind her leading to the dining room and one beside the head of her cot connecting with Della and Bart's room. The fireplace was black-throated from many winter fires but its bottom was swept clean and ornamented by a fan of pleated paper neatly set in its center. There was a little armless rocking chair beside it and a fringed rug with red roses climbing around its edges on the scrubbed floor in front of it. Jincey's Christmas doll stood on the mantelpiece and the clothes she had worn the night before hung straight and smooth on one of a row of black hooks screwed into the wall of the far corner. In the near corner there was a little washstand with a mirror over it and a flowered bowl and pitcher set centered on the crocheted dress scarf which covered it. A slop jar with painted roses and a blue painted ribbon looped around its middle crouched beside the washstand like a docile watchdog.

My room, Jincey thought, pleased. The first one I ever had.

She pulled a hand from beneath the sheet and laid it flat against the smoke-darkened pine boards of the wall. They had been covered with thickness after thickness of newspaper, one layer for every Negro woman who ever kept house there. Some wanted only to keep out the cold and freshen up the room. Others believed the old tale that a hant can't hant you till he has read every word on your walls. But Della in her war against chinches had scraped off all the paper and scrubbed the walls. Some places she hadn't been able to get off all the flour paste and it made little white lacy designs in the grain of the rosin-red wood. The wall, Jincey decided, had a lot for you to see—knots like eyes, dagger-pointed ridges and whorls like fish and birds and stars—the pattern of years of the tree's life running like waves on the beach. She could spend the rest of her life looking at it, she thought.

A second whistle shrilled and even as that sound lifted in the soft morning air another took its place—a steady thrumming, a bum-bum-bumming like a knock on the wall or big feet stepping fast on stairs and then a high, keening whine.

Jincey sat up and listened.

Della, who had been out in the yard, poked her head around the kitchen door and laughed at the expression on Jincey's face.

"Did you think Old Scratch was after you?" she asked. "That's just the sawmill, childee, where we get our bread and meat, I reckon. I'll show it to you when we go down to the commissary for rations. Now you hop up and put on your clothes and come feed Welcome while I fix Uncle Bart's breakfast to take to him. He has to go open up the office and commissary before the whistle blows and he'd rather eat his breakfast later on."

Welcome! To think she had forgotten!

Jincey rushed into her clothes and hurried through the kitchen, where Della gave her a pan of warm milk for the puppy. On the back porch Welcome stood up in his box and put his paws on the edge and wriggled his fat body when he saw Jincey coming and her heart lifted with delight.

"Look at him, he ain't even crying," she said proudly. "Him a good lil' feller," she crooned, picking him up in her arms.

"Him wasn't good all night," Della said dryly. "While you

slept he howled. Bart got up and give him milk. If he don't do better tonight he might lose his happy home."

Jincey looked behind her through the door to see if Della was mad but she was busy stirring a potful of grits and turning frying fatback and she looked cheerful. Relieved, Jincey sat down on the steps and held Welcome, dipping his nose in the milk and watching proudly as he shook his muzzle, snorted, got a taste of the milk and began to lap it up. The competence of the little pink tongue, curving just so, seemed to her to be the finest thing she had ever seen. In a little while Welcome had polished the gray granite pan, sighed heavily, licked his chops delicately and sagged sleepily into Jincey's arms. Not wanting to disturb him, she sat still, her knees high to make a cradle of her lap, and looked around.

From where she sat she could see a sandy road dipping below the red clay bank of the hill on which the house sat and curving past a fenced field, three weathered, deserted looking little houses in a row and a faded but once white-painted board church-house opposite them, all shaded by big live oak trees.

"Ain't it pretty, Mama?" she asked and caught herself guiltily. "Aunt . . . Della?"

"Oh, Lord, we're not gon' make it if you do that again!" cried Della coming to the door. "You *got* to remember, Jincey. Everything depends on it."

Jincey swallowed miserably.

"Yes'm," she said. "I won't do it no more."

"Poor young'un," Della sighed. "It's not right to put that on you at your age. But I didn't know no other way. Just try, do the best you can."

She stood a minute looking over Jincey's head at the yard, not seeing the curve of the road and the big trees, but weeds and a litter of tin cans and bottles and the rusting carcass of an old automobile.

"It's a sorry mess," she said, "but we'll git it cleaned up. I was so busy scrubbing the house and moving in this week I didn't git to the yards."

She glanced at Jincey's sorrel head, now ducked in misery over the sleeping puppy. Every time the young'un took pleasure in something it seemed to be her way to cut her down. She reached down and patted her.

"Come on now," she said briskly. "Put Welcome in his box and come wash your face and hands and eat your breakfast and we'll go."

While Jincey washed and ate Della took a basket off a nail on the wall and set a plate of grits and eggs and crisp-fried white meat in it. She made a well in the grits with the back of a spoon and poured a little grease off the meat into it. She buttered two biscuits and wrapped them up in a cloth and tucked them in the basket, spreading a napkin over the whole thing. With water from the kettle she scalded a fruit jar to heat it and then she half-filled it with coffee, adding sugar and milk from a can.

"Canned milk in the country," she muttered. "We got to fix that."

"How?" asked Jincey.

"A *cow,* for goodness sake!" Della said impatiently. "You wait and see, I'm going to have a cow if I live. Now wrap that towel around the coffee jar to keep it hot and come on. We got to hurry before nothing's fit to eat."

The sandy road that ran past the empty houses and the church-house at one end, ran toward the commissary and the mill at the other. It crossed a little branch with a rattly wooden bridge, passed two more vacant houses and a big barn and climbed a little rise to where a long gray, two-storied building stood on the banks of a big cypress-fringed millpond.

"This here's the office and commissary," Della said. "Over yon-der's the mill and back there," pointing to a silvered house under some pecan trees back of a paling fence, "is what they call the boardinghouse, although I don't know who boards there or what they board on. Ain't anybody there now. Bart's uncle takes his meals there but he's off somewhere now and the cook he had quit, they say."

They stood a minute by the steps, looking at the mill, a long, sprawling, tin-roofed building that stood so close to a big dam the white foam of the falling water blew like egg whites into the first floor, which was creek level. A second floor extended out over the still water of the millpond and some men on a big pontoon raft used poles with hooks on them to push logs on to a moving chain, which carried the logs up to the mill. Jincey saw where the mill got its voice. A little platform on railroad-car wheels ran down a track, going bum-bum-bum and taking a log into the very teeth of a glittering, whirling rotary saw. As the blade struck the flesh of the tree the keening, searing whine rent the air. Almost immediately the little carriage ran back and the men riding it quickly moved levers and turned the log to give the saw a chance at its other side.

"Let's go in," Della said, turning toward the big commissary building, which stood high in the back on cypress blocks like stilts but was level with the millpond in front. "Uncle Bart's rations is gittin' cold."

A gallery ran across the front with heavy double doors opening into the commissary and a regular door opening into two offices, a front office and a back office. Della went to the smaller door and called out, "Breakfast! Anybody want breakfast?"

Uncle Bart got up from behind a big desk in the back room and came to meet them, smiling broadly.

"This is service," he said. "Two women to bring me my groceries."

He kissed Della and hooked an arm around Jincey's neck and pulled her to him.

"How's my little ugly, freckle-faced girl this morning?"

Jincey grinned up at him, pleased but too shy to speak. She had never seen him in his workclothes before. Now he wore faded overalls with no shirt but an out-sized denim jumper over them. His feet were in heavy cowhide high-laced shoes and on his head was an ancient stained panama hat with a brim so limp and floppy it hung around his eyes and ears in a kind of yellow ruffle. He smelled of sweat and tobacco and overall cloth and Jincey could feel heavy tools in his jumper pocket. A row of pencils, big flat lumber-marking pencils, made a fence on his chest from his top overall pocket.

Now he took off his hat and hung it on a rack by the door. "While I eat you all want to do your trading?" he asked.

Della nodded. Bart took his plate out of the basket and went to the high-backed swivel chair behind the desk in the back room to sit down. Della took the basket and moved ahead of Jincey into the commissary.

It was a big, rich-smelling room, so dark with only the light from the door to illuminate it that Della and Jincey had to stand a minute to let their eyes get used to it. While they waited Jincey breathed deeply of the good store smells—tobacco and green coffee, cloth and flypaper, coconut candy and kerosene and the special sweetish smell of old sprouting Irish potatoes close to rotting.

Two big wooden counters ran along the sides of the room with shelves behind them and across the back, opposite the door, there was a glass counter with a high-domed top. Presently they could see it clearly—groceries and a big double-doored icebox back of one counter, bolts of cloth and shoes back of the other, and candy and thread and patent medicines in the glass case. Beside the candy case there was a wire rack holding deep-brown cardboard bins of tea cakes, easy to be seen because every bin had a glass cover over it.

On the grocery counter there was a scarred round wooden turntable with a great golden cheese on it and a fancy iron bar holding a knife blade over it. At the other end of the counter there was a dark plug of tobacco with another swinging blade with fancy iron flowers on it to cut the tobacco.

Little round iron cages swung from the ceiling over all the counters, trailing white twine, and there was a roller—wood and iron—which held brown paper. Flypaper coils curled ceilingward and where the light struck the millpond outside and splashed a bright reflection on the ceiling boards, Jincey could see that they were black-freckled with fly specks. A cluster of barrels toward the back held flour and sugar and lard and green coffee, and a big brown jug with a handle on it held vinegar.

Jincey breathed deeply and looked at Della.

"Is it Uncle Bart's?" she asked, awed.

"No, silly," Della said, laughing. "It's just a place to buy stuff. Uncle Bart has to pay like anybody."

Bart heard them and called out from the office: "You can have anything you want, young lady! Just look around. If it's not there we'll order it from Mobile first passing. And, Sweetheart, don't worry about just buying what you can carry. Flathead will bring everything up in the truck at dinnertime."

"All right," Della said to him, and it was a sober and polite answer but she grabbed Jincey and hugged her and swung her around in a silent, joyful little dance. "Rations, rations, rations, childee!" she whispered, chuckling low in her throat so only Jincey could hear her. "We eat from now on!"

While Della studied the shelves and picked up some canned tomatoes and corn or a bottle of ketchup or pickles and put them in a little pile on the counter, Jincey roamed, looking. Through the gray-frosted glasses of the icebox she could see butter and meat and down at the bottom a kind of reservoir where cold drink bottles stood neck-deep in ice water. There was a meat block by the icebox, its top grainy with salt, and on it, wrapped in clean sacking, there was a side of salt pork.

She moved to the candy counter and leaned against the glass case to study its contents—blocks of pink and white coconut, little peaked Hershey kisses in silver foil, sticks of peppermint, jawbreakers, chewing gum. While she looked Bart came up behind her and put his hands on her shoulders.

"What for you, ma'am?" he teased like he was waiting on a grown lady.

Jincey looked at Della and found her smiling her permission. "Go on, you can have something," she said.

Jincey caught her breath and leaned closer to the case in an agony of indecision. Jawbreakers lasted longer, but she had never tasted pink coconut candy. Chocolate was a sure favorite, but peppermint sticks were mouth-cooling and lasty.

Bart saw her indecision and grinned at her. "Never mind," he comforted. "I'll decide for you."

And he picked up a brown paper bag and opened the candy case and went methodically through the boxes selecting two of everything. Jincey couldn't believe it and she turned to Della to have it confirmed.

Della's brown eyes were sparkling. "I reckon you've struck it rich forevermore," she said.

Bart looked at the little pile of groceries she had on the counter.

"Well, you're not rich," he said. "You've hardly got anything. What else do we need?"

"I was waiting for you," Della said. "If you could cut me a piece of cheese and maybe some beef to fry?"

Bart whistled a little tune and cut and wrapped the meat and cheese and slapped them on the counter. "What next?"

"I wish we had something fresh and green to boil," Della said, "but since we don't, have you got any Yankee beans?"

"All you want," said Bart, swinging a sack of dried white beans to the counter and thrusting a shiny metal scoop into them. "But I think we still have greens in the field. Clewis is the farmer and he should be by the house this morning with a basket of whatever's ready—turnips or mustard most likely. Maybe some new potatoes."

Della was suddenly overwhelmed. Jincey, holding her bag of candy close to her side, looked up in surprise at Della's face. She was about to cry. She was biting her lips and swallowing hard and her eyes were misted over. All these rations . . . it was the richest they'd ever been. To keep Bart from seeing and knowing, she leaned over a big sack of green coffee and let the beans run through her fingers.

"Greens'll be fine," she said off-handedly.

Clewis was waiting on the back steps with a split white oak basket of greens beside him when Della and Jincey got back to the house. When he heard them come into the kitchen he leaped to his feet and swept off his tattered sunhat in a little bow.

"I wishes to greet howdy to the new miss!" he said unctuously.

"Oh . . . well, howdy to you," said Della. "Are you Clewis?" She stood in the doorway and looked at the basket. "My, them's nice greens. Mister Bart said you would be bringing some."

"Yes'm, ever' day the Lord gimme stren'th," Clewis said earnestly. "I be's by wid some of whatever I scrabbles out of the field for the bo'dinghouse. Till the garden make, it be's mostly greens."

"Well, that's good," said Della. "We like greens."

Clewis handed her the basket to take what she wanted and while Della sorted through the turnips, picking out those with the freshest green leaves and the firmest and crispest white roots, Clewis chattered about the weather and the condition of the soil, which, he promised her, was as "sweet'n' ripe as a peach" this year. Della listened, interested.

"I'm gon' have a flower yard," she said, looking at the weedy, littered area around the steps. "And I'd like a vegetable garden."

"With me bringin' you stuff from the big garden?" demanded Clewis.

"We-ell," Della hesitated, "there's land a-plenty and some things I just like to have close to home. Seems like a vegetable patch *makes* a home place."

"You right, you sho' is right," declared Clewis. "You tell Mister Bart you want ol' Clewis to come by here wid the mule and lay you off a garden spot. 'Course it'd take a fence, but they be's wire in the shed and if you cain't git that, they's plenty of slabs for a paling fence on the burn pile."

He interrupted himself to take off his hat and whirl around where he stood. Then he turned to face Della and Jincey again with exaggerated humility.

"Miss," he said urgently, "would you have a cup of coffee you could spare?"

Della gaped at him, bewildered at the sudden change in him from a grownup man who knew about planting a garden to a childlike, too-humble beggar. He made the switch when he turned, like an impersonator closing one skit and starting another. She was to find out later that the scrawny little black man could caper and frisk about like a young'un, preach and sing and pray with the fire and passion of an old saint, and slide into a melancholy so deep and dark it was painful to see. Now she said slowly, "Sit down, Clewis. I'll see if there's some still hot."

Clewis sipped the hot sweetened coffee slowly and looked up at Della over the rim of the gray granite cup.

"Miss, ain't you from Georgy?" he asked after a while.

"Well, yes," said Della, surprised. "How could you tell?"

"Lord Jesus, come out on the front porch of heaven and lemme

145

say my thanks to you!" cried Clewis fervently. "The new miss is from Georgy!"

"Are you from Georgy, too?" Della asked.

"Georgy-born, Georgy-bred!" Clewis assured her. "Cain't you hear it in my talk like I hears it in yo's?"

"I can't tell no difference," Della admitted.

"It be's there," Clewis assured her. "And I sho' is glad to hear it. These Alabamy folks, they don't know how to treat a cullud person like our folks back home. Miss, we gon' git along."

Della found herself smiling with pleasure. Clewis was her first friend. After that it became a morning ritual, Clewis' arrival with garden stuff and Della handing out the gray granite cup of coffee for him to drink sitting on the back steps.

Jincey had a recurring nightmare, the only bad thing about Bayou Bien and Barton's Mill. She woke up at night dreaming that she had called Della "Mama." Sometimes the dreams were so real that she sat up on her cot and listened, waiting for the sound of Uncle Bart getting their things together for them to leave. One night she slept and had a vivid dream of a man coming to the little window at the foot of her cot and reaching in and grabbing her foot. The touch of the man's hand and his face half-smiling at her was so frightening she cried out for Della, and then in the dream she realized she had said "Mama" and that was worst of all.

She awoke sobbing convulsively. The man was not there. The little window with its shutter open to the night air showed only the branches of the chinquapin tree and the night sky. But there was a cold spot on her ankle where his hand had clasped it and she could hear stirring in the next room so she knew she had called "Mama" aloud.

Jincey buried her face in the pillow and held her breath to still her sobs, waiting for a sign that Uncle Bart had heard. It was Della who came and pulled the sheet over her and whispered, "You all right, Honey?"

"Yes'm," Jincey said. "Are you?"

Della laughed softly. "I reckon. Fine as fiddle dust."

146

The days were as fine as fiddle dust. Jincey thought the house was the nicest one in the world.

"Sawmill shanty, nothing but a sawmill shanty," Della scoffed. "They used to have a fine three-story house out there in the field, facing the millpond. Them big oak trees lined the road to it. But it burned down and Cap'n Barton and Bart moved into the rooms over the office and commissary. This will do for us," she said, looking around, "when I finish fixing. Bart told me to pick a house and I picked this one because it's bigger than most and on a hill with no mosquito bogs around and has nice shade trees and a good water pump close by."

There were other houses, the empty, three-room shotgun houses near them, and up the road beyond a grove of hardwood trees and a little branch where bullace vines laced a screen across the road there was a whole settlement of black people. You could smell the smoke from their cook fires and the fires around the wash pots in every backyard. There was always the smell of fat-back frying and coffee boiling and the sound of people calling out to one another from the little front galleries. One pump by the road near the center of the quarters served them all, and there was nearly always a gathering of people around it, laughing and talking while they pumped water for cooking or washing.

Compared to the quarters houses, theirs was fine. It was bigger because a few years back there had been a woods rider with a lot of children working at Barton's Mill, and they had added two rooms and extended the kitchen and front gallery to what had been a regular three-room quarters house. The new rooms, which Della called parlor and dining room, had glass windows. The bedrooms still had shutters only. Uncle Bart was going to send the carpenter from the mill to put in glass windows and screens in the shuttered openings in the bedroom and kitchen when he could spare the time. Even on the hill the mosquitoes were bad. Della and Bart slept under a big net mosquito bar which hung from a swaying frame fixed to the ceiling over their bed. There was no bar to fit Jincey's cot, so before she went to sleep every night they rubbed her arms and legs and forehead and chin with oil of citronella.

147

The mosquito bar was just one of the fine conveniences that Jincey admired about their house. The parlor was so rich and splendid she never tired of looking at it. There was a rug on the floor and centered on this was a big black library table with a crocheted scarf hanging off the ends and in the middle the Aladdin reading lamp with a milky white globe as big as a dishpan and the Holy Bible beside it. Ringed up around the walls was a slick black horsehair settee with a frame carved with grapes and apples, two horsehair-covered platform rockers and a big standing Victrola, its glowing red mahogany cabinet full of albums that looked like picture books but turned out to hold records.

Jincey got to dust it every day and rub red O'Cedar polish into the table and the wood of the Victrola once a week. Della watched to be sure she did it well and didn't get polish on "the art square" rug or the horsehair.

"Belongs to Bart's mama," she told Jincey. "She's in the crazy house in Tuscaloosa and her big old house in Mobile is rented out. Me and Bart took a truck and went and got enough furniture for this house out of a place in the backyard where it was stored. We got to take care of this old junk because it would be just my luck to have her git well and come home."

It turned out that they didn't take care of all of old Mrs. Mc-Pherson's furniture. Della discovered bedbugs in the mattresses and hauled them and the iron bed and coil springs out into the yard and poured gasoline over them and set fire to them. Uncle Bart saw the smoke from the commissary and came running up the road. He was put out with Della for starting such a big blaze. Fire was a constant fear to everybody at Barton's Mill. Fire in the woods could destroy acres of timber, and turpentine and fire in the sawmill or planer mill or turpentine still could be a disaster, destroying property, jobs, even men.

Della was poking at the mattresses with a rake when Bart came up, panting. When he saw what it was he sagged with relief and spoke sharply to Della about the danger.

Della tossed her head, which she had tied up in a now smutty rag, and said accusingly, "Chinches."

"But, sweetheart, that's Ma's good bedding," Bart protested.

"I don't sleep with anybody's chinches," Della said grimly.

The bedstead, being iron, could be saved. When the fire burned out and it cooled off Della scrubbed it and got some meat grease and rubbed away the rust spots. The springs were all right, too. She scrubbed them and dried them in the sun, and before dark a Negro driving a mule and wagon brought a new cotton mattress which Uncle Bart got somewhere and they moved it all back into the house. Jincey's cot fortunately seemed bug-free, but it was not much comfort to her during Della's war on chinches because she swabbed the cracks of the walls with a mixture of sulphur and kerosene that smelled so strong none of them could get to sleep easy the first couple of nights.

But mostly the unpainted house under the oak trees and its fixings were a pleasure to Della. Jincey could tell, although Della herself said nothing about it. For Jincey it was a place of deep content. She stayed close to the house for the first few days, knowing for the first time that she could remember the comfort of looking up from play, no matter what time of day it was, and seeing Della working nearby. The chicken pox scabs on her face dried and fell off, but Della said it was too late to start her to school. She might as well wait for fall. So she built a playhouse under the chinquapin tree at the corner of the house, driving stobs in the ground to hold up the shelves made out of old shingles for bits of crockery play dishes. The day she made the playhouse Della was working on the gallery building long flower boxes to go along the edge and painting them dark green. Uncle Bart marveled at her carpentry. He had never seen a woman turn off the work the way Della did, he said. He sent two women from the quarters to scrub and do the washing for her. They were twins named Louette and Rouette, and although they had identical skin, the yellowish color of cloudy creek water instead of black, they didn't look much alike. Louette, the bigger of the two, was called "Miss Big Sister" in the quarters and Rouette was called "Miss Lil' Sister."

Della, who had never had a servant in her life, welcomed them for their company, sat them down in canvas chairs under a tree and enjoyed a long morning's visit.

The news was all over the quarters that Mr. Bart had got himself a wife with a little girl and that his uncle-employer wasn't pleased about it. The twins' brother, Goat, had been waiting in the commissary to buy rations and had heard Cap'n Barton bellowing at Mr. Bart the day he told about his marriage.

"Reckon ole Cap'n afeared you after his money," Miss Big Sister said.

Della laughed. "I haven't met him so he couldn't know how to judge me. He went on a trip the same time me and Mr. McPherson got married and we haven't had a chance to meet yet. What's he like?"

"He a harsh man," Miss Lil' Sister offered simply. "Bad to cuss and quick to shoot. He shot more'n one hand. None of us, though," she added quickly with an odd flash of pride. "We Barton family. Been on the place since slavery days. Belonged to his grandpa. He don't mess around none with us."

"Well, I'm sure if he's kin to Mr. McPherson he's a gentleman," Della said, remembering belatedly hearing somewhere that it wasn't proper to discuss white folks with black folks.

The twins subsided but not before they dropped one more seed for discord.

"Well'm, but he don' like you," Miss Big Sister said. "Goat heard him call you a venchess."

Rouette wasn't sure what that was but she knew it wasn't complimentary. Della was familiar enough with *Delineator* fiction to know. Cap'n Barton, Bart's Uncle Bob, had called her an adventuress.

It stayed on her mind and that evening when Uncle Bart came whistling up the road, calling out to Jincey and the puppy, Welcome, who were playing in the road, Della didn't go to meet him but hung back in the kitchen, unnecessarily stirring around the stove. She served them their supper silently and then they moved out to the front gallery and the new swing, where Della and Bart sat together. Jincey wanted to stay with them. Uncle Bart would tease her and play with her and Welcome sometimes and she liked to be close to him and Della. But tonight Della threw her a dark, go-away look and Jincey obediently took Welcome and went out to her playhouse under the tree. It was still close enough to hear above the creak of the chains what was being said.

"Why didn't you tell me your uncle didn't want you to marry me?" Della asked.

Bart let out a long, low whistle. "Golly, I knew it was coming," he said. "It's all over the quarters. I bet."

"I reckon," Della said in a low, shamed voice.

Bart put an arm around her and pulled her close to him. "Don't let it worry you one minute," he said. "Uncle Bob didn't know you and when he does he'll see I'm a mighty lucky man."

"He thinks I'm after his money, don't he?" Della asked.

Bart sighed and stood up.

"He thinks so little of me, I reckon, that he can't figure out any other reason a woman would marry me."

Della stood up, too. "I want you to tell him one thing," she said in a quick, angry voice. "I didn't know he had any money and I sure as shooting don't want anything to do with it. He can kiss my foot!"

"Now, sweetheart," Bart protested, grabbing her by the shoulders. "Don't be mad at Uncle Bob. He's been father and mother to me most of my life. I was born out here and spent every summer of my life out here until I went in the Army. When Papa died and Ma had to go to Tuscaloosa I knew I had a home here no matter what. When I came back from the Army you know who was at the train to meet me? Uncle Bob. He's been my only close family for a long time and I'm his. He offered me this job here and he told me if I'd stay with him I'd be his heir."

"Heir to what?" Della said, casting a scornful glance across the road where the line of big oak trees led to a house site now marked only by the rubble of chimneys and a pomegranate tree growing in the midst of a stand of young corn. "What's he got besides the business you run for him? Rooms over the commissary and a bunch of sawmill shanties in the lonesome pine woods!"

Bart laughed at her and put an arm around her to hug her.

"Della, Della," he said softly. "I don't want anything except what I work for. But Uncle Bob is a very rich man. He owns thousands of acres of 'lonesome pine woods,' as you call it, and several blocks of city property in Mobile. I don't count on getting it, of course, because Uncle Bob is still a young man himself and

151

he might yet get married. These trips he takes, I figure there's a woman somewhere."

Jincey, stirring up a sand cake under the tree, stopped listening. She could tell from the tone of Della's voice that things were all right again and from the creaking of the swing chain that they were sitting together and probably hugging and kissing.

Cap'n Barton did come back from his travels driving a Reo touring car and bringing with him a new settled white woman to cook for him. A lot of settled white women came and went at the two-story unpainted house near the mill where Cap'n Barton took his meals and had his washing and ironing done and his chickens and cows tended to. Sometimes they had children— always girl children. Cap'n Barton didn't like boys. And sometimes they were jolly country women who laughed at the typewritten list of housekeeping directions nailed on the wall in the milk room. (Strip beds every day. Shake sand out of sheets every day, etc.) More often they were poor widow women not used to working and felt themselves too good to be anybody's housekeeper, even if the job did pay twenty-five dollars a month and board. Either way, it wasn't a lasty job for anybody.

Louette and Rouette told Della white womens couldn't suit Cap'n Barton and he wouldn't have a black live-in housekeeper. He was so mean nobody stayed any longer than they could help it so there was always a lot of comers and goers.

The day after Cap'n Barton drove back to Bayou Bien in his new Reo Uncle Bart asked Della to come down to the office to see him.

"So he can look me over, huh?" Della said. "Let him come up here if he wants to see me!"

"He won't do that, hon," Bart said pleadingly. "He's been the boss so long everybody goes to him. It won't hurt you to come into the office when you are at the commissary for groceries."

"Foot to that," said Della.

But Uncle Bart looked sad and got very quiet, a system that got his way then and almost every time with Della. Later she would charge him with pouting and "sulling like a sick possum" and would flounce out of the house, refusing to "toady" to his whims. But in the end she couldn't fight silence and hurt looks. A rousing fight with bitter words and name-calling would have suited her fine, but Bart wouldn't fight with her or even answer her back most times and she couldn't stand that.

She told him she would be in to "pay my respects to His Nibs" the next morning, and she got up early to gird herself for the meeting. Jincey hung around, watching her heat an iron on the stove to press a clean cotton housedress and brush her hair, wanting to go too. At first Della said no and then she said impatiently, "All right, Jincey, horn in! I haven't got enough to worry about so you come along too and let the old fool see what a big young'un I've got. Put on a clean dress and some shoes. No use letting him think we're barefoot white trash!"

They walked down the road together, stepping carefully to keep the dust off their shoes.

Jincey stole a glance at Della. She looked pretty, her dark, shiny hair coiled low on her neck and fluffed out around her face. She had put Magnolia Balm on her face so it looked pinker than usual and she had reddened her lips and smoothed the dark wings of her eyebrows with Vaseline.

"Aunt Della," Jincey said, still self-conscious about using the new name, "you look pretty."

"Hmmf," sniffed Della. "Pretty ugly and pretty apt to stay that way. I know how I look in my old rags. If I had the goods I'd make me some frocks, and then I wouldn't be ashamed to set foot out the door."

It turned out that she got some goods almost immediately. The dry goods drummer was in the commissary when they walked in, unwrapping bolts of cloth and showing them to Uncle Bart.

"Come here, sweetheart, and help me pick out dress goods," Uncle Bart called. He introduced the drummer, Brandy Smith, to Della and, grabbing Jincey from behind, he hooked his hands around the side of her face and lifted her from the floor.

"This is my little ugly, freckle-faced gal, Jincey," he added.

Jincey squealed and struggled to get down but the drummer was talking to Della and paid no attention.

"How about old Bart gitting hisself a looker?" marveled Brandy Smith, holding Della's hand and smiling down at her.

"Thought he'd never jump over the broom and I see why he waited now."

Della's eyes snapped. She pulled her hand out of his.

"We did not jump over the broom," she said haughtily. "Just because we live at a sawmill don't mean we had a sawmill marriage."

"Aw, hon," Bart protested, laughing. "Brandy didn't mean any offense. He's joreeing us."

Della smiled uncertainly and reached out a finger to touch a bolt of pink gingham. Seeing her interest, Brandy Smith grabbed up several bolts of goods and led the way to the front door.

"Come over here, if you will, ma'am, and look at them in the light," he invited. "We got some mighty pretty patterns this year."

Della followed, drawn by the cloth more than by the big dark man who had called her a looker.

"Now with your coloring this rose print ought to be just the thing," said the drummer, pulling a length of flowered cotton loose from the bolt and holding it up to Della's chin. He tilted his head and studied the effect.

"With those eyes," he murmured, "you don't need my cloth. God, you could ruin a man with those topaz eyes! Do you ever wear the topaz stone?"

The drummer's hand holding the cloth was touching her chin and Della, holding her head back stiffly to accommodate it, was aware of the dry warmth of the man's touch on her skin.

For a second she looked back into his dark brown eyes and then she jerked her head away and said shortly, "I don't like jewelry."

"Not like jewelry!" cried the drummer. "Bart, did you hear that? What a woman!"

"Interesting, if true," said a voice from the office door.

They all turned to see a tall, heavy-bodied man with a shock of gray hair and bright blue eyes watching them.

"Uncle Bob!" cried Bart, going toward him. "I didn't hear you come in. I want to make you acquainted with my wife, Della."

Della turned from the drummer and went and stood by Bart and Jincey, reaching out one hand to grasp Bart's arm and another to smooth Jincey's hair. Mama's scared, Jincey thought in surprise, real scared. The big man in the office door must be terrible mean to scare Della.

But he didn't look mean. He was smiling and showing a lot of white teeth like Uncle Bart's.

"Welcome to Bayou Bien," he said, holding out his hand. "I'm sorry I wasn't here to greet the bride and..." He looked at Jincey... "the bride's maid. Are you getting settled all right?"

Della put her hand in his and smiled her bright company smile. "Oh, yes," she said in what Jincey recognized as her best mannerly tone. "We're very comfortable, thank you. Did you have a nice trip?"

"Middling," he said, turning away and pushing out his lip petulantly. "I wouldn't have gone if I had been invited to the wedding. Bart didn't see fit to ask me."

Della looked from Bart's anxious face to the older man's with its childishly pouting expression.

"You mustn't blame Bart for that," she said. "It was very sudden. We didn't know we was gon' do it ourselves until the last minute."

"That's what I thought!" said Cap'n Barton triumphantly. "A jumped-up, sneaky affair with nobody there to witness it!"

"Wait a minute, Uncle Bob!" cried Bart.

Brandy Smith, watching and grinning from the drygoods counter, said mockingly, "Hot damn!"

Cap'n Barton turned to the drummer appealingly.

"Like my own son, Brandy, my own son...and Bart didn't even consult me! He brings this woman and this child in and I'm supposed to like it."

Della caught her breath and Jincey knew she wasn't scared any more, she was mad.

"You can like it or lump it," Della said in a low voice. "Bart's a grown man and he'll take a man's part. I mean to make him a good wife, but as for you, Cap'n Barton, you can step straight to hell!"

Della's light dress was a blur as she ran between the counters in the dimly lit commissary toward the square of sunlight that was the front door.

Jincey turned to follow her just as Cap'n Barton threw back

his head and let out a bellow of laughter. Uncle Bart swung uncertainly between the door through which Della had gone and his laughing uncle.

"Go after her, Bart," Brandy Smith said. "You got a woman with spunk. Hang on to her."

Bart went, but not before he threw an anguished look at Cap'n Barton and said, "I'm sorry, Uncle Bob."

Jincey walked slowly up the road toward the house, scuffing her shoes in the soft grainy dirt, now that it didn't matter if they were dusty. Welcome saw her coming and ran to meet her and she squatted in the road beside him and rubbed his ears. Uncle Bart had hurried on ahead of her and caught Della at the steps. They had gone in the house together and Jincey worried over what might be happening, but she knew better than to go and see. Della might be packing their clothes in the trunk. They might be fixing to leave Bayou Bien.

The thought made her drag-footed. A little branch crossed the road at the foot of the hill where the house stood. There was a wooden bridge that rattled when cars and wagons traveled over it, spanning clear water that flowed from a spring back in the woods somewhere and ran between the field in front of the house and the pasture adjoining it to the millpond beyond. Jincey had already discovered it as a play place. She had made dams of sand and mud and fished for minnows with an old holey pot from the trash hole at the edge of the yard. The banks of the little branch were almost solidly carpeted with a thick green moss out of which bluets and cowslips and little white violets grew. Black gum and poplar trees were tall along the stream, and willows and swamp myrtle made a green wall that would hide a person from the house and from the road.

Jincey stood a moment on the bridge with her head ducked down, looking at the water but seeing back of her half-closed lids the house there on the hill. She played the old game. If I don't look at it we won't have to leave it. She knew well what she would see if she lifted her head—the boxlike walls of heart pine that had reddened with the passage of time, instead of weathering gray like a lot of wood did. There would be tear-like amber droplets on the west side where the years of hot afternoon sun had drawn the rosin out of the wood but the front gallery under a scoopy shed-like roof would be cool now and pretty with green-painted rockers and a swing covered with white slipcovers on which Mama had embroidered big "M's" for McPherson. And there would be at the edge of the gallery the long green wooden boxes Mama had hammered together and painted and filled with slips of coleus and wandering Jew. Without lifting her head or moving her eyes from the water she could see the chinquapin tree with its smooth trunk and strong branches placed just right for climbing, and the wide board she had put across two of the strongest limbs to make a seat. From that seat she could look in the bedroom windows and see Della's and Uncle Bart's bed under the mosquito bar in the front room and her narrow cot with a striped, fringed cover in the back room.

She almost couldn't bear to think of the pretty parlor on the other side of the front bedroom and the dining room beyond her bedroom. Della had made cretonne flounces and hung them over the glass windows with even a matching cover on her trunk in the corner of the dining room. The cretonne had birds and flowers and leaves climbing all over it, and Jincey thought it must be the finest goods in the world.

The whole house, she thought, was like that—fine as fiddle dust. And now Della might be packing to leave it.

A brand-new thought came to Jincey and she dropped down on the bridge to examine it. If Della left she might not have to go, too. Uncle Bart had said that she was as welcome as the flowers in May. Almost the instant the idea entered her head she got shed of it. If Della went she would go, too, but oh, she hoped they stayed. Maybe if she hid in the woods and Della couldn't find her they would have to stay.

Jincey took off her shoes and wiped the dust from the toes and set them side by side on the bridge. She slid into the water and started wading and after the briefest pause Welcome jumped in after her.

The sun was warm on her head and shoulders and the water swirled cool around her feet and ankles. Welcome, beginning to lengthen into a leggy puppy with a limp switch of a tail and ears as big and as brown as blackjack oak leaves in winter, drank water and snorted and shook his head, joyfully sending a shower of drops against her.

In a minute they were behind a myrtle bush and out of sight of the house.

"You can quit your worrying," Jincey remarked to the capering puppy. "We sure-god ain't going nowhere now."

On the pasture side of the creek cows coming down to drink had worn a sandy beach-like strip in the grass and Jincey stopped there and sat down to make a frog house by patting a pile of sand on her foot and then pulling it out. The small cave delighted her and she made another and another and then scooped more sand into wet hand-shaped ridges to make a fence around the little cave settlement. Welcome collapsed in the thin shade of a poplar tree and went to sleep.

She had started breaking twigs off the myrtle bush and sticking them in the sand to make trees around the frog houses when she heard voices and looked up to see a black man and woman with fishing poles across their shoulders coming up from the millpond.

Welcome yapped at them dutifully and then ran out to meet them. Jincey bobbed her head shyly.

The woman took it for a proper greeting.

"All right, how you?" she called in a high, sociable voice.

Jincey brushed her bangs out of her eyes with the back of a sandy hand and looked at them without speaking. The woman was tall and broad-shouldered with a round black face under a man's old black felt hat. She wore a starched and ironed flour sack apron on which the words "self-rising" were still pinkly visible. The apron had many lumpy distended pockets across its front. A snuff stick and a box of Railroad Mills snuff and fishing lines and hooks showed at the top of one pocket. The man, short and small-boned and light-skinned, had a solemn quiet face and he leaned over and rubbed Welcome's ears and spoke politely without looking at Jincey.

"How' do, Missy."

"You that chile Mister Bart brought here, ain't you?" the woman asked, switching a string of fish from one hand to the other.

Jincey nodded.

"We be's Barton hands," the woman went on. "Ruth and Matthew Barton. Live in the quarters. I been putting off to come and see you and your ma—or auntie, is it? Matt's sisters, Rouette and Louette, say she a nice lady. Believe I'll stop in now. You goin' that way?"

Jincey stood up reluctantly, brushing at her wet-tailed dress. She didn't want to go but it was beyond her ability to say no to this big, black, smiley-faced woman in the man's hat.

Ruth and Matthew followed a little cowpath along the creek bank and Jincey went along with them. As they rounded a clump of myrtle and came in sight of the bridge they saw Uncle Bart come out the gate and start down the road toward the commissary. He stopped when he saw them and called out:

"Ruth . . . Po' Jack! Where'd you find my gal young'un, Jincey?"

"Aw, playing, Mr. Bart, like chillun do," Ruth answered easily.

Uncle Bart held out a hand to draw Jincey to his side and smiled at the man. "Po' Jack," he said again.

"Po' boy," echoed the man.

"How you making it, Po' Jack?" Uncle Bart asked.

"Mister Bart, I just a po' boy and a long old ways from home," the man answered.

For the first time Jincey looked at the woman and spoke. "I thought you said his name was Matthew," she said accusingly.

"Is," chuckled the woman. "That be's the way him and Mister Bart carry on. Been speaking that spiel when they meets in the road since they was little boys together. Matthew make like he been somewhere with that 'long old ways from home' talk!"

She laughed at Bart.

"Born and raised right here at Barton's Mill, wasn't he, Mister Bart? And never been nowhere else."

Bart smiled at Matthew, who smiled back showing a row of strong, gleaming teeth that made him look surprisingly like the white man in spite of his small stature and the golden cast of his skin.

"Don't forget he went all the way up to Vinegar Bend one time," Uncle Bart said. "Wouldn't a met you if he hadn't."

"That was a po' day's work," Ruth said good-humoredly. "Come on, Jincey, les me and you go find yo' auntie. I ain't made my manners to the new miss, Mister Bart, and this be's a good day to stop by."

"Since the fish ain't biting?" Bart suggested.

"Hoo . . . hoo . . . hoo!" laughed Ruth. "You talking but I got these." She held up a string of small bright perch, waving them in the air as she walked up the hill toward the house. Jincey followed her, and Matthew and Uncle Bart walked along together toward the commissary.

In the house they found Della lying on the bed beneath the mosquito bar with a wet washrag on her forehead and her eyes closed.

Jincey looked at her in alarm.

"Aunt Della?" she whispered, tugging at the mosquito bar. "You all right?"

Della opened her eyes, saw Ruth standing in the doorway and sat up.

"You sick?" Ruth asked.

Della nodded. "Sick headache," she muttered. "Who are you?"

"I be's Ruth Barton, Matthew's wife," Ruth said. "We Barton hands. You lay back down, Sugar, and I'll make you something to ease yo' head. Got the making's right here in my josie." She patted one of her bulging apron pockets.

"Come on, Jincey, you can hep me."

Jincey cast an anxious look at Della, but she had closed her eyes and eased her head back on the pillow. She went in the kitchen where Ruth was poking up the fire in the wood stove and filling the kettle from the water bucket.

"First we makes her some creepin' Jenny tea," Ruth said. "Then we makes her a creepin' Jenny tussie to snuff up her nose and clear her head."

The big black woman emptied one of her pockets of some pungent green leaves and stems and spread them out on the kitchen table.

"You a doctor?" Jincey asked.

"Some calls me that," Ruth said. "Up yonder where I was raised at warn't no doctors and we larn to treat what ailed us with granny woman remedies from the woods."

The fire caught and burned brightly and by the time Ruth had washed the leaves and stuffed them in a cup the water in the kettle was boiling. Ruth poured the water over the leaves and set a saucer over the cup to let them steep. She pulled a bit of string out of her pocket and tied another bunch of little green plants together, crushing the leaves a little as she worked. Then she strained the water from the leaves into a clean cup and took it into Della.

"Set up, Sugar," she said. "Ruth gon' make you a well woman. Here, you sip this."

Della obediently sat up and took the cup and, grimacing a little at the sharp, leafy smell, wet her lips with it.

"Take a lil' drink," directed Ruth. "Hep you."

Della took one drink and then another and smiled wanly at Ruth.

"When you got that in you, you lay back and sniff this," Ruth said, putting the little bouquet of creeping Jenny on the bed beside Della. "Me and Jincey cook Mister Bart's somepin' t'eat."

"Oh, would you?" asked Della. "I don't believe I could stand to do it."

"We gon' fix his dinner and take it to him when the noon whistle blow," Ruth said.

The big woman stepped out of her shoes and set them on the back gallery and hung her apron with its bulging pockets on a nail nearby. Then she moved quickly and competently around the little kitchen, putting on rice and scaling and gutting and frying the little fish from the willow switch. When the fish were brown and crisp she dropped spoonfuls of cornmeal batter into the skillet and almost immediately lifted out thin golden cakes, which she buttered and stacked on a plate for Jincey to take to Uncle Bart.

When Jincey climbed back up the hill, carrying the empty basket and hurrying to get her own dinner, she found Della sitting up on the gallery talking with Ruth and nibbling at a bit of fried fish herself.

"Go eat yo' dinner, honey," Ruth said. "It be's waiting in the warming closet."

Jincey ate sitting at the kitchen table and listening at Della and Ruth's talk. Della had apparently recovered from her sick headache and was enjoying the company. She laughed often at the big black woman and Jincey could tell why. Ruth was doing an imitation of Cap'n Barton.

"Oh, they think they be's better'n anybody else," Ruth said. "But the old man ain't above you-know-what."

"Now what did he say?" asked Della, laughing.

"It was right after me and Matthew got married," Ruth related. "I was in the commissary to git rations and warn't nobody in there but the cap'n. I axed him for a can of Alaga syrups and he say, 'Come here, girl, and lemme pick your peaches and I *give* you some syrups.' "

"Your 'peaches' he called 'em," Della repeated.

Ruth giggled. "First time anybody ever act like these big titties of mine be that sweet," she said. "I kep' steppin' around to git out of his way and he kep' follering me saying, 'Now girl, don't be so wild! I just want to pick yo' peaches!' 'Bout that time Mister Bart come in and the old man lemme alone."

Della laughed so hard tears streamed from her eyes and she wiped them away with the back of her hand.

"Way he talked to me, I can't believe it," she said. "Biggety thing."

"Sugar, they all be's biggety," said Ruth. "Barton niggers as bad as Barton whites. Matthew act too good sometimes but I whittles him down a notch. You got to figger to know how to best 'em all—figger and figger."

Della sighed. "I'm not sure I can do it. I just want peace and a good stay-place."

"Aw, you smart," Ruth said. "Ain't none of *them* smart as they think. They loons—not foxes."

"You mean there's others besides Mrs. McPherson in the crazy house?" Della asked.

"Not to say right now," said Ruth. "But the old mother, the cap'n's ma—Mister Bart's grandma—they kep' her on the third floor of the old house in a little locked room. She was that crazy. That was before I come to Barton's Mill but I heerd plenty about her. Say they treated her good, killed chickens every day to cook for her and made her broths and puddings and all. Matthew's mammy was her servant and took prime care of her, bathed her and brushed her hair and babied her. She died before the house burned down."

"And Mrs. McPherson . . ." prompted Della.

"Miss Annie Katherine," Ruth said. "Yes'm, she got it, too. They thought craziness might skip her and light down on her brother, Bob, but 'bout time her chillun, Mister Bart and Miss Mary, growed up she come down with it too and had to be put in Tuscaloosa."

"Bart . . ." Della began and stopped.

"Oh, you don't have to worry none about Mr. Bart," Ruth said easily. "No more'n I worries 'bout Matthew. Barton blood's been thinned down to a puny trickle in them. They be's stout of mind."

"Well, I don't worry, of course," said Della, turning proper. "I *know* about Mister Bart."

"Sugar, you don't know 'bout no man till you's fed him and bedded with him many a long year," said Ruth. "But you learns. That headache today . . . when you had a headache before?"

Della shrugged. "I don't know."

"I knowed it," said Ruth triumphantly. "You be's smart jus' like I thought. Woman let her mouth run her into a corner, bad headache be's bes' thing to git her out."

"There wasn't anything else I could have done down yonder," Della said. "He stood there insulting me, that old man did. Acting like I was common trash or something."

"You do's right," Ruth said. "Talk up to him. That what he require. That more'n the rest do—his kin and all. He say frog and they jump. Now if you git 'em all on yo' side, you be's all set."

"All who?" asked Della.

"All the kin, Sugar, what I'm talking 'bout. Miss Mary and the Mobile kin."

Jincey had long since lost interest in the conversation and climbed to the board seat in the chinquapin tree. It did look like Della was planning on staying and it was safe for her to look at the house and into the windows from her perch and like everything that she saw.

RUTH CAME to the house often after that, sometimes to help out with the washing and ironing or whatever project Della had going, but more often to sit and talk or toll Della off to the creek bank to fish. Della loved to fish but she was afraid of snakes and wouldn't go by herself or just with Jincey.

When they saw Cap'n Barton at the commissary Della spoke to him coolly and got out as fast as she could. But she began to talk more often of Uncle Bart's sister and mother and his aunts and cousins who lived in Mobile. She would be glad to have them come and visit, she said, and one day Bart came home from the commissary and told her that his sister Mary was driving up to see them.

"I telephoned her for you, sweetheart," he said. "We haven't been close in a long time but she's family and it's right that you all meet and be friends—if you can."

"What do you mean, 'if we can'?" Della asked defensively. "I can be friends with the devil if he'll give me half a chance. Mister Big Britches Barton don't want to be friends!"

"Now Della," Uncle Bart said soothingly, "don't get your hackles up. I was thinking about Mary. She's not the easiest person . . ."

Not long after that a blue Hupmobile roadster rattled over the bridge and came up the hill and Uncle Bart's sister Mary walked straight into the house calling out in a husky, sweet voice, "Where's my new sister? Where is the lovely Della?"

Before Della could get out of the kitchen and into the front room Mary ran into Jincey on the gallery and grabbed her and hugged her and held her off and looked at her.

"I know who you are!" she cried. "You're Jincey, sweet Jincey! It's high time I got my hands on you."

Jincey squirmed but not much because she was such a pretty woman with soft, rose-tipped hands and she smelled not of flowerdy talcum powder but of something richer and rarer and altogether fine.

When Della came in, taking off her apron and pushing at her hair, Mary let Jincey go and held out her hands to her.

"Oh, you are all that Bart said—gorgeous!" she cried. "I am thrilled, absolutely thrilled, to welcome you into the family. I've always wanted a sister and now I get a sister and a new niece, all in one package. Della, this is wonderful!"

Della looked unexpectedly shy to Jincey but she smiled and said that she was glad to meet Mary and suggested that they go sit on the porch where it was cooler, while their dinner finished cooking.

Mary plumped down in the swing, kicked off her shoes and tucked her feet in pale-cream silk stockings under her short, pleated, cream-colored skirt.

"Isn't this grand?" she asked, looking around her. "And you've done it all since you've been here! My Lord, it took courage to move into a sawmill shanty and fix it up. If only you had the old home, with your talent you'd make it a showplace!"

Jincey could see Della easing down and opening up, ready to smile and to talk and to like this woman. She made herself as small as possible in the rocking chair behind Della and didn't let it rock so Della wouldn't notice her and tell her to go play. She wanted to get as close to Mary as possible and hear her talk and touch her silken clothes and smell her perfume.

But it wasn't long till Mary was out of the fine pleated silk dress. The noon-time heat pressed down on the tin roof and just before the mill whistle blew for dinner she said, "Della, have you got something I can stick on? Any old rag will do, just so it's cool. Pongee is supposed to be cool, but it's hot as Hades and besides, I don't want to perspire on it. It's new, of course. Bought it at Gus Mayer's yesterday—just to impress you."

Della grinned at her delightedly.

"You didn't," she said.

"Of course I did. Paid twenty-five dollars for it. Or rather promised to pay. Charged it, naturally, to Prince Edward."

"Prince Edward?" said Della, puzzled.

"Oh, you know. My royal husband, Edward Taylor. I call him Prince Edward because he's so grand. Reminds me of Lord Gotrocks in "Maggie and Jiggs," except that he hasn't any rocks. More like Count de Change."

Della stood up and led the way into her room to look for a housedress for Mary.

"Twenty-five dollars for a dress sounds like money to me," she muttered.

"I told you I charged it," Mary said. "That doesn't cost anything!"

Della laughed but she didn't say anything about Askin-Marine Credit Clothiers, her only experience with charging. She got her new pink gingham out of the wardrobe and held it out to Mary, who had peeled off her dress and spread it on the bed and stood there before them in a brief cream-colored slip that was half silk and half lace. She reached up under it and unhitched her stockings and took them off and did a little dance step in her bare feet before she slid the gingham over her head.

Della and Jincey, watching, laughed at her and she made a face at Jincey and held out her hands.

"You know the Charleston? Come on, I'll teach you a step."

Jincey hung back and looked at Della and Della smiled.

"Go on," she said. "Learn it and you can teach it to me."

"You've got a Victrola, put us on a record," Mary directed.

And Della wound it up and put on the "Yellow Dog Blues" before she went to the kitchen to see about dinner.

Jincey felt clumsy and lumpish. Her hands in Mary's cool ones were hot and sweaty and her hair kept falling in her eyes. But she enjoyed the dancing lesson, especially when she found she could do a toe-heel step that Mary showed her. The Victrola was blaring and they were thumping briskly about the art square in the parlor when Uncle Bart came home to dinner.

He stood in the door looking at them and laughing. When they stopped he clapped his hands and cried, "Encore! Encore!"

"Bubba!" cried Mary running to hug him. "I'm enchanted with your new family, you lucky bum!"

Uncle Bart smiled at her, patted Jincey and headed for the kitchen.

"I like 'em myself," he said, "especially at dinnertime."

Della had worked over dinner and she felt hot and flustered as she dished it up and set it on the dining-room table.

"Oooh, fried chicken and hot biscuits and rice and gravy!" cried Mary, pulling out a chair. "Della, you shouldn't have done it—all that cooking in this heat—but oh, I love it!"

Mary ate a lot of everything, including the creamed corn and the butter beans and the coleslaw and the chocolate cake. But during the meal she did mention that cold plates were a new thing in town—for "luncheon," she said—and Della should think about trying them when the summer heat came on.

"Three Georges, the ice-cream parlor on Dauphin Street, started them," Mary said. "You get a plate with cold sliced ham and potato salad and crackers and maybe a little lettuce and tomato for decoration for fifty cents. With a glass of iced tea it's very cooling and oh, so smart."

"Sounds like monkey junk to me," Uncle Bart said, serving himself another piece of fried chicken and ladling gravy over it. "I like a good hot dinner. Cold supper is all right, but you need a hot dinner."

Mary made a face at Della.

"Tacky," she said to Bart. "All the smart people now eat dinner at night and have a light lunch at midday. It's the thing in Mobile now."

"Is it?" Della asked with interest.

"I don't know about the old Government Street crowd," Mary confessed. "They probably have their cooks in there fixing a log-rolling dinner at noon and then they sleep all afternoon just like they used to do. But the new crowd, the country club set, they came in from other places and started dinner at night, dressing up and all. Very smart."

Her eyes fell on Bart's bib overalls with his cotton undershirt showing.

"Bubba," she said, "I hope you don't come to the table like that often. Gracious, mother used to make you wear a collar and tie and your jacket when you sat down to a meal and here you are eating like white trash. What will Della think of us?"

Della didn't say anything but her eyes rested on Bart thoughtfully. It would be a long time before she overed Mary's visit. She was disgusted with herself for not thinking of cold plates for their lunch and spoke of it to Jincey.

"All that hot food steaming on the table and the kitchen stove roaring and heating up the house! I should of knowed better. Trouble is, I never knew how to do anything proper!"

"Aunt Della, it was good," Jincey insisted. "Everything was good and she et a bait of it."

"Ate, not et," said Della. "At least I know that much—and next time I'll do better with the rations."

In the weeks that followed Jincey heard a lot of Mary in Della's talk. Words she never used before came out again and again. "Marvelous" and "gorgeous" and "grand." She spoke often of what was "smart" and Jincey saw her combing her hair down and fluffing it up around her face, trying to get the effect of Mary's stylish "windblown" bob. It happened that Uncle Bart caught her doing the same and he knew what it meant.

"Don't do what you're thinking about, sweetheart," he said, smoothing the long red-brown mane with his hand. "A woman's hair is her crowning glory. I'd hate for my wife to be a bobbed-headed flapper."

"Foot to that," Della said, but she coiled her hair back into a knot high on her head because it was cooler off her neck and let it alone for the time being.

Mary came often to Barton's Mill, driving up in her blue roadster with the top down and her short, fair hair blowing in the breeze. Sometimes she brought a bathing suit and they went in the millpond in front of the commissary. The first time they went swimming was close to five o'clock whistle time and Uncle Bart came out of the office and asked his sister to either stay under the water or put on a robe until the hands had done their trading in the commissary and gone on to the quarters.

"Why?" asked Mary.

"That suit," said Uncle Bart, looking embarrassed. "You're half naked."

Mary's suit was a bright blue one-piece wool, unlike Della's, which was longer and full-skirted with little sleeves, and Jincey's, which Della had made out of wool dress goods. It was held together by thin straps and showed a lot of bare leg above the little yellow rubber bathing shoes she wore.

"Oh, Bubba!" Mary protested, laughing. "You're so quaint! Everybody wears one-piece bathing suits now." She struck a pose like a bathing beauty. "Why not give the natives a treat, huh?"

Uncle Bart looked irritated but Della, sitting in the water with her full skirt billowing around her, laughed.

"Come on in, Mary," she said. "If you don't he'll sic your uncle on us and we'll have to get out of the water. At least it's cool in here."

Mary cut the coffee-colored water cleanly in a quick, graceful dive from the bank. She swam fast and easily and Jincey looked after her longingly. If only she could do that. Della had never learned to swim and the idea of teaching Jincey how had never come up.

Mary knew how to do everything.

"Come on, Puddin', I'll teach you," she said, swimming back toward the bank.

But in the end it was Uncle Bart who taught Jincey to swim. Mary tried and lost interest when Jincey splashed and kicked furiously and still couldn't stay afloat.

"Maybe if we pushed her off the bank into the deep water she'd come up swimming," Mary suggested to Della one day. "I've heard of people who started swimming when they thought they were going to drown."

Uncle Bart heard her.

"No, sir," he put in. "I won't have her scared like that if she never learns to swim!"

He looked out at the millpond, a placid, dark mirror fringed by pines and big-boled cypress trees and reflecting the rose and green streaked sunset sky. Up toward the head of it an alligator croaked hoarsely and closer by there was the sound of rushing water where it spilled over the dam by the mill. Toward the opposite shore half a mile away an H-shaped raft supported by big metal drums awaited the next day's crews to float logs to the mill for sawing. And tied up near the swimming place was a flotilla of small boats—a motor launch used by logging workers, a rowboat and two cypress pirogues.

Bart's eyes were loving as he looked and he said gently, "Water's a friendly thing. I've loved this pond all my life and I want Jincey to love it. She'll swim soon enough and paddle a boat and fish, if she wants to, and I won't have fear put into her."

Della smiled at him gratefully but Mary had lost interest in the subject and was floating on her face with her eyes open looking for green jelly-like masses of frog eggs that drifted just below the surface in the rushes near the shore.

One day after dinner Mrs. Bates and her three children walked up the hill to make a visit. They were Della's first white callers and she hurried to take off her apron and make them welcome on the front gallery, pushing a rocker toward Mrs. Bates and inviting the children to sit in the swing.

"Can I offer you some iced tea?" she asked.

"You got ice?" Mrs. Bates said, surprised.

"Plenty," said Della proudly. "Bart sent a man with fifty pounds this morning."

"Then I don't care," said Mrs. Bates, "just so you don't disfurnish yourself."

The three children, Zack, Lula and Virgie, set the swing swaying and jerking and squeaking in anticipation.

"Jincey, you come help me," Della called. "Hand Miss Eva that palmetto fan off the library table and then git out a tray."

Mrs. Bates, called Miss Eva in the quarters, rocked and fanned briskly and the children swung wildly while Della chipped ice on the back porch and Jincey set out the glasses and sugar.

"Lucky we got a lemon to go with it and some tea cakes," Della muttered, brushing a strand of dark hair from her moist face with the back of her hand.

She let Jincey carry the plate of little cakes and she set the tray down on the edge of the gallery and handed around the tea.

"Have a tea cake, Lula? Virgie?" Della asked, motioning to Jincey to pass them. "Here, Zack, you like tea cakes, I know."

"I don't care," said Lula, the eldest, with the studied casualness of country etiquette.

"I don't care," echoed Virgie, reaching for a cookie with her free hand.

But Zack was engrossed in his glass of tea with the lemon wedge on the side and a gleaming line of sugar in the bottom. He held it to the light and tinkled the ice against the side.

"Ma," he said, awed, "ain't it purty—and don't it rattle?"

Miss Eva smiled at him and then at Della.

"You'll have to overlook us," she said gently. "We don't git ice and we ain't never had iced tea before."

"Well, we don't have it all the time," Della said. "It's hard to keep ice all the time 'way out here."

All the Bateses had curly, syrup candy-colored hair, but they weren't pretty children, Jincey decided, looking at them from her seat on the top step. As much as Della liked blond curly hair she couldn't say the Bateses were pretty. They all had big mouths full of big mule-sized teeth and pale skin. Of them all, Virgie was the one she thought might catch Della's eye. Her curly hair was worn in long corkscrew shapes, three on each side and one in the back—all freshly dampened and combed around somebody's finger, Jincey could tell.

They finished their tea and sat silently staring at Jincey for a long time. She carefully looked away and moved to the bottom step, making circles in the dirt with her big toe.

Suddenly Lula said, "Les play!"

Jincey stood up uncertainly. She was so accustomed to playing by herself she didn't know what children played together. But the Bates children knew. They saw her playhouse under the tree and Lula said, "Pretend we run a commissary. Want to?"

"Hey, I'll git the goods!" said Zack and ran off to the dump hole at the edge of the yard to pick up bottles and cans.

Virgie got a stick to draw a bigger room than the one Jincey had drawn off. Lula asked for a pencil and paper for a ledger in which to write down charges and they drove new stobs in the ground and laid longer boards across them to make counters.

Lula knew all about how the commissary operated and she set the rules. The others were hands, working for twenty-five cents an hour wages and charging their rations until the end of the week. They picked up pebbles in the ditch beside the road for checks, the imitation money which was used at Barton's Mill. It was the first Jincey knew that workers weren't paid with real money but with lightweight metal discs stamped with the name, Barton's Mill.

"Used to be U.S. money out here," Lula explained, "but t'warn't no use in Cap'n Barton keeping that on hand when ain't nobody going nowhere but the commissary to spend it."

"We seen money, though!" Virgie put in eagerly. "Cap'n Barton gives Papa and our grandpa five-dollar gold pieces evva Christmas."

"Aw, gold ain't regular money," scoffed Zack. "That's Christmas stuff. But I seen plenty of the regular kind. Over at the post office at Bayou Bien Mr. White (he's a Yankee from Kentucky) runs a store and he takes in copper cents and silver dollars and green paper money, all like that."

"You still have to use real money in town," Jincey offered, glad to know something to say.

"I reckon," Lula agreed. "We ain't been that fur yet. But we going someday, Papa says. He's been. Twice."

They played until the five o'clock whistle blew and Mrs. Bates got up to go. Jincey thought commissary was the most interesting game she ever saw and although she had not learned figgering in school she made up her mind to take a crack at it. Lula Bates showed her a lot about how it worked. If you bought many rations out of the commissary and charged them, at the end of the week you didn't draw any pay and you still owed Barton's Mill.

Virgie had whined around trying to buy and charge some pretend coconut candy and Lula, as stern a commissary operator as Cap'n Barton himself, wouldn't let her.

"God'amighty, woman!" she had cried in a gruff, grown-up voice. "Don't you know hit's rained all week and nobody working? You cain't charge frivel things like candy!"

"Well, sowbelly then—to cook with my greens," Virgie compromised.

"Sowbelly's different," said Lula, sawing an oak leaf in half to represent a chunk of meat. "Got to have seasoning for your vittles, if you eat to work."

Mrs. Bates called them and they left, after making Jincey promise to come across the creek beyond the lumberyard to play with them.

When they had walked a way with the Bateses and waved them out of sight Della went in the house to start supper and Jincey followed her to tell her about the game, commissary.

"And if you don't work you cain't buy frivel things," she explained.

"What's 'frivel things'?" Della asked absently.

"Coconut candy," Jincey said promptly.

Della laughed, pushed Jincey's damp bangs back and leaned over and kissed her forehead.

"You are enjoying life, ain't you childee? But I think that's 'frivolous' things you're talking about and it must mean anything fancy that you're not bound to have to stay alive."

She was quiet a moment.

"I believe I'm about ready to have something 'frivel' myself," she murmured. "I'm going to speak to Bart about going to Mobile tomorrow."

It turned out that Uncle Bart couldn't get off to take them to town except on Saturday afternoons after the mill closed down and he had paid off the men for the week and sold them what they wanted out of the commissary. But he saw no reason why Della shouldn't drive the car.

"Me drive!" Della cried. "Bart, you crazy. I'll never be able to do it."

Bart's eyes rested on her hands which had been white and smooth when she worked in the overall factory but now showed stains and blisters and small hacked places from the labor of hammering, sawing, painting and digging and raking in the yard.

"Sweetheart, you the most do-something woman I ever saw," he said. "If an ignorant nigger like Percy can drive a truckload of lumber to Mobile and see it loaded on a boat at the dock, I bet you could drive a Model-T Ford anywhere in this world."

"We-ell," said Della dubiously, "when could you show me how?"

Why not then, as soon as they finished supper, Bart asked.

So it was that every evening after supper Della slid under the steering wheel of the car and waited for Bart to crank it up and jump in beside her. With him in the front seat and Jincey in the back seat she drove all around the country roads. There was a gas pump by the commissary for filling the mill trucks and some- times they bought five gallons, a whole dollar's worth, and Della drove it up before they went home to bed. The no-bannister bridge between the mill and the post office settlement of Bayou Bien on the gravel road was the stretch Della dreaded most and she always stopped just before she got to it and made Jincey and Bart get out and walk.

"You funny woman," Bart said, shaking his head. "If you fell off the bridge, do you think Jincey and I would want to be high and dry and safe?"

But she wouldn't take her foot off the brake until they were out of the car and safely on the other side of the bayou.

"Got to have somebody able to go for help," Della muttered between clenched teeth.

Then she drove slowly and nervously, gripping the steering wheel so hard her knuckles were white and holding her head out the side to peer around the windshield and watch the front tires to be sure they stayed on the board runners.

Because she was so afraid of the bayou bridge Bart showed her the back road to the highway, a little-traveled woods trail through the quarters and Fever swamp. In rainy weather it became im- passable through boggy parts where the water stood, but in dry weather the sandy ruts were firm enough for the light car. When Bart felt Della was skillful enough to turn her loose with the car, the Fever swamp road became her favorite route. She and Jincey drove to the post office and Jincey saw the white two-room school

174

across the road from it, where she would start the third grade in the fall. They met the Yankee storekeeper from Kentucky and his wife. He was a quiet, soft-spoken man who wore glasses and spent a lot of time sitting in a rocking chair in the back of the store reading. His wife was from an even more northern state—Illinoy, she called it—a plump, pink-faced woman who had been a schoolteacher before her marriage.

"Missus McPherson!" she cried in a high nasal voice. "I must apologize for not calling on you. I don't drive and Aaron can seldom leave the store long enough to take me anywhere."

The way she said it made Della almost sorry that she had learned to drive. To be able to take yourself anywhere you wanted to go somehow seemed common. It was more ladylike to hang back and be driven by your husband.

Jincey could tell Della admired the way Mrs. White talked, saying "Missus" instead of "Miz" the way everybody else did, and making some words last longer like the sound of a plucked guitar string lingering on the air with a kind of "Zing" instead of just easing down into silence. She knew Della would be trying to talk that way next.

"Go-innguh," Jincey tried it herself while the Yankee lady talked on and on. Not "gon' " like everybody else said, but "go-innguh."

"You folks must come to meeting Sunday," Mrs. White went on, and Jincey thought that was odd. "You folks" not "you all."

"We hold Sunday school for the children in the schoolhouse," Mrs. White continued. "We've been thinking of organizing a church if we can find a minister that would give us a Sunday, say once a month. So many of the people out here are poor and ignorant."

She glanced at a group waiting for their mail in the front of the store by the post office window and lowered her voice. "It would be such a help if you folks would come and give us a hand."

"W'y, we'd be more than glad to help," said Della, beaming. "I've been wanting to git Jincey back in Sunday school and I know Bart—Mr. McPherson—will want to help any way he can."

It turned out that there was a whole nest of Yankees at Bayou Bien. Some land salesman had traveled over the north and sold people who were tired of the cold on moving to south Alabama where the winters were mild and the farmland deep and rich. They were a funny breed of folks to most of the bayou people. They built high-backed, compact little houses, more often than not without galleries front or back to sit on, and painted them and put up water tanks with windmills to whirl around in the air and fill them. They even painted their barns, and some of them had purebred cows which they kept in planted pastures, fenced, instead of the piney woods heifers and bulls that roamed freely in the pine barrens and swamps and were sometimes killed by the trains or cars on the gravel road.

Della admired just about everything about the Yankees and right away made Jincey stop using the word "Yankee."

"Northerners. Call them northerners," she directed. "They cain't help it if they was born up yonder."

"In the 'narth'," put in Bart, grinning. "You ever notice how they say 'narth'?"

"Oh, you hush up," Della said, making a face at him. "Them's nice people over at the Front and I reckon if they want to start up a church we ought to help them. I don't want Jincey to grow up like a heathen with no religion at all."

Uncle Bart grumbled some about having to get up early on Sunday morning and go to the churchy doings over at the Front. He and Della had been lying a-bed late on Sunday and Uncle Bart seemed to like it a lot. Della would get up and hand Jincey some raisin bread and a glass of milk and send her out to play and then she would go back and get in bed but not always to sleep. Jincey heard them laughing and talking low and she figured they did a heap of hugging and kissing, which suited her fine. When they were hugging and kissing she did not have to worry about Della taking a notion to pick up and pull out from Bayou Bien.

The Whites posted a sign on the door at the post office to tell all the people at Bayou Bien that a church was going to be started up in the schoolhouse the very next Sunday. Della made a lot out

176

of starting off with it. She hadn't taken much interest in the church in town where Jincey went with Uncle Tee but this was different. They were not to be just goers to this one. Mrs. White had asked Della to teach the beginner's class in the Sunday school and Bart, since he was already a bookkeeper, to be the secretary and treasurer of the Sunday school and the church when it got going.

Della spent the week getting things ready. Bart had a drawer full of white shirts but none of the exact whiteness and crispness that Della wanted for church. She picked out the best and worked on its bosom with lemon juice and salt to bleach it before she put it on to boil in lye water. Then she made starch so thick that when the cuffs of the shirt dried and were ironed they were of a celluloid stiffness to match the collars, which Uncle Bart kept in a leather drawstring bag on his dresser.

For herself there was a flowered voile she thought would do if she raised the hemline to make it look newer and crisped it up with a light starch. She polished their shoes and tried Jincey's yellow Easter dress on her to be sure she had not outgrown it, with all the eating she was doing. On Saturday afternoon she moved the car from its customary place under the oak tree at the edge of the yard to the pump and she and Jincey drew water and washed it and polished the black painted body to a high sheen.

When they finished washing the car they had to take all-over baths themselves in a washtub, where Della had water warming in the sun all day. She scrubbed their heads, rinsing hers in rainwater and leaving it loose around her shoulders to dry in the sun. Jincey's, done up on rags to dry, made rusty knobs on Saturday, which Della intended to be soft curls on Sunday.

When Uncle Bart finished the Saturday chores of paying off the men and selling them rations for Sunday, Della sent Jincey down with a basket of clean underwear and soap and a towel so he could go down under the dam behind the mill and scrub himself under the running water.

Jostling about on the back seat of the car as they drove to the Front, Jincey felt the crispness of her organdy dress and saw

Della's broad-brimmed straw hat with its wreath of cloth daisies and Uncle Bart's straw katy hat and it was all a piece of Sunday morning cleanness and solemness.

Mr. and Mrs. White and an old man in a black suit were already at the schoolhouse when Bart drove up to the door, and a dozen children of all sizes straggled up the steps or stood around the hard-packed yard. They were all clean with wet-combed hair but they weren't as dressed up as Jincey was. The little ones didn't wear shoes and their feet were dusty from the walk from home. The boys' heads were white-ringed with high, home-done haircuts.

Mrs. White, remembering her days as a teacher, rang the brass bell on the teacher's desk in the bigger of the two schoolrooms and the children obediently filed in and took their seats. Then she introduced the old man in the black suit as Brother Doby Webster, a railroad engineer weekdays and a Methodist preacher on Sunday.

"Brother Webster is going to set our feet in the path," Mrs. White said, "and if you children will get your parents to come we will organize a regular church with meetings every Sunday. Failing that, we'll go ahead with our Sunday school and have church once a month."

Brother Webster had a long, sad face but merry dark eyes and he believed in more singing than praying and preaching. Since there was nobody else to play the old upright piano in the corner of the room, he said he would "give her a whirl" himself, and he sat down and fingered around until he found chords to go with every song they sang. They were all bright and bouncy songs and Brother Webster kept one of his feet on the loud pedal of the piano and stomped time with the other, sometimes taking one of his hands off the keys to swing it at the congregation.

"*Evva*-body sing!" he would cry and light into the song himself in a booming baritone that made even the shyest singer in the room feel safe about jumping in.

On the front row three little dark-haired, dark-eyed girls, squeezed together in the same seat, sang with him in such true, sweet voices he stopped playing and looked at them.

178

"I believe the Lord has sent us some real talent here," he said. "You girls come up here and hep me."

Instead of giggling and hanging back, shy and embarrassed, the three pushed out of the desk and obediently went to the piano, solemn and poised.

"Now let me git yo' names," Brother Webster said.

"Delight . . . Sunshine . . . Joy Boudreaux," said the older one in one breath.

"Whoa!" said the preacher, laughing. "Let's start over. Now you," pointing to the tallest of the three.

"Delight Boudreaux, nine going on ten," she said seriously.

"And you?" pointing to the next tallest.

"Sunshine Boudreaux, eight going on nine," she said in a carrying voice.

"And now," pointing to the smallest.

"I Joy," said the little girl shyly.

"Joy Boudreaux, five going on six," said the older sister.

"Well, that's just fine," said the preacher, smiling and winking at the congregation. "They're pretty names and y'all are pretty girls with mighty fine voices. Now let's worship the Lord with 'Beulah Land,' page four hundred fifteen, if you've got a book. If there ain't enough to go around, look on with your neighbor."

He wheeled around to face the piano and the Boudreaux girls lined themselves up to face the room. "Beulah Land" went off fine with Delight singing alto and throwing in "Praise God!" when they hit the part about feasting on the manna of a bountiful supply.

Preaching and praying and collection-taking followed but the singing was the best of all and when the service was over and everybody stood on the steps talking, Della spoke to the Boudreaux girls.

"You all give us some mighty pretty music," she said. "Where did you learn it?"

"Up at D'Iberville Chapel, where we used to live, was where we learned the words," Delight said. "But our papa teaches us to sing."

"What's your father's name?" Bart asked.

"Pierre Boudreaux," said Delight. "Our mama, she be called Reenie."

Later, when they had spoken to everybody and promised to be back next Sunday, Bart told Della they were driving to Mobile for Sunday dinner at a restaurant.

"Bart, we got stuff at home," Della said. "It would be a saving to eat what we got."

Bart smiled on her approvingly. "That's the ticket," he said. "I like a thrifty woman. But I thought if we ate in town we might make it to the ball park in time to see the Mobile Bears play the Birmingham Barons."

"Oho!" said Della, laughing. "It's the ball game that's getting us out to dinner, huh? Well, you go and maybe me and Jincey will stop by and sit a spell with Ina and Tee. Or maybe you'd like to ask Tee to go to the ball game with you?"

"I'll ask him," Bart said, and they rode along in contented silence for a long time.

"I thought church went off nice, didn't you?" Della said.

"Well, it ain't Government Street Presbyterian," said Bart, smiling. "Flighty and talky, compared to our church, but I reckon it's one way of worshipping and it's close."

"But wasn't the singing pretty?" Della persisted. "Them children sounded practically *trained*."

"Boudreaux from D'Iberville Chapel," Bart said reflectively. "You know what they are?" he asked suddenly. "They're Cajuns. I thought they talked a little that way and that's what they are, cajuns from D'Iberville! That explains the name, Pierre Boudreaux, and I bet Reenie is Renee."

"What's a Cajun, Uncle Bart?" Jincey asked from the back seat.

"They're what our people at the mill call 'no-nation folks,' " Bart said. "They're neither black nor white but a mixture. Before the Frenchman, Bienville, settled Mobile in 1702, he sailed up the river to 21-mile bluff looking for a place away from the mosquitoes. He found Indians already there. Some of his Frenchmen got mixed up with the Indians and later on with some of the Nigra slaves and that's where we get our Cajuns. The Louisiana ones are supposed to be all white, they say, but I wouldn't know."

180

"You mean Joy and Delight and Sunshine have Nigra blood in them?" asked Della, shocked.

"I wouldn't be surprised," Bart said. "You haven't met Ace at the mill but he's from D'Iberville and he's married to a Nigra woman with white skin."

Jincey's mind dropped away from Cajuns and fell to dreaming ahead about the unaccustomed adventure of eating in a restaurant.

The visit at Aunt Ina's house started off fine, Jincey could tell. Everything was in a furniture-moving stir of the kind Della liked.

Aunt Ina greeted them from the old leather davenport in the hall when they walked in the front door.

"Bless the Lord, look who's here! Tee, Cora, Mabel, come a'running. You can quit your moving, here's Della and Jincey and Mr. McPherson!"

"Moving?" cried Della. "Where to?"

"Aw, nowhere," said Aunt Ina, disgusted. "Just here. Tee's giving hisself airs. Got promoted to sergeant and . . . *he wants a par-ler!*"

She lapsed into a mocking falsetto. "A front room with a bed in it ain't good enough for a police sergeant, we got to have a *par-ler!*"

Della laughed and they spoke to Uncle Tee and Cora and Mabel, who were in the front room, knocking the bedstead apart. Bart mentioned the ball game and Uncle Tee was glad to hand the hammer to Mabel and reach for his coat.

"Tee, don't you think you're going out that door till you've got me some place to lay my head tonight!" Aunt Ina called after him.

"Aw, Ina, let him go," said Cora. "We can finish by ourselves."

"You ain't talking to me," said Aunt Ina. "Finish if you want to. I'm a-laying right here."

The men left and Della took off her hat and borrowed a kimono from Cora so she wouldn't get her church voile dirty, stepped out of her shoes and pitched in to help get the bedroom furniture into hers and Jincey's old room and a new living-room suite in its place.

"Glad to have you instead of Tee," said Cora, taking one end of the mattress Della was lifting. "Menfolks ain't no hand for moving furnitoor around. If they got the back, they ain't got the will. Hate it so bad they drag their feet without meaning to."

"Well, Tee Walton didn't have to bring this *par-ler soot* here," said Aunt Ina petulantly. "We was gittin' along all right with a bedstead and two rockers."

"Ina, you'll be glad to have a living room," Della said. "We got one out at the mill and it's just as nice as can be. Everybody has living rooms nowadays."

"What I been telling her," said Cora. "Tee's gon' be a big man, may want to bring some of his friends home with him. Where's he go'n' set 'em down? In the hall or on the bed?"

"Little I care," said Aunt Ina, giggling.

The three women worked at arranging the new wicker living-room suite, placing it this way and that to get the best effect, and Jincey helped them by sweeping out the corners of the room, which Aunt Ina had never got to, and taking up the puffballs of dust and lint on the coal shovel and hauling it to the kitchen garbage can. Finally, Aunt Ina pulled herself out of the davenport's broken-springed embrace and said she would put on the coffeepot and maybe set out some of that chocolate cake, if Jincey would help her.

From the kitchen Jincey heard Della's voice lifted in talk and laughter. Then the three women came to sit around the dining-room table and drink coffee and talk.

"Good cake, Ina," Della said. "Did you make it?"

"You must be sick," said Aunt Ina. "Did I *ever* make a cake? Cora made it for Tee. She makes him something just about ever' week. And then her and Mabel fixed him his par-ler."

"Trying to garntee our stay-place," said Cora, grinning. "It's not evvabody that would let women in our line of work live in their home."

"How you garnteeing your stay-place, Della?" Mabel asked idly. Jincey had to tell them.

"Oh, it's the *best* place!" she said in a rush. "It's the best place ever you saw. Uncle Bart got me a puppy named 'Welcome Jincey' and I got a place to go in bathing and we got a real pretty house with a room just for me and rations all the time!"

She ran out of breath and all the women laughed.

"Well, now you've put in your oar about something that wasn't even asked of you," Della said sternly. "You can take your cake and go outside and play."

Jincey felt shamed for having said too much but she couldn't help it. All her pleasure in Barton's Mill and Bayou Bien was there choking her, pushing to get out.

"And Sunday school and car-riding and children to play with!"

She stopped at the kitchen door and said it in a rush and then ran outside, finally sitting down on the steps nearest the dining-room window where she wouldn't be seen but could hear.

The women were laughing again and then she heard Della say, "Oh, she loves it, all right. Bart is good to her and to me. But it ain't *garnteed,* if that's what you want to know, Mabel. Anything could happen to queer the whole deal for us. Bart's uncle is against me and . . . well, you know, the *other one* is alive and walking the earth and likely to make trouble if he can."

"You ain't done anything about Howie yet?" Cora asked.

"Do?" said Della. "What is there for me to do except lay low and hope for the best? I haven't even written to my people— Titter or Aunt Sweetie—and told them where we are for fear *he* would inquire of them and they'd feel like telling him. You never know about them. They may think it their duty to tell him."

"Oh, Della," put in Aunt Ina, "you ought to write to them. They the only blood kin you got. You know they'll always help you if you need it—and you may need it, you can't tell. Don't ever turn your back on your kin, Hon."

"She's right," Cora said soberly, and Mabel nodded her dark head.

"But suppose I do and then Howie shows up there asking questions?"

"If I remember Sweetie aright she'd run him off the place with the battling stick," Ina said, laughing.

Della laughed, too. "I reckon," she said. "It sounds like her."

Cora's chocolate cake should have tasted good to her but Jincey couldn't finish the slice she had. Her stomach had started hurting when Della said they might have to leave Bayou Bien and she shivered, although the wood of the step where she sat was heated through from the summer sun, which now fell on her shoulders. If she didn't eat the rest of the cake or go back in the house maybe Uncle Bart would come and take them home and tell them they were as welcome as the flowers in May and he wanted them to stay forever.

Della must have thought about what Aunt Ina and Cora said about kinfolks because a few days later she got out a pen and a bottle of ink and a blue-lined tablet and sat down at the dining-room table to write them a letter.

Jincey hung around, trying to read over her shoulder.

"What you writing, Aunt Della?" she asked. "What does it say there?"

Della picked up the start on her letter and read aloud:

"Dear Titter and all, just a few lines to let you know that we are fine and hope you are the same. We now have a good home and plenty at it at Barton's Mill out from Bayou Bien, Alabama. On the eighteenth day of April last I married the nephew of the owner. His name is Barton McPherson and he is the dearest man."

"That's all so far," Della said. "Now quit hovering me and go play while I think what to say next."

Jincey was glad to go because she wanted to think about the words of the letter. *"Fine and hope you are the same."* It had a good ring to it but best of all was, *"He is the dearest man."* She hadn't known there was such a word as "dearest" but it sure-god fit Uncle Bart right down to the ground.

Jincey climbed up to her seat in the chinquapin tree to think about it and was there when two cars of company drove up the road practically together. One was Mary in her blue roadster and the other was a new Ford touring car with Aunt Ina and Uncle Tee. Della dropped her pen and ran out to greet them— first Mary, who was just ahead of the others, and then Aunt Ina and Uncle Tee.

"You've got a car!" she cried. "When did you git a car?"

Aunt Ina, wearing a new hat with pink velvet ribbon and clusters of little pink berries on it, got out of the car smiling.

"Told you Tee is Mister Big Britches, didn't I? First a par-ler, then a car. How you like it?"

Uncle Tee, wearing his policeman's uniform with the new sergeant stripes on the sleeve, climbed out proudly and led them all around to inspect the fine upholstery and the cunning little toolbox, which was built on to the running board. He sounded the horn and lovingly wiped a film of gray dust off the windshield with his pocket handkerchief.

Della introduced them to Mary and Jincey could tell she was proud to be able to say, "*Sergeant* Walton, Mrs. Walton, my sister-in-law Mary."

Mary caught the emphasis on the word "sergeant" and she smiled prettily at Uncle Tee and let her hand lie a long time in his.

"Are you *really* a sergeant—with the Mobile Police?" she asked.

"Yes, ma'am," said Uncle Tee, gruff with pride. "Just got my stripes."

"Oh, my!" breathed Mary, awed. "That's an *important* position."

Aunt Ina giggled. "Not as important as Tee thinks it is," she said.

Uncle Tee wanted them all to take a ride down to the commissary to show the car to Bart, and Della and Jincey climbed into the back seat but Mary begged off.

"I'm dying from the heat," she said. "If you have any ice water, Della, I believe I'll stay here and get a drink and try to cool off."

There was ice in the box and tea in the blue crockery pitcher, Della told her, and she'd find a breeze in the shade on the south side of the house.

"I'll be right back and fix us a little cold supper," she said, pleased that she had caught the hang of cold plates since Mary's first visit.

When they came back Uncle Bart was with them, riding in the front seat of the car beside Uncle Tee and very interested in the working of the new Ford. They stayed outside to lift the hood and look at the engine while the women went inside to start supper. Mary was at the dining table sipping iced tea when Della sent Jincey in to put out the plates and knives and forks.

"Put up my letter stuff," Della called from the door, and then she saw Mary sitting beside it, reading it.

"Well, Mary . . ." she began, irritated.

Mary looked up and grinned her happy, pleased-child grin.

"You write a beautiful hand, Della. You should have some nice stationery to show it off, instead of this old tablet paper. I'll bring you some the next time I come."

Mollified, Della smiled and went back to slice the cold roast and devil the hard-boiled eggs.

Aunt Ina and Uncle Tee left right after supper because they didn't want to be out on the road after dark. Mary, lounging in the canvas chair under the chinquapin tree, asked if she could spend the night.

"Why, you know you're welcome!" cried Della, pleased. "You can sleep on Jincey's bed and we'll put her down on a pallet."

"We'll both sleep on a pallet," said Mary, smiling at Jincey. "We'll be company for each other and it's always cooler on the floor than anywhere else. If you'd screen that porch, Bubba, that would be the best place of all to sleep."

Della looked at the porch thoughtfully and then at Bart but she didn't say anything. Jincey knew she would get to porch-screening sooner or later. If Uncle Bart didn't do it, Della'd figure out a way to do it herself. There was hardly anything Mary suggested that Della didn't latch on to right away.

But then Mary hurt her feelings.

"I was glad to meet those friends of yours, Della," she said, clinking ice in what must have been her sixth glass of tea. "They're really sweet. Wasn't he cute about being a police sergeant having a new Ford?"

Della paused before answering her, puzzled by the words and the patronizing tone. She had thought being a police sergeant and having a new car fine things. Now Mary made her uncertain.

Bart answered. "I don't know about 'cute,'" he said. "Sergeant Walton is a good man and policing is an important line of work."

"Oh, Bubba, re-ally!" said Mary. "You know policemen and firemen are tacky. Invariably poor whites get those jobs, hoping to move up in the world."

"Mary!" Bart said sharply. "Sergeant Walton and his wife are our friends. They were good to Della and Jincey before I even knew them."

"Oh, sorree," murmured Mary, getting to her feet and dropping a kiss on the top of Della's head. "I wouldn't disparage your friends for the world. Anybody you like, sister of mine, Mary likes."

She reached up a hand to Jincey on her branch in the tree overhead and said lightly, "Come on, jaybird, and let's fix our pallet."

Bart and Della sat on in the yard, Della stiff-faced and stunned. Bart reached for her hand and squeezed it.

"I'm sorry, sweetheart," he said. "Mary is capable of a lot of nastiness. I don't reckon you know that but I've been knowing it all my life. It's one of the reasons we haven't ever been close. She can be sweet and a lot of fun and then she turns mean."

"But is it true, what she said, that people look down on policemen?" Della asked in a low voice. "I'm asking you because I don't know, I honestly don't know. I thought . . . well, anybody respectable . . ."

"Well, I don't know what Mobile society thinks of them, if that's what you mean," Bart said. "I reckon that's what Mary was talking about. She puts a lot of stock in what she calls the Government Street crowd. I'm a working man myself and I *like* Tee Walton."

Della was silent a minute and then she said, "Bart, you don't like him. You say you are a working man but even I know that it's different with you. You are working in your family's business and that's not as though you was sawmilling for somebody else. You're nice to Tee and Ina for my sake but you think they're tacky, too, don't you?"

"Sweetheart, this is a silly conversation," Bart said impatiently. "I think enough of Tee Walton that I am going to a Ku Klux Klan meeting with him Sunday night."

Della drew a long breath and let it out slowly, happily.

"You are? Bart, that's nice! You *are* friendly to Tee. I shouldn't of said you wasn't!"

She reached for his hand in the darkness.

"Besides, I bet you'll be proud you joined the Klan. It's a important organization, I know, and I think it would be nice to belong to something."

Bart stood up, slapping his jumper pocket for his cigarettes.

"Well, I haven't joined yet. But I will go and see what it's like. Miss Mary can put that in her pipe and smoke it."

The prospect of going to a Ku Klux Klan meeting was uppermost in Della's mind all week. She planned a picnic supper and worried about clothes and what to do with Jincey.

"Just regular clothes this time," Bart said. "I haven't got to the sheet stage yet. And I reckon it'll be all right for Jincey to go with us. Tee said we'll meet at his house and eat supper and go on to Creacy Branch Church, where the Kluxers are going to present a pulpit Bible to the preacher."

"Aw, that's nice," said Della, glowing. "Them's good people."

"I reckon," Bart said. "They filled a need once—back when General Bedford Forrest organized them. I don't know about now."

Bart fed the stock early Sunday afternoon. He always did it himself because he didn't believe in asking Clewis or any of the hands to work on the Sabbath. And then he put back on his church clothes and cranked up the car, where Della and Jincey, already dressed, waited.

Della was excited over the outing. She talked and sang, persuading Bart to chime in on the chorus of "Golden Slippers," and she fussed at Jincey only lightly about keeping her head inside the car so the wind wouldn't blow the curls straight, after all her work to wash and roll them on rags on Saturday night.

There were three cars in front of Aunt Ina and Uncle Tee's house, and the new parlor was full of people. Jincey made a quick check and saw there were two other children, a baby asleep in a clothes basket in the corner and a big boy in knee pants.

Neither of them counted. You couldn't play with a sleeping baby, and a big boy—maybe thirteen or fourteen years old—sure wouldn't want to play with you. She sat stiffly beside Della on the wicker sofa and waited to be told what to do.

The men and women were separating, the men going into the dining room to drink coffee and the women gathering around the new Victrola.

"It's orthophonic," Aunt Ina explained to them. "Tee bought it yesterday and I want you to listen to Gene Austin a-singin'. Why, it sounds like he's purely in this room!"

She put a record on and all the women sat listening expectantly. There it came—an orchestra playing sweet and mellow and then a man's voice so close and clear and sad Jincey thought he might be getting ready to cry.

"Girl of my dreams," he saing. "I love you. Hon-est, I do! You are so sweet."

Mushy love stuff, she thought restlessly, and looked up and saw the boy was looking like he was thinking the same thing. He stood up and started toward the door. Then he stopped and looked at her.

"Wanta go outside?" he asked.

Jincey looked at Della and Della turned to Ina. "How much time we got?"

"Aw, they don't go nowhere till after dark," said Aunt Ina.

Della nodded her permission.

Outside the boy didn't pay any attention to Jincey for a long time. He picked up a stick and sat on the curb and dug into the hot tar, which covered the wooden paving blocks. A mockingbird came and sat on the edge of the roof and started singing and the boy rolled up a pellet of black tar and threw it at him. The bird hushed and flew away.

"Le's go back here," he said after a while, pointing toward the backyard.

"I know a shady place in the alley," Jincey offered.

"Show me," said the boy.

Jincey was pleased to lead the way to the snug little path between a big signboard advertising Camel cigarettes ("I'd Walk a Mile for a Camel") and the brick side wall of Mr. Bostwick's store. She had been through there many times and knew it well— a cool, shady place the sun never reached with hard, sour-smelling dirt—just big enough for a small person to squinch by.

"This'll do," said the boy. "Take off your drawers."

"What we gon' play?" asked Jincey, obediently reaching up under her yellow organdy skirt for her elastic waistband.

"I'll show you," said the boy, smiling at her for the first time.

Jincey thought about it a minute. She had on her best dress and shouldn't be in the alley anyhow. Della would be mad as fire if she got it dirty before the Ku Klux Klan meeting.

"No," she said. "I got to stay dressed up for the Ku Klux Klan meeting."

"You're a sissy," said the boy, disgusted.

"Am not!" said Jincey furiously.

"You *am!*" said the boy.

"I can just about swim," offered Jincey hopefully. "I got a pirogue and a pond to paddle it in and a place high up in a tree where I climb when I want to. I got a horse to ride."

The boy was interested.

"You lying or joking? How far from here?"

"Not far if you got a car," Jincey said.

"We got one," the boy said. "My daddy's a deputy sheriff."

Jincey didn't know what that was but it sounded important.

"Uncle Tee's a policeman," she countered.

"Aw, I know that!" said the boy. "Don't you reckon I know that? Him and my daddy been Kluxers together a long time."

"Yeah," said Jincey. "I know it."

"Aw, you don't know nothing!" said the boy. "I bet you don't even know what Kluxers do to people!"

"I do!" insisted Jincey. "I sure-god know."

"What?" jeered the boy.

"They give 'em Bibles!" she cried triumphantly.

The boy was seized by a spasm of mirth that threatened to flatten him out between the signboard and the brick wall. It belittled what she had said and shut her out and all Jincey could think to do was to draw her stiff yellow skirt closer to her, so it wouldn't brush the dirty wall, and walk out into the sunshine.

As she did she heard Della calling her and another voice, that of the boy's mother, joining in.

"Jincey!"

"Alsace!"

"Where are you?"

The two women were on the side porch and the minute they saw Jincey the boy's mother, a plump little woman with dark curly hair, said suspiciously, "What you all been up to?"

The boy, no longer laughing, was coming out of the alley behind Jincey.

"Fooling around," he said. And then, fixing his eyes on Della, "Your girl says she's got a pirogue to paddle and a place to swim and a horse and a dog. Is she lying or joking?"

"Why, neither, Alsace," said Della, smiling. "We live out in the country where it's easy to have things like that. You'll have to come and see us and play with Jincey some."

"When?" said the boy. "And don't call me Alsace. Call me Al."

Della turned toward his mother, who said tiredly, "We'll see, Alsace. You play nice and we'll see."

She and Della turned back to the house and Jincey heard her say, "He hates his name. His father got it overseas when he was in the war."

The sun went down and the tar in the street slowly cooled. A fresh breeze sprang up in the bay and the streetlights came on.

Jincey and Al, now friends, had started catching lightning bugs and putting them in milk bottles when their mothers called them in to eat. All the women had brought food for the pre-meeting supper, which was spread out on Aunt Ina's dining-room table and, although the grown folks had started first and nearly finished eating, there was plenty to choose from when Jincey and Al got there. Fried chicken and sliced pork and potted meat sandwiches and potato salad and three kinds of cake and a banana pudding.

"Where's Mabel and Cora?" Jincey asked.

Della threw her a quick, shut-up look.

Aunt Ina heard her and giggled. "Hiding in their rooms," she whispered. "Tee would have a conniption fit if they come out before his fancy KKK friends!"

Uncle Tee moved back and forth between the dining room and the parlor, pleased to have so much company and to see them enjoying themselves.

"See, Bart," he said, "there's more to it than high ideals and serious purposes. These fellers like to get together for a little fellowship."

Uncle Bart smiled and nodded. "It's nice," he agreed.

When they had finished eating all the men and women except Bart and Della got out their white robes and put them on.

"Leave off the hoods and masks till we get to our destination," directed Uncle Tee.

"Listen to that!" giggled Aunt Ina. "He thinks he's the Grand Cyclops or the Imperial Kludd!"

"What is your position, Tee?" asked Della.

"I can't tell you," said Uncle Tee. "Ours is the Invisible Empire. What I am is a secret."

"It's a nothing!" laughed Aunt Ina. "Tee would love to be the Grand Dragon wearing that satun suit with the spangles on it but that job's took."

"Ina, it ain't no bad thing to be a plain Knight," said Uncle Tee severely. "I'm proud to be a Knight and you should be proud to be a Kamelia."

"Oh, I am," said Aunt Ina, rustling her own white robe about like it was a dancing dress.

It wasn't a good idea for the cars to go in a procession, Uncle Tee said. So they would take different routes but try to wind up at Creacy Branch Church about the same time, after the singing and prayer had already started. There they would all put on their masks and pointed hoods and line up outside the door and march in together.

"Bart, you and Della precede us into the sanctuary," said Uncle Tee importantly. "The children, Jincey and Al, will go with you. We'll leave the baby in the car, if it is sleeping. After the ceremony, be prepared to get up quietly and depart."

Bart complained mildly about having to spend Sunday night driving around the countryside in the dark, looking for Creacy Branch.

"Oh, but it's exciting," Della said.

"I'm sleepy," said Bart. "All that food, I reckon. You know I'm bad to go to sleep at the wheel at night. If I doze off, reckon you could drive us home?"

"Oh, Bart!" cried Della. "This is a important occasion, and you talking about sleeping!"

But since he had mentioned it, she worried some. Bart was bad to go to sleep at the wheel. She stopped being excited about the Ku Klux meeting and started watching Bart's driving, urging him to go slow. When they drove into the yard of the little clapboard church, now weathered gray and sagging on the cypress posts which served as pillars, the others had already gathered. A small congregation inside sang thinly to the accompaniment of a tinny piano. KKK members had parked their cars off the road in a grove of live oak trees and put on their masks and hoods. They were walking through the little graveyard to the front steps.

Jincey shivered to see them, the faceless, pointed heads, the blank, black holes for eyes. They were so ghostly white walking under the trailing tatters of Spanish moss hanging from the live oak trees and through the rows of white tombstones.

Then she thought she saw Uncle Tee's policeman shoes beneath one white robe and she felt better.

She was right. It was his voice that said to Bart: "Proceed."

Bart took Della's arm and motioned to Jincey and Al to follow him and they walked up the rickety steps and into the half-filled church. They took seats on a splintery bench in the back and reached for hymnbooks to join the singing.

"Blessed assurance, Jesus is mine," sang the congregation. Della, knowing the words, joined in.

There was a light rustle on the front benches as people turned to see who had come in. A woman across the aisle leaned out and handed Della a palmetto fan.

The song ended. The gasoline lamp hanging over the pulpit hissed and a hard-shelled light bug thumped against the white globe. The preacher, a tall man in a black suit with thick, black hair growing from a point on his forehead, stood up and announced the scripture lesson from the book of Isaiah.

"Ah, sinful nation, people laden with iniquity," he read. "A seed of evildoers, children that are corrupters! They have forsaken the Lord, they have provoked the Holy One of Israel unto anger. They have gone away backward ..."

Jincey shifted on the hard seat and peered over her shoulder out the door. The Kluxers were nowhere in sight.

"Your country is desolate, your cities are burned with fire; your land, strangers devour it in your presence," read the preacher.

Somewhere outside there was a stirring. A woman laughed and was shushed. Somebody coughed. The preacher finished reading and closed the Bible.

"And the Lord bless to our hearing and understanding His holy and inspired word. Let us pray."

It was a long prayer that covered sin and backsliding and the sick and the grieving and came along to the one Jincey always liked the best—the Stranger Within Our Gates.

Suddenly there was the sound of feet on the sandy, warped boards of the doorsteps and the little church was full of strangers within its gates.

The pianist, as if on cue, struck up "Onward Christian Soldiers" and the Kluxers, moving solemnly two by two, filled the aisle with their white robes and peaked hoods.

The preacher stared at them fearfully, his mouth agape. Somewhere a woman's voice screeched, "Oh, my God!" A child near the front row whimpered and a man in front of Jincey took his pocket handkerchief out of his hip pocket and mopped his brow.

The march ended and for a moment there was no sound in the church but the whindling of the baby and the beetle bodies hitting against the hot light and dropping to the floor.

Then Uncle Tee was talking. He had told Bart that he copied some of his speech out of the Klan newspaper, *The Kourier,* and Jincey thought it sure-god sounded fine. He talked for a long time about Woman and her being "God's greatest gift to man." Every Knight of the Invisible Empire, "one hand upon the flag and the other upon the Holy Bible," stands pledged to protect her, Uncle Tee said.

After he finished with Woman, something he liked, he lit into three things he said were going to be the ruination of the United States of America—niggers, Jews and Catholics.

The Catholics want to turn this country over to the Pope of

Rome, Uncle Tee announced, and Jincey sat up straight and listened.

"The Roman Catholic owes his allegiance to the Pope of Rome, the Jew renounces Jesus Christ. (He's a businessman and to him one flag is as good as another provided the shekels come in!) And the nigger, he's still speaking the jargon of the jungle, just a generation removed from savagery!"

There was more, but Jincey was embarrassed for Uncle Tee standing up there using the word "nigger" in front of people. Della had said you only said it in private, if at all, and it was better to say "colored." Some of the people in the church seemed to be enjoying it though, especially when Uncle Tee said their church, their white Protestant church, was just about the only thing that stood for one hundred percent Americanism and "the sanctity of the white race."

He folded his speech and motioned to a Kluxer who was holding the big pulpit Bible.

"And our foremost reason for visiting you tonight is this," said Uncle Tee, taking the big Bible with its gold edges and purple-ribbon marker dangling from its side in his hands. "We are here for to give away a Bible."

The preacher, his hands trembling, held them out to receive it and cleared his throat to speak, but Uncle Tee waved a hand to stop him.

"Don't talk," he said gruffly. "Do! This is a gift and a warning!"

And turning majestically, he signaled the fat lady at the piano to resume her playing and began his march back up the aisle. It was a minute or two before the pianist caught on and picked up the tune—"marching as to war, with the cross of Jesus going on before"—and most of the Kluxers were practically outside the door.

Suddenly somebody yelled "Fire! God'amighty something's burning!"

The people in the church were on their feet pushing and straining toward the door. Bart took Della's arm and thrust Jincey and Al out ahead of them.

A flaming cross, eight feet tall and smelling rankly of kerosene, stuck in the ground in front of the church, licking at the moss on the live oak trees, lighting up the little gray building and the bleached bone tombstones.

The Kluxers were in their cars, starting up and moving toward the highway.

"Hurry," Bart said to Della and Jincey. "Al, run find your daddy's car—quick! We'll wait by the road to be sure you're with him."

The engine, being hot, started with one turn of the crank, and Bart ran and jumped into the seat over the front door without bothering to open it.

"What you running for?" whispered Della. "Are you scared?"

"Scared of fools with matches," muttered Bart.

Della said she thought the ceremony had been very impressive and the fiery cross was "just beautiful," but Bart concentrated on driving and didn't answer.

Uncle Tee asked him several times to join his Klavern of the KKK, but Bart never would. Uncle Tee said the purpose of the visit to the church had been to scare the black-haired preacher into behaving himself and quit running around when he had a wife. Bart said that might be a good thing but it wasn't any business of his and he wouldn't join. He told Della it was because driving around the country after dark made him so sleepy it was dangerous to be out on the road.

Della decided suddenly one morning that she wanted to go to Mobile to buy a few things.

"Jincey, you stay here and clean up for me," she said. "I might bum around a little with Aunt Ina and it's too hot for you to put on shoes and a starched dress and drag around the streets and stores."

"I wouldn't be too hot," Jincey said.

"Well, I say you would," Della told her in a tone that closed the subject. "You spread up the beds and finish washing these few dishes and then you can go on down to the commissary and stay with Uncle Bart. He'll git something out of the commissary for you all to eat today. Now come help me crank the car."

Jincey regulated the gas and the spark and when the engine was running she got out of the car to make way for Della and stood on the steps and watched her drive away. She hadn't been left alone all day before and she felt a little quivery about it. She might have cried to go if Della had given her time. Now, alone, there didn't seem to be much point in it.

She spread the bed and poured hot water from the kettle over the dishes to scald them and dried them and put them on the shelf and hurried outside to call Welcome and head for the commissary. Uncle Bart was waiting for her on the gallery and he started waving as soon as she was in sight.

"Pick 'em up, Jincey!" he called. "I got to go up to the head of the pond and you can go with me. Come on, jump in the boat."

The big launch was tied up in front of the commissary steps, its motor running. Uncle Bart got in first and held out a hand to help Jincey, with a squirming Welcome in her arms, step off the bank and onto the broad seat in the stern.

"Hang on!" Uncle Bart called, smiling at her. "I don't want to lose you all."

The pond was as smooth as water in the mule trough in the early morning, reflecting the trunks of pines and cypresses and every branch and leaf as truly as a mirror. There was a little marshy island in the middle, and a white crane stood on one leg at the water's edge studying something on the bottom with single-minded concentration. Only when the launch came close enough to send waves lapping against his leg did he put down the other leg and slowly and without alarm lift great white wings and flap up to the cypress tree overhead.

"He wasn't even scared," Jincey called out to Bart, and he cut the motor so he could hear her. "That bird," she repeated, "he wasn't even scared."

Bart nodded.

"This is where he lives," he said. "He knows nothing's going to harm him."

Jincey turned in the seat to watch the crane, serene and still on his high perch. Welcome, trying to keep his balance on the swaying stern of the boat, whimpered and Jincey put her arms around him to steady him and make him feel safe. "You don't have to worry none," she murmured against his droopy brown ear. "This is where you live."

There was a skinned place on the bank at the head of the pond. No marsh grasses or willows grew there and the raw earth was littered with pine bark. Uncle Bart cut the motor and let the launch drift up to the bank and a man came out of the woods and reached down to catch the rope he threw him. Jincey saw it was Matthew, Ruth's husband, and she waved at him.

"Po' Jack!" Bart called, and the man, busy tying the rope to a little sapling, echoed automatically, "Po' boy."

Bart leaped to the bank and pulled the boat around so Jincey and Welcome could get out.

"You didn't finish it," Jincey said. "You didn't do the spiel."

"Too busy this morning," Bart said. "Now you and Welcome can stay around here where Po' Jack can see you while I go back here with Flathead."

Jincey peered over a pile of logs at the top of the bank where a second man, wearing a battered straw hat, was busy brushing a kerosene bottle with pine needles stuffed in its mouth to make a bristle over the blade of a big crosscut saw. She tugged at Bart's jumper and whispered, "Is his head really flat?"

"What?" Bart asked, and then he laughed aloud. "Miss Ugly, you won't do! No, I don't reckon his head is especially flat, is it, Flathead? That's his nickname—one they give all timber cutters. It just stuck to him so long nobody remembers his real name."

The man turned from getting rosin off his saw and smiled at Jincey.

"My name be's John Seymour Edgerton, chile," he said quietly. "I remembers it."

Bart laughed again. "With an aristocratic handle like that, you ought to. We got to stop calling you Flathead."

Bart and the two black men walked back into the woods and, after sitting a while, Jincey decided to follow them. Bart and Flathead were not in sight but Matthew was there with four mules and a big eight-wheel wagon, loading logs left by the cutting crew.

"Can I stay with you, Matthew?" Jincey asked.

"Sho' can," said Matthew cordially. "I be glad to have company. Take you a seat somewhere and watch old Babe and Bathsheba do they job."

Two of the mules were hitched to the wagon and standing quietly, but two others, Babe and Bathsheba, were hitched to big, shiny chains which were looped around a pine log. They were on one side of the wagon and the log was on the other and when Matthew spoke to them they moved lightly away from the wagon, pulling the log toward it.

"Ba-abe!" Matthew said. "Ba-ath. Easy . . . hunnh!"

The log slid up two slick poles leaning against the wagon and slipped into its place on the pile of logs already loaded.

"Whoa!" Matthew called, and the mules stopped. He turned to Jincey with a smile. "See? Babe and Bath knows they business."

"They so smart!" agreed Jincey. "Did you learn 'em that?"

Matthew nodded modestly. "They was born knowing they had to work, just like me. But I broke 'em to the fine points. You take Sal and Jeeter there," nodding toward the pair hitched to the wagon, "they good pulling mules but they flighty. Ain't steady like Babe and Bath."

Jeeter and Sal flicked their ears as if they knew they were being talked about and flapped their tails at a persistent horsefly.

Jincey sat a long time watching Matthew and his mules load logs. When one pile was on the wagon they moved on to another one until the big, heavy-wheeled wagon was loaded. Then Matthew hitched Babe and Bath to the wagon in front of Sal and Jeeter.

"Now we gon' haul 'em to the pond," he said. "Come clime up here, chile. You ride wid us."

Matthew lifted Jincey to the topmost log and then he climbed up himself. He spoke to the mules and they moved, pulling the loaded wagon along a sandy road and then down the hill to the scarred bank of the pond, as easily as if it had been a sack of clothespins.

"Will they unload 'em too?" Jincey asked.

"They could," Matthew said. "Don' have to. We turns 'em a-loose and lets 'em slide."

He halted the mules at the top of the slope and lifted Jincey to the ground, warning her to get Welcome out of the way. Then he took a hammer from a box suspended under the tongue of the wagon and knocked loose two iron pins, which held the logs on the wagon. From somewhere under the wagon he brought forth a peavey hook and pushed off the top log and it rolled down the bank to the very edge of the water. One at a time he nudged the other logs with his pole and they lunged off the wagon and flopped down the slide.

When the last log lay on the ground, Matthew clucked to the mules and turned them back toward the woods, walking alongside because the wagon was not really a wagon at all but a metal frame on wheels. Jincey followed, and when they got back to the road Matthew stopped the mules and boosted her to Bath's back, climbing on Babe himself. They rode along to the next pile of cut logs and there they alighted and Matthew unhitched Bath and Babe and began the loading pattern all over again.

The sun was hot on Jincey's head and Matthew, noticing, worried about it. Finally he stopped the mules and went off in the bushes and came back with two big blackjack leaves and a thorn off a hog saw bush.

"Heah, pin these together and make you a sunshade," he said, handing them to Jincey. "Us don' want you falling out from the heat."

Jincey was so pleased with the leaf hat that she began looking around for more leaves and more thorns and had made a hat for Welcome and a second one for herself when Matthew said the wagon was loaded and called her to come ride to the pond.

They had just finished unloading the logs at the pond when the noon whistle blew, sounding sweet and sharp across the little body of water.

"Well, knock-off time," said Matthew to the mules, and he unhitched them and led them to the edge of the pond to drink and, leaving them there to drop to the water-greened grass, he dipped his hands in the pond and washed them and splashed water on his sweaty face, drying on a blue bandanna handkerchief. Then he reached under the wagon and brought out a tin bucket.

"Le's see what Ruth gimme today," he said, lifting the lid.

"Um, um, plenty meat and bread for bo'f us. Wash yo' hands and we'll eat."

Jincey hurried to wet her hands in the tepid pond water and dry them on her skirt, then sat down on a log by Matthew.

"I sets heah," Matthew said from some sense of what was fitting. "You sets theah." He pointed to a stump in the shade and handed Jincey a biscuit with a piece of cold fried fatback in it.

It had been a long time since breakfast and she was hungry and the biscuit and fried meat tasted salty and good to her. She ate it fast and was about to take the second one when she heard a whistle in the woods behind her and Uncle Bart appeared at the top of the slope.

"Aw, Jincey," he said, "you got so hungry you're about to eat up Po' Jack's dinner. I'm sorry, Jack. I was gon' feed her in the commissary but I got busy trying to see how them rednecks got in here and got our timber and got out without us hearing them. There are truck tracks leading back along the branch, so you know they had to make noise. I appreciate you and Fathead telling me. I'll get somebody out to watch after this."

He touched Jincey's leaf-covered head and motioned her toward the boat. Jincey remembered Della's admonition about thanking people, especially men, and she turned back and faced Matthew shyly.

"I want to thank you for a nice time," she said. "I enjoyed myself very much, 'specially your dinner."

Matthew laughed aloud with pleasure and Bart smiled. Aunt Della was right, Jincey decided, menfolks liked to be thanked.

It was cooler back in the commissary, shut away from the sun's heat and the glare on the water, and it smelled good. Uncle Bart took off his floppy old hat and washed his face and hands and set about putting them a good lunch out on the counter. He lifted the big blade and cut them thin, sweet wedges of cheese. He opened a can of sardines and dumped then in a little thin-wood lard carton, decorating them with rings of white onion, which he peeled and sliced with his pocketknife. He let Jincey fish bottles of the peppery gingerale out of the cold water well of the icebox and set out honey-jumble tea cakes, both the white-iced and the pink. Matthew's biscuit and meat had just whetted Jincey's appetite and she ate ravenously until everything was gone. Uncle Bart opened a second can of sardines for Welcome and put it on the floor, and then he yawned and stretched and pulled himself up on the counter.

"When I'm here by myself I usually catch a nap before the whistle blows," he said. "You want to pull up a counter and catch you one?"

Jincey hated naps but she wanted to do what Uncle Bart was doing. It seemed important. She crawled up on the counter beside him and he edged over to make room for her and put his arm under her head for a pillow.

Jincey slept through the second whistle and when she woke up Uncle Bart was in the office, hollering into the telephone on the wall. It was his day to call the packinghouse and order meat for the commissary and she heard him bellow: "That's what I said— fifty pounds of *salty sow sides!*"

Uncle Bart smiled at her when she wandered into the back office with Welcome at her heels. He finished the telephone call and then asked her if she would like to have some paper and a pencil and stay in the office with him and draw pictures or would she rather go across the bridge down below the mill and play with the Bates children.

"When is Aunt Della coming back?" she asked.

"Oh, I don't know," Bart said. "She probably got to trading and decided to stay till the stores close."

"I could go home and see," Jincey offered.

"Aw, no, I'd hear the car come in up there. It's too early for us to start worrying about her. Why don't you go play with Virgie and Lula until you hear the five o'clock whistle?"

"I'd rather stay with you," Jincey said. She didn't want to tell him but she felt like she'd better be where Della would come when she did get back. She didn't want to miss her.

"That's my girl," said Bart. "You know I need help and I believe I've got it. How about getting that broom and sweeping out the commissary for me?"

Jincey swept the commissary and the front gallery and the offices and then Uncle Bart showed her how to take cans of beans and tomatoes out of the big boxes in the storeroom, climb up a little ladder and stack them on the shelves. She worked until the five o'clock whistle blew and then she stood by his side back of the counter and ran to get things for him when he filled the orders for the men who came flocking in from the sawmill, the planer mill, the turpentine still, the lumberyard and the pond.

All of them spoke politely to Jincey. She recognized a few of them, especially the farmer, Clewis, who was walking up and down outside, slapping a Bible and making a speech to a little crowd which lingered on the gallery.

Jincey slipped out the door and listened to see if he was preaching a sermon but he seemed to be only talking up the revival, which was starting at the quarters church that night. "Heah me, you backsliders!" Clewis yelled. "Heah me, you skin-gamers and poontangers! The kingdom of heaven is at hand —and if you all stay away from meeting tonight you is gon' feel the wrath of the Lord God Almightee! You wid yo' baccy chewing, yo' snuff-dipping and shinny drinking..."

Jincey eased back inside the door and went and stood by Uncle Bart. When trading slacked off she said, "Is Clewis a preacher?"

"Clewis is a flimflam artist," he said lightly. "I expect he picks up the collection at meetings. That's why he's determined to get everybody there."

"Aunt Della likes him," Jincey said. "She always gives him coffee and they talk about gardens and Georgy."

"Oh, he's all right," Uncle Bart said. "He's a good farmer and I reckon he gets lonesome since his wife left him last year. He hasn't got anybody to laugh at his clowning."

The men finished buying rations and straggled up the road toward the quarters, sweeping Clewis and his Bible along with them. Bart locked up the commissary and straightened up his desk and went out on the gallery to wait for Della. He sat on the floor and leaned up against a post and looked out across the mill-pond, which was stained verbena-rose now with the setting sun.

His floppy panama hat pushed to the back of his head, he squinted to see the opposite shore.

Jincey sat on the floor, too, leaning against another post, her feet near his. She thought he might be thinking about the timber stealers across the pond, but she had to ask him the question:

"Do you reckon Aunt Della's coming?"

"Any minute now. Quit your worrying."

He looked at her freckled face and saw it was pinched with waiting and listening. The green-flecked eyes were on the road and the skinny little body was stiff with straining to hear the sound of the Ford over the sound of water falling over the dam.

"Tell me something, Ugly," he said gently, "Do you always worry like this when Della's away?"

Jincey looked at him and swallowed. She never had told anybody. It wasn't safe to tell anybody the big fear, it might make it come true. She knew Della might go away and not come back, might die and be buried in the ground. But she couldn't say it.

Instead, she turned her face away and looked out at the pond. The rose-verbena sky was darkening and the water of the pond, where a fish jumped and rippled it, was blood-red. A cotton-mouth moccasin slipped off a log and swam toward the little marshy island, pulling the water in bloody pleats behind him. Jincey looked and didn't answer and finally Bart said, "Well, come on, I'll get my tackle box and we'll see if we can catch us a fish or two."

Uncle Bart had a rod with a reel on it and he tried to show Jincey how to hold it and flip it and send a little false wooden fish with hooks in him whirling out into the water. But she tangled the line and got the false fish caught in the bark of a floating log and finally she burst into tears.

"I want to go look for Aunt Della," she whimpered.

"Golly, Jincey, you're getting to be a pain in the neck," Uncle Bart said. "You go sit over there on the gallery and let me fish for a little while."

But Jincey couldn't sit still. She walked down the bank to the road and as far as the bridge. Then she walked in the other direction, thinking to see if the car was in front of the house. The house was dark and still and the car was not in sight. She trudged back down the road toward the commissary, walking around the cows which lay in the warm dust.

Uncle Bart was walking to meet her and when he reached her he took her by the shoulders and shook her.

"Young lady, you know better than to go off like that without telling me. It's getting dark and I didn't know which way you went."

The touch of his hands on her shoulders and the sternness of his voice set Jincey off again. Tears poured down her dust-streaked face and her body jerked with sobs.

"Le's go look for her!" she begged. "Le's git in a truck and go look for her!"

"Now, Jincey," Bart began. "Della's all right. She'll be along in a little while. You're acting silly."

"*You're* acting silly!" Jincey cried. "Please le's go! Please!"

"Jincey, shut up!" commanded Bart, exasperated. And he slapped her face.

Jincey stopped crying and looked at him. Her hand traveled up to her cheek and she caught her breath to stifle a sob.

"I'm sorry, honey," Bart said. "I didn't mean to hurt you but you got to straighten up and behave. You're not getting Della home any faster with this carrying on. Now we'll walk as far as the Bates's to meet her, if that will satisfy you."

It didn't satisfy Jincey, but it was better than standing still, so she set off beside him toward the Bates's house. They had gone only as far as the bridge when they heard voices on the road.

"Hello?" called Bart.

"Hello, yourself!" called Della. "Have you got our supper ready?"

"Who's with you?" asked Bart.

"Ina," said Della. "I brought her for company and I've really given her a workout."

"Bart McPherson, if you got a stretcher crew, send them to git me!" said Aunt Ina, giggling. "I never have walked this far in all the years of my life put together!"

Jincey raced down the road to meet them and flung herself at Della, sobbing and knocking bundles out of her hand.

"Bless my soul, the young'un's gone loco," said Della, hugging her. "Did you think I wasn't coming home?"

Jincey couldn't answer for crying. Bart came up even with them and started asking questions about the car and why they were walking.

"Wheel run off over beyond the Front," said Della. "I was driving along just as fine as fiddle dust and I looked and yonder went a wheel rolling off in somebody's cornfield. I pulled over to the side and sure enough, only three wheels. Front one missing. So we got out and left it there and here we are."

She swung her shoes in her hands and laughed again.

"Sore-footed, but here."

"I'm sorry you had that trouble," Bart said, stooping to pick up the fallen packages. "If the car's all right where it is, we'll let it stay till morning and I'll get Percy to take me over there in the truck to work on it.

"It's safe, I think," Della said. "There was a colored house close by and I asked them to watch out for it."

"Safer than I am," sighed Aunt Ina. "I wore blisters on my feet before I took off my shoes. Now my feet is wore off at the knees."

They all laughed at Aunt Ina and walked along together toward the house. Jincey, limp with relief, clung to Della's hand and didn't care what was in the packages for her.

Later from the pallet they spread for her by the cot, where Aunt Ina was to sleep, Jincey heard Uncle Bart tell Aunt Della that he had slapped her.

"She was acting wild and irrational and I lost my temper," he said. "I was sorry right away."

"You hit Jincey?" Della said in a low voice.

"Yes," said Bart. "I did."

Della was quiet for a second and she said in a low, angry voice, "Don't you ever let me hear of you doing such a thing again!"

"You mean I'm not to punish her, even when she needs it?" Bart asked.

"Nobody punishes Jincey but me," Della said. "It's not like she needed punishing. She never does. But if she does, I'll whip her myself. I don't want you to ever do such a thing again!"

Jincey lay still on the cot and thought about it. She hadn't minded Uncle Bart slapping her. She wouldn't even have told Della about it. Maybe if he couldn't slap her he wouldn't let them stay.

MARY WAS the one who told them that old Mrs. McPherson was getting out of the crazy house.

"Whatever she's got won't get any better or any worse," she explained to Della. "They think she might improve some at home."

"Will she be living in her house in town?" Della asked.

Mary looked at Bart and back at Della.

"You didn't tell her? Honey, she's coming to live with you!"

Della saw Bart's red face and sheepish look and she knew that he hadn't wanted to tell her his mother was coming home. She hated that but she hated worse Mary's jibing at him.

"Why, certainly she'll live with us!" she said heartily. "It would be awful for her to be alone in that big house. We'll be more than happy to have her here."

Bart looked at her gratefully and reached a hand across the table to take hers.

"I thought—I hoped—you'd say that," he said. "But," looking around him at the red pine walls of the dining room, "we haven't got much room, have we?"

"All we need," said Della. "With family you don't worry about room. There's always enough."

"I got me a good woman," said Bart humbly. And Mary picked up her knife and fork and tossed her head.

"Better than I am. I have two bedrooms in my apartment and I know I should offer to take her but, Della, I know her and I know we couldn't live together. Bubba was away during the war and I was the one who had to crawl under the house at night and hide all the hatpins and knives and scissors. She was going to kill me."

Bart glanced at Jincey and shook his head at his sister.

"She's not dangerous, Mary. The doctor wrote that in his letter. She's an old woman now—nearly seventy years old—and whatever lunacy she had is all burned out."

Mary shrugged. "Maybe. I'll help you with her. I'm going up to Tuscaloosa to get her. Edward and I will provide her clothes while she's here so you won't have to worry about that."

It was settled that Mary would bring Mrs. McPherson home on the train the next Sunday and Bart and Della would pick her up in Mobile at the railroad station.

Jincey was curious about her and eager to know what her relationship to the old lady would be. Della, busy clearing out the dining room to make a bedroom for her mother-in-law, wasn't interested in discussing it.

"She could be my grandma, couldn't she?" Jincey asked.

Della was turning the dining-room table end over end to get it through the front door to the gallery, where she said they would eat the rest of the summer since Bart was sending a man to screen it. The table was big and it got wedged in the door, pinching Della's fingers.

"Jincey, if you don't git out of this house and leave me alone I vow I'll whip you!" she cried, sucking a bruised finger. "Now git! And don't ask me what to call that old buzzard, because I don't have the least idea what to call her myself!"

"Why is she a old buzzard?" Jincey asked, backing slowly toward the yard.

"She's a old woman," said Della. "And all old women's mean. Don't you remember Aunt Sweetie?"

Interested, Jincey stopped her backward movement to talk about it.

"Aunt Sweetie's awful mean," she agreed. "But Aunt Elvie's not. Aunt Elvie's good."

"Well, that's because she's colored," explained Della, tackling the table again. "Nigras is different."

"I didn't think Aunt Jessie and Aunt Ruby Pearl was mean," began Jincey thoughtfully.

"Well, I don't care," said Della. "They as mean as anybody'll let 'em be. Go sweep the dining room. I'm gon' scrub and put up that single bed in there and hang the drapes."

"The what? What you gon' hang?" asked Jincey. It was the first she'd heard of drapes and she sure-god didn't know what they were.

"Drapes! Drapes!" said Della impatiently. "You saw me make them. New cretonne ones."

Jincey had thought Della had made curtains and she said so.

"Well, they call 'em drapes now," Della told her. "Remember that."

Jincey swept the Congoleum rug in the dining room, admiring once more that pattern of leaves and flowers in it. And then she stood by while Della mixed up suds with the broom and a bucket of water and scrubbed it.

"It don't take Congoleum long to dry," Della said, "so we'll be setting up the bedstead. Come help me."

When it was finished Jincey thought it was as fine a room as she ever saw. The cretonne drapes made straight panels of climbing blue flowers by each window and Della had cunningly stitched a border of the same goods around the edge of the white bedspread.

There was a crocheted centerpiece in the middle of the washstand in the corner and a flowered bowl and pitcher set in the middle of it.

"Oh, it looks fine, Aunt Della," Jincey said.

Della stood in the doorway looking.

"Not to say fine," she muttered. "But it'll have to do. She's probably used to better but it's the best I can do with what I got to do with. Now to git in rations and we'll be ready."

As a special treat for his mother Della asked Bart to send up an extra fifty pounds of ice so she could make ice cream. She had in mind fresh peach with a pound cake, which would take a pound of butter, sugar and flour and a dozen eggs.

"You going to a lot of trouble," Bart told her, when she kept the kitchen fire going late Saturday night and stood over it slowly stirring the custard for the ice cream. "I don't want you to put on the dog for Ma."

"It's not putting on the dog," said Della, mopping her dripping face with her apron. "I just want to have things nice. Where she's been maybe she didn't git homemade cream and cake."

"Let me do something to help you," Bart offered unexpectedly. Jincey and Della both stared at him. Helping around the house was not man's business and Bart had never suggested it before.

"You can freeze the cream in the morning before we go to church," Della told him. "We'll leave it packed in the shade and it'll be just about ripe when we come home from the depot."

In the excitement of meeting Mrs. McPherson Jincey didn't take much interest in Sunday school, although Sunshine and Joy and Delight Boudreaux were there and had a new song to sing. Since they had a Sunday school to go to, their papa was teaching them a new song every week so they could sing especially for the meeting. Bart and Della didn't hang around the front steps talking to Brother Doby Webster and the Whites either. They barely had enough time to get to the station before the train from Tuscaloosa was due in.

Jincey saw them first and in a sudden fit of shyness she couldn't speak but tugged at Della's dress and nodded toward the train step.

"Oh, they come on the Pullman!" cried Della. "There they are! I was watching the day coach."

"Mary would never ride on the day coach," said Bart over his shoulder as he hurried toward the back of the train, where Mary and a porter helped propel an enormously fat, white-haired woman down the steps.

"Parlor car," whispered Della to Jincey as they walked past the glittering windows of the train. "I do believe she come in the parlor car."

Bart was hugging and kissing the old lady, who was patting him and crying. Mary was counting baskets and boxes and traveling cases as the porter handed them down.

"Mama," said Bart, "I want to make you acquainted with my family. My wife, Della, and my little girl, Jincey."

Jincey could feel Della stiffening up to give the old lady a mannerly handshake but without bothering to wipe away the tears which had cut rivulets in the white powder on her plump, pink cheeks, Mrs. McPherson opened wide her cushiony arms in their blue taffeta sleeves and cried, "Hey-o! There you pretty things! Come to Ank!"

Della and Jincey went forward awkwardly and Della kissed the flour-pasty cheek. Jincey butted her head into the soft bosom and drew away as fast as she could.

"Mary told me I am to stay with you at the old home place," the old lady burbled to Della. "Do you know how happy that makes me? Say? The happiest days of my life were spent there! Picking scuppernongs and dancing with my beaux in that lovely, graceful room!"

"Mother!" said Mary sharply. "You know the old house is gone. Bubba and Della live in the woods rider's little house. That's where you'll be staying."

The pink face crumpled and the china-blue eyes filled with tears. "Gone . . ." she murmured brokenly. "Gone . . ."

Della turned helplessly to Bart.

"Ma . . ." he began, but the old face had cleared as fast as it had clouded and now the old lady was smiling broadly, showing a mouthful of brilliant white teeth, every one perfect.

"No matter," she said airily. "My little feet can't waltz anymore anyway." She made a face at Jincey. "Bunions."

Jincey glanced down at her feet and they were little, the kind of little feet that Della admired, and they were crammed into child-size navy blue silk slippers with ribbon ties across the instep.

Mary winked at Jincey and took her mother by the arm. "Come on, twinkle toes. Let's get out of this heat."

"Twinkle toes," repeated the old lady, allowing herself to be drawn along toward the station. "Sticks and stones may break my bones but names can never hurt me. You know that, Jenny?" She stopped and clutched Jincey's shoulder. "Come on. I'll teach it to you. 'Sticks and stones may break my bones but names can never hurt me.' Now you try it."

Jincey looked at Della and repeated the rhyme in a low voice.

"Tolerable," said Mrs. McPherson judiciously. "But let's get it perfect. Now repeat after me, 'Sticks and stones . . .' "

"Oh, for God's sake, Mother!" put in Mary. "Shut up and walk. It's too hot for you to start acting crazy."

Mrs. McPherson lifted her white head in its blue silk toque imperiously, but she did start moving again.

"No matter what you think, Mary," she said after a cool silence, "it's important to teach children things. I'm going to earn my place in my son's home by teaching Jenny. You knew I won a prize in German at Barton Academy, didn't you?"

"Yep," said Mary good-humoredly. "You've told me time and again. Now, Bubba," she said, as they reached the car, "you've got all you can haul if you get Mother and her stuff in here, so I'm going to take a taxi home."

She kissed her mother on the cheek, patted Della on the shoulder and winked at Jincey.

"You all gon' have a picnic," she promised them and walked away.

Della insisted that Mrs. McPherson ride in the front seat and she sat in the back with Jincey and the boxes and baskets. Bart tied a big steamer trunk to the running board.

"Should we stop and get a cold drink on the way home?" he asked Della.

"You don't have to on my account," put in his mother. "Those frivolous things cost money and I'm not used to them."

"Let's do have one," said Della. And Jincey was glad. She had been remembering how nice it was to drive up to the curb at Five Points and have the boy bring out drinks filled with crushed ice. The sun on the canvas roof of the car seemed hotter than she ever felt before. Maybe because the steamer trunk on her side blocked any breeze they might have gotten.

"What would you like, Ma?" Bart asked his mother.

"A chocolate malted milk with an egg in it!" the old lady said promptly.

Della caught her breath and rolled her eyes at Jincey. They had never ordered such a thing. It must cost a quarter if it cost a cent.

"Sweetheart? Ugly?" Bart turned to them.

"Oh, root beer as usual for us," said Della.

"You must not call that child 'ugly'!" said Mrs. McPherson. "I don't care if she is ugly, you must not call her that. It is discourteous and unkind."

Bart burst out laughing and reached in and rumpled Jincey's hair.

"Jincey knows that's a pet name," he said. "If she wasn't the prettiest little girl I ever saw I wouldn't call her that, would I, Ugly?"

Jincey smiled at him and bobbed her head. It was a special name nobody else called her and it meant he liked her. As for how she looked, she hadn't thought about that. But if he said she was the prettiest little girl he ever saw, it must be so, even if she was greenish and freckled and stringy-headed, like Della said.

The curb boy was slow to come so Bart went in the drugstore to get the drinks and Della said, "Speaking of names, what do you want us to call you, Mrs. McPherson?"

"Names, names, what's in a name?" cried the old lady shrilly. "A rose by any other name would smell as sweet!"

Della rolled her eyes at Jincey again.

"I was christened Annie Katherine, my brother and sisters call me Ank. The man . . ." She faltered and her voice dropped. Della leaned forward to hear her better. "There was a man who called me Mrs. McPherson . . ."

"Well, we don't want to call you that," Della said quickly. "It makes a stranger of you. It's for Bart to call you 'Mama.' How about me and Jincey calling you 'Motherdear'?"

"Motherdear?" The old lady tried the name in her mouth, pursing her full pink lips to taste it. "Why, it's charming. Something like the darkies, but it has a nice sound. Affectionate."

She turned around in the seat and rested her big blue eyes on them thoughtfully.

"I do want to be loved," she said earnestly. "I've been trouble for people all my life and I expect I'll be trouble for you all—but I don't mean to be. I want you to love me."

Almost as fast as her serious tone came it was gone and she was shouting gleefully to see Bart coming out the door followed by the curb boy with their drinks on a tray.

"Hey-o there, son! Hey-o!"

Bart smiled at her and she waved her handkerchief at him.

"They're going to call me 'Motherdear'! How's that?"

Bart smiled at Della gratefully, handing her her five-cent root beer and his mother the frost-beaded glass of chocolate malted milk, which was so big there was even some of it left over in a tall, shiny metal cup. Jincey, sucking her own root beer through a paper straw, watched as the old lady greedily drank of the foaming liquid and then spooned out the little mound of ice cream heaped in the bottom of the glass. For the first time she thought Della might be wrong to say that you must never order more than a five-cent drink. Uncle Bart plainly didn't mind that his mother wanted something rich and expensive.

Between the station and the mill Motherdear forgot that her old home, the three-story house which had been in the field, was no more and that she was going to live in a regular quarters house. When Bart stopped the car under the oak tree by the door, Jincey was watching to see if the old woman would admire the newly screened front gallery with the flowerboxes full of coleus and the swing and chairs with their white covers embroidered with big red "M"s.

"Well, here we are, Ma!" Bart said, leaping over the door on his side and going around to help his mother out of the car.

"We are?" asked the old lady. "Where are we?"

"This is your new stay-place, Motherdear!" Della said gaily. "Get out and come and see. Bart had the front gallery screened for your coming."

"And Della has you a room all ready," put in Bart.

There was no sound from the front seat for a minute and Jincey knew the old lady was crying.

Bart and Della stood by the car, looking at one another helplessly. Jincey shifted some boxes aside and climbed out and stood beside them a minute and suddenly she felt sorry for them and all their wasted preparation. She moved closer to the old lady with the idea of shaming her, as Della was forever shaming her for not being thankful enough. But the old face, even pinker in the noonday heat, was as wet and as crumpled as a washrag and the blue eyes were shut tight.

"Motherdear?" said Jincey, trying the new name for the first time. "We got some peach ice cream."

Motherdear's eyes popped wide open and the crumpled face smoothed into a wide smile.

"No, no. None for me," she said cheerfully, beginning to pull herself together and get out of the car. "They served us a pure spate of it Up Yonder. I'll never eat ice cream again as long as I live."

But when her boxes and baskets were stacked in a corner of her room and Della had persuaded her to take off her taffeta dress and her corset and put on a plissé kimono, Motherdear settled down on the screened front gallery and ate everything that was put before her. Della's fried chicken and rice and gravy and butter beans and fried okra vanished before her drive with knife and fork. Then she ate a soup plate full of peach ice cream with a side wedge of cake.

"Naps," said Della, when she was done. "I think we all need naps, don't you, Motherdear?"

"I never could sleep in the daytime," Motherdear said. "But I will lie down for a minute—as an aid to digestion."

Bart had already gone to stretch out under the mosquito bar and Della turned back the new spread and drew the cretonne drapes against the sun in Motherdear's room. She helped the old woman off with her shoes and stockings and, sighing heavily, Motherdear settled her hefty old body on the new mattress.

"Come and kiss me goodnight," she called to Della and Jincey.

Della cut her eyes at Jincey and obeyed. Jincey slipped around the door facing into the kitchen and out of sight. She plumb hated the notion of kissing the slippery, wet old face.

Both Bart and Motherdear were snoring by the time Della and Jincey had cleared the table and washed the dishes, so Della gave up the idea of a nap for herself and Jincey was glad. She hated naps, especially when Della took them. Sometimes when Della slept in the afternoon Jincey would be seized with the idea that she was dead and would tiptoe into the room and watch to see if she was breathing. Della was a light sleeper and Jincey's presence was usually enough to awaken her and that made her mad. So either way, naps were a plague. If Della slept, Jincey was scared. If she awoke, Jincey was in trouble.

"Let's walk up to the grove," Della whispered as they stood a minute listening to the snoring. "It'll be cooler than here and we won't have to listen to the old hog snort and snarf."

"Why do you call her a old hog?" Jincey asked when they were a little distance from the house.

"Did you ever see anything human eat like that? She's a fattening hog, all right."

Walking wide to put her bare feet down in the shady spots on the road and avoid the burning sand, Jincey thought about it. Della liked to see people eat her cooking, but when Motherdear shoveled it in, she called her a hog.

"I reckon we ain't gon' like her, are we?" she said after a while.

Della's eyes rested on her thoughtfully.

"We better try to," she said after a while. "Our stay-place could depend on it."

A few minutes later up at the grove Della found a bullace vine hanging over a deep sandy ditch and her face lit up.

"Look, childee, a swing! I remember when I was a little girl about your size, me and Titter had a bullace-vine swing in the woods behind Aunt Sweetie's peanut field. We'd noon out there in the shade and when our dinner was eat we'd stir up a breeze swinging. Come on, I'll show you."

She kicked off her shoes and pulled down her stockings and folded them carefully and stuck them in the toes of her shoes for they were silk and costly. Then she grabbed hold of the tough old vine, which was bigger than her own arms, tested it to see if it would hold her, and then swung out over the ditch, landing on the other side.

"Come on, childee, you try it," she called, sailing the vine back to Jincey. "Here, catch it. I'll git me another one."

Laughing delightedly, Jincey caught the vine and hung on, letting it carry her to the other side of the ditch. Della loosened another vine, which had wound itself around a little sapling, made a loop in it for a hand-hold and swung back and forth across the sandy gorge, laughing as she met and passed Jincey in the crossing, and the little breeze they stirred up flipped at her skirt and pulled her hair loose from its pins.

The sun shining through the leaves of the big trees made a green-gold light. The July flies' song sizzled in the rooftree above them. Jincey's hands hurt where they grasped the scaly bark of the vine and her arms felt stretched and sore, but she didn't know when she had been so happy. Della's cheeks were pink and her eyes sparkled and her bare feet and legs, now sandy from the bank, looked like a young'un's feet and legs as she wound them around the vine and went sailing through the air.

"Diamond Joe, come git me! The one I love's done quit me!" she sang as she swept by Jincey, going faster and higher with every sweep.

"Diamond Joe!" echoed Jincey, missing the tune and not caring as she swung out after Della, trying to catch her.

Suddenly there was a cracking sound in the big oak tree above them. The branch holding the vine Della was on broke, the vine tore loose, and before Jincey could see what was happening Della lay on her back at the bottom of the ditch.

"Mama!" cried Jincey, dropping her vine and sliding down the bank. "Mama, are you dead!"

Della's eyes were closed but she was breathing hard and she kicked a bare leg impatiently.

"Don't you 'Mama' me," she said. "Of course I ain't dead. But I ought to be. A woman my age cutting the fool like this."

She sat up and started pulling the pins out of her hair and holding them in her mouth while she twisted the loose hair into a new knot on top of her head. Her dress was covered with sand and her face was red and angry, but she looked at Jincey's face, pinched with anxiety, and she laughed.

"Come and sit down," she invited. "It's cool down here. We'll rest awhile before we go back to old Motherdear and her boy."

Jincey slid the rest of the way into the ditch and sat down. A growth of live oaks and sweet gums and haws, interlaced with bullace vines, made the bottom of the ditch dim and shady. Spring rains flowing through it to the millpond had swept it free of leaves and grass and its sandy bottom was soft and clean.

Jincey looked around at the clay walls. Tree roots pushed through them here and there, making crevices where fern seed, blown by the wind and washed by the rain, had caught hold in little lacy green patches.

She shoved her toes into the sand and sighed happily.

"It's a good place, ain't it?" she asked Della.

"Right good," agreed Della. "But don't come up here by yourself. It's too close to the quarters and you don't know what old man or boy will be wandering loose looking for trouble. Besides, you might run into a snake."

Jincey didn't say anything but she knew she would come back. It was a good secret place, so well hidden by the bullace vines overhead no trouble could find it.

Della sat with her hands clasped around her legs and her chin resting on her knees.

"One good thing," she said thoughtfully, "*she* didn't notice her furniture all over the place. I don't know what we'd do if she decided to cut up jake over that. I reckon I ought to be thinking about gittin' stuff of our own, just in case she decides to pull out and take her old junk with her."

Jincey hadn't thought about Motherdear ever leaving them and turned the idea this way and that, examining it.

One good thing about having Motherdear there was that Della had walked out with her and found this good play-place and had swung on the bullace vines with her.

It was something she had never done before, but in the days after the old lady came, the house didn't hold Della like it had. She had been wrapped up in it and its fixings. Now Motherdear and her voice seemed to fill the five rooms and spill out into the yard and Della fled to the outdoors as often as she could.

"I vow she's noisier than the sawmill," Della remarked to Jincey one day. "Listen at her."

They were chopping down weeds in the backyard and Motherdear was by herself on the front gallery, talking at the top of her voice.

"Go see what she's saying," Della said. "Maybe she's talking to us."

But Motherdear was talking to the heavy summer air which enveloped the tin-roofed house and pressed down on her, causing her fluffy white hair to lay in damp yellow skeins on her skull.

"And my dear papa said to me, 'Annie Katherine, my angel, you are the prettiest one . . .' "

"Hi Motherdear," said Jincey, coming around the corner of the house and taking a seat on the steps. "What you doing?"

The big blue eyes rolled Jincey's way, rolled heavenward and then came back and focused on Jincey's face. She smiled broadly and patted the swing beside her.

"Hey-o! Come sit with me, child. We'll talk."

Jincey didn't mind the talk like Della did but she didn't like to sit next to the fat, sweat-damp old body. Still, she didn't know how to refuse, so she wedged herself in the little space left in the swing and felt a white, sausagey old arm settle damply around her shoulders.

"You help me unpack my trunk," Motherdear said. "I might have a little present for you."

"I'll help," Jincey said, "and you won't have to give me a present."

"O-ho!" cried Motherdear, pulling herself out of the swing. "You don't know what darling pretties Ank has!"

They started on the trunk, pulling out and hanging up a lot of rustling black taffeta before they got to the interesting things. There was a papier-mâché parrot, all red and yellow and green, with a great gold bow on his neck. He sat on a perch in a gold hoop. Motherdear wanted him hung in the window so he could see out. There were boxes of powder and little bottles of cologne, all half-empty. Her sisters and Mary had sent them to her at the Tuscaloosa hospital and she had used a little of this and that, never finishing and discarding any bottle. There was a tin box of candies wrapped in waxed paper. Motherdear offered them to Jincey, and then put one in each jaw, sucking noisily as she pulled out silk bloomers and sweet-smelling soap.

It was an interesting trunk, Jincey thought, and she was enjoying squatting on the floor beside it, letting the sweet peppermint flavor fill her mouth and trickle down her throat.

Suddenly Motherdear shrieked happily.

"Hey-o! This is what I've been looking for!"

She pulled out a little gilt-edged Bible and clutched it to her breast.

"My Bible, yes, my Bible! I'm going to give it to you, child, and I want you to read it and memorize a passage every day."

Jincey looked around helplessly for Della. She didn't think she ought to take Motherdear's Bible and she didn't know how to refuse.

"Listen!" cried the old lady. "Here are the Beatitudes. Can you say them?"

Jincey shook her head. Motherdear held the Bible closed on one finger to mark her place, turned her eyes heavenward and shouted:

"*Blessed* are the poor in spirit for theirs is the kingdom of heaven. *Blessed* are they that mourn for they shall be comforted. *Blessed* are the meek for they shall inherit the earth. *Blessed* are they which do hunger and thirst after righteousness for they shall be filled. *Blessed* . . ."

"What's this, Sunday school?" asked Della from the doorway.

"Wait a minute! *Blessed* are the merciful for they shall obtain mercy. *Blessed* are the pure in heart for they shall see God. *Blessed* are the peacemakers for they shall be called the children of God. *Blessed* are they which are persecuted for righteousness' sake for theirs is the kingdom of heaven. Blessed are ye when men shall revile and persecute you and shall say all manner of evil against you falsely for my sake . . ."

She paused and smiled broadly at Della. "*Rejoice* . . . I say . . . *rejoice* and be exceedingly glad for *great* is your reward in heaven!"

"Well . . ." said Della uncertainly.

"I want Jenny to commit the Beatitudes to memory," Motherdear said. "That's her first bit of memory work. I'll check you on it after supper," she said to Jincey, handing her the Bible. "Now I'm gon' rest my eyes a minute."

Stepping around the trunk and the litter of possessions on the floor all about it, she headed for the bed and sagged down on it, without even turning down the new spread.

Della made a face at Jincey and beckoned her out of the room.

"Go play," she said. "I'm gon' rest while she's quiet. God knows it's seldom enough."

But Jincey thought Motherdear's recital had been fine, full of big, pretty words, and she couldn't wait to climb up in the chin-quapin tree and start trying to memorize the Beatitudes herself.

The garden grew and with it Della's pleasure in life grew too, expanding and glowing until Jincey, caught up in it, felt a one-ness with everything that moved or flew or skimmed through the water. She skipped when she walked and sang when she climbed trees or hid in the gully up in the grove to lie on her back and dream.

That was the summer Bart taught her to swim and paddle the little double-end pirogue, which, shallow and pointed at both ends, glided smoothly and swiftly over the surface of the mill-pond. Occasionally a cottonmouth moccasin glided along too, and although Jincey knew that they were poisonous, causing peo-ple to die if they bit them, she somehow felt immune to danger. Nothing bad could happen to her here. Nothing bad could hap-pen to anything or anybody.

Once when she drifted in the pirogue near the head of the pond a deer came down to the water's edge to drink. When he lifted his head he saw Jincey and stood a moment looking at her with clear, calm eyes that recognized no danger. When he had drunk his fill, he turned and moved lightly but without fear up the slope and into the woods.

Another time when she lay on the sandy bottom of the gully, looking up at the trembling shadows in the green canopy of gum and bullace leaves above her, a skunk came and stood at the top edge and looked at her for long moments, curious but unworried, before he went away. The phoebe bird singing down in the woods at dusk seemed to Jincey to have a special message for her. Once when Della was gathering young onions and tomatoes from the garden, Jincey perched on top of the fence post, watching her and the way the sunlight left the earth first and then slowly edged upward in bands of pale gold to the tops of the trees, where it lingered until the last. The phoebe bird in a bay tree down in the branch began, and Jincey's freckled face with its too-long bangs, stiff from sweat and uncombed since morning, was radiant with pleasure.

"What you think he's saying, childee?" Della asked.

"I know," said Jincey. "Hey, Jin-cee! Hey, Jin-cee!"

Della listened and smiled, her apron full of ripe red tomatoes. "I believe he is," she said. "Or maybe it's 'Sweet Childee! Sweet Childee!' "

Central to Della's content was the plentitude of food. Her garden was part of it. But the commissary was there, stocked with things she could have for the asking. The woods were filled with blackberries and mayhaws, free for the taking, and she and Ruth and Jincey spent every afternoon in the fields and fence rows filling buckets with the fruit. Every morning, long before the sun was up, Della had a fire in the stove, making jellies and jams and baking for Bart's dinner a big blackberry cobbler. Sand pears ripened out in the field and she made pear preserves. Figs on the trees around the old house site began to turn from green to great rose-touched, honey-dripping globules of brown and Della, hitching up her skirt, clambered through the tough old branches with Jincey, filling a dishpan to make Bart's favorite preserve of all— whole figs, caught in a thick, dark syrup the color of topaz.

Motherdear, who wanted to help at everything else, would have nothing to do with picking berries or mayhaws.

"Hey-o, you ragamuffins!" she cried when she saw them with sunhats tied under their chins and their arms covered with old stockings to keep them from getting sunburned. "You go along. I'm gon' stay here and say my prayers."

Red bugs, well-nigh invisible, burrowed into the skin, itching furiously, but Della dusted everybody with sulphur before they left home.

"If I had to dust Motherdear with all her gobs and creases it would take more sulphur than they've got at the commissary," she told Jincey.

When they returned with buckets brimming with blue-black berries, Motherdear dipped into them greedily, filling and refilling a soup bowl and topping them with sugar and cream.

"Where do you find these, Della?" she asked.

"On briars," said Della. "On mean, scratchy old briars."

"Oh, I couldn't pick them," said Motherdear, refilling her soup bowl. "It would be too hard on the hands."

"Yes, ma'am, it is," said Della, picking a stubborn thorn out of her own bleeding thumb. "It is that."

But she was glad to have the time away from the house, free from Motherdear's chatter. She really enjoyed the picking, and as long as Ruth was with them she wasn't too afraid of snakes.

The jars and glasses of things Della canned and jellied and preserved overflowed the kitchen shelves and crowded the cook table.

"I need a pantry, Bart," she said one day.

"Where would you put one, sweetheart?" he asked absently.

Della had that figured out. The little back porch was too small to sit on and really served as a catchall for tools and old shoes they wore in the garden and a place for Welcome, who was now big and smelly, to sleep. Flies clustered on the floor, and when the back door was open they swarmed into the kitchen.

"We could enclose the back gallery," said Della, "and make shelves along three sides."

"Well, but what would we do for a gallery?" asked Bart. He couldn't imagine a house without a back gallery of some kind.

"Git me the pantry first and I'll tell you my idy about the gallery," said Della, smiling at him so fondly he reached across the table and took her hand.

But Bart had forgotten the pantry until he came home one day and found Della out on the gallery nailing up shelves along the wall of the house.

"What are you doing?" he asked.

"I got to have some place to put my fruit and stuff," said Della, around the nail in her mouth. "I'll put 'em here and if the Nigras don't steal 'em and the winter don't freeze 'em, they'll be all right."

That afternoon Bart took the carpenter off a job at the mill and sent him up with a load of lumber to wall in the gallery, and while he was there Della got him to cut another back door in the kitchen wall and lay off a foundation for a bigger back porch to run all the way across the house.

In between canning tomatoes and corn and beans, Della worried about meat and milk. One day she went to town and came back with a calf in the back seat of the car.

"Woman, you are crazy!" yelled Bart when he saw the cream-colored head sticking out over the car door. "What you doing to my car? Wouldn't a kitten or another puppy be a better pet?"

"Foot to pets," said Della. "This is gon' be my milk cow. I give five dollars for her at the dairy. Purebred Jersey."

"But how you gon' raise her?"

"You gon' help me with that," said Della, smiling. "Git me milk every day from your Uncle Bob's cow, Sylvia. She's fresh and they don't use half that milk. Feed it to the chickens."

Della named the little calf Alice, and twice a day she warmed milk, sweetened it slightly and poured it into a vinegar bottle, topping it with a rag-stopper the calf could suck on while she held it.

"Let me, Aunt Della, let me!" begged Jincey.

"All right," said Della reluctantly, giving up a chore she enjoyed herself. "But don't let her step on you. Her little hooves are like knives."

Alice would take her nursing bottle from Jincey, but Della was the one she loved. When she heard the back door slam she ran, looking for Della, and following her about the yard like a dog. If Della sat on the steps, Alice would put her big head in her lap or lick at her hands with her long, rough tongue. She had the run of the yard, and Della cheerfully collected her plops every morning, piling them at the edge of the garden to season for use as fertilizer. But the day she reached over the garden fence and started cropping the cucumber vines, Della started campaigning for a separate cowpen.

"Alice is big enough now to go in the woods with the range cattle," Bart objected. "She'll come up at night for her feed."

"She is not a pine woods range cow," Della said. "She's a Jersey. Purebred. Besides, winter is coming and she'll need a shelter of some kind. Just a little shed with a pretty good-sized pen around it."

Bart grinned and agreed. He couldn't oppose Della on anything she wanted because she worked so hard herself, and some of her sense of comfort and plenty was reaching him.

"While Josh is here . . ." Della began, and Bart got to his feet and pretended to run for the front door. Jincey and Motherdear laughed and he poked his head back in the room and said, "While Josh is here, what?"

"Well, I was thinking," said Della, "Mrs. Bates's old sow has nine pigs. That's too many for them to raise for winter meat. She would sell me two for a dollar each. Our kitchen slop would easily feed them but we need . . ."

"A pen," finished Bart, laughing. "All right. Tell Josh."

"You plan to have more livestock?" Motherdear asked. "Child, let the darkies raise that for you. There's plenty of meat already being raised on the place. Caring for animals is not woman's work. Why, my papa . . ."

From the door Bart flapped a hand at Della and she nodded back. They knew what was coming and they didn't want to stay and listen. But Jincey did. She never tired of hearing what Motherdear's papa wouldn't let her do. For it seemed that Della would not only let Jincey do every lick of work that had to be done but she would stand beside her, working herself, showing Jincey how to do it better than she already knew and fussing if she didn't do it right.

When the pen was finished and Della and Jincey walked across the creek to the Bates's to get the pigs, they took advantage of the time and stayed to visit. The Bates children were playing that summer in Old Pa's car, which sat under a shed at the edge of the yard. They invited Jincey to come out and play checkers with them. They propped a homemade checkerboard on top of the front seat and the players sat one in the front, one in the back, with the others looking on and advising. Jincey didn't know how to play checkers, but they were patient about teaching her, giving her the Chericola tops for her men while Virgie played with the grape Nehis.

When she was ready to go, Della walked out with Mrs. Bates to look at the car. It was an early Ford, and except for the fact that its canvas top was in tatters and its tufted leather upholstery was torn and sprouting springs and dark, hairy stuffing in many places, and whitened here and there with droppings from the chickens roosting on the rafters overhead, it would have been handsome. So much of its hood and dash were brass.

"Does it run?" Della asked.

"Lord, I don't know," said Mrs. Bates. "I reckon it would if it was cranked up. But my man ain't had no use for it since he hit a bunch of cows down by the commissary the day he got it."

"They wouldn't git out of the road," Zack put in, giggling. "Pa forgot the horn." He whammed down on the klaxon by the door to show what he meant. "So he just hung out the winder slapping the side of the car and yelling 'Hoey! Hoey!' Them cows didn't move a inch, just switched their tails and chewed their cuds and stayed put. Pa couldn't stop the car, so it hit one cow and climbed over another and turned over on the next one. Pa ain't druv it since."

"Hitched the ox to it and hauled it up here and built that shed over it," Mrs. Bates said. "Young'uns use it for a playhouse."

It was a nice one, too, Jincey thought, opening the door to get out. Sheltered from the sun and the rain, with good places to sit or even to lie down if there was only two of you. She would have liked to have had an old car for a playhouse herself.

When they went to pick up the pigs, which the Bates had separated from the old sow and had washed clean with soap and water and tethered to the back steps for them, Della's eye fell on the fat dominecker hens strolling across the gallery, messing and walking on it.

"Shoo!" yelled Mrs. Bates without surprise, mechanically taking a dipper of water out of the bucket on the shelf and pouring it on the chicken manure and grabbing a sedge broom and sweeping it off the porch. "I cain't stand nastiness," she explained to Della.

"I reckon you can put up with it if they are good layers," Della said. "How many eggs do you git?"

"Oh, a-plenty," said Mrs. Bates. "Brown ones. Do you all need eggs?"

"I am thinking about gittin' a few chickens myself," Della said. "Looks like having a rooster to crow for day kind of makes a place. And having your own eggs fresh and handy . . . well, you just ought to have chickens, that's all."

"Good woman, why didn't you say something?" cried Mrs. Bates. "I got a old hen and eight biddies I'm gon' give you!"

"No," said Della, "I'll buy 'em, but I don't have anything but the pig money with me. I'll give you a note to Bart and he'll give you the cash at the commissary. How much do you want for them?"

"Well, I ought to give them to you and Mist' Bart for a wedding present," said Mrs. Bates slowly. "But if you mean to pay, I could take it out in dress goods for the gals' school-starting. What do you say to fifty cents for the hen and fifty cents for the biddies?"

It was a bargain, Della said, and she and Jincey walked all the way through the lumberyard and across the creek, past the commissary and up the hill, carrying a pig each and taking turns carrying the old hen with her feet tied together and her head hanging down from a basket of peeping biddies.

The comfort of plenty encompassed Della about. Her cheeks filled out and had color in them. Her slim body was fuller, and sometimes when she hurriedly dressed to begin the day's work she caught a glimpse of herself in the mirror and thought she saw that her bosom, which she considered too small, and her legs, which she thought were too thin, had plumped up some.

If she got away from the house she sang, but she warned Jincey against singing within Motherdear's hearing because the old lady would be reminded of something and get off on a day-long reciting spree.

Della discovered some old chairs in the barn and she asked Bart if she could clean them up and use them. They didn't look like much to Jincey, but the *Delineator* magazine had a series on what it called Early American furniture and right away Della recognized the old chairs as ladderbacks. She scrubbed them and rubbed furniture polish into them and made ruffled cushions for the seats and then looked around for a place to put Motherdear's horsehair rockers to make room.

Jincey thought the carved grapes and the slick horsehair seats much finer, when she watched Della pushing them out of the way.

"Victorian. Tacky," muttered Della.

"Where did you get these lovely pieces?" chirped Motherdear, looking at her own furniture.

227

"Why, from your house," Della said in surprise. "Didn't Bart tell you? They was in a lot of stuff in that little house in the backyard."

"That's those renters!" cried Motherdear. "They moved into my house and they have thrown out my beautiful things. I never did want strangers in my heaven, my home. I'm going to tell Bart I want those people out of my house immediately. A woman who has been through what I've been through, should be surrounded by her treasures."

"You're right," agreed Della, pushing one of the now hated platform rockers into Motherdear's room.

"You want to play a game of setback?" Motherdear asked Jincey, and Jincey was glad to spend the rest of the afternoon sitting at the table on the porch trying to beat the old lady at a game she had learned imperfectly, but which Motherdear had spent years in the crazy house practicing. She had never won and sometimes she thought if she did it would kill Motherdear, who couldn't stand to lose even at a babyish game like Old Maids or Go Fishing.

There was something funny about Motherdear's playing cards, in fact, all of her things, her books and even her handkerchiefs. They had "Property of Lady Sheridan-Brown" written on them in India ink.

"Motherdear, who is Lady Sheridan-Brown?" Jincey asked once, and the old lady threw down her cards, burst into tears and tottered from the room.

A subject so terrible was too awful to bring up again and Jincey never did. Nor did she mention it to Della. But one day when Mary was visiting, she picked up a card and saw the words, "Property of Lady Sheridan-Brown" written across the back, and she motioned to Della to look at it.

"What do you know?" said Mary softly. "She's still a peer of the realm!"

"A what?" asked Della, who had never heard of such a thing.

"I guess Bart never told you that one of the signs that she had lost her marbles was that Lady Sheridan-Brown business?"

Della shook her head.

"Well, Bubba doesn't talk. Or maybe he doesn't remember. Anyhow, when Father died Mother started getting the idea that she had been married to a British lord and she wanted everybody to call her Lady Sheridan-Brown. The only Brown we knew was old Pete Brown, who used to run a grocery store in our neighborhood in town. I don't remember a single Sheridan. But it has a kind of tony, hyphenated ring, doesn't it? I thought they had brought her back to being just highfalutin Annie Katherine Barton McPherson at Tuscaloosa, but I reckon she couldn't erase that India ink."

Della didn't mention it to Bart, but one afternoon when Ruth went fishing with them she asked her if she had ever heard Motherdear called Lady Sheridan-Brown.

"No'm," Ruth said. "But I knowed she didn't want to marry Mr. McPherson. Matthew's nanny told us many a time that Miss Annie Katherine was made to marry him by her papa. Somebody else she loved, but her papa pick Mr. McPherson. You ever seen that big rock up on the hill at the head of the pond?"

"No, what about it?" asked Della.

"Well, the Sunday before Miss Annie Katherine's wedding her and the man she love ride their horses up there to say goodbye and they cut a heart and they initials in that rock."

"Let's go see it!" said Della.

"Hoo-hoo! Ain't no fish up there!" laughed Ruth.

But she was willing to go, and they leaned their fishing poles against a tree and took the rough path through the pine woods and away from the water. It was the highest hill around the place and when they got to it, the biggest rock Jincey had ever seen.

"What a rock!" said Della when they had it in sight. "Where do you suppose one that size come from in this flat, piney woods country?"

"Matthew say it be the only one he ever see," Ruth said. "And he know this country 'round Barton's Mill better'n anybody."

They reached it, the brown sandstone rock jutting out from the hill, and Della searched its grainy flank for initials, brushing off pine needles and old poplar leaves that had settled on it.

There on the top, eroded by time and the weather, was a crooked heart and the unmistakable letters: "AKB-JCS."

"Ah," said Della with a rush of sympathy for Motherdear and her old love, "JCS. It could have been Sheridan!"

Sympathy for the young girl Motherdear had been, pushed into a marriage she didn't want, made Della treat the old lady with special kindness for several days. Jincey noticed it and Della sighed and admitted it.

"Ain't anybody got it easy," she said. "Even the rich and well-to-do have to take bitter medicine sometimes."

Bart asked Della and Jincey to ride into the Southern railroad depot at the Front with him to meet the new housekeeper and her daughter, who were catching the up train from Mobile. (The night train going south was called the down train.) While they waited by the little yellow station, Bart handed Della the woman's letter to get her name, which he had forgotten.

"She writes a pretty hand," Della said, opening the pale pink envelope. She read aloud: " 'I am a settled white woman with one daughter, age fifteen. Neither drink nor smoke. Until my husband's death I ran my own home and am a expert domestic scientist.' "

"What in the world is that?" demanded Della suspiciously, looking up.

"It's what they call keeping a house and cooking and all like that," explained Bart. "Maybe sewing, too. I don't know."

"Domestic science," repeated Della. "Foot to that. She'll find her work here is more like slopping hogs."

"Get to her name," directed Bart, suspecting what Jincey was sure of, that Della was referring to feeding his Uncle Bob. There were no hogs at the boardinghouse.

" 'Also a Christian. Could come at once,' " Della finished. " 'Yours truly, Allie Stynchcomb.' Be blessed if I wouldn't change my name if it was Stink-comb."

"Stynchcomb, Stynchcomb," repeated Bart. "You better not be playing around with her name. She might be the type to scratch your eyes out."

But she was a wispy little woman, small-boned and frail, with an old face but a girlish look about her, matching her pink dress, hat and stockings and the two precise wood-shaving-like curls in front of each ear. A dark-haired girl in a blue middy suit with red braid on the collar and sleeves and a big red butterfly bow on the top of her head followed her off the train, carrying a suitcase. Della and Jincey waited in the car while Bart went forward to greet them and take their suitcase.

As they came toward the car Della opened the back door to let them in beside Jincey and smiled her welcome.

"Mrs. Stynchcomb, Miss Reba," said Bart, "I want to make you acquainted with my wife, Della, and my little girl, Jincey."

Della held out a hand and said elegantly, "How do you do?"

It was new to Jincey and she knew right away Della had learned it from Mary. Not "Glad to meetcha" or "Pleased to make your acquaintance, I'm sure," as in former times, but an airy and offhand "How do you do?" She was so caught up in this new greeting of Della's she was slow to slide over to make room for Mrs. Stynchcomb and Reba.

"Jincey, *move!*" ordered Della.

"S'okay," said Reba. "We got room."

They squinched in beside her, smiling uncertainly. Mrs. Stynchcomb sighed a shallow, fluttery sigh and took out a pocket handkerchief and daintily wiped the dust off her patent-leather pumps.

"It's nice to be in the country," she said in a high, little-girl voice. "Ain't it, Reba? So restful."

"S'okay, I reckon," Reba said, looking at the yellow depot and the little cluster of Yankee houses facing the railroad. "I like town myself."

"So restful," repeated Mrs. Stynchcomb, now dabbing at her face, which Jincey could see, on closer inspection, ran heavily to wrinkles filled with powder and pink rouge, now dewed over with sweat.

"You might not find it as restful as you think, when you git to your new stay-place," Della said lightly. "Cap'n Barton hasn't had a housekeeper in quite a while now and the house may be a mess."

Mrs. Stynchcomb threw an anguished look at Reba who said stolidly, "S'okay. We'll manage."

Without her loose middy blouse Reba turned out to be what Della called "well developed." She had breasts which defied the flat-chested fashion and thrust out the front of her tight little everyday dresses and bounced when she walked. The only thing about the new stay-place that got more than a resigned "s'okay" from her was the millpond. She loved to swim and every afternoon she met Jincey in front of the commissary wearing a skimpy bathing suit the texture and color of wash-faded cotton stockings. When it got wet it clung to her like her own skin, causing Della to offer to help Mrs. Stynchcomb make her a new one out of wool.

"Why, I don't know," said Mrs. Stynchcomb uncertainly. "I never made a bathing suit."

"Well, I made mine and Jincey's," Della said. "Wool turns the water and is less revealing."

"But she's only a little girl," Mrs. Stynchcomb said plaintively. "A mere child."

"With that royal booziasm!" scoffed Della, nodding toward Reba's chest. "She may be just fifteen but she could pass for older. I don't think it's safe for a young girl to ... *bounce* around like that in front of menfolks."

But it made Mrs. Stynchcomb tired to think about it and Della dropped the question of the bathing suit. It was just as well because Uncle Bob came back from a trip and he seemed to approve of everything about Reba. He had not gone swimming with Jincey and Della before, although he sometimes swam by himself in the early morning, but now he took to their afternoon sessions, snorting and splashing and sometimes lying on his back and floating with majestic dignity toward the old makeshift diving board, where Reba spent most of her time either diving or jumping lightly, stretching her arms and flexing her shapely young legs, getting ready to dive.

"Old fool," Della remarked to Bart one night. "You can see his comb is red."

Bart laughed. "You talk like a woman with some experience with roosters!"

Then he turned serious. "Uncle Bob just feels for Mrs. Stynchcomb and Reba. They've had a hard time. The mother is not strong and she's never had to work before, so the girl does just about everything. Mrs. Stynchcomb has pride and needs the money. She doesn't want Uncle Bob to know the work is too hard for her."

Bart himself tried to ease the load for Mrs. Stynchcomb. He took to sweeping out the office and commissary himself, a task expected of all previous housekeepers. Instead of coming to the commissary to get groceries, Mrs. Stynchcomb frequently sent a list with Reba or somebody passing from the quarters. A couple of times Della saw Bart lift a box of rations to his shoulder and take them to her himself.

Della was glad to have another white woman close by and expected to enjoy neighboring with her, but the little housekeeper never seemed to finish the work Cap'n Barton expected of her and never had any interest in fishing or hunting for fruit and berries in the woods or even sitting under a tree and doing fancy-work.

"That list ... that *list!*" she moaned to Della. "I cain't catch up!"

"What list?" asked Della.

"In the milk room," sighed Mrs. Stynchcomb, flapping a lace-edged handkerchief to cool her face. "Come in. I'll show you."

On the wall in the little room next to the kitchen, where milk was strained and pans were washed and bowls of milk were set to turn for churning, there was an old fly-specked sheet of paper on which somebody had typed all the things expected of house-keepers.

"Shake sheets every day, removing every grain of sand. Air pillows daily. Change sheets once a week, pillow cases every day. Sweep all floors every day. Scrub kitchen, milk room and back porch three times a week. Feed chickens, gather eggs, milk cow, care for milk. Cook three meals a day."

"Aw, that's not too bad," Della interrupted reading the list to say.

"The meals," whimpered Mrs. Stynchcomb. "He eats three hot meals a day."

"Well, you and Reba git to eat too," Della said cheerfully. She had an idea Mrs. Stynchcomb had short rations before they came to Barton's Mill.

"I cain't," faltered Mrs. Stynchcomb. "He expects me to eat in the kitchen . . . like a Nigra. He invited Reba to sit at the table with him but . . . not me."

"Oh, the old fool!" said Della. "Like I told Bart, his comb is red."

The housekeeper looked puzzled. "His comb?"

"Don't tell me you haven't seen roosters when they are ready for a hen," said Della.

"I think he just . . . likes children," Mrs. Stynchcomb said weakly. "Reba is a little girl."

"Not so little as you think," Della said. "With that shape you'd better watch her. You might do better to send her back to stay with your folks, if you got any."

"No," said Mrs. Stynchcomb with more firmness than she had shown before. "No. We'll manage here. Reba's a lot of help to me. She can milk the cow and I cain't . . . even . . . get near her!" Her voice ended in a whimper and she twisted her lacy handkerchief.

"Foot to that!" said Della. "I'll be blessed if I'd let a old piney woods heifer best me. If Reba can git to her and milk her, why can't you?"

"I don't know, I don't know," sighed Mrs. Stynchcomb. "I never milked a cow before and she must know it. She shakes her horns at me."

"That Sylvia is a mean cow," Della admitted. "I've heard that in the quarters. You just have to show her who's boss."

"Maybe you could show me what to do," said Mrs. Stynchcomb. "In case Reba don't git back before dark. She rode in to Mobile with Cap'n Barton and I don't know when they'll git back."

"Grab you a stick," said Della. "If she so much as shakes a horn at you, whop her one."

Mrs. Stynchcomb shuddered delicately. "I couldn't strike . . . anything. It's so coarse. Unfeminine."

"Foot to that," Della said again. "Come on. If she's up yet I'll show you how to handle the old hussy."

Sylvia was at the lot gate, waiting to be turned in and fed and milked. She was a piney woods cow, not as smooth and fine-boned looking as Della's Jersey, Alice, but she had a full bag of milk and that plentitude took Della's eye. Della approached her with only the milk bucket in her hands.

"The stick," faltered Mrs. Stynchcomb from the other side of the gate, where she seemed decided to stay.

"If she gives me any trouble I'll slap the daylights out of her," said Della.

Della put shorts and cottonseed hulls in the feed box and turned Sylvia in. Sylvia cut a wild eye at her as she went by but she was otherwise peaceful. Della tied a rope around the cow's neck as she ate and hitched it to the stall wall. Then she let down a board across the stall behind the cow to keep her from being able to back out or turn.

"Somebody's already fixed a stanchion so she has to stay put while you're milking her," Della pointed out. "Come on now and try it."

Mrs. Stynchcomb had trouble opening the gate and she came slowly, putting down her little slippered feet with great care in the manure-filled lot. She approached the stall fearfully and seemed uncertain how to get past the barrier board Della had put up or by the cow's rear end.

"Aw, come on in," directed Della impatiently. "Climb over or crawl under. If she kicks you, kick her back."

"I cain't . . . I cain't!" wailed the little woman. "Even if I was where you are and reached for one of her tits she wouldn't let me have any milk. She *hates* me!"

Della burst out laughing, causing Sylvia to turn and roll her big eyes nervously.

"Maybe she does," Della said when she could talk for laughing, "my Aunt Sweetie always said cows is like humans. Could be Sylvia's taken a grudge to you. So-o, Sylvia, so-o cow."

And Della squatted down with the milk bucket between her knees and a teat in each hand and started pulling down twin streams of milk that made rich music against the side of the bucket.

"Look at that," she said to Jincey, who had climbed the lot fence and was watching. "Good milk going to waste for lack of somebody to tend to it. Why I bet they let the calf strip Sylvia of the cream every blessed evening of the world!"

Mrs. Stynchcomb had wandered off out of earshot and was standing fearfully and uncertainly on the other side of the gate.

That night Della told Bart about milking the cow for Mrs. Stynchcomb, making a funny story of the housekeeper's timidity.

But Bart didn't laugh.

"Poor little lady," he said sympathetically. "She's too refined for the job, I expect."

"Refined!" scoffed Della. "She's whey, pure whey—thin and green."

Later Della found out that Bart had told Mrs. Stynchcomb she could ask Ruth or one of the twins, Louette or Rouette, to do the milking for her when Reba wasn't there and send them to the commissary for pay. Mrs. Stynchcomb took that to be authority to have other help.

"Why, she's as good as got a hired girl!" marveled Della when she heard about it. "Ruth is scrubbing for her and washing the clothes and even helping with the cooking!"

"Poor little lady," said Bart in a tone which made Della turn and look at him again. "She needs help."

Reba was gone more and more with Cap'n Barton on his trips to town. He even asked her to ride with him when he drove over to the Front to pick up the mail or around the country roads to check on stands of timber.

They often came back from town with new dresses and shoes for Reba and there was talk of her learning to drive a car so she could go to high school in Mobile when fall came.

Only Della saw anything wrong with the relationship. She tried to talk to both Bart and Mrs. Stynchcomb about the looks of the thing and both of them were shocked that she saw anything amiss.

"Reba's a child," Mrs. Stynchcomb insisted stubbornly. "Nothing but a child."

"Uncle Bart wouldn't do anything ... questionable," declared Bart. "He's a lonely man and the little girl is company for him."

"Foot to that," said Della and dropped the subject. But when Bart spoke of the loneliness of Mrs. Stynchcomb, a new light came into Della's eyes.

One night Bart worked late at the office on end-of-the-month bookkeeping and Della and Jincey walked down after supper, taking along a sandwich and a piece of cake for him. Bart was in the back office bending over a ledger and Mrs. Stynchcomb was in the front office with a broom in her hand.

"Mrs. Stynchcomb!" cried Della, almost making it "Stinkcomb." "What are you doing here?"

"Reba's gone to the show in town with Cap'n Barton," the little woman said, turning her head uneasily. "I saw Mister Bart's light on over here and I thought it was a good chance to do the sweeping I didn't get to today."

"I bet you did!" said Della sharply, plunking down the sandwich and cake in front of Bart. "Come on, Jincey, let's go back home."

She wheeled and started out the front door and Bart called after her.

"Come back. Sit down and wait for me. I won't be long."

"No-o!" cried Della haughtily. "I'll leave you two to do whatever you're doing. But," she turned to the housekeeper, "Mrs. *Stinch*-comb, you ought to be careful about sweeping the floor after dark! I've always heard it was bad luck."

Della and Jincey were outside the door when Mrs. Stynchcomb came skittering after them looking frightened.

"What kind of bad luck?" she begged.

"Somebody in your family will *die!*" Della said darkly and ran down the steps.

Bart had to work late several nights in a row but Della would not go to the commissary with him, although he suggested it. A few days later she announced that she was going to town for the day.

"Me, too?" asked Jincey.

"Hush," said Della.

Later she explained. They were going to pretend that they were going to town, driving past the commissary to the Front. But they would come in the back way through Fever branch. Jincey would stay at the house and Della would go down to see the housekeeper "about a little business," she explained.

"Why?" asked Jincey. "Can I go too?"

237

"Hush up, Jincey, for the Lord's sake!" Della said. "You will stay here. This is grown folks' business and nothing to concern you!"

Motherdear was in town visiting her sister and that meant Jincey would have to stay by herself. She worried less about that than about what Della was up to.

Della looked bright-eyed and lively when they told Uncle Bart they were leaving for town and she hummed lightly to herself when she cut off the highway south of the Front and guided the car through the low trickle of water which was Fever branch. She waved at Ruth and two or three other women as they passed through the quarters and then she parked the car around back of the house and went in and changed her high-heeled shoes for some low canvas ones.

"Don't you budge from this house till I git back," she told Jincey and took off toward the commissary but through the woods back of the house, instead of using the road.

Jincey played paper dolls and read and finally put a fire in the stove and made a pot of runny fudge. It was late when Della got back, looking tired and exasperated.

Jincey knew better than to ask questions and hurried to put on the coffeepot when Della told her she was perishing for a cup. Ruth came by and got her a cup and they sat on the gallery together. Jincey heard Della laughing and talking and she left the fudge pot to soak and climbed to the seat in the chinquapin tree.

"I wish you had come by sooner and tolled her off!" Della was saying to Ruth. "I must of been stuck there back of that sideboard for two hours."

Ruth was shaking with laughter.

"I seen yo' foot! Scared me for a minute and then I knowed what you was up to. Then's when I tolled the lady to the back yard."

"If you hadn't come when you did," said Della, laughing, "I'd a fell out of there with a case of Saint Vitus's dance."

They laughed some more and finally Ruth, wiping her eyes, said, "Well, did you find out anything? What did you see?"

"Not the rapping of my finger," said Della. "I slipped in while she was gathering eggs and wedged myself back of that sideboard. I heard Bart come whistling up the path and saw her run to the mirror in the hall and push at her hair and put some more rouge on her pukey face. A-ha, I thought, he's coming to see her!"

She bit her lip and grinned.

"But he didn't. He stopped on the front gallery and called out, 'Mrs. Stynchcomb, how about your meat order? I'm fixing to call the packinghouse.' She run to the back of the house and got a list and read it off to him and he wrote everything down and went back down the path to the commissary, whistling again!"

"And what did she do?" Ruth urged her on.

"Do? Old Stinky didn't do a thing but take her seat at the sewing machine, not four feet from where I was back of that sideboard, and stitch away on something all afternoon! At least, till you come."

They doubled up with laughter again.

"Lord, Miss Della, you don't do!" Ruth said, wiping her eyes on a corner of her many-pocketed apron. "Man be crazy to try to fool around on you!"

Della felt so cheered up by Ruth's appreciation of the story, she sang when she cooked supper and was extra loving to Bart when they sat in the swing before bedtime. Jincey heard her whispering to him and he sounded surprised and hurt when he answered.

"You mean you doubt me, Della? Why, Sweetheart. I don't know what to say!"

"Say nothing," said Della happily. "You a man, ain't you? I'd be a fool not to worry sometimes."

She kissed him and smoothed his hair and he looked at her in wonderment. Even after they were in bed Jincey heard him say, "I still don't understand . . ."

The matter seemed to prey on his mind because the next afternoon he and Della and Jincey were walking home from the commissary together and he stopped in front of Cap'n Barton's house.

"I'm gon' set your mind at ease for good," he said. "I'm gon' call Mrs. Stynchcomb out here and let you talk to her."

"Don't you dare, Bart McPherson!" muttered Della between clenched teeth. "Don't you dare say one word to that firkin of whey! I wouldn't have her know . . ."

But it was too late. Mrs. Stynchcomb had seen them and was walking out to meet them.

"Mrs. Stynchcomb," said Bart gravely, "my wife thinks there is something between you and me. I want you to tell her the truth."

Della was shaking with anger.

Mrs. Stynchcomb's rouged face, which had been sagging weakly, got starch from somewhere and firmed up haughtily.

"I'll have you know," she said icily, "that I am a Christian!"

Della put her hand on Bart's arm and leaned close to the little housekeeper.

"I *eat* little Christians like you!" she whispered very distinctly.

Late summer was on them and the earth seemed to have a ripeness. The sun had a tawny glint in it, the garden was making a last-minute push toward harvest. The purple spikes of ironweed and the little blue heal-all Ruth collected for her poultices were blooming along the roadside and at the edge of the field.

Scuppernongs came in on the big arbors in two of the fields and everybody went out to pick them.

"Eat all you want," Bart said, "but we've got to have a couple of washtubs full for Uncle Bob. He always makes scuppernong wine for Christmas and New Year's."

Della was immediately interested. She hadn't thought about wine, it being Prohibition, but if Uncle Bob could do it she certainly wanted to try it.

"Ask him for his receipt," she said.

"Oh, no, Della," said Motherdear. "That scuppernong wine receipt's a secret, known only to the oldest Barton man in every generation. No woman in our family has ever been entrusted with it."

"Hmmpf," sniffed Della. "Silliest thing I ever heard of. I bet I can make as good scuppernong wine as he can any day. Why, my grandmother had the biggest scuppernong arbor in our part of the county and I'll never forget the wine she made for Christmas."

Jincey looked at her steadily but silently. She didn't know how she knew it but she was certain that Della made that up. There was something about the way her dark eyes widened and grew brighter when she told a tale.

But after she had picked enough grapes for some jelly, Della left the picking to Jincey and the Bates children and stayed in the house making Jincey school dresses, forgetting all about the wine.

Uncle Bart paid five cents a quart for all the scuppernongs the children brought to the commissary and Jincey was so pleased with the dollar she made in commissary checks she decided to save it and maybe find other work to do to earn a total of $2.50 to buy Della a birthday present in November.

"Ask Mister Bart," Lula suggested. "We git ten cents a hour for hoeing out the fence rows in the big field. I saved up enough for my schoolbooks. Zack dips gum with Mama and Daddy and he makes the most money of all."

It seemed that job opportunities were plentiful and you could earn all kinds of money if you tried. Jincey especially hoped that she could work with the Bates children because whatever they were doing they stopped and played. None of them could swim but they knew the best wash holes in the creek, sandy-bottomed places where you could splash and wallow and cool off. They weren't allowed to go in the millpond because it was deep, but also because their parents were uneasy that Cap'n Barton might not like it.

When Zack wasn't along the girls took off their dresses and went in the creek in their bloomers. If Zack worked with them, they tucked their dresses in the bottom elastic of their bloomers and waded as deep as they could. Sometimes they stopped picking grapes and looked for arrowheads. One day Zack found one, setting high and dry on a little hillock of sand in the field, and after they had all admired it a while they gave it to Jincey. She promised the Bates children she would keep it all her life and she took it home and put it on the mantel shelf beside her doll.

When scuppernong picking ended, Jincey went to the commissary and found Bart talking on the telephone to Mobile. She waited a while and finally he put the receiver back on the hook on the wall and walked around the desk to hug her.

"What you need today, ole Ugly? Something from the commissary?"

"No sir, I want a job," Jincey said. "Could you let me hoe fence rows or dip gum with the Bateses?"

"Both lines of work are slacking up for the summer," he said seriously. "But let me see. Why are you so anxious to work? You just like being with the young Bates?"

"I like Lula and Virgie and Zack," Jincey admitted. "But mostly I want to make some money to buy Aunt Della a birthday present in November."

"How much you shooting for?" he asked.

"I need another dollar and fifty cents," Jincey said.

"Oh, well!" He opened the desk drawer and reached in it and then, reconsidering, he withdrew his hand and closed it.

"School's starting Monday so it'll have to be something in the afternoon or on Saturday," he said, half to himself.

"I know what. Cap'n Barton has been talking about getting the goats that roam in the woods penned up at night. They're sleeping in the vacant houses in the quarters and under the quarters church, putting their smell and their fleas everywhere. How would you like to round 'em up in the early evening and drive them into that pen down yonder at the edge of the pasture?"

"Oh, and Welcome could help me!" cried Jincey happily. "I'd like that, Uncle Bart. But do you pay for it?"

"Sure do," he said, smiling at her. "Fifty cents a week."

It was a fine lot of money, so much that Jincey worried she might get it in commissary checks and the present she wanted for Aunt Della was in the window of Grant's in Mobile, where it took real money. Six little stemmed dessert glasses of a color like soap bubbles, delicate and iridescent.

"Would you pay me in cash money?" she asked.

"I sure will, young lady. You'll get Number One U.S. cash, if you can pen up them goats satisfactorily."

Jincey started out the door, but Bart called her back.

"Tell Aunt Della that they got storm warnings up in Mobile. I just called down there to the Weather Bureau. There's a hurricane in the Gulf."

The day was hot and still and the sun so bright Jincey forgot about storms and wouldn't have thought to give Della the message but Della got up from the sewing machine on the porch and stretched and looked out at the sky and said, "Hmm, feels like the heat of a oven or the breath of a storm one, I don't know which."

"Oh, I forgot," said Jincey, "Uncle Bart said storm warnings is up in Mobile."

"I bet we're in for a hurricane," said Della. "What you think, Motherdear?"

"Hey-o," said the old lady, pulling out of a catnap that had caught her where she sat in the swing. "Make a cake, bake a ham, fill the lamps . . ."

"And board up the windows," said Della. "You know the program, don't you?"

"Well, I've seen many and many a hurricane," Motherdear said. "I lived in town during the 1906 storm. Mobile bay came up in the stores and warehouses on Water Street. Roofs going off and trees going down everywhere you looked. A lot of people went up to Spring Hill but we went down to the customhouse. Built out of granite and the strongest building in town."

"I remember the 1916 storm," Della put in. "I was on East Bay just . . ." She looked at Jincey and caught herself. She might have been ready to say she was "just married." Jincey, listening, held her breath and waited.

"Just visiting," Della said.

"And what happened?" asked Motherdear.

"Oh, it was awful. People I was staying with put everything up in the attic and the water come up so high in the house we had to git out by skiff."

Even as she talked Della's eyes moved over the house, considering what to do to get ready for the storm. The sun had a coppery glint to it and the air was so still not a leaf on the chinquapin tree stirred.

"At least we won't have to worry about high water," she said.

The rain started during the night and by the next morning a brisk wind was blowing, tossing the tops of the trees and turning the feathers on the old hen backwards on her back like a woman's skirt, as she clucked her biddies out of the rain and into the little coop Della had built for them. Della fed Alice and the pigs early, putting extra feed out for them in case the weather got too bad for her to get to the cowshed and pigpen later. She had a fire in the kitchen stove all morning, baking a ham and a chocolate cake and cooking a big pot of beans and potatoes.

Jincey filled the kerosene lamps and wiped the chimneys clean with wadded-up newspaper and made several trips to the commissary to get things Della felt they might need if the storm hit and they couldn't build a fire in the stove.

"Git a loaf of bread and crackers and cheese and potted meat, Jincey," Della directed. "And be sure and ask Uncle Bart the latest on the storm."

But the telephone line to the weather bureau was busy and Bart had no new information. The mill stopped at noon to let the men go home so Bart closed up the office and commissary early and climbed the hill to the house, looking as chirked up and lively as Della and Motherdear were looking.

"We ain't scared, are we Aunt Della?" Jincey asked once to be sure.

"Ah, no," said Aunt Della cheerfully. "We used to hurricanes. I don't like thunder and lightning but a hurricane's not that kind of storm. Rain and blowing, not snapping and crackling."

"Is my brother down there by himself?" Motherdear asked.

"Not exactly," said Bart. "The housekeeper and her daughter are there and the lady's about hysterical over the idea of a hurricane. Said she's never been in one before. I asked him to come up here with us, but he wouldn't do that."

"No," said Della shortly. Bob Barton had never been inside that house since she came.

"He thought he ought to stay close to try to calm Mrs. Stynchcomb and her daughter. He'll either go over to the house or let them come sit it out in the office."

"My brother is sweet and thoughtful," put in Motherdear.

"Ah-h," muttered Della, turning away.

"If it should get bad," Bart called after her, "we should be prepared to go down to the planer mill. That's the safest place here. The dam could go and flood the sawmill but the planer is built against the side of a hill with a good dry basement and no trees close to blow down on it. We always go there."

"Hey-o, that's something new!" put in Motherdear. "I didn't know we had a planer mill. You built it when I was Up Yonder?"

Bart nodded. "Most of the lumber we sell now has to be planed."

"Not like in Papa's day," said Motherdear, getting excited. "Why I recall my papa said every inch of the lumber for our home had to be hand-planed by slaves."

"Yes'm," said Bart. "You know you ought to put on any jewelry you have in case the house starts to go and we have to get out."

"That's right, that's right!" cried Motherdear, clapping her hands. "You know I forgot all about that. And I'll need to pack a little bag with dry clothes and shoes to take along, won't I?"

"You remember fine, Miss Annie Katherine," Bart said, smiling at her.

"Come on, girl," Motherdear called to Jincey. "You can help me with my jewels."

Jincey went happily. Motherdear's steamer trunk was a musty, sweetish-smelling tower of wonders she had not looked into half enough.

The sky turned dark and they lit some lamps. The wind blew harder and Della poked worriedly at the fire in the stove, willing it to die so there wouldn't be danger from fire if the chimney blew down or the stove blew over. Motherdear and Jincey squatted in front of the steamer trunk, rummaging through boxes and little chamois bags and bedecking themselves with breastpins and bar pins, with lavaliers and lockets and rings. Jincey's fingers were too thin for the rings but her chest was armored with enameled birds and rhinestone flowers. Her head was heavy under the weight of fancy combs and barrettes.

"Lord help us!" cried Della when she saw her. "All that is junk. Pure junk. Why is she bothering with it?"

"Motherdear said if I help her save it from the storm she might give me some of it—the birds, I think," said Jincey, fingering with pleasure the big bluebird and three little bluebirds in full flight across her chest.

"I see," said Della. "Well, do try to keep it from blowing away, by all means."

They lost track of time. The clock stopped and there was no whistle to blow to tell them when it was five o'clock. But Della set places at the kitchen table and they ate their supper, knowing one of the rules of weathering a hurricane was to be well-fed in case.

About dark the wind stopped and the rain fell slowly, tiredly, as if it had lost whatever force pushed it out of the sky. The trees were still and there was a tremendous quiet on the earth.

Jincey and Motherdear closed the trunk and went and stood with Bart and Della on the front gallery, listening to the stillness and waiting.

"Son, do you think this is it, the center?" Motherdear quavered after a time.

"Yes'm," said Bart, "or a lull one."

Della reached out an arm and held Jincey close to her. Rain had blown in through the screen and the chairs were all turned up against the wall, looking like people praying.

Nobody wanted to sit down, anyhow. They simply stood and waited. Jincey thought it might be getting on toward bedtime but she knew they wouldn't be going to sleep now. Even in the quiet and waiting, excitement quivered in them, keeping them alert and watchful.

Suddenly somewhere in the woods beyond the creek back of the house there was a rush of wind. They heard it one minute and the next minute they felt it roaring and tearing around them. Sharp, pistol-like reports sounded in the pine thicket and almost at the same time there was a crash in the kitchen as one of the new glass windows blew in. In the field across the road there was a tearing, sobbing sound and another crash and Bart said, "One of the big oak trees leading to the old house."

The rain came back in full force and Della hurried to grab the oilcloth off the table and hang it over the opening where the window blew in.

Now they sat in the living room listening to the rain on the roof blowing in gusts against the tin like gravel thrown by a strong hand, and then settling down to a steady drumming.

The flame in the kerosene lamp flickered and was steady and Bart said, "How about another piece of that chocolate cake, sweetheart?"

"You think it's about done its do?" Della asked, standing up.

"Just about," said Bart.

Motherdear's eyes had grown heavy and closed and she nodded where she sat in one of the old rockers.

"Come on, Ma, I reckon it's safe to tuck you in your bed now," Bart said, taking her arm and helping her up.

Jincey yawned and headed for her cot, too tired to find her nightgown but unable to sleep in her clothes because of the weight of all the pins and necklaces.

Bart sent Clewis up with a mule to plow a fall garden spot for Della. He came at a good time because Motherdear, in an effort to be helpful, was driving Della wild.

"I vow I'll be as crazy as she is before this is over," Della prophesied darkly to Jincey. "I can't stay in this house."

Everything Della started to do, the old lady took a hold of, trying to help. If Della made up a bed, Motherdear was on the other side of it, tugging at the sheet, too. When she put on something to cook, Motherdear got a spoon and stirred it, whether it needed it or not.

Because she suspected that bedbugs came home with the clothes when they were washed and ironed by Louette and Rouette, Della decided to do the washing herself. She bought an iron pot and four No. 2 galvanized tubs and knocked together a wooden bench to hold them under a tree by the pump.

"Before winter I want you to build me a washhouse," Della told Bart. "A regular bench to hold the tubs and a shutter across the back that I can lift up to dump the dirty water."

"By winter we might have running water," Bart said. "Uncle Bob is getting a waterwheel for the mill to generate electricity and that'll mean we can have an electric pump and plumbing."

"Lights, too?" asked Della. "Oh, my, that'll be the ticket!"

But Bart still didn't see why she insisted on doing the washing herself. The twins only charged seventy-five cents a week.

"Chinches—bedbugs," said Della. "You don't know what-all's in their house. It's a chance you take—and I don't want it. I'll do the washing myself and maybe git Ruth to come here to iron."

"I'll help you," said Motherdear, and Della sighed.

The old lady had never washed a garment in her life and she did not know the first thing about putting clothes to soak the night before, soaping and rubbing them on the corrugated tin washboard till your knuckles hurt, boiling the sheets and white clothes first and then Bart's workclothes. She laughed and splashed in the bluing rinse water when she first saw it.

"Where do you get this pretty-colored water, Honey?" she asked Della. "Is it out of my papa's sulphur well?"

"No, ma'am," said Della tiredly, "it's bluing. You buy a stick of it at the commissary and whip it through the water to take the yellow tinge out of white things."

"Hey-o!" cried the old lady. "I believe I'll dip my hair in it."

And she did, holding her nose and ducking her head, hairpins and all. Jincey squealed with delight, but Della didn't want hairs in her rinse water and she walked away, saying over her shoulder to Jincey, "Git her a towel and help her take her pins out and dry that mess. I'm gon' make starch."

As it turned out, the bluing water worked so well on Motherdear's hair she asked for some every other washday. And Della was careful to mix it in the little foot tub and set it on the steps to warm so there'd be no chance of hairs in her rinse water.

When Motherdear attempted to slosh the clothes around in the first rinse water and wring them she got her dress sopping from neckline to hemline and filled her shoes with water. The clothes she worked with were too soggy to hang up. Della always had to wring them again. Jincey loved to watch while she did it. She would grab a sheet or a towel midway its length and whirl it around in the water until it was wound up tight as a top. Then she would grasp it in both her hands and turn the ends in opposite directions until the water came pouring out. The strength in Della's hands was an unfailing marvel to Jincey because she really meant to keep her hands soft and her fingernails long and buffed to a shell-like pinkness, but sometimes she forgot and sometimes she was too tired.

But Motherdear took pride in her weakness, not her old-lady weakness, because that was expected in her, but in her born-nice weakness.

"I never had to lift a finger to do for myself," she said, smiling archly at Della, as if she hadn't already said the same things many times a day for months. "My papa had darkies to wait on me."

"Yes, ma'am, well you don't have to do anything here. We'll take care of you."

"I don't want my poor boy having to hire anybody to wait on me," Motherdear said. "Wages being what they are and him with a ready-made family, it's too much. I will not let myself be a burden."

Della sent a dark, help-me look to Jincey, and Jincey knew what to do.

"Motherdear," she called, "you got time to sit on the porch with me and recite?"

"Hey-o!" cried Motherdear. "You have chosen the better part. Anybody can wash clothes but it takes Ank to enrich your mind, doesn't it, Jenny? Come on and let me hear you say the Beatitudes."

Jincey hadn't learned all the Beatitudes but it didn't make much difference because Motherdear never wanted to hear her recite anyhow. She liked to do it herself. She would set the swing going fast and high, clap her little feet in their silk slippers together and, holding on to the chain with both hands, she would shout:

"The boy stood on the burning deck
When all save him had fled."

She knew a lot of poems, relics from Friday speaking days at school, and Jincey really enjoyed hearing her say them. Sometimes she interspersed poetry with Scripture, reminding Jincey of Howie. She knew a lot of wise sayings but, unlike Howie, who would spout one out in the middle of any conversation, she kept hers together and sang them out in a loud, high-pitched voice that caused Negroes passing on the road to stop and look toward the house, wondering if there was drinking, a skin game or a revival going on there.

If Jincey could keep Motherdear away, Della worked happily. She loved washing clothes. Pinning the sheets taut and snowy white on the line pleasured her eyes. She was careful to put the colored clothes in the shade of the mulberry trees to save them from fading by the sun. She dipped many things in a starch, which she made from flour, cooking it slowly and stirring it gently until it was silver gray and luminous-looking as a pearl. She loved passing a line of starched doilies and aprons and dresses and flipping them with her finger to see how stiff they were drying, gauging in her mind how crisp they would be when they were dampened down and ironed the next morning.

When she had finished washing, Della saved the water in the tubs for the garden. From early spring when it came up, a minute stitching of pale green along the dark, rich rows, until time to plant turnips and collards for fall, she saw that it got plenty of water. Because it was near about new ground, untilled since the days before the boll weevil, when the Barton family planted cotton, she had asked Clewis to plow it twice and she stood by, urging him to lay off the rows arrow-straight. Corn here, beans there, a faintly purple ruching of beets, silvery green blades of young onions, tomatoes, feathery carrots, and now, with fall coming on, a wide bed for sowing mustard and turnips, a long row for collards, and a rectangle nearest the house where she planned to plant strawberries.

Clewis had taken as much pride in the little garden as Della did, checking it when he brought by whatever they had in the field for her to choose from—never as crisp or fresh as hers!—and stopping by again after work to look and talk. Sometimes she had the feeling that Clewis was paying more attention than was needful to her garden because he wanted something.

When he finished laying off the rows for the fall garden he told her. He wanted to know if Mister Bart had an old suit of clothes he could have for church.

"Why, Clewis, his clothes would be too big for you," said Della, looking at the narrow, stringy old body in the ragged overalls and jumper. "I think he's got a suit, blue serge, that he won't be able to wear anymore, the way he's putting on weight. But it would be too long and too wide for you."

"No, ma'am, no ma'am," said Clewis, eager and unreasonable as a child. "If it be's give to me, I can wear it."

"I thought clean overalls would be plenty good enough for your church. If you're the preacher, maybe you ought to set the style."

Clewis laughed heartily, slapping his leg as if Della had said something particularly smart and funny.

"You see it ain't jes' church," he explained after a minute. "We's got some town folks in the quarters and it don't seem right for the preacher not to have a suit."

"You finish planting this row," Della said, "and I'll go see about the suit."

She took the blue serge out of the wardrobe on a hanger and then looked through the drawers for a silk shirt Bart's mother had given him for Christmas. He would never wear such a thing, Della knew, and wouldn't even recognize it if he saw it on Clewis. She picked a tie off his rack and went back to the garden with them.

Clewis's face, so often showing what he wanted people to think he felt, reflected genuine joy at the sight of the clothes.

"Hold 'em, missis, till I can rench off my hands," he cried, dipping earth-stained palms in the bucket of wash water and wiping them on the seat of his overalls. He held the hanger up to him and rolled his eyes heavenward. "Thank you, Lord and Jesus, and thank you, Miss Della."

When he had gone off down the road Della stood a minute watching him. It felt good to be able to give somebody something, even if it wasn't hers, and the old fellow was really grateful. His gratitude seemed one with the cooling earth, the smell of the fresh-turned soil and the sun on the pine thicket just beyond the clearing.

She heard Motherdear's voice high and mad careening through First Corinthians, 13th Chapter. She had hit the part about "Charity suffereth long."

"Just call me Charity," Della said to herself, and walked out to the road and down toward the commissary. "I suffereth,

suffereth. Anything, Lord, to git away from the sound of that voice."

But she felt so good Motherdear didn't get to her bad. Her eyes fell on the vacant house beyond the little branch. It really was a nicer shape than theirs and closer to the mill. She could do something with that yard. Dam up the little branch to make a pool and maybe have lilies in it or build a fancy little bridge to span it—for looks, because it wouldn't go nowhere. The trouble was that there were no shade trees anywhere about the house so it looked raw and resiny where the sun had baked it. The branch sounded cool and pretty, but it would likely draw water moccasins and it was sure to be cooler up there on the hill, where they were. Della never saw a house that she didn't mentally move in it and start fixing it up, and she didn't reject this one until she had looked in the window.

It was jammed with furniture and boxes, piled to the ceiling. She saw a piano and a long wicker lounge, a sewing machine and a phonograph, a high chair and a baby's bed. One of the open boxes held pots and pans and there were pictures in frames on the floor leaning against furniture and the wall.

It was getting late, close on to suppertime, and Della turned from the window and started toward the gate. Over beyond the field, where the old Barton house had stood, beyond the pecan grove and the millpond, the sun was going down in a Mardi Gras of color, all purple and gold. She stood a minute looking at it, and then she heard Bart's whistle on the road.

They walked to the house arm-in-arm, and Jincey was glad to interrupt Motherdear's recital of "Maude Muller on a Summer's Day" to cry, "Yonder comes Aunt Della and Uncle Bart—le's go meet 'em!"

Over supper Della thought to tell Bart about giving away his suit to Clewis.

"The blue serge? Sweetheart, that's my best church suit!"

"Oh, it's *not!*" scoffed Della. "It's gittin' too tight in the waist, even if you do use galluses to hold your pants up. I want you to have something younger looking anyhow, Bart. You wear old man clothes, high-top shoes and galluses and dark colors. Why don't you buy a white linen for church or maybe something gray?"

"Son, you should," put in Motherdear. "With your blue eyes you should have a suit to match. Mother will go with you and help you choose."

But Bart was still thinking about the blue serge.

"What in the world will Clewis do with a suit of clothes?" he asked.

"He said he wanted it for church," Della said. "And you know with him being a preacher ... he said some people from town would be there and he wanted to look good."

"Oh, now I see!" said Bart, laughing. "It's not 'some people.' There's only one here—a little high yaller gal from Prichard. I thought Clewis was showing out for her in front of the commissary the other day. He shows out anyhow, but this must be serious if he's coming here relieving me of my good suit."

Jincey, listening, worried. Della shouldn't have given away Uncle Bart's suit. It was a very risky thing to do. But it seemed all right because he was laughing.

"Old Clewis courting!" he said.

"Well, he's lonely," Della said. "He works hard and he has to do his own washing and cooking when he gits home. He should have a wife."

"Yeah," said Bart, still laughing. "A fifty-year-old two hundred-pounder would be about right. This little gal can't be more than seventeen or eighteen years old. About right for Clewis's daughter or granddaughter."

"Well, if he gits her," said Della, smiling good-humoredly, "it'll be because of your suit."

After the table was cleared and they sat on the porch Della remembered the house full of furniture across the little branch. She asked where it all came from and what it was doing there.

"Belonged to a lawyer in Mobile," Bart said. "Had his house and everything in it mortgaged to Uncle Bob and got in a tight and had to let it go."

"You mean your uncle took that woman's piano?" cried Della. "And her baby's bed?"

Bart nodded. "He had a right. Why, would you like to use some of it?"

Jincey saw Della's face change. It had been stiff with anger at the man she disliked. Suddenly she was beaming.

"You mean I could bring some things here?" she asked. "Even the piano?"

"Sure," said Bart. "Uncle Bob don't care anything about that junk. He just didn't want to let a smart Mobile lawyer get by with something. He don't even know what's there. I'll ask him to be sure, but pick out anything you want and I'll get some of the men to bring the truck and haul it over here for you."

Jincey knew right away that Della would choose the piano. She loved playing and singing—and there was a chance it would drown out Motherdear's talking.

THE SCHOOLHOUSE and most of the children at Bayou Bien were already well known to Jincey when school started. Only Miss Upton, the new teacher of the three lower grades, was strange and she was beautiful. Slim and red-headed and just out of Montevallo College, she wore high-heeled pumps and pretty dresses and she smiled a lot and all of the children loved her. But Jincey thought that Miss Upton loved her best.

Right away she raised the question about Jincey's name, just as soon as she had lined the children up according to their grades —eight in the first grade, six in the second grade and five others in the third grade with Jincey.

"What a wonderful class," she said, looking them over. "And all so pretty!"

Some of the children looked at Tucky Upshaw, who was cross-eyed, and giggled back of their hands, but Miss Upton said it was the sure truth, they were all pretty and they were going to have a fine time learning some mighty important things. And she wanted to get acquainted with them as fast as she could. So she would go down the rows, asking their names. When she got to Jincey McPherson, she said:

"Real name or nickname?"

Jincey started to say real name. But then she remembered the fortune-teller, Madame Zillah, who had asked the same question, and Della had told her it was Genevieve or Virginia or some such foolishness. No telling what Della would tell Miss Upton. She decided not to take the risk of picking one herself.

"I think I have another name," she said pitifully. "But I'm not sure. I'm a orphan."

"Oh, honey," said Miss Upton, putting an arm around her. "I'm sorry." And all the children in the room looked at her enviously.

"She's not a orphan!" said Sunshine Boudreaux. "She's Mister Barton McPherson's girl—out at Barton's Mill."

Miss Upton smiled, a moist, melting smile. "Well, I'm sure she knows, darling, and she's very lucky to have such nice foster parents."

She didn't say any more about Jincey's name, but Jincey kept the role of orphan in mind, thinking she might use it again sometime. People pure-tee liked orphans, she reckoned, and she fell to dreaming over her "real" parents and how they must have died. Then she got scared that the Lord would punish her for lying by causing Della and Uncle Bart to die and she dropped the orphan idea. She was beginning to forget that Howie was her father.

Walking to and from school was one of the best parts of it. She hurried over to the Bateses every morning, getting there about time Miss Eva finished twining Virgie's hair around her finger to make curls. Virgie fidgeted and whined and Miss Eva tugged at the syrup candy-colored hair and scolded them all, yelling, "Be still, Virgie! Make 'aste, Lula! Make 'aste, Zack!"

Once on the road they walked fast to get to school on time. But when school was out and they started home, tying their sweaters around their waists by the sleeves and taking off their shoes, if it was warm, they dawdled and played games. They took side trips to see if the persimmons were beginning to ripen and to check a spring Zack knew about where his uncle had leaned over to get a drink of water and lost three dimes one time. They always ran their hands around in the sand where the water bubbled out of the ground, expecting to find the dimes, although they had been lost many years ago.

Crews from the mill had cut new ditches along parts of the road to let the winter rains drain off, and they explored every inch of them. A man from a candy company put a tin sign on a pine sapling—a daring violation of Cap'n Barton's rules—advertising "Oh, Henry!" candy bars, and they took turns chunking pebbles and pinecones at it. Jincey and Virgie could never hit it but Zack and Lula could make the tin go "ping!" and they looked for bigger and bigger stones to try to get a louder sound out of the sign.

Once a little grass fire broke out in the woods and two truckloads of men from the mill came to fight it. Zack ran to help them, but the girls were told to stay away from the fire and go on home. They played fire-fighting all the way to the mill, flapping pine tops at the dusty road and pretending the burning woods were about to entrap them. Lula remembered a bad woods fire when all the wild animals—the deer and 'possums and squirrels and painters, even the snakes—rushed into creeks and branches to save themselves.

Jincey wondered if she had really seen them, but Virgie always believed everything her older sister said and she loved to hear her tell about the fire and the animals.

"An' no fightin', huh, Lula?" she prodded her to tell a part of the story she had heard many times.

"No, they didn't fight," said Lula. "They was so a-skeered of the fire they stopped being a-skeered of one another. Even them big diamondback rattlers cooled theirselves in the branch, peaceable to everything."

The truck drivers were not allowed to pick up the children. Uncle Bart explained that they could be hurt riding on the piles of lumber, which were being hauled to the Southern railroad or to the dock in Mobile for shipment to faraway, pineless places. One or two of the drivers, new on the place, obediently passed them by. But Percy always slowed down and pretended not to see when they ran and caught a hold of the scantlings that stuck out the back and pulled themselves up on the sweet-smelling new lumber. When they rounded the curve just before they reached the gravel road he slowed down again so they could jump off. They all knew somebody at the Front might see and report to Cap'n Barton.

Jincey was believed to be a smart girl at Bayou Bien school. She knew it and it was a wonder to her. She hadn't been smart in school in Mobile nor at school in the old store building in Epoch. Della and Bart took an interest in her schoolwork, but sometimes she thought it didn't have anything to do with her. She thought it might be Uncle Bart, who gave her the reputation for smartness. Most of the children had parents who could barely read or write, if at all. Everybody knew that Uncle Bart had graduated from high school in Mobile and gone away to college for a year before the war. He could write and figure with such speed and knowledge he was a bookkeeper. He might even be smarter than many a schoolteacher. Having education at home had to be a help with teachers, Jincey thought.

It was also a help that she wore the nicest dresses, always with clean socks and whole shoes, that she had good lunches and that Della wasn't shy about walking up and talking to the teacher. Most of the mothers, aware of their lack of education and ashamed of their clothes, stayed away from the school. But Della dressed herself up and walked right in the door and asked Miss Upton home with them for Sunday dinner.

Several days before Miss Upton was due to visit them Della sent Jincey to the Bates's to borrow Lula's English book.

"Why, Aunt Della? Why you want a old school book?" Jincey asked.

"Tell Lula I want to use it to teach you," Della said.

Jincey was flabbergasted. "Teach *me!* Why, Aunt Della I couldn't learn seventh grade stuff. Lula's in the other room— the seventh grade!"

"For pity's sake, Jincey!" said Della impatiently. "I don't care where Lula's at! I want a book I can study out of myself!"

Jincey couldn't believe that, a grown-up person who didn't even have to study, doing it.

"I didn't have the chance at schooling that you've got," Della went on. "I know I don't talk right. I got to find out how to do it. I figure any fool can learn it and I sure don't want that school-teacher coming here and hearing me talk like a ignorant nobody of a person. Git me that book, but don't you tell nobody what it's for."

The English book sure-god looked hard, and Della agreed that it was. Since it had to be returned she spent the afternoon copying out a lot of things about correct speech, trying them out on Jincey before venturing to spring them on Bart.

"One person *was*," she told Jincey, reading from her notes, "unless that person is *you*. It don't make sense, but you *were*. And two or more people *were*."

She pronounced it "wear," instead of "wur," the way Uncle Bart said it. And that seemed to confuse both Uncle Bart and the schoolteacher when Della started saying "people wear" and "you wear" at supper. Finally Miss Upton asked Della where she was from.

"Georgy," Della said promptly, and then quickly caught herself. "As the darkies say." The next time she pronounced it, she called the state Georg-ee-ah.

They talked of Miss Upton's school, Montevallo, and Uncle Bart said he'd love to be able to send Jincey there someday. He spoke of his time at Alabama Polytechnic Institute, and then Miss Upton turned to Della and asked, "And where did you go to school, Mrs. McPherson?"

Jincey caught her breath. Aunt Della wasn't gon' tell nobody that she didn't go to school. She'd die first.

Della served Miss Upton a second piece of the jelly cake and said airily, "Oh, I was privately educated!"

Christmas, the way Jincey had known it before they came to Barton's Mill, had been a sometimes kind of day. She didn't really remember much about the ones on Intendencia Street in Pensacola, before Della and Howie parted, and the one at Aunt Ina's and Uncle Tee's had run heavily to Grape Nuts and keeping warm in bed. Now, it seemed, Christmas was an all-out celebration, which even grown folks took a hand in preparing for.

There was to be a play at school—a wonderfully funny play, Jincey thought. It was called "Christmas Comes to Skaggs Skewl" and, as Jincey explained to Della, that was something called dialect, the way country folks talked.

"Not any I ever heard of," said Della. "I never in my life heard anybody say 'Skewl' for 'school.' Are you sure that's dialect?"

To be sure, Jincey asked Miss Upton and the teacher said she

259

thought country people up north talked that way but it didn't really matter. The play was a fine comedy and all the parents would enjoy it, the funnier the talk the better.

Jincey was going to play the part of the smart-alecky bright girl in the class, a hateful role, she thought, but one that had a lot of talk to it so Della was very pleased about it. She memorized Jincey's part with her and then helped her practice over and over, putting "expression" into it.

"I sure-god act mean," Jincey brooded, after having to put her hands on her hips and stamp her foot at one of the boys in the play.

"Stop saying 'sure-god,' " Della directed, "and be glad you're taking such a good part. Would you rather be that sugary-sweet girl Sunshine is playing?"

Jincey would have loved to have been the sweet girl, but the directions in the playbook said a girl with long curls should play that part and Jincey, examining her straight hair in the mirror, realized that she looked the part of a mean girl, all right.

When they weren't practicing the school play, all the children at Bayou Bien practiced Christmas carols for Sunday school. Della was in on that, too, teaching Jincey the words and singing alto to what passed for the melody with Jincey.

"I vow you got the voice of a crow, Jincey!" she said, exasperated. "You couldn't carry a tune in a bushel basket! Listen ..." and she would sing it again and Jincey would try again. The songs sounded pretty in her head but when she opened her mouth the tune seemed to get wedged sideways and wouldn't come out.

"Never mind," said Della. "There'll be enough voices there to cover yours. I don't know why you can't sing. I always could. Me and Titter went to singing school in the summertime in Georgy—George-ee-ah—and learned Seven Shape singing. Titter nearly caught her singing school teacher one year!"

She laughed at the memory.

"He was a prissy old maid of a man and we used to laugh at the way he would sound out, 'Fal-oh-sal-sing-Miss Latitia! Sal-oh-fal-sing-a-little-louder!' "

Caught up in the pleasure of remembering, Della would forget her disappointment in Jincey's singing and get on with the big

Christmas cleaning and cooking she had going, humming to herself as she worked.

She washed the windows, polishing each one with wadded-up pages from the *Mobile Register* dipped in vinegar. The vinegar cut the soap, she explained to Jincey, and the ink from the newspaper polished the glass. She cleaned every inch of the kitchen, putting up new shelf papers and spreading a new length of pure white oilcloth on the kitchen table, folding it up and tacking it under the table's wooden skirt the way the Yankee women at the Front did.

Jincey, missing the old complicated patterns of flowers and birds in the oilcloth, asked why white.

"More sanitary," Della said crisply, as if she had thought of it herself instead of copying the Yankees. "You ever notice how stuff drips down the side of them old oil cloths and dries and sticks there? You can't see it for the flowerdy pattern and you can't keep it clean. This looks as up-to-date as one of them porcelain-top tables they're selling now."

It looked and smelled new and fine and Christmasy to Jincey, as did everything about the house. Della was planning a lot of cooking. The weather turned cold a week before Christmas and Bart came home from work to find Della with her head tied up grinding dried red peppers and sage together.

"What you up to, woman?" he asked, looking around for signs of supper cooking.

"Fresh pork for Christmas!" cried Della. "If the cold holds I want you to kill a shoat tomorrow."

Bart looked uncomfortable. "Sweetheart, I reckon I could shoot one in the head—but I've never cleaned or dressed a hog before."

"You haven't?" Della was surprised. "Lordamercy, Bart, where'd you git your sausage and souse meat? Don't tell me, I know. Haas-Davis Packing Company! Well, we gon' have our own meat this year, if I got my strength and my head is hot. I'll git Ruth to help me—and can you spare Clewis?"

"This weather, there's not much for him to do anyhow, after he's fed the stock," Bart said.

Della stopped turning the food chopper and smiled at Bart approvingly.

"Wash up then, your supper's in the warming closet. I got the kitchen so raddled up, why don't you sit in that rocker by the fireplace and let me bring you a plate?"

It was something Della had learned from Mary, serving plates by the fire or in the yard or wherever it was most comfortable— buffet style, Mary called it. Bart didn't like to hold his plate in his lap, so Della pushed up a little table which she had found in the barn and scrubbed and varnished.

The next day Jincey awoke to the smell of smoke from the backyard. Della had the washpot boiling and she and Ruth were digging a hole in the ground to sink a barrel in which to dip the pig for cleaning and scraping when he was dead. Jincey hurried to get dressed and get out of the house, not wanting to know which of the little Bates's pigs was to die or to hear his cry when he was shot.

When she came home the air was richly pork scented. Ruth stood over the washpot, turning the little squares of white fat meat, which she was carefully frying out to make lard and cracklings. Della, her face smoke-smudged, was back at the food chopper, grinding lean portions for sausage, which she mixed with sage and red pepper and shaped into patties and fried before she packed them in fruit jars and poured in hot grease to fill them before she sealed them. The pig's head was now denuded of hair and unrecognizable, waiting, clean-shaven and eyeless, to be boiled and converted into hog head cheese. Two hams cooled on clean sacking on the screened back porch.

"Jincey, you just in time to help me!" Della called out. "Change your dress and come poke up the fire. A hog killing, even if it's just one little old shoat, takes more hands than we've got. Next time, I'm gon' have plenty of help. You wash some sweet potatoes and put them on to bake for Uncle Bart's supper and we'll fry some pork chops when the whistle blows. That bucket with the liver and lights in it, set it outside to keep cool. I've give it to Clewis, his share for helping me, and Ruth gits the brains, the chittlings and some middlings."

She paused, looking at the dishpan full of pig's guts regretfully.

"If I'd had more time I'd a taken them to the creek and washed them to use for sausage casings. But it takes a heap a-washing to clean hog guts and the weather could change on me before I git all this meat taken care of."

The weather didn't change but held, still and cold through Christmas, and for days the fresh pork filled the house with the smell of plenty. Della baked one of the hams for Christmas dinner. There was sausage for breakfast and spareribs and rice simmered on the back of the stove for Christmas Eve. The hog's head, frightful to look at whole, was a wonder to Jincey when Della got through with it. She cooked it all night over a slow fire and when the meat was so tender it fell off the bones, she chopped and ground and seasoned it with pepper and sage and packed it in loaf pans, pouring strained juice from the boiling over it. By morning the juice had cooled and turned to gelatin and one of the ornaments of the Christmas table was the loaf of souse meat, turned out on a platter and decorated with hard-boiled eggs.

Motherdear, stuffing herself on all of it, paid Della an unexpected compliment.

"I do believe," she said grudgingly, "that you are as good a cook as my papa's old servant, Hester."

Della, pink-cheeked from the Christmas preparations, and happy over the abundance of food, smiled contentedly.

"Cooking's only a little part of it," she said proudly. "I raised that pig and butchered it myself. That's got something to do with the flavor of the meat."

The pork wasn't all they had for Christmas. It seemed to Jincey there wasn't anything they didn't have. The Saturday night before Christmas Della and Bart went to the stores in Mobile to buy presents for the people in the quarters.

"I figured on spending about fifty dollars," Bart said. "Do you think you can get something for everybody for that?"

"Fifty dollars?" cried Della, aghast. "Bart, that's a fortune! Are you sure you want to spend that much? Why, I've seen the time when you could pay down on a house and lot with fifty dollars!"

Bart nodded. "It's a lot but they don't have much and it's Christmas. See what you can do. Uncle Bob is giving the old-timers five-dollar gold pieces and a pair of goats for a quarters barbecue. He'll send a crate of apples and oranges up to be divided among all the children. I've written down all the names, except the children. I can't remember them all. Let Jincey help you with that."

In the end they bought beads and scarves for the women and pocket handkerchiefs and tobacco for the men. Della shopped carefully to have enough money left over for a doll for each little girl and a mouth organ or a pocketknife for each little boy. She bought yards of red tarleton to make small drawstring bags and Bart sent a wooden bucket full of hard candy from the commissary to fill them.

Motherdear and Jincey sat up late helping her fill the bags and sucking away on cinnamon drops and peppermint pillows as they worked.

Della insisted that Bart wrap the presents in the holly-sprigged paper she'd bought because of his skill gained in years of sacking up dried beans and meal and tying them into neat packages in the commissary.

"And write cards," she directed. "You write such a pretty hand."

Bart protested, but he fell to and seemed to enjoy thinking about each black recipient as he tied the packages and labeled them.

"Old Aunt Hester," he mused. "Ma, haven't you always heard how she nursed Grandpa through the fever during the Civil War?"

Motherdear nodded. "She nursed them all through everything. Papa was a young man, home from the war wounded, when the Yankees came riding up in the yard. He got out of bed, leaning on his body servant—Matthew's grandpa, it was Della—and he walked out on the upstairs gallery and said, 'Gentleman, the place is yours.' While he was doing that Aunt Hester was running through the cornfield with a coop full of young pullets she had penned up just in case the Yankees came."

They all laughed to think of Aunt Hester, now old and senile, as a young woman, agile and fly enough to beat the Yankees.

"Where she hid 'em, they never found 'em," Motherdear went on. "But they took all the corn and they burned the sawmill."

Bart tied up another package and nodded.

"They had to. Great-Grandpa and the slaves were supplying Admiral Semmes and the pitiful little Confederate Navy with lumber."

Bart went on to wrap another package. "Po' Jack," he said. "Seems like we ought to have a little something more for him and Ruth, Hon."

"Well," said Della thoughtfully, "they're gittin' fresh pork and fruit and candy. What more do you want to give them?"

Bart reached for the scissors. "I don't know. Just seems like with family . . ."

"Barton McPherson," said Motherdear shrilly, "you watch your tongue! My grandfather . . ."

Bart smiled at her. "I'm not saying a word about Grandpa, Ma. You know Po' Jack is the closest thing I have to a brother."

Motherdear sniffed and popped another peppermint into her mouth and Della, grating sweet potato for one of her dark, rich, syrup-sweetened potato pones, said placatingly, "I know how you feel—and blood ain't got nothing to do with it, necessarily. Ruth is like a sister to me."

"Darkies," said Motherdear severely, "are not kin to white people!"

Bart lifted an eyebrow at Della, winked at Jincey and said nothing.

When they had been through the list from Barton Negroes to Clewis and the other fieldhands to turpentine workers and mill-workers and lumberyard workers, they stacked the neatly wrapped packages on the library table in the front room.

Before she went to bed Jincey went to the door two or three times to look at them.

"Shut that door, for the Lord's sake!" cried Della. "You're letting in the cold."

Then she saw that Jincey was looking at the Christmas packages and she came and stood beside her and put an arm around her shoulders.

"Look pretty, don't they, childee?" she whispered. "It's the first Christmas we've had anything to give anybody."

"Are we gon' git anything?" Jincey asked.

Della laughed and hugged her. "You wait and see. Tomorrow we git our Christmas tree!"

The next day was Christmas Eve and Ace was at the kitchen door early—a bandy-legged little man with a long yellow beard, brown-stained in streaks where tobacco juice dribbled on it. He wore a coat patched with many different colors and kinds of goods, and as he stood waiting for Della and Jincey he kept looking over his shoulder at the young bull he had tied to the gate and yelling "Whoa!"

It came out, "Missy, I come to take you tree-hunting . . . whoa! Got Walter my newest broke yelling . . . whoa . . . wid me. Best you and that lil' gal wrap . . . whoa! . . . good, 'case it's gitting colder . . . whoa!"

Ruth, in the kitchen drinking coffee, got to laughing so hard she put her head down on the table to keep Ace from seeing her.

"Do Jesus," she whispered to Della. "Voncile's turned him into a crazy quilt . . . whoa!"

Threatened with giving way to the giggles herself, Della quickly poured Ace a cup of coffee and handed it out the back door.

"You stay with your ox," she said. "We'll be there in a minute . . ." and then she doubled up with laughter.

"Stay with your ox . . . whoa!" said Ruth and they laughed harder.

Impatient to get in the oxcart and on with the Christmas tree hunt, Jincey didn't see anything to laugh about. She kept tugging at Della's hand. "Le's go! Walter might leave us!"

"Ruth . . . whoa! . . . you got to go, too . . . whoa!" said Della. "You crazy thing, you set me off. Now you got to see it through."

"Not me . . . whoa!" said Ruth. "That lil' bull yelling and that lil' cart ain't stout enough to haul this tub of lard . . . whoa. I stay here and hep Miss Annie Katherine make the ambrosia."

As soon as Della could straighten her face she tied a scarf around her head and put on an old coat and followed Jincey out where Ace and his spotted bull yearling, Walter, waited.

"You got a hatchet and a saw, Ace?" she asked.

"Yes'm, an' a rope, too, case we needs to tie de tree on," Ace said.

"Well, let's go across the creek and git the Bates young'uns and then we'll be on our way," Della said.

Jincey and Virgie rode in the cart, but Lula and Zack walked alongside with Della and Ace, talking about places they knew where cedar and holly trees grew in abundance in the woods back of the turpentine still. The day was cold with a heavy frost encrusting the weeds by the roadside and turning to silver where the sun struck it. The bull yearling moved lightly on his little curved hooves, his breath a plume of whiteness ahead of him.

Ace walked beside him, his hand on the heavy wooden yoke, talking to him quietly and nudging him along. They forded a little creek and climbed a hill and Zack yelled, "Miss Della, look-a-yonder!"

"Oh, Zack," said Della, "let's rest a while and just look at them. They're so pretty it's a shame to cut one. We ought to just have our Christmas here in the woods."

Jincey looked to see if she was serious. They'd never had a Christmas tree before and she wouldn't have minded not having one, except that Della had promised and she'd set her mind on it. She reached out a hand to the nearest one, its prickly greenness cold to the touch and sharply fragrant.

Della was watching her.

"Go on, childee, choose one," she said. "But remember how low the ceiling is and don't pick one too big for the front room."

Jincey and the Bates children wandered around the little hill in pleasant indecision while Della took the hatchet and chopped off some holly and pine branches for decoration and Ace gave Walter a handful of hay to munch.

The Bates children didn't want a tree for themselves, they said. They had never had one and their mother told them there was no use to start anything. But they had definite ideas about a tree for Jincey. Lula held out for a medium-sized tree, Zack the biggest one on the hill, and Virgie, a little one. Jincey finally made her choice, a tree of such perfection she had to circle it three times to be sure it didn't have a bad side. Zack estimated that it was six feet tall and ran to get the hatchet.

The tree and the holly and pine branches filled the little cart so they all walked home, Jincey as close to the Christmas tree as she could get so she could smell it and reach out and touch it now and then.

"Le's sing," said Lula.

"Yes, let's," said Della.

They sang "Silent Night" and "Angels from the Realms of Glory" and Ace stopped mumbling to Walter, buttoned his crazy quilt coat against the cold and marched smartly ahead to the music, a gaudy, golden little figure of a man.

Jincey didn't believe Christmas Day itself could be any better.

Della decorated the tree after she had gone to bed and it was the first thing Jincey looked for in the cold early morning darkness when she awakened. The fire had died on the hearth, but she found the tree by its fresh, cedary smell and went and stood before it, groping for its ornaments and tinsel and tiny finger-length wax candles like a blind man.

Della, a light sleeper, heard her and called out, "Jincey? You up? Wait a minute and I'll make a light."

And what a light it was. Della struck a match to a fat splinter from the hearth and touched the tip of every tiny candle, bringing it into instant, golden life.

"Oh-hhh," whispered Jincey, taking a deep breath. "Oh, it's the prettiest thing!"

She squatted on the floor, filling her eyes with the wonder of it, the unexpectedness of it—a live green tree in a house, of all places. And wearing such things as a tree never wore. A star on its topmost branch and glass ornaments like strange and wonderful fruit and a silver web a spider might have spun. All this and the little baby candles with their steady yellow flames.

Della came and squatted beside her and in the cold, dark room it seemed to them that this, their first Christmas tree, was ahead of anything they had hoped and worked to have.

One day shortly after Christmas Jincey stayed home from school with a cold.

She was uneasy about it and tried to hide it for two or three days because Della always talked mean and blamed her for any illness she got.

"Yes, you fool around out in the wind without your sweater

and shoes and take a nasty cold so I'll have to wait on you!" she would say. Or, "That's right, run out in the dew barefooted and when you git sick you'll be here on my hands!"

Jincey wouldn't have admitted to having a cold but now there was no getting around it. Her nose was running, she had a bad cough and her chest hurt. Still, when the six o'clock, go-to-work mill whistle blew she sat up on her cot and reached for her clothes.

Della came in from the kitchen with a cup of cocoa for her and saw her running eyes and red face.

"Aw, childee," she said. "Feel bad?"

Setting the cocoa on the hearth to keep warm, she laid a hand on Jincey's forehead.

"Um, feverish. You git back under the covers and let me see if I can't git you to feeling better."

She brought a pan of cool water and bathed Jincey's face and hands. She laid a stack of Bart's big white pocket handkerchiefs within reach for Jincey's runny nose and put another pillow to her back so she could sit up and sip cocoa in bed.

"I'm gon' take Uncle Bart his breakfast and I'll bring a dose of castor oil back for you," she said.

"Do I *have* to have castor oil?" cried Jincey, thrashing about on the bed and starting to get up. "I'm not that sick. I can go to school!"

Della pushed her back.

"You are that sick, honey. I wouldn't give you oil if you wasn't. I know you hate it. I do, too. But I'll fix it so's you won't even taste it. It'll clean you out and make you well. And when it's worked a time or two I'm gon' kill one of my little broiling-size roosters and make you some gruel."

Jincey loved gruel, but she couldn't think about it for remembering the nasty greasy feel and vomity smell of castor oil. Della couldn't make it tasteless, no matter what she tried. She had an idea that heating it made it work better and Jincey thought she couldn't stand the hot oily stuff oozy and ropey in her throat. She listened to the back door slam as Della left the commissary and burrowed miserably into the covers.

She dozed and when she woke Della was in the kitchen, poking up the fire in the cookstove and rattling pots. In a little while she came to the door with a bottle of castor oil wrapped in a dish towel.

"Here, you drink this," she directed, "and I've got a treat for you afterwards. Something to cut the grease."

She held up her other hand and showed Jincey a lemon with a little stick of peppermint sticking out of it.

"Drink. And then you can suck lemon juice through the stick candy and it'll be cooling and sweet."

The lemon and the peppermint helped, but they didn't do away with the evil oil entirely. Jincey slept and woke up and used the slop jar Della brought her and slept again and the taste of the castor oil, only slightly overlaid with lemon and peppermint, was there in the back of her throat all day long.

In the late afternoon Della went in the yard to catch a young rooster to kill for the gruel and Jincey heard a car pass on the road and stop near the pump. She sat up and looked out the window and saw it was Cap'n Barton's Reo and he and another man, a small, white man in city clothes, had got out and were walking toward the house.

Della didn't seek out Cap'n Barton but now he was practically in her yard so she went to meet him. Jincey lay back and waited. It could be trouble for them but she felt too bad to worry. She closed her eyes and willed the castor oil to stay down and finish its work.

She must have slept again because when she opened her eyes again the smell of chicken stewing was in the kitchen and Della sat by the fire contentedly sewing on something.

Jincey remembered Cap'n Barton and she wanted to ask Della what he had come for but she wasn't sure she could bear to know. She reached for a handkerchief and Della saw that she was awake.

"You feeling better, honey?" she asked. "I got some nice gruel made and I've put together a new dress for your doll. And Jincey, the best news! Cap'n Barton and a electrician from town come to see about a place to put the new water tank! This hill we're on is the highest spot around and so they're gon' put a big tank right out there beyond the chicken coop. They're starting to put a waterwheel in the mill to make electricity and they'll pump water into the tank. We'll have a sink in the kitchen and a bathroom just like city folks!"

The oil seemed to have gone, taking with it whatever sick-making evils Jincey had within her. Della brought a bowl of the yellow broth, thickened with a little cornmeal and bits of chicken, and Jincey ate it, sitting, wrapped in a quilt, in a rocker by the fire. Della finished a gray silk dress for her doll and they dressed and played with her and talked through the twilight about where to put the new bathroom and if Bart would build a new kitchen to have room for the sink and maybe a little electric stove to use when it got too hot for the wood stove in summer.

The mysterious feat of sinking a big old greasy iron wheel into a box set down in the mill and making electricity was endlessly interesting to Bart. The little man in the city clothes was an electrician from Mobile and he came out and moved into the boardinghouse for weeks to supervise the installation of the generator and the wiring of the houses and the commissary for lights.

Bart brought him home to supper one night.

"Sweetheart, I want to make you acquainted with the feller that's going to do away with smoking kerosene lamps," Bart said, making a joke. "Mr. Brown. My wife, Della, Brownie."

Della hadn't known that he was coming but when she found that he wanted to look over the house and get an idea of how much wire and how many insulators and outlets he would need for the job, she was glad to see him.

"Brush up the hearth, Jincey," she whispered, "and git out the white cloth. We'll set a table in your room."

Since Motherdear had come to stay they had no dining room and ate either in the kitchen or by the fire in Jincey's room in winter and on the gallery in summer.

Della had meant to talk to Bart about that. Every house needed a set room for eating and if they were to get a new kitchen, big enough to house a sink and maybe an electric stove, they could cut off part of the old kitchen for a bathroom, saving most of it for a dining room.

Now, with Mr. Brown there, seemed a good time to mention it.

"Brownie, see what you got me into!" Bart said, laughing. "I married me the buildingest woman in Alabama. Every time I turn around she wants me to move an old wall or put up a new one."

Mr. Brown was busy sopping up the brown juice from his second plate of liver and onions with a hot buttered biscuit and he smiled at Della, a quirky, monkey-like melding of sun-browned face, black eyes and sharp-pointed teeth.

"I'd give her what she wants," he said. "Lady cook like Mrs. Mc. deserves the right place to do the job. Before I come to start wiring would be the best time to add on that room. And while you at it, had you thought of making it big enough to accommodate a electric icebox too? They're the coming thing. You'll be gittin' one before too long. Ain't that right, Mrs. Mc.?"

Della shook her head.

"No, much obliged. I'm not gittin' any high and mighty ideas like that. A two-burner electric stove for summertime would be nice but we git ice when we need it and that's plenty good enough for me."

Two or three of the younger men in the quarters showed an aptitude for electrical work and were assigned to help Mr. Brown. Old Pa Bates wasn't working in the woods because of the winter rains and Bart asked the electrician if he could use the old man.

Mr. Brown had bands and pockets sewed to his work pants to hold pliers and screwdrivers and he clinked when he capered up and down ladders and in and out of attics. Now he paused in the doorway to the commissary and looked at Mr. Bates, red-faced, gray-haired and stoop-shouldered from hauling buckets of gum on his shoulders and bending to pull a crosscut saw.

"You know electric?" he asked.

Old Pa shook his head humbly. "No, sir, and I'm a-feared of it. Them little glass globes that hold it, ain't they dangerous if they break?"

Brownie laughed. "Naw. No more'n any other broke glass. Stick with me and I'll learn you about it. To start, you can bore the holes and set in insulators and I'll run the wire through."

"Yes, sir," said Old Pa. "I thank you, fer I need to be a-workin'."

By the time the electrical crew got up the hill to their house, Della and Ruth were tickled to hear Mr. Brown calling Old Pa

"Batesey" and, as the slow-moving older man trudged about, setting up ladders and getting out his brace and bit, the electrician would yell, "Snap it up, Batesey, sugarfoot! Hand me them pliers."

"Do Jesus, 'Batesey, sugarfoot,' " murmured Ruth as she threw her plump body into a sly imitation of the old man's slow progress through the house, his face lifted anxiously and uneasily toward the ceiling.

"What you reckon he think he see up there, Jincey?" Ruth asked. "Electric popping out or Elijah coming in on his fiery chariot?"

Della and Ruth could laugh at anybody, but Jincey didn't like to see them make fun of Mr. Bates. Some feeling of loyalty to her friends, Virgie and Lula, and a liking for Miss Eva, his wife, kept her respectful to the old man. Besides, she thought the electric might be dangerous. Mr. Bates had told everybody he didn't want none of it in his house, and Jincey thought he might be wise. She had seen wires giving off fire, where there was no fire, when Mr. Brown touched them with a screwdriver.

The rainy weather slowed down the building of the new kitchen but there was enough of it up, a roof and walls and a floor, for Mr. Brown to get in the wiring. The rearrangement of walls was indoor work, and every day when Jincey came home from school she found something different about the house. One end of the old kitchen housed a big shining white bathtub with faucets, now dry but ready to bring in water when the wheel in the mill started working. With the tub in place, they had built a wall and a door and Della, her hair tied up in a towel to protect it, was busy brushing something called calcimine on every surface. The trouble with using the old kitchen for a dining room was that it now had no windows, Della pointed out. And it was small.

"A man needs a place where he can put his feet under the table to eat and then push back with plenty of room when he's done," she told Bart. "A light, sunny room. Don't you think?"

Bart sighed and pretended self-pity he didn't feel. "What now?"

"Nothing," said Della. "Not if you don't want it too."

She walked out of the room.

Bart winked at Jincey and chuckled.

"Come back, sweetheart," he called after Della. "Come back and tell me what my new building project is."

Della stuck her head around the door facing and said seriously, "Come here and see what you think."

Two days later when Jincey got home from school the screened back porch had been framed in and a man was building a brick flue for the big wood heater that Della planned to have there. It was to be the new dining room.

Jincey wasn't at home the day they gave the big dynamo in the mill the final test and the lights were turned on but she never forgot her first glimpse of them. Walking home from school, she had said goodbye to the Bates children and gone down the road through the lumberyard and toward the creek when she heard a new kind of rumble coming out of the mill. It was not the regular, everyday sound of the steam boiler, nor the low throb of the carriage, and certainly not the whine of the big saws. She paused and listened. Above the rush of water falling over the dam there was a low and steady hum, louder than an automobile, steadier than the launch on the millpond.

She started running.

As she crossed the bridge she saw a light burning on a tall pole in front of the commissary. The mid-afternoon sun was bright, rendering the little streetlight weak and useless, but it seemed unbelievably bright and grand to Jincey.

She tore up the hill to the office door and burst in, crying, "Uncle Bart! Uncle Bart, the lights are on!"

He poked his head in its floppy old panama hat out of the commissary and his blue eyes and white teeth blazed in a smile.

"You don't mean to tell me!" he said, and waved to the usually dim room behind him.

Every five or six feet an electric bulb on a drop cord showed up the shelves and the counters with yellow light, brighter than the sunshine.

"Ooohee," said Jincey, squinting against the brightness and seeing things in the long room she had never seen before, patterns of the cloth on the yard goods shelf, the red of Prince Albert tobacco cans, the gilt whorls and loops on the handle of the big cheese cutter, cobwebs on the ceiling and a little silver drip from the spigot on the kerosene tank.

"Oh, Uncle Bart, ain't it a sight?"

Bart hooked an arm around her neck and hugged her.

"Progress, Ugly, just progress. We'll be just like Dauphin Street, Mobile, any day now. You'll see it's the same at the house when you get there. By the way, we got company and your Aunt Della wanted me to send up a few things by you."

"Company? Who?"

"Mary came to bring Motherdear back from her visit and is talking about spending the night. Wants to make the most of the new bathroom and dining room and kitchen, I reckon. Della wanted some cheese and some of the new tea cakes that came in today."

Electric lights *and* tea cakes *and* Mary, thought Jincey, hopping a little in her haste to get to the house. Some days there was almost too much good fortune.

There was a streetlight on a pole at the edge of the yard and in the house a blazing light bulb hung from the ceiling in every room. Before Jincey reached the door Mary was out on the porch to meet her.

"Come in this house, pretty one!" she called. "This is the Great White Way—Broadway, Alabama! The lights came on an hour ago and we've been afraid to turn 'em off, afraid they'll never be persuaded to shine again!"

"It's a waste, I'm sure," said Della worriedly.

"How could it be?" asked Mary. "With that new thingamajig generating it in the mill? This ought to be one place on earth where I'll never have to turn off another light. Ma, just think, you can't nag 'em about 'dousing the light' the way you've done us all our lives. It's free, like the gentle rain from heaven!"

Jincey had an idea Mary had said something from a poem and it would set Motherdear off and it did.

"And God said, 'Let there be light,'" she cried, "'and there was light. And God saw the light, that it was good; and God divided the light from the darkness. And God called the light day and the darkness he called night.'"

"Enough, enough," said Mary. "I didn't mean to crank you up. Let's see what treat Jincey has brought us from the commissary. I'm starved."

They went in the kitchen where Della had the coffeepot on, leaving Motherdear saying Scripture to herself. Della arranged the new tea cakes on a flowered plate and led the way into the new dining room with its newly green calcimined walls.

The door to the new bathroom was open, showing the gleaming white rim and the elegant claw feet of the new tub.

"All this you're doing around her, Della dear, is Bubba paying for it or has somebody persuaded old Uncle Gotrocks to shell out?"

"I don't know," said Della slowly. "I just ask Bart and he sends materials and somebody to do the work. I hadn't thought to ask him about the cost."

"Oh, you innocent!" cried Mary. "I bet Bubba is paying for every lick of it out of his own pocket, and you know you all don't own the land, the house or any part of it. If Uncle Bob fired Bart tomorrow, you'd have to leave—and I'd like to see you take that clawfoot monster in yonder with you!"

Della sat very still, her coffee and tea cake untouched.

"Why, Mary," she said after a long silence, "I don't know. I didn't think. I suppose it could happen."

"You durned tooting it could happen," said Mary cheerfully. "But it probably won't. Bubba's the heir apparent, and unless somebody throws a monkey wrench into the works I suppose you all will sit right here in your little nest until the old boy kicks off. Then, maybe we'll all be on Easy Street!"

Della turned to the kitchen to start supper, but her eyes didn't seem to be on the food she prepared. And for Jincey, some of the glow had dimmed in the new electric lights.

Motherdear did ask Bart to move the renters out of her house.

"But Ma, they pay good money," he protested. "And they're

taking care of the place. It's not good for a house to stand vacant."

"I could move back in there and take care of it myself," she said.

"Aw-w," said Bart, distressed. "Aren't you happy here with us?"

"Happy?" Motherdear repeated the question. "Happy? Son, don't you remember the poet said of happiness, 'Within our breasts this jewel lies'?"

Bart shrugged and turned away restlessly. He knew the signs. Motherdear had latched on to something to recite and nothing would stop her. She rolled her eyes ceilingward and was shouting:

> *"They are fools who roam,*
> *This world has nothing to bestow.*
> *From our own selves our joys must flow.*
> *And this dear hut, our HOME!"*

"But it's not a hut," Bart pointed out. "It's a big two-story house and it will be hard to take care of and you'll be lonesome there."

"What, in my heaven, my home?" cried Motherdear. She turned coy, smiling at him with her eyes wide and all her white teeth showing. "Why, I'll be as happy as a jaybird in whistling time!"

"Well, let me think about it," said Bart. "Maybe we could get somebody to stay with you there."

As it turned out, Mary and Edward were looking for a place to stay.

"You are giving up your apartment?" asked Della. "That pretty apartment!"

"Well, it really isn't big enough," began Mary, and then she interrupted herself. "What the hell, we can't afford it. Edward's business is off. I don't mean 'off.' I mean gone. He's not making a dime."

Shocked, Bart and Della were silent. Jincey was unbelieving. They never saw Edward but he did something high-paying and mysterious in an import office near Water Street and he always looked rich and well-dressed enough to be Prince Edward, which was what Mary mostly called him. And Mary in her blue roadster with all her pretty clothes, how could she not be rich?

"So if the old girl is set on going back to heaven, her home, we could move in with her for a while. God knows, I'd rather be dead, but it is a way out for all of us. I bet you could use a little peace and quiet in your heaven, your home, couldn't you, Della-dear?"

Della smiled at her. "She's welcome here. We enjoy having Motherdear."

"Boy!" said Mary. "What a beautiful liar! Let's take a walk and see if any other way out comes to us."

No other way did, and Bart finally called up the renters and asked them to move. They were already of a mind to do that, they told him. They had found a more modern house in a better part of town and they could get it immediately. The old McPherson house needed paint and a new roof anyhow. Bart told Motherdear that and asked her if he should draw money out of the account where he had put the rent money for her.

"Hey-o," she said cheerfully, "fix the roof . . . paint the house? That's a foolish frill, son. Let's not bother with it. Just get me back in my old room and if the roof leaks, why I'll put something to catch the water."

She smiled at Jincey and tapped her on the shoulder. "The chamber pot," she whispered.

"She'll need her furniture," Della told Bart, looking at the horsehair loveseat and the platform rockers.

"I don't think so, will you, Ma?" Bart said. "That house must be full of stuff."

But they decided to load a truck with her things and move them anyhow, and Della was glad because she had been reading about house-fixing and Victorian stuff was tacky. She wanted an overstuffed sofa and a club chair and something that was called an occasional chair and she knew the best way to get it was to strip the house of Motherdear's furniture. Meanwhile, there were things in the barn salvaged from the fire at the old Barton house years ago that she would fix up and use.

Mary met them at the old house on St. Stephen's Road when they took Motherdear and her trunk and boxes and baskets in.

She sat in her blue roadster looking at the place where she had grown up, with a marked lack of enthusiasm.

"Buff and brown, jigsaw special," she said, waving at the faded yellowish walls, the fringe of wooden flowers and teardrops trimming the porch, and the round little room where a corner should have been, with a steeple on top of it. "A study in tacky."

Della looked at the house with new eyes. She had thought it grand in a sad, neglected way. The old crape myrtle trees, which made a jungle of the yard, needed pruning, she thought, and she would have preferred to see the house painted white. But it *was* a two-story house, and that spelled class. Now she wondered why it was tacky, taking it for granted that it was, if Mary said so.

Motherdear had decided that she would live upstairs and let Mary and Edward live downstairs.

"Thank God," said Mary to Della. "I was afraid we'd have to be bedfellows."

Bart didn't think much of the idea because of the steep stairs but Motherdear cried, "Hey-o! I'll get up there and I won't come down."

"Pray God," murmured Mary.

The renters had not used the upstairs rooms, finding space a-plenty in the high-ceilinged double parlors, library, dining room, breakfast room and vast kitchen with its big coal range. They had stripped the rooms of all Motherdear's furniture that was not too heavy to move, and put down Gold Seal Congoleum everywhere.

"It's nice where there are children," the renter woman explained to Della, as her husband rolled up a livid yellow strip in the hall to take with them.

They had set up beds in the back parlor and the dining room and library and put a wicker living-room suite in the front parlor. They had spread oilcloth over the coal range, using it as a cook table, and installed beside it a blue Florence kerosene stove. Della looked at these things wistfully. She thought the wicker furniture with its cretonne cushions and matching fernery was the prettiest she had ever seen.

"What will you do for a kitchen?" she asked Motherdear when they had climbed the stairs and toured the four big, dusty,

crowded bedrooms, which had not been touched since Motherdear left for Tuscaloosa in 1917. "There's not a flue up here. You
gon' have a gas stove?"

Motherdear had it planned. Every bedroom had a small dressing room adjoining it, and the one next to Bart's childhood room
was on the back of the house. That would serve as a kitchen,
Motherdear decided, because it was near enough to the bathroom
for her to draw water to cook and it opened to the back gallery
where she could set out her garbage.

"What about a stove?" Della worried.

Motherdear smiled mysteriously.

"I'm on to something better than a stove. A lady Up Yonder
was caught cooking in her room, against the rules. And guess how
she did it—Sterno canned heat! It's the newest thing."

Only Jincey had heard of canned heat, and that was from the
old lady who took her to the banana wharf and to the city jail.
Canned heat was used by the old lady's son for drinking purposes.
She had not known it was used for cooking and Mary, who knew
practically everything, had never heard of it either.

"The funny farm's educational," she whispered to Della as
they toured the big, dark rooms with their heavy, dark furniture
and dusty, curtained windows.

Motherdear saw no reason to clean or rearrange the rooms before moving in, but Della and Mary opened windows and set to
work, airing and dusting and mopping. They decided that Mary's
old room at the top of the stairs would be most convenient as a
sitting room-dining room and persuaded Bart to take down the
big ornately carved golden oak bed and bring up a desk, a clawfoot, round dining-room table and some chairs.

Motherdear, unpacking in the bedroom, was only slightly interested.

"Hey-o," she said, bringing out her papier-mâché parrot and
hanging him by the window. "We are at home at last."

The path from the new sitting room to the kitchen was a pre-
carious trip through the room which had been Bart's as a boy.
Boxes filled with parts of clocks, which he had taken apart and
failed to fix, were piled high. There was an old cage where he

had kept a pet raccoon and a glass bowl where he once had a goldfish. Jincey was attracted to a shelf of books, and Bart came and stood beside her, pleased with her interest.

"Here's *Treasure Island*," he said, pulling out a little gray volume on which he had written in his fine, flowing script, "Barton McPherson, Grade 6." "And here's *Kidnapped*. Boy, I liked that one!"

Jincey opened it and started reading and when Della called that they were ready to go, she couldn't bear to put the book back.

"Why don't you bring it with you?" Bart asked. "In fact, I'll get a box and we'll bring all those books if you'd like to have them."

"You mean, to keep?" Jincey asked, unbelieving. She had not owned a book before, except for school books, which she read the minute she got them and which were not lasty, any way you looked at it.

"Sure, I mean to keep," smiled Bart, taking down the dusty volumes and stowing them in the box. "We better take the shelf, too."

Della looked at the ornate hanging shelf without much enthusiasm, but she didn't say anything. Between what Mary said and the things she had been reading in the magazines, she knew that anything with fancy, unnecessary curves and ornamentation was what they called "Victorian" and Victorian was regarded as pretentious and tacky. Mary had a white-painted bedroom suite with a new thing—a dressing table with three mirrors, two of them movable so you could see yourself front, back and side. When she and Edward moved, she wanted to sell it for twenty dollars. Della was planning to ask Bart to buy it for Jincey's room. She would paint it some pretty color, maybe the new color, orchid, which was what they now called lavender, and trim it in green. The little shelf, painted either color, might be "fun" or "not bad," Mary's terms for near-approval.

Jincey loved the shelf as it was, with a chunk of dried glue Bart had spilled there when he was a little boy. She proudly arranged and rearranged the books he gave her, knowing for the first time in her life the rich security of having something stacked up ahead to read. They hung the shelf over the washstand at the foot of her bed, and the books were the last thing she saw when she went to sleep at night and the first thing on awaking.

Part Three

THEY WERE going to celebrate Valentine's Day at Bayou Bien school and Jincey was so happy she thought she might sail through the air in little pitchy pieces like a stump set off with a stick of dynamite. She was bound to get a lot of valentines, she knew, and she wanted to send a lot of them, one, maybe two, to everybody in school and the biggest and prettiest one to Miss Upton.

Her room had been cutting out heart shapes and coloring them blood red for two weeks. There were hearts glued to every windowpane and marching around the top of the blackboard and they had a valentine mailbox nailed to the wall in the little hallway between the two rooms. Miss Upton showed them how to cover it with white crepe paper and everybody took turns sticking red hearts on its sides. There was a slot cut in the top where you put in your valentine, to be handed out on The Day by one of the bigger boys, who would be appointed postman.

She wanted to make an especially pretty valentine for Sunshine Boudreaux, who was her very best friend and who had already let her get a glimpse of one she was making for Jincey. The Boudreaux girls could all draw wonderfully well, but Sunshine drew the prettiest of all—houses and flowers and horses of breathing likeness but colored the most magical colors like no horse that ever lived. When Miss Upton asked Sunshine why she made pink and lavender and pale-yellow horses when she had never seen horses of such colors, Sunshine looked dreamy and said there must be horses like that *somewhere*.

Miss Upton smiled at her because she liked the little girl and didn't want to discourage her.

"I think Sunshine's horses are a sin," put in Ella Sutton. "God and Jesus make horses black and brown and that's not good enough for Sunshine. She thinks she can choose a better color."

"I do not!" cried Sunshine, who was very religious. "Horses get to be pretty colors when they go to heaven."

A side argument over whether horses went to heaven at all sprang up and Miss Upton had to halt it. Artists, she told the class, had leeway in choosing colors they painted with and Sunshine was an artist.

The dissenters shut up because it was true that nobody in the room could draw anything as fine as Sunshine or any of the Boudreaux children or wield the crayons with such delicacy and subtlety, getting shades and variations of shades that nobody else could manage.

Jincey worked late on a valentine for Sunshine one night by the fire, and it kept coming out crooked with nothing about it the least bit pretty. At last she appealed to Della for help.

"Why, I never made a valentine in my life," Della said. "But we're going to town Saturday and I'll give you some money to go to the dime store and buy some. How's that?"

A storebought valentine! Hardly any child at Bayou Bien school could expect anything as grand as that. Jincey couldn't wait for Saturday to come.

Their system when they went to Mobile was to park the car at a filling station run by friends of Bart's on Jackson and St. Michael streets and go their separate ways, Della to look at clothes she might copy at Gayfer's and Hammel's and Jincey to browse through the ten-cent stores. If Bart was along he visited lawyers and real estate men and shipping agents responsible for sending Barton's Mill pine lumber and turpentine off. He inevitably wound up at a hardware store. They always said in parting, "Meet back at the car."

Sometimes Jincey got tired of waiting in the car, but not the day of the valentines. She had found for twenty-five cents a box of twenty-five valentines, which came half-finished with a whole perforated sheet of paper lace to be poked out and glued on, framing each picture, each declaration of love. Jincey especially enjoyed the valentines which came shaped like vegetables and fruit—a great pointed carrot with the words, "Do you carrot at all for me?"; the leafy green cabbage which said, "You go to my head"; the big red apple which promised, "You're the apple of my eye."

Storebought valentines, Jincey decided, were deliciously, unbelievably clever. She couldn't get enough of sorting through them, lining them up on the car seat and trying to decide who would be lucky enough to get each one. Pansies for Miss Upton, a serious valentine. But for Sunshine it had to be the brightest and funniest and she leaned toward the carrot.

"Do you carrot all for me?" she asked herself, giggling and hugging her knees in a convulsion of amusement and delight. "Do you *carrot* all for me?" That was the funniest of them all, for sure.

She had been through the valentines a dozen times with undiminished pleasure when she saw Della coming. She scrambled out of the car and ran to meet her, carrying the carrot valentine.

"Look Aunt Della, look what I got for Sunshine!" she cried, holding it up. "Do you *carrot* all for me? Git it? Do you *carrot* . . ."

"Jincey, for God's sake, shut up and git back in the car," Della said in a low, tired voice.

Jincey stopped, stricken. Something was wrong, bad wrong. She could tell it from Della's face.

"Aunt Della . . . ?" she whispered anxiously.

"Git in the car," Della said again.

Without a word, Jincey turned and crawled back in the front seat, collecting the spread-out valentines and putting them in their box.

Della sat, gripping the steering wheel but not moving to start the car. She was staring at the brick wall of the house next door, biting her lip. Jincey straightened the box of valentines on her lap, waiting.

Suddenly Della turned in the seat and faced her.

"It's your fault," she said in a low, mean voice. "Old Sorry

Sorelegs has started up on us again! He wrote the police department a letter asking them to find you!"

Jincey didn't ask how it was her fault. She knew somehow that if they lost their stay-place at Barton's Mill it would be her fault.

"If you had written him a letter instead of ..." Her eyes fell on the box of valentines. "Instead of playing with valentines, it would have lulled him into letting us alone. But no, you had to have *valentines!*" The word came out of her mouth in an ugly, high-pitched imitation of Jincey's voice.

Jincey's hand on the valentine box trembled and she felt a sob building up in her chest.

"Aunt Della, will Uncle Bart ..."

"Make us leave?" Della finished it. "You know he will if Howie shows up looking for his 'kidnapped' young'un! Barton McPherson is too good for trash like us. If you had only written to him, Jincey, one letter now and then ..."

Jincey couldn't say Della hadn't told her to write a letter. She had never heard of such a thing before, but in the face of Della's anger she thought she *might* have heard of it and failed to do it. She felt numb with guilt and grief. The box of valentines fell to the floor, unnoticed. The sob in her chest moved to her throat, choking her.

Della was talking now.

"I ran into Tee on the street and he give me the letter. He had been fixing to come to the mill with it. The police chief knew he knows us and he told him to handle it. Lucky for us—but no credit to you, Jincey. You could have written him a letter and lulled him. Now, the Lord knows what we'll do. Tee says if I don't git to Howie myself he'll have to answer the letter and tell him where we are. You know what that would be. I can see him now, walking up the road, the sorry, good-for-nothing son-of-a-bitch!"

Jincey knew Della had used a bad word, showing more than anything else how serious their trouble was. She wanted to cry and couldn't. She wanted to touch her, to hold a fold of her skirt, but she didn't dare.

Della sat a minute longer and then she sighed and said, "We might as well go. I'll git out and crank. When I turn her once you push down the gas lever, not the spark, you hear? All I need now is to have it kick and break my arm!"

Jincey was well used to helping Della start the Ford by pulling down the spark lever and pushing up the gas but her fingers felt thick and unmanageable now. She wasn't sure she remembered which was which and she couldn't see for the tears in her eyes. Della, waiting in front of the car, saw her distress and dropped the crank and came back.

"Oh, childee, I'm sorry," she said, leaning in to put her arms around Jincey. "It's not your fault, none of it."

Jincey, clinging to her, could cry at last. The sobs in her chest ripped through her throat and came out her mouth jerking and racking her body.

"Baby, baby," murmured Della, pushing her over and getting in the seat beside her, the better to hold her. "Don't cry, it's not your doing. It's mine. I didn't tell you to write to old Howie. I thought about it, thought it might be a good idea, but I didn't. Don't worry about it, I'll think of something."

They were the words Jincey needed to hear—"I'll think of something." Della always got to that when they had troubles and she always did think of something. It meant she had not given in, she would find a way.

Jincey's sobs eased and Della handed her one of her own white, sweet-smelling handkerchiefs, the kind she always had tucked in her purse or a pocket, no matter what.

"Here, blow," she said.

Jincey blew her nose and wiped her eyes and straightened up in the seat. Della returned to the front of the car and the crank and in a little while they were on their way back to Barton's Mill.

Della sure-god thought of something, Jincey marveled when she heard about it. They were going to see Howie! She told Bart she wanted to take Jincey and go see Aunt Sweetie and them in Epoch.

"My aunts are gittin' old," she remarked at the supper table. "I'm of a mind to drive over there and see them."

"Would you take Jincey out of school?" asked Bart.

"For a day or two is all," Della said. "It won't hurt her. She's ahead in everything but arithmetic and penmanship and you can help her with that."

It was true and it pleased Uncle Bart so he made no more objection.

Motherdear would come out and keep Bart company while they were gone, cooking up terrible messes for him to eat. But he never complained, even if the rice was gluey and the meat smelled tainted. It often did when Motherdear had anything to do with it because she didn't believe in throwing out anything.

"Has the bowels of a fattening hog," Della would mutter to Jincey. "Nothing makes her sick."

Della packed a lunch and Bart put up the side curtains because the weather, which had been warm, had turned off cold and rainy again. They got out the two lap robes, a big one for the back seat and a little one Della could use to cover her legs without getting it tangled up in the foot pedals, and early one morning they took off for the dock in Mobile, where the *Bay Queen* was tied up.

Driving on to the deck of the big stern-wheeled ferryboat made Della nervous, and the sight of the wind-roughened water made her nauseated.

"I'm gon' be sick, Lord God, seasick," she muttered to Jincey between clenched teeth, as the *Bay Queen*'s deckhands chocked the wheels of the car and ran big ropes out from the iron cleats over and under the body of the car.

When the ship's big wheels started turning and they were well out into the bay the people in the other cars went up the steps to the lounge, where it was warm, but Della was afraid to go.

"Heat will git me, sure as the world," she said. "You could go, but I better stay out in the air. It's only a couple of hours to cross and I won't freeze here in the car."

But Jincey wouldn't go and presently out in the open water, the wind blew stronger and colder and they were shivering in their coats under the lap robes.

"My feet are chunks of ice," Della said. "How about yours?"

"They ache pretty bad," Jincey said.

"I know what," said Della, "We'll warm each other. Let's git in the back seat and take off our shoes and put our feet together.

We'll cover with both the lap robes, instead of one each."

The wind was against the *Bay Queen,* blowing from the east, and the trip across Mobile Bay took a long time. Della closed her eyes and leaned her head against the car's canvas side. Her face was very white and Jincey, watching her, worried so her own stomach ached and seemed chancy. Did anybody ever die from seasickness? she wondered. The waves grew so high they peppered the top of the car with pellets of spray. The old ferryboat wallowed and lurched and creaked. But Jincey could see the deckhands standing in the shelter of the stairs, smoking and talking and they didn't look worried.

When they reached the eastern shore and the *Bay Queen,* paddles going in reverse, sidled up to the docks and the deckhands began moving the ropes and the chocks which had kept the cars from rolling off the deck, Jincey thought Della would feel better. But there was a new worry—the long, steep, mucky clay hill, which seemed to go straight up from the water.

"I got to drive up that?" Della asked a deckhand and he laughed.

"No other way, ma'am, unless you're going back to Mobile with us."

"Not today, not after that crossing I just had!" said Della. "I'd camp on the beach first."

The other cars on the boat were going up the hill and Della cranked up and got in line with them. The rain was still falling and the ruts ahead of them were streams of clay-thick water the color of dried blood.

"Stay in the ruts and give her the gas, lady!" the deckhand yelled as they passed him.

"Oh, God, it's always something I don't know how to do," moaned Della. But she did it. She pushed up on the gas lever, gritted her teeth and guided the little car into the ruts behind a big, glass-enclosed sedan so powerful it surged ahead of them. Suddenly the sedan was out of the ruts and floundering across the muddy road in a zigzag pattern.

"Look!" screamed Jincey, "It's gon' wreck!"

"Let it," muttered Della, gripping the wheel harder and keeping her eyes on the ruts ahead.

While Jincey watched, horrified, the sedan flipped over. Della caught a glimpse of it out of the corner of her eye but she didn't turn her head or slow down till they were at the top of the hill, where a cluster of other cars was already stopped and men were getting out and going back to the overturned sedan.

"Can we do anything?" Della asked a man going by.

"No, ma'am," he said, tipping his hat politely. "There's enough menfolks here to turn him right side up, if that's all he needs. I just hope him and his folks ain't cut to pieces by broken glass. It's the reason I'd never buy a sedan-type car, all that glass."

Della nodded and eased the Ford around the parked cars and into the road to Milton.

They reached the little town by the river in the middle of the afternoon and Della went first to the house of one of Howie's cousins, a pink-faced, barefooted woman with a wad of hair as yellow as butter pulled into a tumbled mass on the back of her head and two diapered young'uns clinging to the faded and stained dress she wore.

"Look at them," Della said in a low voice as they crossed the hard-packed yard. "Not a stitch on except hippens—and dirty hippens at that."

But to the woman she was friendly, almost loving.

"Vury, how on earth are you?" She hugged her and stooped to pat a yellow head at her knee. "It's been a coon's age."

Vury asked them in and offered them coffee from a big blue pot setting on the coals at the edge of the fireplace. It was strong and black and they sweetened it with can syrup out of a jar on the oilcloth-covered table.

"Ain't you and the young'uns cold?" Della asked, looking at the big woman's bare feet and the diapered children.

"Lord, no!" laughed the woman. "We run like this a-purpose to git tough to the cold. Grandpa Hinson always said Floridy cold ain't a patch on cold in Sweden. He called it plumb balmy, even in winters when it fruz up."

Della cut her eyes at Jincey without cracking a smile but Jincey knew she'd be mocking this woman when they left, talking about weather that "fruz," when it froze.

"Well, I'm glad you got a fire for I'm cold to my bones," Della said. "Speaking of Grandpa Hinson, when have you seen Howie?"

"Lord, Howie just left her!" Vury cried. "Not more'n a hour ago. Are you looking for Howie," her voice dropped and she smiled slyly, "to git back together?"

"Not on your tintype!" cried Della. And then, because Vury was Howie's cousin, she softened her tone. "I am taking Jincey to see him, that's all. And I didn't know where to find him, the way he goes here and yonder. Which way was he headed when he left here?"

"Why, right across yonder to the Yellow River Road," Vury said. "In that car you driving you can surely catch him before he gits to the river. He was a-planning on staying all night with Uncle John and them and gittin' some of 'em to row him across the river tomorrer morning."

Della was on her feet, motioning to Jincey to move and telling Vury and the young'uns goodbye, even as she hurried out to the car.

The road was flat and even in the drizzling rain you could see a good distance ahead. They saw him walking along slowly miles before he got to his kinfolks' house in the Yellow River swamp— a thin, lonely figure in the drenched pine woods.

There were no other cars on the road so he heard the Ford a long time before they got to him and he stopped walking and turned and stood by the roadside waiting politely for the car to go by.

"Look at the sorry thing," Della said. "Ain't got sense enough to git in out of the rain nor to lift his hand and flag a ride. Too 'umble to ask, too sorry to earn, that about sums up Howie."

But when she stopped beside him she was as pleasant as could be.

"Howie," she said cordially. "How are you?"

Rain dripped off the bill of his cap and splattered on the front of his overalls and his eyes widened and his jaw fell slack to see them. He looked at the car and back at their faces through the isinglass windows in the side curtains.

"Git in," said Della, "and we'll take you where you goin'."

Jincey moved the folded lap robes to one side of the back seat and unlatched the back door and Howie, bending forward to accommodate his long body to the room under the canvas top, had his head close to hers.

"Jincey, Della . . ." he said at last. "The Lord God in his mercy and majesty sent you. I been a-praying."

"Foot to that," said Della, giving the car so much gas it lurched ahead. "You been writing the police, that's what you been doing."

"Was that wrong?" he asked humbly. "I was worried. Jincey is mine, as much as your'n. You had no call to take her off and leave me a-worrying."

Jincey could smell the wetness of his overalls mixed with old sweat and the plug of tobacco, which was sticking out of the pocket on the bib. She felt sorry for him because he looked so humble and shamefaced and worried. She put out a hand and touched the top of his big wet hand, which rested on his knee, and he smiled at her and covered her hand with his other one.

"I'm proud you come," he said gently.

Della pulled into a clearing under a stand of live oak trees with gray moss hanging low and stirring mournfully in the rain.

"We'll talk here," she said. "I've come to do the right thing— to give you a chance to see your young'un and know that she's all right. Look at her," she directed. "Meat on her bones from plenty of rations, shoes on her feet and clothes on her back. Have you ever done that much for her?"

"Man shall not live by bread alone," began Howie.

"Howie, if you start that mess I'm gon' shove you out in the rain and leave this place! You can Bible-talk all you want to but I'm the one that sees that Jincey gits to Sunday school and church. I even teach a class myself. If it was left up to you she wouldn't have shoes to wear out of the house, much less to church."

He bobbed his head at Jincey and looked ashamed.

"Now what I want you to agree to," Della went on, "is to git a divorce. Go see a lawyer in Milton. Do you know one?"

He nodded. "Colonel Avery. Was a friend of Pa's."

"Go see him then," said Della. "He won't charge you much. Tell him I've deserted you. That's good grounds. And the swap I'm gon' make is this: I'll take care of Jincey, no calls on you for nothing, and I'll see that she writes to you regular and can come to see you when she wants to."

"You'd want to, wouldn't you?" Howie asked Jincey, taking her hand between his and gently splaying out the fingers. "Blood is thicker'n water and you got my blood in your veins."

It was almost more than Della could take.

"More's the pity!" she snapped before she thought. And then she softened. "I don't mean that, Howie. You got good blood. Grandpa was as fine a man as ever lived. The Swede side was all right, too. Good people, hard-working and right-doing. It's just that we can't live together and a girl young'un's place is with her mother, you know that."

It sounded logical to Howie and he nodded. But he looked sad.

"You wouldn't consider coming back, would you, Della? I got a chance at a job at the fish house in Milton, night-watching and rat-catching. I never thought to live in town, but if you'd come back I'd take it. It'd be better than being parted like this."

For a minute Jincey almost hoped that Della would say yes. He was so sad. But she saw Della's head go up and her eyes flash with laughter or anger or both.

"Not a chance, Howie, not a chance. What do you say to my proposition?"

Howie leaned back in the seat, his cap scraping the top of the car. He looked out the back isinglass at the rain and then at Della who had turned to face him.

"What would you think if I said I didn't want to live without you?" he asked softly. "What would you say if I said I didn't want you to live without me?"

Startled, Della looked at his face and what she saw there caused her to grasp the steering wheel so hard her knuckles were white. He was smiling dreamily.

"What do you mean?" Della asked. "You know what the situation is. We can't live together. I *won't* live with you. That's all there is to it."

"We don't have to live then," Howie said. "Neither you nor me nor Jincey. We can make that great journey into the beyond, go to join my Ma and My Pa and little Woodrow. I got the means right here."

He patted his overall pocket and Della, to her horror, saw the handle of a pistol there.

"Don't you talk about joining little Woodrow!" she shouted, now thoroughly mad. "You let him starve to death. He wouldn't be glad to see you in heaven. But if you want to go somewhere— hell most likely—I'll be glad to send you there!"

She lifted her pocketbook. "I got the means right here and I ain't scared to shoot one damned bit!"

Howie put the hand that had been hovering near his pocket back on his knee and looked scared, swallowing hard.

"No call to use bad language, Hon," he said pitifully. "You really got a gun in there?"

"You want to see?" demanded Della. "If I pull it out I use it."

He shook his head and gave her a sickly smile.

"You right. Shooting ain't the answer. I'll do what you want."

"A divorce?" said Della.

"Like you want," he said.

"Well, let's go see Colonel Avery right now," said Della. "I'll go with you."

He looked uncertain. "I ought to have on better clothes. A suit maybe."

"You got a suit?" demanded Della.

He shook his head. "These all I got. I been sick with my legs."

"I thought so," said Della. "Well, git out and turn the crank and let's go."

He climbed out and only then did Jincey notice that Della was shaking. In the rain he motioned to her to retard the spark and advance the gas and Della snorted contemptuously.

"Like he knows something about a car!"

The lawyer was locking up his office when they got there, but he recognized Howie and opened up and asked them in. Jincey sat in the waiting room, glad to be warm and dry, and listened to the murmur of their voices back of the closed door.

She must have dozed because it was nearly dark when they came out.

"Well, that's settled then," Della was saying brightly. "Howie gits the divorce and he pays your fee. I git the child with him gittin' the right to see her some. I'm glad it's settled."

She turned to Howie.

"Well, Howie, good luck to you."

He was fumbling in his pocket and he finally brought out a little lockjaw pocketbook.

"Wait a minute," he said. "I got something here for Jincey."

He moved closer to the light and poked a finger in to the long, dark tongue of leather, stirring at something and trying to see what it was. Finally, his face cleared and he smiled.

"Here's what I been looking for, Jincey. I want you to have it."

He extended a finger bearing a three-cent stamp.

Jincey smiled back and moved to take it—just as she heard Della choke and run for the door.

Later when Howie had walked out into the darkness and they were sitting in the car, Jincey wondered aloud where he had gone, back down the Yellow River Road or to his cousin Vury's. But Della was slumped down in the seat, limp from laughing and she merely shook her head from side to side and didn't try to answer.

That night when they pulled up at the New Milton Hotel to spend the night, Jincey found the box of valentines on the floor in the back. They were wet and muddy and the paper lace was torn where Howie's feet had been. It was all right, Jincey decided, because she wasn't at school on Valentine's Day anyhow.

Della had sent a telegram to tell the aunts that they were on the way, so when she stopped the car under the oak trees in front of the picket fence three old women popped around the corner of the house like they had been doing nothing but waiting.

From the car they all looked the same, bonneted and aproned and wearing sweaters against the February chill. They came toward the car like young'uns in a play, doing a slide-slap kind of dance, whirling around, dipping and slide-slapping again. As the engine died, Jincey caught their old voices raised in a song:

"Oh, my little darlin',
I'm sorry for you!
Told you that I love you
But I don't believe I do!"

Della was laughing so hard she couldn't get out of the car for a time. When she could, she went to meet them singing, too.

"I'll tune up my fiddle,
I'll rosin my bow.
I'll make my sweet music
Wherever I go!"

Then they all came in together: "Oh-h, my little darlin', I'm sorry for you-u . . ." before they started hugging each other, leaning together and laughing. Aunt Titter and Aunt Elvie came out on the front gallery and looked on, laughing and waiting their turn to hug Della.

Jincey hung back, watching. This singing and dancing was different from the way they had greeted her when she come to stay and she didn't know what to make of it. Aunt Titter and Aunt Elvie finally got to her, but Aunt Titter's mind was on the show the others had put on.

She wiped the tears of laughter out of her eyes and kissed Jincey.

"They all crazy, Jincey. Your mama brings it out in them."

Aunt Elvie was patting her with her nubbin arm and hugging her with the other one.

"Bless Elvie's child, she home at last. You hongry, Honey?"

Aunt Sweetie looked from Della to Jincey and said, "Well, the old cat's the same. How's the kitten?"

"Cat and kitten, my foot!" said Della. "We your rich kin come to stay a spell. How the beds in this house? How the rations? We may not favor you with a visit if things ain't up to snuff!"

All the aunts laughed and Aunt Sweetie slapped her side in mock astonishment. "Wish I may drap dead if she ain't airish!"

"You see my fine rig here, don't you, Miss Sweetie?" Della

asked. "Well, let me git my readies out of it. Jincey, grab a hold of that box. I'll git the grip."

Aunt Sweetie was studying the car with interest.

"Where did you steal this, Miss Priss?" she asked Della.

"Down the road apiece," Della said. "Seen this man off pissing in the blackjacks. Car just setting there. So while he was busy I got in and drove off."

"Lor-rd!" laughed Aunt Sweetie. "I wouldn't put it past you!"

The others laughed and trailed along as Della and Aunt Sweetie walked to the front door.

Supper was ready and Jincey ate hungrily of chicken and dumplings. They had been eating out of the food box Della packed since they left the mill and hot rations tasted good. Della had changed to her kimono and slippers and she was bright-faced and talky, asking about Aunt Jessie's children and Aunt Titter's Rose, and sitting long at the table over a cup of coffee.

After supper she opened the box they had brought and passed out candy from the commissary and lengths of dress goods for each of them. The old women compared the patterns and the colors and finally agreed that Della had chosen well. She knew that Aunt Sweetie liked gray and black, that Titter fancied blue, Aunt Jessie was partial to brown and Aunt Ruby Pearl loved any goods with roses in it. The dark red of Aunt Elvie's was so pretty, she decided, she would make it up into a church dress.

"Well, I reckon you have struck it rich," Aunt Sweetie said, after they had settled around the front-room fire and Jincey had gone into the next room with Aunt Elvie to go to bed.

"Not to say rich," Della said. "Bart's a working man. But we got a good home and plenty at it."

"Not like Mister Howie, huh?" put in Aunt Ruby Pearl.

"That sorry thing!" said Aunt Sweetie. "He warn't fit to bell a buzzard!"

"Nor to tote guts to a bear," echoed Aunt Jessie.

"Let me tell you about him," said Della, laughing. "He put on that he cared something about Jincey, wrote the police that I had kidnapped her and all. So I had to tell Bart that I was coming here—he don't know nothing about Howie, you understand—and go look for Old Sorelegs. Well, sir, me and Jincey found him, poking along in the rain like dead lice was falling off him, and got him in the car to talk to him. I want you to know, ladies, what the good-for-nothing tried to do!"

They all stopped rocking and waited.

"He had a pistol in his overalls pocket and put on that he was going to kill us all!"

"Lord God!" cried Aunt Sweetie. "He *didn't!*"

"Yes, he did," said Della, enjoying the story. "Sounded like a ballad—if we had to live apart, we'd better go to glory or something like that. He even had his hand on the pistol and was smiling crazy-like."

"Della, what on earth did you do?" asked Titter. "Wasn't you scared?"

"Scared green," Della admitted. "But the fool made the mistake of mentioning my baby Woodrow and 'going up yonder to join him.' Lord, I seen red. Him that let my baby starve to death talking about going to be with him! I could of killed him!"

Jincey, listening, knew Della wasn't laughing now. Her voice was low and sad.

In a minute she went on. "I grabbed my pocketbook, which was by me on the seat, and shook it at him and told him I'd shoot him first. He backed down."

"You bluffed him," said Aunt Sweetie with satisfaction.

"I sure did!" said Della, laughing.

"You didn't have no gun after all?" asked Aunt Ruby Pearl.

"I got Bart's pistol. He made me bring it along, but I'm scared of the thing and I carry it under the front seat. I didn't have nothing in my purse."

"Lor-rd!" said Aunt Ruby Pearl, awed.

"You couldn't a reached Bart's gun if you'd tried?" asked Aunt Sweetie.

"How could I?" demanded Della. "Me and Jincey was sitting on it!"

They all laughed and slapped their sides in amazement and approval.

"And let me tell you the rest," said Della. "When we got everything settled and was gittin' ready to leave, Old Sorry made a big show of pulling out his lockjaw pocketbook and probing around in it. I thought, 'Well, sir, at last he's gon' give Jincey something —maybe the price of a coat or some shoes.' You know what he pulled out?"

"No, what?" the aunts said together.

"*A three-cent stamp!*"

They laughed till tears streamed down their cheeks. Every now and then somebody would say, "Three-cent stamp" and they were off again, doubling up in convulsions of laughter.

Jincey, in Elvie's big bed, which Della would share with her, stirred restively and Aunt Elvie reached up her good hand from the cot and patted her. Jincey thought it was fine that Daddy gave her a postage stamp. It meant that he wanted her to write to him and it was likely all he had. It made her want to cry to hear the old women laughing at him. Aunt Elvie understood that.

But laugh the old women did. Everything everybody said after that tickled them.

"Jincey needs a coat, tell her to wear that postage stamp!" cried Aunt Sweetie.

"Jincey needs shoes . . ." began Aunt Ruby Pearl, and they all said together, "Tell her to wear that postage stamp!" And they cackled and screeched with laughter again.

"Cold in her chest—make a plaster with the postage stamp!"

No telling how long it would have gone on but Aunt Jessie happened to say, "Oh, my little darlin', I'm sorry for you," and they all picked it up and started singing. In a little while somebody brightened the fire with more wood and Aunt Sweetie reached up on the top shelf of the armoire and brought down her fiddle. They pushed back the chairs and Jincey drifted off to sleep to the sound of fiddle music and their feet sliding and slapping in a dance.

IT WAS still winter but spring was edging in, an inch at a time, greening up the tips of the cypress trees in the swamp, setting the frogs to singing in the marshy places in the early evening. Jincey, still trapped in sweater and long socks and shoes, watched eagerly for each new sign and couldn't decide which of them was spring's finest work.

There were six new kids in the goat herd she rounded up every evening—dainty, pink-nosed, fey little creatures that let her pet them and nuzzled her legs and followed her instead of their mamas in the drive to the pen. She asked to bring one home with her for a pet and Della stood at the gate and looked at the bleating babies and thought about it a while before she said no.

"They cute little fellers now," she said, "but when they grown, Jincey, they the biggest pests you ever saw. They eat everything in sight, clothes, shoes, furniture, and climb—you know how they climb. They mess, too. You'd never git one even yard broke. You'd better not separate one from the herd. Just pet 'em when you can, but don't take one away from its mama. Goat mamas are notional anyhow. They'll go off and leave their young'uns for anything or nothing. And one that has your smell instead of theirs on it, why Jincey it'd be deserted in no time."

Jincey reluctantly pushed the babies along with the rest of the herd, which was well accustomed to the evening ritual now and went along to the pen with hardly any wild scampers in other directions. But there was a little one, smaller than the others, that seemed to stumble and totter on its delicate, fine-boned legs, bleating piteously. She picked him up and carried him. When she closed the gate on the pen and turned to leave, he stood beyond the wire and cried after her.

"Go eat, little 'sing," she urged him. "Go suck your mama."

But as long as he could see her he cried and, fearing that his mama would reject him, Jincey slipped into the kitchen after supper and mixed some water with some canned milk and poured it in a bottle with a rag-stopper the way Della had for Alice. She hurried back and fed him.

He sucked eagerly, switching his tiny tail excitedly and rolling his pinkish eyes at Jincey in an ecstasy of hunger satisfied.

"Pretty 'sing," she crooned to him, thinking about the can of milk she had depleted. "I'm gon' name you Carnation."

In no time at all he knew his name and answered to it when Jincey called out to him. He depended on Jincey for milk, apparently forgetting which one of the mama goats was his.

Her pleasure in Carnation was a private thing, kept that way because she was disobeying Della. But her pleasure in spring flowers, especially violets, was sociable. All the children at school brought handfuls of limp violets to Miss Upton every morning. But Jincey and the Bates children felt that they brought her the prettiest bouquets of all. Lula, being experienced in violet-picking, showed Jincey and Virgie how to look for violets in the tall grass, that way getting those with the longest stems.

"Hold them with the ends of the stems together," she directed, "and the tops won't be crowded. Mix in a few leaves."

The road from the mill to school was rich with violets, deep purple ones, blue ones as pale and delicate as Della's bluing rinse water, and along the creek banks and the marshy places, little white ones with golden hearts.

So exciting was violet picking that the school customarily closed early one Friday afternoon so all the children could go to the woods and pick together. The one with the prettiest bouquet got a prize.

Jincey thought of little else in the days before the violet picking. She knew she wouldn't win the prize because of the bigger girls like Lula, who had been to violet pickings before and were skilled in making bouquets. But she thought about it a lot and mentioned it to Della.

"I know what," Della said. "You can make a nosegay. You can take a pink rose to school on that day and put it in the center of the violets you find. We'll fix you a frill of lace to go around the outside and I'll give you a piece of pink ribbon to tie the stems together. Nobody else will have anything like that so you'll most likely win the prize."

With Della's help, Jincey practiced making violet nosegays in the old-fashioned way for several days. Then Mary's letter came.

Bart was not whistling when he came home to supper that evening and he didn't eat any supper. He went straight to the back gallery and called to Della.

"I want to talk to you," he said, and something about the tone of his voice caused Jincey to stop fiddling with violets and walk around the corner of the house to listen.

"Well!" said Della, sticking her head out of the kitchen. "You slipped up on me. I didn't hear you coming."

"I don't think you gon' hear me coming again," Bart said angrily. "Look at this!"

From where she stood, Jincey couldn't see but Della said, "A letter from Mary. What in the world?"

"Read it," said Bart.

There was a paper sound and then silence. And then Della said in a low voice, "The mean, hateful bitch!"

"Is it true?" asked Bart.

"Why don't you ask your sister, Mary, if it's true," said Della angrily. "She seems to know everything."

"I'm asking you," said Bart. "Were you married before? Is Jincey your child?"

"Yes," said Della quietly.

Jincey heard the scraping of a chair as Bart sat down. She wanted to sit down herself because her legs suddenly felt too weak to hold her but she couldn't move.

"Della, why did you deceive me?" Bart asked in a tired voice. "Why didn't you tell me the truth?"

"Would you have married me if you'd known?"

There was a silence and she answered herself. "You damned sure wouldn't of—and you know it!"

Bart stirred restively. "I had a right to know. That day before we got married, when we talked in front of the justice of the peace's house, we were supposed to tell one another everything. You lied to me."

"That's right," said Della. "I lied to you and made you look like a fool in front of your family. Ain't that what's bothering you? Your family knowing?"

"You should have told me," Bart said stubbornly. "I had a right to know."

"Well, now you know," Della said sharply. "And I see how you feel about it. Me and Jincey will git out tomorrow."

Bart sighed. "No," he said.

But even to Jincey it sounded weak. He was gon' let them go. Jincey looked around her frantically. They'd be leaving everything. Her eye fell on the seat in the chinquapin tree and she stumbled toward it.

"What about *him?*" Bart was asking. "Where is he?"

"I haven't the faintest idea!" snapped Della. "I haven't seen him in years—since Jincey was a little baby, since the divorce!"

Oh, Aunt Della, mourned Jincey to herself. You're telling him another lie. You made me write *him* a letter last week. You know where he is. You know there may not be a divorce, even now.

From her seat in the chinquapin tree Jincey could hear their voices but she couldn't make out the words and she didn't want to. She felt as limp as the pitiful green stems, crumpled and forgotten, of the wilted violets, which were falling out of her dress pocket. She leaned her head against the gray trunk of the tree and waited. Tomorrow they would go, leaving behind everything. She thought of Welcome, asleep by the front steps, and Carnation and the millpond and her pirogue, and the neat, pretty room beyond that window with its shelf of books. She thought especially about the books, all the ones Uncle Bart had loved and written his name in when he was a little boy. He wouldn't want her to have them now.

Oh, beg him, Aunt Della, beg him to let us stay, she prayed silently. Tell him I'll be good.

She remembered suddenly that she was supposed to polish Bart's Sunday shoes once a week and she hadn't done it. Now she wanted to. She wanted to so much she couldn't sit still on the board seat in the tree but climbed down and hurried into the front room and found the brown shoes and the little polish kit he had given her from his boyhood room.

Her hands shook as she clutched the shoes and the little box to her chest and hurried out on the front gallery.

She was sitting in a corner rubbing the Sunday-smelling ox-blood paste-polish into the leather and crying silently when Della came looking for her.

Bart had gone back to the office, although it was past closing time.

Della wandered through the house, looking about her distractedly.

"What you doin', Jincey?" she asked. Then she saw.

"Aw, childee," she said, stooping down and pulling Jincey to her. "You heard it all, didn't you?"

Now Jincey was crying in earnest, spilling tears on the shoes and sobbing in long, noisy, racking jerks.

"Don't cry, don't cry," begged Della, smoothing her hair and kissing her. "It's all right. It's gon' be all right."

"Do we have to go?" Jincey asked when she could speak.

"No," said Della and she sighed. "No, we can stay. You know Uncle Bart don't want to lose you. Why, he loves you, childee."

"He knows!" Jincey sobbed. "He knows!"

"It's all right," said Della. "He don't know everything and he don't want us to leave. He's mad, sure, but he'll over it. Anyhow, we gon' make the best of it till you're older and had your schooling."

"But I don't want to go—ever!" cried Jincey.

"I know, I know," said Della tiredly, turning away and moving to sit down in the swing. "But quit carrying on now. We'll do what we have to do—when the time comes. We don't have to decide anything right now."

The swing chains creaked. Welcome awoke and shook himself with the snapping sound of his hide which had made Jincey laugh in the past but somehow seemed like a sad and weak thing now. A dog belonged to have a snugger-fitting hide than that. Down the road the barn door creaked shut and Jincey heard Clewis start toward the quarters singing.

As he came closer to the house she heard the words, the mournful, lonesome words of the song from the colored church:

> *"I was 'way down yonder all by myse'f,*
> *An' I couldn't hear nobody pray!*
> *Lord, I couldn't hear nobody pray!"*

"Poor Clewis," said Della, "I reckon he feels worse than we do. His little ladylove left him for a gambler from Prichard."

Della remembered the next morning to give Jincey the pink ribbon and the rose and a white frill to make her nosegay of violets, but the rose wilted and she left the ribbon and the frill in her school desk. She went with the others on the violet hunt but the urge to pick violets and win a prize had died in her. She gave Virgie the few violets she found. As soon as the hunt was over she started for home ahead of the Bateses.

Uncle Bart seemed to treat her and Della the same, but Jincey couldn't be sure. She searched his face every time she was around him for a sign that he no longer loved them and wanted them to leave, but he gave none. He was quiet a lot of times, but not always. She watched Della more intently than ever, alert to any sign of sadness in her. It was hard to see because Della worked as much as ever, getting in a spring garden and sewing and cooking and cleaning. She sang as she moved about the house and yard but Jincey, listening, wasn't cheered by the songs. They reminded her a little of Motherdear's singing, not happy so much as anxious to be the one making the noise.

Jincey's report card was not good and she dragged her feet, bringing it home.

"Two D's!" shouted Della when she saw them. "Now, Jincey, that's the limit! I'm staying at this sorry place killing myself working to git you a education and what do you bring home? D's! What will Uncle Bart think? Him feeding you and clothing you and sending you to school—and you bring home D's!"

The prospect of showing her report card to Bart made her uneasy, but not so much as hearing Della call it a sorry stay-place.

"This is not a sorry place," she mumbled.

"Well, thank you, Miss Priss, for telling me!" Della mocked. "I reckon I know what it is. A cage, a pure cage. I git to clean out the droppings but I don't go nowhere. You—you, now—you don't have to do anything but enjoy the good beds, the cooked rations, the starched and ironed clothes. And make D's at school!"

Trouble had come to them, Jincey felt it and tried to push it away and not think about it. They weren't going, Della had said, but something had happened to the happiness she had known there. She couldn't understand it and she didn't want to try.

One warm night when they were almost asleep Della's canary bird started squeaking frantically. Della had covered his cage with the little cretonne bonnet she had made for it and it had been asleep a long time. Now it was awake and making a funny noise.

Jincey heard Della's feet hit the floor and saw the light go on in the front room.

Suddenly she was screaming, shrill, piercing, frightful screams. Bart and Jincey hit the floor at the same time and ran to the room. Della stood in the middle of the library table, clutching her nightgown around her knees and screaming.

"There! There!" she cried, pointing at the cage.

A brown spotted snake was coiled around the stand, which held the cage, with his head between the wire sides—inches from the little bird.

Bart started laughing and looked around for the broom.

"It's nothing but a chicken snake," he told Della. "It won't hurt you."

"It's horrible," cried Della, beginning to cry. "It's gon' kill my bird!"

Bart poked at the snake with the broom handle to loosen its hold and then lifted it off the stand and carried it outside.

"Kill it!" cried Della. "Kill it!"

"Aw, he's a friendly fellow," objected Bart. "Keeps the rats down."

"I want it *killed!*" shouted Della, jumping up and down on the table. "I don't want that thing coming in this house!"

Bart obediently found the hoe and chopped the snake in two just as it attempted to make its way under the house. He helped Della off the table and after they had gone to bed Jincey heard her say a little shamefacedly, "I hate to be hysterical."

Bart mumbled something and was snoring in a little while.

The next morning Della took the canary bird to the edge of the yard and set it free.

"You let him go," Jincey said, surprised. "He won't come back, will he?"

"Nope," said Della calmly. "He's gone and I'm glad. I don't want to have nothing in a cage."

There was also trouble outside the house which had not touched them before but seemed to reach in and get them now. Everybody in the quarters knew that Clewis had lost the girl he wanted to marry and that he was sad and lonely. But it had been a distant sadness until one night Bart suddenly sat up in bed and whispered, "Listen!"

"What do you hear?" Della whispered back.

"Wagon," said Bart, getting up and reaching for his overalls. "Somebody's up and out in a wagon at this time of night."

Della turned the flashlight on the clock, which showed three o'clock. She reached for her clothes, too.

"Stay here," Bart said, taking his pistol out of the drawer.

Della waited a minute, but when he had put on his shoes and tiptoed out the door and off the porch she finished dressing and made no objection when Jincey stumbled out of her room and started for the door with her.

The sand in the road felt cool to her bare feet and a pale sickle of a moon, riding high over the barn, gave enough light for them to make their way between the fences and the trees lining the way to the commissary. They could hear the wagon ahead of them moving down the road toward the creek beyond the commissary. Bart yelled, "Stop!" and turned on the flashlight. "Stop or I'll shoot!"

"Lord, cap'n, don' shoot me!" cried Clewis. "Ain't nobody 'cept me."

Della and Jincey caught up with Bart as he walked up to the wagon. Clewis, huddled in Bart's old suit, sat on the wagon seat behind a strange mule and in front of a pile of house plunder. In the bright beam of the flashlight Jincey could make out a stove, a bedstead and mattress, a deal table and some chairs.

"Where you think you sneaking off to this time of night?" Bart demanded sternly.

"I ain't sneaking, boss," whined Clewis. "Just gon'. Happened I could borrow me a mule and wagon this time of night—not in the day. So I thought it bes' to load up and go."

"Where you going?" asked Bart.

"Mist' Cushman down Bayou Gennette need han's," began Clewis. "I thought . . ."

"I don't care what you thought," said Bart, emphasizing his words by shaking the hand that held the pistol. "You can go if you want to. I can't hold *you*. But your household goods ain't leaving Barton's Mill till you've paid your commissary bill. You know it's a big one, dating from the time you bought all that candy and drinks and dry goods for that little gal."

"Yes, sir," said Clewis meekly.

"So if you want to go," went on Bart, "just pull up to that shed over there and unload this plunder and then you'll be free to drive that old mule wherever you want to."

"Cap'n Bart," pleaded Clewis, "I needs my bed and my stove. Ain't no place to go 'thout 'em."

"They don't belong to you till you've paid your bill at the commissary," said Bart.

Clewis sat a minute, holding the reins loosely in his hands and blinking at the light. He seemed to shrink even deeper into the blue serge suit.

"Lord Jesus, help me!" he mumbled.

Della, standing by Bart's shoulder, said softly, "Why don't you let him go? His stuff ain't worth all this!"

"You don't understand, Della," Bart said coldly. "It's the principle of the thing. If we let the hands go running off with their plunder every time a commissary bill got too much for them, Barton's Mill would have to shut down."

"That might be a good thing!" Della said angrily.

"Whatever you think, it's Uncle Bob's rules," Bart said over his shoulder. And then to the old man in the wagon, "Just back the wagon up to the shed, Clewis, and start unloading."

Clewis waited and then he sighed.

"Look here, Mist' Bart, I changed my mind. I believe it be bes' that I stay at Barton's Mill. You care if I go put this stuff back in my house?"

"That what you want?" asked Bart.

"Yessir, yessir, dat it," said Clewis as fast as he could speak.

"All right," Bart said. "You better start now. Time you get unloaded it's gon' be daylight and time to start to work."

"Hoo, hoo, hoo!" laughed Clewis. "Ain't it so? But I ain't gon' be late on the job. You watch and see."

He turned the wagon back toward the quarters and Bart and Della and Jincey followed it as far as the house.

"I hope he sneaks out the back way," Della muttered to Jincey, but Bart heard her.

"Why do you hope that?" he asked. "You want him to get away with stealing?"

"A lot of pitiful old plunder not worth the rapping of your finger!" scoffed Della. "Poor stuff nobody else would want—and him trapped like a caged coon. It's ugly, Bart, and God don't love ugly!"

"Well, I don't make the rules," sighed Bart, dropping his shoes by the side of the bed. "But I don't see what's wrong with them."

A few weeks later Jincey came home from school and Della wasn't in the house. The old worry arose in her as she began to search the yard. Signs that she had been there were all around— a coffee cup on a post, the hoe leaning up against the fence, where she had just finished marking off a row and planting something, her apron on a chair on the porch.

Jincey turned toward the road to the commissary and was plodding slowly back toward it when she heard Della calling her from the vacant house by the branch.

"I'm here, Jincey, in here."

Jincey went around the house and Della waited for her at the kitchen door.

"I just got to looking at this stuff," she said. "Stuff old Cap'n Barton has taken off people. I vow it makes you want to cry. There was a woods rider couldn't make it and he had to go off and leave every last thing he brought here, even to letters from his wife."

She sighed and sat down on a box.

"The way I got it figured he moved in here with all their furniture and was to git settled and her and the young'uns would come later. Only he got sick. There's letters from his wife, worrying about that. He run up a bill at the commissary and must not of liked the place anyhow because he decided to leave. They wouldn't let him take anything with him."

Jincey backed toward the door. She didn't like the dim room jammed with other folks' house plunder. She wanted to get back to their ordered house and find something to eat and change from her school clothes and go pen up the goats. She didn't want to hear Della go over other folks' troubles and sadnesses.

"I reckon we'll go," Della said, standing up. "I think I'll take this calendar with me. The woods rider's wife must of kept it the last place they lived. She wrote down everything—when she put a hen to set, what they would have for dinner, what they paid out money for, even recipes. There's one here for a cake I think I'll try."

Della, who usually moved rapidly on light feet, with her shoulders back and her head up, now walked slowly, heavily, like all the energy was drained from her. Jincey, walking beside her, thought wonderingly, Aunt Della could get old. She who danced and sang and could climb fences and swing on bullace vines like a young'un, could get drag-footed and slow like a old lady. It was the first time she had thought of that and she didn't like it. To push back the idea she rushed ahead to change her clothes before Della told her to, calling out as she ran, "Why don't you play the piano, Aunt Della?"

"Aw, I can't play," Della said listlessly, walking into the front room. But she lingered a minute by the shiny, well-polished upright that had belonged to some other woman, fingering the keys. She played mostly by ear but she knew the notes and if she practiced . . .

"Marchita . . . Marchita!" sang Jincey to prompt her to start the latest song she had.

Della smiled at the tuneless little voice.

"You sing like a tree frog."

Jincey poked her head around the door, grinning. "I like the way tree frogs sing," she said.

"Well, they all right, I reckon," said Della, "but they ain't venturesome about trying new notes."

She sat down and played a few bars of her favorite, "Marchita." Satisfied that she had cheered Della, Jincey headed for the kitchen to make herself a cold biscuit and onion sandwich.

Something happened to revive the spirit and push in Della and for a little while Jincey was glad about it.

They stopped at the post office over at the Front and Mrs. White called Della back into the storeroom to talk. Jincey, hovering near the candy case, didn't hear the whispered conversation, but as the two women walked back into the store she heard Mrs. White say, "You understand, I have nothing personal against the girls."

"I know," said Della, "it's the principle of the thing."

"Why, yes, if you let down the bars my cook Coreen's children would be coming!"

Della's eyes were bright and her walk was purposeful as she picked up the mail and turned to the door.

"Let me know what you find out," she said. "I'll be glad to help any way I can."

Della drove fast on the way home and sang as she fed the animals and cooked supper. Whatever it was, Jincey was glad.

That night at the table Della told Bart that Mrs. White had found out that the Boudreaux children had Negro blood in them.

"Well, I told you that it was likely, I think," said Bart.

"Yes, but it wasn't for sure," said Della. "But now Mrs. White has seen their grandmother from up at D'Iberville Chapel and the old woman was practically black. Kinky hair and everything. They come in asking directions to Pierre Boudreaux' house and Mrs. White asked them outright if they was kin. The man said bold as brass, 'He's our son.' "

"So the Yankees are mad about it, huh?" asked Bart.

"You mighty right they're mad," Della said. "I am, too. I don't want Jincey going to school and church with Nigras."

"You let her go to church with Ruth and Matthew across the road," Bart said. "Their church."

"Well, that's different," snapped Della. "She goes over there for the singing and for fun. It's not as if she was a member of their church. The Boudreaux children are *members* of our church and our school and I think Mrs. White is right. She asked the little pickaninnies not to come to Sunday school any more and she has a petition to the school board asking that they be taken out of the white school and sent to the nearest Nigra school. I signed it and I'm gon' get others to."

"Pickaninnies!" gasped Jincey. "Not Sunshine!"

"Well, I'm sorry," said Della, getting up to clear the table. "I know she's your friend but right's right. I promised Mrs. White I'd help."

"What can you do?" asked Bart. "Put on a sheet and burn a cross in front of their house?"

"That might help," Della said calmly. "But we don't have any good KKK's around here to take over. Us women will have to handle it ourselves by circulating a petition."

"Oh, Aunt Della, I don't want Sunshine to leave school," put in Jincey. "She's my best friend."

"Git you a white friend," Della said briefly, heading for the kitchen.

"She's mad," Bart said to Jincey. "So mad she's busting with it."

Jincey left the table and headed for the back steps. Della didn't have any right to be mad at the Boudreaux children—the clever, gifted Boudreaux children, who were the best singers and the best drawers and painters in school. The anger, she thought wonderingly, was already in Della and Sunshine had accidentally gotten in the way of it. Welcome lay on the step below her and she rubbed his side with her bare feet and tried to think what to do.

Della passed by her with a bowl of scraps for the chickens and she stood up to follow her.

"Aunt Della," she said hesitantly, "Sunshine and Joy and Delight look as white as I do."

"I know it, Jincey," she answered briskly. "They look white and they're very pretty little girls. But the fact remains, they are *not* white. They have a Nigra grandma so they have colored blood in them."

"Well, I don't see . . ." Jincey faltered.

"No, you don't see," interrupted Della. "You don't need to see. This is grown folks' business and you just don't worry about it."

Jincey did worry. On the long walk to school she and the Bates children discussed it endlessly. Their parents had signed the petition when Della brought it to them. And they thought it was a fine thing she was doing. Zack was one of the crowd of boys who gathered around the Boudreaux children when they went out for recess crying, "Nigger, nigger, hicky sticky stigger . . . highball, lowball, bald-headed nigger!"

Some of the girls avoided the Boudreaux girls but one or two of them went with Jincey when she took her lunch and followed them to the seat under the oak tree. Jincey would have preferred going down in the myrtle thicket with just Sunshine and playing church but now that there was trouble in the air some sense of danger caused the Boudreauxes to stick together. They sat side by side on the bench, their thin shoulders touching, their hands still on the lunch buckets they didn't open.

One of the boys passing on the way to the baseball diamond yelled at the little group of girls sitting on the ground under the trees.

"Hey, y'all gon' sit on the ground and let the niggers have the bench?"

"You shut your mouth!" Jincey yelled back, and Roberta Larkin, a seventh-grade girl, took it up. "You talking about your betters when you talking about us!" she jibed.

The boys went on to play and Jincey tried to get Sunshine to take a walk with her. They often walked with their arms entwined. Now Sunshine shook her head and sat still.

"I know what," said Roberta, "Le's play jump rope."

"I'll run git the rope," said Jincey eagerly. She went off at a trot and was back in a minute with the long rope.

"Me and Lula'll turn," directed Roberta, "and you littler ones can jump first. Joy?"

The littlest Boudreaux started to get up. She loved to jump rope and could hardly be stopped on even "Red Hot Pepper," her little legs pumping like pistons and her curls bouncing. She looked at Delight and settled back down, shaking her head.

"Come on, Delight, you go first," invited Roberta.

"Don't feel like it," answered Delight.

"Sunshine?"

"Me neither," said Sunshine.

"Well, Jincey, you go ahead," directed the older girl.

So Jincey jumped through "Cinderella-dressed-in-yellow." But she was never good and she knew she was going to trip on "How-many-kisses-did-he-give-her" without even getting to the numbers.

"Aw, she didn't git a kiss," said Roberta good-humoredly. "You turn, Jincey, and let me jump."

Roberta was good but the game had gone sour and they stopped long before the bell rang and sat glumly on the ground under the tree, poking at ants with brown live oak leaves and not talking.

The Boudreaux girls weren't at Sunday school on Sunday, a thing which Mrs. White and Della noted with satisfaction, although the singing was mighty poor without them. On Monday the petition came back with a letter from the school superintendent saying that the Boudreaux case had been investigated and the children found to be white. They could not be removed from school.

"Did you ever hear of such a thing?" demanded Mrs. White, showing Della the letter.

Della glanced at Jincey as she read it and when she finished she folded it up and handed it back, saying slowly, "Well, I reckon that's that."

"Oh, Missus McPherson, I'm not ready to give up that easy!" cried Mrs. White in her high nasal voice. "I am not a mother, of course, but I feel that you mothers should make yourselves heard. There are ways, you know."

Della listened while Mrs. White whispered. Jincey couldn't hear and she felt so low she didn't much want to. She drifted out on the store's front gallery and climbed up on the bannister. Sunshine and her sisters had come to school every day but they had stopped playing altogether and barely spoke to anybody but the teachers. Sunshine had not once slipped Jincey a note or a drawing or twined arms with her at recess.

When Della came out of the store her eyes were bright and her step brisk.

"Come on, childee, you're going to school today but you might not make it tomorrow!"

Jincey didn't know what she meant then but the next morning she found out. Della and Mrs. White spent the day driving around the country talking to the other women and they had agreed to boycott the school till the Boudreaux children were removed. Because there was a telephone at the mill Della had accepted the assignment of calling the school board office in Mobile and notifying them of the boycott.

Bart, sitting in his swivel chair, listened to the plan and shook his head.

"I hate for you to be mixed up in this," he said. "It's the kind of thing the red-necks over at the Front love. I don't know what's so bad about the little girls."

"It's not the children," said Della. "It's the principle of the thing. You know that, Bart, don't act like you don't. Now let me use the telephone."

Jincey and Bart sat quietly while she turned the crank on the wall and shouted her number to the voice which answered, "Mo-beeuhl." She was crisp and efficient in her talk to the board office and Jincey couldn't help being impressed and proud of that. To call the superintendent himself, the very head of all the schools in Mobile County, and tell him the Bayou Bien school was gon' have to run with nobody there but the Boudreauxes, took nerve, and Della snapped and crackled with nerve.

The next day the school opened with nobody but the Boudreaux children. Most of the other children came and their mothers with them, standing around in the yard or sitting on the gallery at White's store, waiting and watching for the three little girls. There was an air of sociability about the gathering. Most of the women were in fresh starched and ironed dresses with their hair damp-combed and shoes on their feet, if not stockings. They talked, shyly at first and then with increasing confidence. Miss Eva had ridden over with Della and their children and since she was kin to several of the other women she led the talk of spring gardens and fishing and sickness in the community.

They had gotten there long before school was due to open and had settled down to enjoy themselves when an old Ford rattled up to the school door and the Boudreaux children climbed out.

"There's that nigger, Pierre Boudreaux, now!" whispered Mrs. White, pointing.

They all were still, watching.

The three little girls climbed the steps and disappeared into the schoolhouse.

"That settles it!" cried one of the women. "My young'uns ain't going a step!"

"Mine neither," echoed another.

The old Ford moved from the schoolhouse door, turned and crossed the gravel road to the store. The driver got out—a thin little man with dark hair and a bushy black moustache. His overalls were patched, pretty patching, Jincey noticed, the kind that would make Della say he had a good wife. Patches and all, his clothes were clean and slick with starch and ironing.

Boudreaux was taking off his battered black felt hat.

"Good morning, misses," he said.

Some of the women nodded. One said "Good morning" in a low voice, but most of them were silent.

He stood on the ground looking up at them, and Jincey thought his eyes, as blue as Bart's, were sad.

"I come to tell you all," he began and choked to silence. "I come to tell you my little girls are gittin' their books. They won't be going to your school no more."

The women on the porch seemed to expel one long, pent-up sigh together.

"I'm sorry for the trouble you've had. They didn't tell me. They wanted to stay in school so bad."

He choked again and turned back toward his car, his hat still in his hand. Then he turned again and faced them. "The school supervisor woman come to my house and told us. They got a right, she said, they belong in the white school. But my wife, she say 'No,' not if they gon' be hurt like this."

"You know you're wrong," Della said quietly. "You know your mother is colored. Mrs. White saw her."

"Ma'am, Miz White saw my stepmother," he said gently. "But I ain't denying her, black as she is. She raised me from a baby and I honor her for it."

He got back in the car and picked up the little girls who were waiting in front of the school with their books in their hands.

Bart heard the news without enthusiasm.

"I reckon you did what you set out to do," he said and then he grinned. "Where old Boudreaux made his mistake was to *marry* the colored woman, if that's what he did. Pierre wasn't any different from the rest of us, being raised by a Nigra woman. I reckon you're to be congratulated though, you and Mrs. White."

But Della seemed uncertain and more restless and dissatisfied than ever. Jincey no longer enjoyed school and Della thought that might be her fault. But the most she said, when she saw her out the gate one morning, was, "I'm sorry about Sunshine, Honey. You want to let's go see if we can find her and git her to come over and play with you?"

But Jincey knew it was hopeless. The Boudreauxes had loaded up the Ford and moved out of that country and nobody knew where.

Della lapsed back into listlessness. She kept the house and cooked the meals and spent time in the garden, but the urge to change and rearrange and fix up seemed to have left her. She took longer and longer naps, still times of anxiety for Jincey, and sometimes when she was in the yard or the garden Jincey looked out and saw her standing, not working but just standing, looking off toward the woods.

Except for worry over Della, Jincey was happy. The closing of school, the beginning of summer with all its pleasures—swimming in the millpond, playing with the Bates children, paddling her pirogue—kept her busy. Bart let her ride Dan, an old sleepy, slow-paced horse, that summer and she spent a lot of time hanging around the barn with Clewis, who had apparently given up the idea of leaving Barton's Mill for good. He taught her how to feed and curry Dan. Unlike old Beck, Aunt Scam's horse on which she had ridden long ago, Dan had a saddle and the complication of putting it on him and cinching it tight was absorbing to her.

"Let me, Clewis," she begged. "Let me do it myself."

"Ain't work for a little gal young'un," Clewis told her. "Saddle too heavy for you to lift, and if you don't git them belly bands right the whole thing gon' come swerving off and dump you on the ground."

So Jincey stood back and watched and made up her mind that the first time Clewis wasn't there she would saddle Dan herself and go galloping through the quarters.

Dan was too old and too spiritless to gallop, but he would move, and the novelty of seeing the familiar places from the new eminence of horseback kept Jincey contentedly plodding through the quarters and around the lumberyards and past the planer mill and the turpentine still through many of the long, hot days. Moonlight nights came, nights so silver-bright Jincey felt she couldn't stay still and begged Bart to let her take Dan and ride.

"Not by yourself and not on old Dan," he said. "It's too hot for that old horse to have to work night and day. Wait till it's cooler and you are a little better rider. Then I'll saddle up Nancy for you and Rip for myself and we'll ride together."

"Aunt Della, too?" Jincey asked.

"Not me," put in Della. "My horseback riding days are over, I hope. When Henry Ford got his flivver going he saved me from horses."

They sat in the chairs in the yard, the better to enjoy the

moonlight and whatever breeze was stirring because every time she got a new gallery tacked on to the house, Della started in immediately to get it screened. And there was no doubt about it, screen wire cut out some of the air and grayed the whiteness of the moonlight. Even Della, who loved having everything screened, admitted that.

But the usefulness of a gallery that was enclosed with wire mesh made up for the disadvantages. The big back porch, which she persuaded Bart to add, was now screened and served as a summer dining room. Della had moved her sewing machine out there and a cot with a cretonne cover, where she often lay down to rest now in the morning after she had sent Bart's breakfast to the commissary.

Jincey, seeing her lie down one morning, lingered on her way to the barn to ask, "You sick, Aunt Della?"

"Side hurts," said Della. "It'll be all right. Run along."

But it wasn't all right. The hurting got worse, so bad that sometimes Della would go back to bed. She finally started keeping Jincey home from the pond and the woods to help around the house more. But she cautioned her not to say anything to anybody about it. Always, before Bart was due in for dinner or at knocking-off time in the evening, she would pull herself out of bed, comb her hair and put on a fresh housedress.

"Menfolks can't stand ailing women," she told Jincey. "You've got to help me so Bart won't know. You set the table for me and come here and let me tell you how to put on the rice and the fried meat."

She told Jincey so carefully and in such detail that Jincey could build a fire in the cookstove as well as Della could in no time at all, and she knew how to wash the rice under the faucet in the new sink and put it on in the granite pot with half an index finger of water above it.

"Let it come to a boil," Della directed, "and then push it to the back of the stove where it'll cook slow. Don't touch the lid, you hear? Keep it covered till the whistle blows. When you git that done, come back and I'll tell you about the meat."

Fried steak was something they had often because Bart liked it and it kept better than hog meat during the hot weather.

"Spread the steak out on the table and take that crockery saucer, the heavy one with the thick edge. Beat the steak with the edge of the saucer till it's criss-crossed all over and take about this much flour . . ." She made half a handful sign . . . "and spread it on first one side and then the other, beating till you've got it all beat in. Bring it and let me see it when it's ready and I'll tell you the rest."

Wincing from the pain, she would push up on an elbow to look at the steak and judge if it had been beaten to a tenderness. Did Jincey remember the salt and pepper?

"Well, put on the iron skillet, front of the stove over the hottest eye, and take a gob of lard about as big as a hen's egg and heat it till it smokes. Lay the steak in carefully so's not to splash hot grease on the stove or yourself. Now Jincey, be careful. When the steak is brown on one side, turn it to the other and take the dishrag—a dry one, Jincey—and slide the skillet to the back of the stove, where it will cook slow. Then come back and I'll tell you about the gravy."

The only part about cooking that Jincey didn't like was peeling and chopping the onions. Uncle Bart liked lots of onion gravy with his rice and Jincey fought eye- and nose-stinging tears every way she knew. Della told her to put a piece of raw potato on the end of her knife and it would absorb the onion juice. Ruth, who happened by one day when she snuffled and cried over onions, held a piece of cornbread between her lips so it stuck out a couple of inches and vowed the onions didn't bother her. The bread absorbed the fumes before they could get to her eyes.

Nothing worked for Jincey, but she peeled and chopped and cried for weeks, worrying all the time that Bart would tell the difference between her onion gravy and Della's and learn that Della was sick and they'd have to leave. She asked Della about it, when she went to her bed with a sample of gravy one day.

Della was white-faced and sweating, but she stuck a finger in the saucer of gravy and licked it.

"All right," she said. "Next time brown your flour a little more and don't let your onions cook quite so much. But you've done good enough today. Just slide the skillet back where it'll keep hot and chip some ice for the tea. Fill the glasses and set them close to the block in the icebox so they'll be cold when Uncle Bart gits here."

"If he knows you're sick, will he make us leave?" Jincey asked, standing in the door with the saucer of gravy cooling in her hands.

"God knows," sighed Della, turning her head tiredly. Then she saw Jincey drooping against the door facing and she said, "Aw, now, you know better than that! Do you think he'd turn against us just because I'm sick?"

"No, ma'am," Jincey began uncertainly. "I reckon not. But you said he wouldn't like a ailing woman."

"Jincey, go finish dinner," said Della impatiently. "No man likes his womenfolks to be sick. It's tedious to come home to a whining, limp-around of a woman. But that don't mean he'd throw us out, so quit your worrying. Bart McPherson wouldn't throw a sick dog out."

That was true, Jincey knew, and she went back to the kitchen feeling cheered up. When the whistle blew for noon she heard Della's feet hit the floor and by the time Bart came whistling up the path from the commissary Della was sitting in the swing wearing a fresh dress, her lips and cheeks pink from rouge, her hair, which had been limp and damp, brushed and coiled high on her head.

But summer wore on and Della didn't get any better. She lost interest in food and grew so thin Bart finally noticed and asked her what was wrong. She said she had a hurting in her side.

"Why, Della, Sweetheart, you might have something serious wrong with you!" he cried. "I'm taking you to Dr. Willis tomorrow."

Jincey went with them, waiting in the car in front of the drugstore at Plateau while Della and Bart went to the doctor's office in the back room. When they came out, bringing ice-cream cones from the soda fountain, they were talking of other things, and Jincey decided that Dr. Willis had made Della well.

But the next day Della sent Uncle Bart's breakfast to him and went back to bed. Jincey hung around the door, watching her when she closed her eyes to be sure she was still breathing. Finally, Della noticed her and lifted the mosquito bar and asked her to come and get in bed with her.

"I want to talk to you, childee," she said, facing Jincey and smoothing her hair. "I've got to go to the hospital and have a operation. I might be gone a good while, but you'll be all right here with Uncle Bart and Motherdear. She'll come stay here and they'll take good care of you and bring you to see me as often as they can."

"You'll be gone and I'll be here?" Jincey asked in a low voice, barely able to get the words out for the tightness in her throat.

"Oh, Honey, don't start gittin' the down-yonders over that!" said Della, trying to hold back her impatience. "That's the way it's got to be now and maybe from now on. Who knows?"

"You might die," Jincey said flatly.

"I could," said Della. "But I probably won't. If I should, Jincey, you're to stay on here and be Uncle Bart's little girl. He wants you and he promised me he'd take care of you."

Jincey reached for a fold of Della's dress and held on to it as hard as she could, fighting tears which were stinging her eyes.

"Listen, Jincey," Della said sternly, "You are not to cut the fool over this, no matter what happens. Why, lots of children don't even have a mama. Or, if they do, they've got one so crazy she might as well not be. Look at Uncle Bart and old hateful Mary, what kind of mother you think they had in Motherdear? Loony!"

She turned onto her back and stared at the top of the mosquito bar where it all came together in pleats, making a kind of rosette.

"I should talk about 'loony,'" she said more to herself than to Jincey. "My own poor ma was crazy—is crazy, if she's yet alive."

Jincey waited and in a minute Della sighed and went on.

"If I come out of this all right I'm gon' try and find the old thing and help her if I can. I bet she's prowling the earth somewhere just like she did when I was a young'un, turning, turning, walking, walking, never staying at the same place more'n a few days at a time. Jincey, I didn't have a good stay-place like you got, when I was a young'un. Me and Ma went from pillar to post, Dan to Beersheba, first this relative and then that one, after

Grandma died and they sold the farm. I was always welcome where they had a new baby so's I could wash shitty diapers for them. I reckon I washed the weight of that sawmill in shitty diapers by the time I was your age."

She turned her head and smiled at Jincey.

"You'll git to go to school, too. I never did. Titter did and when we landed up at Aunt Sweetie's, Titter learnt me to read and write. When I fell in there, after I was about grown, Miss Lucy Merritt, a schoolteacher, was boarding at Aunt Sweetie's and she give me and Titter hand-writing lessons, big as we was. We took 'em because we wanted to write letters to boys and if you wrote a pretty hand, it amounted to something then."

She was quiet a minute.

"It still does, Jincey. I want you to be educated, to talk proper, to read and write as good as anybody in this world. You can learn it here. Uncle Bart got schooling himself. His whole family did, as far back as anybody knows, and they believe in it. Why Jincey, you can go to high school in town when you finish at Bayou Bien and maybe after that even teacher's normal school! Wouldn't you like that?"

Jincey was momentarily diverted. To be a schoolteacher when she grew up? It sounded so fine she eased her hold on Della's dress and lay still dreaming about it. She'd be exactly like Miss Upton.

But Della went on, as if she couldn't stop, as if she had to pull everything from the past and show it to Jincey.

"If my Papa had lived I might of had a chance. He was a educated man, well-to-do, too. His folks had a big white house on the main street of Willacoochee, Georgy, where I was borned. But he was old, forty or fifty, I reckon, and Ma wasn't but sixteen. So as soon as she was able to travel, after I was born, she took me in her arms and walked—walked, mind you—all the way to Grandpa's farm, fifteen miles out from town. Grandpa didn't want us. He had made Ma marry Old Williams, as he called him, with the idea of bettering herself in the world. But Grandma made Grandpa let us stay—or let me stay—and Ma took off, going here and yonder, first one's house and then the other's. I remember my Papa come to Grandpa's once a-looking for us, but Ma wasn't there and Grandma hid me in the backroom and didn't let on that she knew where Ma was."

She was silent, thinking.

"I often wonder what would have happened to me if he'd found me and taken me to raise in town. I expect I'd a been educated and wouldn't have had to marry Howie for a roof over my head and rations to eat, like I did. That's what you got to do, Jincey, git a education so you won't be beholden to no man in this world."

"Yes'm," Jincey said miserably, thinking about the little baby Della had been with a loony mama and no stay-place of her own. She wished Della would hush, but she couldn't seem to.

"My Papa died soon after that. People said from a broken heart." She laughed. "I think that's a fancy and he probably had the TB. Everybody else in his family did. But they say he loved Ma and I reckon she was a pretty little thing—sixteen years old with a head full of red curls. And dance . . . Lord, I remember her dancing and drinking whiskey when we didn't have bread in the house! When I was big enough to walk she come for me. A lot of men wanted to marry Ma and once when I wasn't much older than you, she got a job with an old feller out from Waycross, Georgy.

"Lord, that was a fine place! Big house with magnolia trees in the front yard and a smokehouse plumb full of meat in the back. He hired Ma to keep house for him and his ailing boy and then he got the notion of marrying her. I was tickled . . . Lord, I thought I had struck it rich! But Ma wouldn't stay. They got the license and the preacher was set to come the next day and perform the ceremony in the parlor. The old man's married daughter was gon' play the organ and his sisters had come and cooked till Hosea-hoe-the-row!"

She smiled dreamily. "Hams and baked hens and a shoat barbecuing over a pit out under the trees, cakes stacked up like stovewood and even a freezer of ice cream and a five-gallon crock of lemonade. He sent into Waycross and got clothes and shoes for me and Ma so we would do him proud at the wedding. But wouldn't you know, Ma got me up before daybreak the day of the wedding and we took off walking! Without even our new clothes."

She was quiet, staring at the top of the mosquito bar for a long time.

"It wasn't long after that I run away. We was staying at Aunt Jessie's out from Jacksonville, Georgy, and Ma decided to go. By that time I knew the signs. Walking, walking, singing and talking. A lot like Motherdear. She would be gittin' me up before the day to take off and I wasn't going with her no more. I had that settled in my mind, young as I was. When she felt for me on the cot at the foot of her bed the next morning I wasn't there. I was hiding in the woods. I had one dollar Uncle John, Aunt Jessie's husband, had give me, and as soon as it was day I walked to the railroad track and flagged a train and rode it to Aunt Sweetie's near Pearson. It was enough money, but I wasn't sure it would be so I hid in the toilet so the conductor couldn't ask me for any more, until the train pulled into Pearson.

"Uncle Dit and Aunt Sweetie was fixing to move with a new railroad that was going through Epoch, but they let me stay until Grandma came for me. Until Grandma died I had a place to stay and plenty at it. But when she died, I was back to being pore kin on Aunt Sweetie and Uncle Dit. That's how I come to marry Howie."

She laughed and leaned toward Jincey, taking hold of the hand, which clutched her dress.

"Talk about driving your ducks to a bad market, Lordy, Lordy! But the reason I'm telling you all this, Jincey, is so you'll be content to stay here, no matter what happens to me. Bart McPherson will raise you right, Sunday school and church and all the learning you can jam in that squirrelly-looking head. Git up and go comb it."

She took a deep breath and sat up. "Then help me smooth up this bed and cut out some nightgowns for the hospital. I'll need so many we won't have time to do anything fancy. You can help me with them."

The rest of the morning Della sat in a chair and directed while

Jincey spread out lengths of voile and nainsook and pinned the nightgown pattern to them. Della started to cut but a pain caught her and she sat back down and supervised while Jincey followed the pattern shapes with the scissors. When they had six of them cut out they moved to the porch, where the sewing machine was, and Jincey, squatting on the floor, worked the foot treadle while Della guided the goods under the needle and presser foot.

They made mistakes and Della got tired and impatient but by the time the noon whistle had blown they had all the main seams sewed up, ready for the handwork which Della could do sitting in a deck chair under a tree.

Now that he knew Della was ailing, Bart got his dinner out of the commissary and sent Clewis up to the house with a cold watermelon for them, hoping to tempt Della to eat. The crisp, bright melon flesh did tempt her some, and she ate a small piece, sitting under the chinquapin tree with Jincey, before she went in the house to lie down.

Moving the folded, nearly finished nightgowns from the bed, she sighed tiredly and then smiled at Jincey.

"You're a good hand to help, childee," she said. "No matter what, you gon' be somebody."

It wasn't anything Jincey wanted—to be somebody—but she felt comforted by Della's approval. If she practiced she might be able to help Della hem the gowns and whip the lace on the edges of the collars and sleeves.

Going to the hospital was a big, terrifying, expensive thing, even to Della, who had had an operation before. She didn't think Jincey should be there, but on the day of her operation, Bart had insisted on bringing her. She let it go, too tired to raise much objection.

"It's no place for a child," she said once as Bart and Jincey stood by her hospital bed. "She should be home playing. Ruth and Matthew could look after her, if Motherdear's not out there yet."

"No, no, Aunt Della!" cried Jincey, fearful that she'd have to leave. "Let me stay. I'll be good."

Bart looked pale and worried himself, but he put an arm

around Jincey and said, "I need her company while you're in the operating room."

"Well, do something besides waiting," Della said. "Go somewhere. They said I'll be out for hours and there's no need for you to hang around here. You hear?"

Bart nodded. "When they come for you, we'll go," he promised. Della reached for his hand.

"I'm sorry about this," she said thickly from the shot they had given her. "All this expense to you. I wouldn't have let you in for it . . . if I could of stood the pain."

Bart squeezed her hand. "I just want you well, that's all. No more pain."

Della dozed and in a little while they came with a rolling stretcher and lifted her on it and wheeled her away. Jincey followed until it disappeared beyond a swinging door and then she turned to Bart, searching his face anxiously.

"She's gon' be all right," he said. "Just fine. Don't you worry."

She's gon' die, Jincey contradicted him in her mind, her freckled face frozen with anxiety. But she couldn't say it to Bart, even ask it, for fear of making it true.

"Tell you what we'll do," Bart said. "We'll go get an ice-cream soda and then we'll ride down to McGown-Lyons and look at hardware."

Jincey couldn't finish the fifteen-cent soda and at the big hardware store, which was one of Bart's favorite places, she could only stand and wait. Bart wandered among the kegs and bins of screws and nuts and bolts. He looked at racks of paint and rolls of screen wire and he called to Jincey to look.

"See this," he said. "Didn't Della say she thought the house ought to be stained dark green?"

Jincey nodded. "Yes, sir. That's her favorite. Except white."

"Paint won't do on that rough lumber," muttered Bart. "But stain will. And if you're sure it's dark green she wants, that's what I'll get."

Jincey went back and stood by the door. She couldn't think of green stain or anything else but the still, white-sheeted form on the rolling stretcher back at the hospital. They said an operation meant cutting a person with a knife. She could smell the acrid hardware smells—new rope, floor-sweeping compound, oils and ointments used to keep machinery going—but her eyes saw a great gush of red blood spouting up from Della's side, where they would slice in with a knife. A person couldn't live after that.

She was seized with a certainty that she had to go back to the hospital and tell them not to do it, to make them stop, to get Della back as she was. She willed Bart to stop looking at hardware and pricing paints and take her back to the hospital. He didn't look her way, didn't see the greenish eyes fixed on him, the sun-speckled face screwed into mute plea. Instead, deciding slowly, he bought the house stain—a great box filled with many cans of it, and then he talked with the man back of the counter about brushes. Finally, the matter was settled. A porter went out to put the paint and brushes in the car and the man at the counter entered the sale in a charge book. Bart began to walk toward the door and Jincey thankfully opened the door to make their leaving faster. Then she saw him stop to examine a rack of wrenches.

It was too much. Her disappointment at another delay overwhelmed her. Tears rushed to her eyes and were spilling down her cheeks when Bart looked up from inspecting a wrench and saw.

"Oh, Ugly, what's the matter?" he asked, dropping the wrench and coming to her side. "Do you feel bad? Where hurts?"

"Aunt Della . . ." blubbered Jincey, now really crying. "They taking a knife to her! I want to go back!"

"Aw, sure you do," said Bart. "I do, too. I just thought we might spend a little time looking at stuff here and maybe buy her a surprise for when she comes home. But if it'll make you feel better to be at the Mobile Infirmary, that's where we'll go."

The Mobile Infirmary wasn't any better. Jincey couldn't go looking for Della. Bart explained to her that well children weren't supposed to be in a hospital. He had broken a rule to bring her. And now she would have to stay outside and wait for a chance to see Della when the operation was over and she was back in her room. He talked of doctors and how good they were to take care of pains like Della's.

"Dr. Willis is a very good doctor," he said, as they sat on the hospital gallery and rocked in some funny-shaped chairs. "He's the kind of doctor I wanted to be."

Jincey pulled her mind out of the hospital long enough to ask, "You was gon' be a doctor?"

Bart smiled, glad to have found something she was interested in talking about to keep the hunted, frightened face turned his way instead of fixed on the opening and closing of the front door of the infirmary.

"One of my grandfathers was a doctor," he said, "and I always thought I'd go to medical school, too. When I was a little boy," he chuckled at the memory, "I used to tell my mother I was going to be a doctor when I grew up and I would have a goat wagon to drive around the streets of Mobile and would take her riding in it."

Jincey laughed at the picture of Uncle Bart and Motherdear riding in a little goat wagon.

"I got the goat wagon, all right. We always had plenty of goats at the mill and it's little trouble to break one to the harness. But I didn't make it to medical school."

"Why didn't you?"

"My father died and Motherdear was sick and the war came along and I joined the army."

"But you still doctor," Jincey said, remembering his books and the shelf of medicines in the office.

"As much as I can get by with, having no license," smiled Bart. "I take splinters out of your feet and treat burns and prescribe calomel and quinine to folks in the quarters. I'd like to have been a surgeon because I believe I could have done that well."

Jincey didn't know what a surgeon was and, when he explained, the bloody picture of Della and the knife came back. But he talked about it so calmly and seemed to put so much stock in the good it did, Jincey began to feel better.

Then he talked of goat wagons and what it would take to train a goat to pull a wagon and finally, in a rush of confidence, Jincey told him about Carnation.

"Carnation?" said Bart, laughing. "You didn't name a wild and smelly little goat 'Carnation'!"

Jincey nodded. "I think he smells good. Maybe not like a flower but like a baby . . ."

"A baby goat," finished Bart, laughing harder. "Oh, Ugly, you won't do! Wait till I tell Uncle Bob you've adopted a goat and named him Carnation."

"You won't tell Aunt Della, will you?" worried Jincey.

"No," said Bart, "but I think you should. In a family we shouldn't keep things from one another, especially if you are pretty sure you're doing something she won't like. It usually makes trouble later."

Jincey fell silent. She and Della had kept things from him and it sure-god made trouble. She didn't know how it worked, but bad things had been happening lately.

The day had nearly ended when they saw Della again. The nurse let them in her room, talking brightly and loudly of how well she was doing, but Bart and Jincey tiptoed to the side of the bed and whispered when they spoke her name.

She opened her eyes and looked at them and smiled and closed her eyes again.

"She's gon' be drowsy a while yet," the nurse said. "She'll be nauseated some from the ether but the operation went fine and she'll be able to talk to you tomorrow. Why don't you go on home now?"

Jincey would have stayed but when Bart smiled at her and held out a hand she put hers in it and went docilely. She was too tired to do anything else. She slept all the way home.

Della's strength was slow to come back. The operation, Dr. Willis told them, was a success and she should be back on her feet in two weeks or a month. But every time Bart and Jincey went to the hospital, Della seemed thinner and paler and more tired.

She didn't like the hospital food and hardly ate enough to keep her alive, the nurses said.

"What do you think," Della said tiredly, pointing to a dish on her supper tray. "Cream of Wheat they call it—and me a-wanting grits and gravy. Not flour gravy," she amended after a moment, "fried meat grease. A little pool in the grits, made with the back of the spoon, and it filled with piping-hot meat grease."

"Aw, you kidding," the young nurse said, laughing. "All that grease will kill you."

Della shook her head and smiled weakly.

"Well, you eat a good supper," said the nurse, "and you can go home sooner and cook that grits and fried meat."

She left the room and Della handed the little bowl of white cereal to Jincey.

"Yankee food," she said. "They put milk and sugar on it. You try it. I can't."

Jincey did try it and liked it very much, almost as much as grits and gravy. But she felt guilty about eating it when Della needed it.

"If you eat it maybe you can come home soon," she ventured.

"I'll git there soon enough," said Della, and turned on her side and closed her eyes.

Uncle Bart came in the room and with him—Motherdear and Mary! Jincey's eyes darted to Della's pale face. After what Mary had done to them she sure-god hoped Della wouldn't see her.

But Mary was hugging Jincey and calling her "Pretty One" and Motherdear, who had ridden in to town with them for a visit to her house, was puffing around to the window side of the bed to peer into Della's face and be sure she was sleeping.

Before she succeeded in getting Della awake, Mrs. White from Bayou Bien came in and all of them stood around Della's bed whispering.

Della heard them and stirred, looking up into the faces of the three women. To Jincey's surprise, she smiled and moved her hand on the counterpane toward them.

"Hey-o, daughter, you're looking fine!" cried Motherdear, leaning to kiss her.

"Della, Honey, I'm so sorree!" cried Mary and kissed her too. "I brought you a get-well present. Jincey, ask the nurse for an extra pillow. I want to prop up our invalid and show her my bag of tricks."

Jincey looked at Della and she nodded. She was going to be

nice to Mary! Jincey left the room, shy about having to speak to a strange nurse and ask her for a pillow but, more than that, worrying about Della's funny-acting ways. Mary had found out and told on them—and now she might have come to do more harm so they'd have to leave, after all. And Della, who never believed in being nice to people who did you bad, was smiling and letting herself be kissed. Maybe ... Jincey stopped on the hospital's rubber hall runner and turned back uneasily. Maybe Della was fixing to die! Didn't folks always sweeten up before they died?

She turned and ran back in the room. Mrs. White and Mother-dear were sitting in the two chairs and Mary was perched grace-fully on the foot of the bed. Della, her eyes bright and interested, and Uncle Bart, standing and shifting from foot to foot, listened to Mrs. White's high voice going on and on about a gall bladder operation she had suffered through once.

"I can't stay long," she said, looking at the fancy metal brace-leted watch on her plump wrist. "Aaron had to go to the whole-sale houses and he should be downstairs looking for me right now!"

"Aw," said Della in polite protest. "I wish you could stay a while. It's such a long way to come."

"And a long way to go," said Mary, getting up. "I don't blame you for wanting to get started, Mrs. White. Let me walk down with you and say hello to Mr. White."

She put an arm about Mrs. White's shoulders and expertly guided her out the door, cutting off any lingering goodbyes. As she went she rolled her eyes and stuck out her tongue at Della behind Mrs. White's back.

Della laughed so hard she had to grab her stomach to staunch the pain in her incision.

Bart glanced at Motherdear, who had taken her New Testa-ment out of her reticule and was studying it, evidently with the idea of finding a passage to read aloud to Della when things quietened down.

"I tried to get Mary not to come, Della," Bart said worriedly. "She had Ma outside when I got to the hospital and I told her to let Ma come in and for her to wait downstairs. She wouldn't do it. I'm obliged to you for treating her nice."

"Pushy heifer, ain't she?" said Della in a low, weak voice, but she smiled. "Well with Mrs. White here I couldn't jump up and scratch her eyes out. Don't worry about her. She can't hurt me unless you let her."

Bart took her hand.

"And I'll never do that—her or anybody else," he said earnestly.

Jincey, standing by the door, felt the knot of worry that made a hard chunk in her middle dissolve and come up in a long sigh. She went back out to try again for the pillow.

Mary's "bag of tricks" was a little suitcase full of Elizabeth Arden creams and lotions, rouge, lipstick, a blue leather-cased vial of Djer Kiss perfume, and a pink silk-and-lace thing she called a "boudoir cap."

"My goodness, your skin is dry," she said fussing over Della's face with creams. "You're recovering from your operation all right, but if Mary hadn't rushed to the rescue, darling, you might of died of the uglies! Here, I'm patting in some orange skin food. Now, you do it every night. Here's the eye cream and the throat cream, and while you're here in the hospital with no man to be frightened by it, you should grease up good and wear this mask at night."

She shook out a little cotton mask with holes in it for the eyes and mouth.

Della held it up to her face and laughed. "You're making me a Ku Kluxer," she said.

"I hope not!" said Mary, fluffing out the boudoir cap and bundling Della's long, red-brown hair into it. "Talk about tack-pots, it's that crowd!"

Della lifted her eyes to Bart's and smiled.

Whatever Mary's stuff did, she looked better, not just rosier in the face, but livelier.

"Mary," she said, looking at herself in a hand mirror, "all this must have cost a fortune."

"Didn't cost anything," said Mary flippantly. "I charged it.

And what's more, I charged a fur coat, too. Figured before the word gets out that Edward is out of a job and we haven't got a dime, I'd better get everything I can."

"Oh, my," said Della enviously. "A fur coat?"

"Not just fur, darling, beaver. Verry good this year."

Bart was looking at her thoughtfully, a troubled crease between his eyes.

"They say we're in a depression," he said. "I know business is falling off for everybody. Do you think it's the year to buy a fur coat?"

"Oh, Bubba!" cried Mary, reaching up to kiss him on the cheek. "Any year's a good year to be warm. And it's now or never for us. Do you think Gus Mayer will let me have a fur coat when he finds out we're broke?"

"But you'll have to pay for it somehow," Bart said.

"Don't be sil!" said Mary. "Gus Mayer and I'll both wait—and I'll be warm till good times come again. Come on, Mother," she said, turning to Motherdear, who was dozing over her New Testament. "Put up your Scripture and let's go home."

"But I was gon' read something to Della," the old lady protested.

"We've done enough to Della today," Mary said. "Get on your horse."

When they had gone, Della handed the mirror she had been studying to Jincey to put back on the white dresser and turned to Bart.

"What's that you said about business being bad?" she asked.

"It is," he said. "There was a stock market crash that set things off. We didn't pay much attention to it at the time. What happens in New York to rich people doesn't seem important to poor sawmill folks in Mobile County, Alabama. But it had an effect. Uncle Bob is talking about shutting down the mill one or two days a week."

"I'm going home," Della said suddenly.

"What you talking about?" said Bart. "You can't do anything about business. You stay in bed and get well."

"I'm well enough. This hospital is costing a fortune. I know that. I'm going home and we'll see what we can do. If I put in a fall garden and we get another cow . . ."

"Sweetheart, sweetheart!" said Bart, laughing a little and reaching for her hand. "You think of everything in terms of food."

"Well, we got a roof over our head, ain't we?" Della asked sharply. "What else is there to worry about?"

Della did come home two days later, weak but determined. Ruth was there to welcome her with the bed freshly made up and the pillows standing up straight in sharply starched cases. She had a fire burning in the kitchen stove and the smell of green coffee parching in the oven.

There was chicken pie for supper and Della insisted on sitting up at the table to eat, although Ruth had fixed a tray for her.

"No more eating in the bed for me," Della said. "It's weakening. I've come home to take a hold—and I can't do it from the bed."

Thereafter she got up and put on her clothes when Bart did every morning, lacing her corset tightly to support the sagging stomach incision, brushing and coiling her hair high on her head and reddening her lips with the lipstick Mary had brought her. Jincey, moping around, dressing for school, looked at her in astonishment.

"You sure are fixing up. Do you feel good?"

"Nope, not yet," Della admitted. "But I will. No use dragging around here like dead lice are falling off you. Uncle Bart's got enough to worry about."

The mill was shut down, not one or two days a week but three. Many of the hands went looking for more work at other mills. There was one at Three-Mile Creek, they heard, that was running full tilt, six days a week. But it, too, cut down and some of the Negroes came straggling back, willing to take whatever Cap'n Barton had to offer.

Jincey was at the commissary when a wagonload of them crossed the bridge. Cap'n Barton heard the rattle of the bridge and looked out the window. He stood up and walked out on the commissary gallery to meet them.

Flathead, from the woods, was driving a mule so old he was gray and stumbled as he came up the hill. His wife, Jerusha, and Easter, a little girl Jincey's age, sat on the seat beside him and three other men, whose names Jincey didn't remember, sat in the back. They looked dusty and tired, but when they saw Cap'n Barton they straightened up and began smiling.

"Evening, Cap'n," said Flathead. And from the woman beside him to the men in the back the echo came, "Evenin' ... Evenin', suh ... Evenin', Cap'n.

Easter ducked her head and smiled shyly at Jincey and Jincey lifted her hand and said a barely audible, "Hi."

Cap'n Barton didn't say anything for a while but stood on the top step with his legs spraddled out and his arms folded over his big belly.

"Where you all been and where you think you going, Flathead?" he finally asked.

"Us been looking for work, Cap'n," Flathead said, climbing stiffly down from the wagon and taking off his frazzled straw hat. "I tol' Mist' Bart us couldn't make it on one day a week and he said it was all right to go a-lookin'."

"What'd you find?" asked Cap'n Barton, smiling like he enjoyed the question.

"Nothing ... nothing. We don't find nothing!" cried the woman shrilly. "Rations is gone and nobody working. We be's hongry, Cap'n!"

"Yessir, that be's the truth," Flathead said soberly. And from the back of the wagon came the echo, "Sho' is. Sho' be hongry."

"Well, there's no more work here," Cap'n Barton said. "You just as well to keep traveling. We running one day a week and I got more hands than we need for that."

Flathead slumped against the wagon, ducking his head to study his ragged hat, which he kept turning between his hands.

Cap'n Barton scratched his stomach and looked out across the millpond. He started to whistle and then he coughed and spat in the yard. Inside the commissary they heard Bart's voice raised in his cheerful salesman's cry, "Tell me something! Tell me something!" as he waited on half a dozen hands who were working.

Flathead lifted his head.

338

"Boss man, my woman be's poly and dis old mule 'bout to fall out. How it be if we go back and sleep in our old house tonight?"

Cap'n Barton watched a water chicken paddle halfway across the pond before he answered.

"All right. You can sleep there tonight. But no more credit in the commissary and you got to move on tomorrow."

He turned and walked heavily back toward the office. Jincey jumped down from the porch and skittered off up the quarters road before Flathead could get the mule and wagon moving.

She was in the kitchen telling Della and Ruth about it when they heard the wagon go creaking by.

"And they hongry, Aunt Della. They all said they hongry."

"Hungry," said Della, correcting her automatically. But her eyes were on the fruit jar of tomatoes she had put up the summer before and was getting ready to open for supper. "I'll git 'em something together for tonight and Ruth, you take it when you go."

"Jesus, what us gon' do?" sighed Ruth. "It could be me and Matthew. Or any of us. Miss Della, when times gon' git better?"

"Lord knows," said Della. "We just have to spread out what we got till they do. Git that basket and let's see what we can put in it."

She measured out flour and lard and cut off a chunk of side meat from her own supply in the smokehouse. She put in a small sack of grits and jars of tomatoes and corn and a little bottle of cane syrup. Turning distractedly, she looked at the stone sugar crock and passed it by. Then she lifted the lid on the coffee can and put it back.

Sugar was high. Coffee was her own luxury. She bought it green and lovingly washed and dried the beans, picking out culls and an inevitable pebble or two. Every Saturday afternoon she spread the green coffee out in a baking pan and slowly roasted it in the oven, watching it carefully and stirring it with a wooden paddle to make sure it didn't burn. The first thing she did when she got up in the morning, after building a fire in the stove, was to put on water for the coffee and then measure out a cup full of the plump, shiny brown beans and grind them in the little black tin mill on the wall.

Jincey often awakened to the sound of the coffee mill and the smell of the coffee. Now she watched to see if Della was going to give away part of her coffee.

Della put her hand on the coffee-can lid twice more before she finally grinned at Ruth and said, "Foot, if anybody ever needed coffee, them pore people do. Take it all to them, Ruth."

It was to Jincey the first measure of what folks were calling the Depression.

Flathead and Jerusha and their little girl, Easter, didn't leave their house in the quarters the next day. Nobody said anything about it so they turned the old mule out to graze and stayed on. Flathead fished in the creeks at the head of the pond and Ruth told Della the working ones in the quarters shared what they had with them, meal and lard and a cup of dried beans occasionally.

There weren't many working ones left. Matthew, a Barton, born and bred on the place, never thought of leaving. Nor did his brother, Goat, his grandmother, Hester, or his sisters, Rouette and Louette. They had never lived anywhere else and it did not occur to them that there was any other place to go. Matthew continued to hitch up the mules and go to the woods daily, moving what logs were cut to the millpond. But the sawyers weren't working. The mill ran but one day a week and then not at all. And after a time the pond was jammed and crisscrossed with logs there was no use in sawing. The people in Mobile who had wanted yellow pine lumber no longer needed it.

Clewis put in a spring garden in the big field and brought the mule by to plow Della's patch. He sat on the back steps drinking coffee and complaining about the lack of help.

"Mist' Bart done fired every fieldhand on the place," he said. "Got a wagonload sweet potato sets—and who gon' put 'em in the ground? Me, that's all. Ain't a soul out there in the field 'cept me!"

"Well, Clewis," said Della soothingly, "I'm gon' put mine in myself. Me and Jincey. Why don't you git them that's not working in the quarters to help you? Mister Bart would pay 'em ten cents a hour for fieldwork, I reckon, and that's better than nothing."

"Say they ain't fiel'hands," said Clewis bitterly. "Ack lak they too good to scrabble in the ground and make some'teat. I axe Fireman to help me and he say I ain't got no steam boiler out there in the fiel'. Up there laying on the front gallery joreeing wid the wimmen."

It was true of all of them. They were turpentine-sawmill hands and they didn't know about plowing and planting. Even the Bates family surprised Della by their lack of interest in a garden. Beyond a few collard plants, they planted nothing.

"Why, they'll eat canned tomatoes out of the store instead of growing and putting up their own!" she told Bart.

He didn't seem surprised at that. He wouldn't have planted a garden himself. Farming was something done by other people—a little side enterprise and of slight importance compared to the real work of harvesting rosin and distilling turpentine and cutting and sawing and planing and stacking and hauling the gleaming golden flesh of the pine tree.

Now there was no market for lumber or turpentine and the people who had manned the swift and sometimes lethal sawmill carriages, who had fired the boilers and dipped the gum, who sang while they pushed dollies loaded with lumber down the long runs, were no longer needed. Their hard-forged skills were valueless.

The women were more adaptable. They would work in the fields and Della had all the house and garden help she could use in exchange for a note to Bart to let the workers have some flour or meal or sowbelly out of the commissary.

Tramps from the Southern railroad over at the Front started showing up at the back door. The first one to come was a neat old man in faded but clean overalls and a broad-brimmed, black felt hat. He carried a pack on his back in which he had fitted a long-handled straight razor, a worn army blanket, a well-scrubbed coffeepot and tin skillet and a bar of soap.

Della saw him come out of the woods back of the house, shortly before dinnertime one day. He paused at the cowpen, looking at Alice carefully, and then came around the fence toward the kitchen. She met him at the back steps.

"Good morning, ma'am," he said, tipping his hat politely. "My name is Elias Hascall and I'm a private first-class in the army of the unemployed."

"A what?" asked Della.

The man laughed, showing broken yellow teeth. "A little joke, ma'am. I mean to say I am temporarily out of work and I wonder if you have some wood I could chop or some hoeing I could do for a meal?"

Della shook her head. "I got more help these days than I need," she said. "But if you're hungry . . ."

"I see you have a cow, ma'am," the old man said. "I'm purely perishing for a glass of milk. Buttermilk, if you can spare it. Seems like the stuff I been eating since I left home in Georgy don't agree with my stomach."

"Put your bundle there on the steps and come on in," Della said. "I got plenty of buttermilk. My husband'll be here in a few minutes and you can have dinner with us."

"I see a pump out yonder," the old man said. "I'll just walk out there and wash up."

Jincey started to say, "We got a bathroom now," but Della threw her a look that stopped her.

"Do that," Della said to the man. "And here's a clean flour sack you can dry on."

When the man had walked a little way from the house toward the pump Della said, "Better let him stay outside till Bart gits here. He's a Weary Willie and we don't know what he's up to."

"But you said come in . . ." Jincey began.

"Well, I thought better of it!" snapped Della.

The noon whistle no longer blew but they still marked the shape of the day—6:00 A.M., work starting time, noon, 5:00 P.M. quitting time—by beating the hour on a piece of an old rusty and broken rotary saw, which had been bolted to a post set in the ground in front of the commissary. Bart had few people to wait on in the commissary so he got to the house almost before the old man had finished washing and wiping his hands and pinning the sack Della gave him to the clothesline to dry.

Della met him at the door and whispered, "We got company, a Weary Willie, I think. Old man from the railroad and hungry. Go talk to him."

Bart hurried out the back door and went up to the man holding out his hand.

"Barton McPherson," he said. "How are you?"

"Elias Hascall," said the old man, grabbing his hand and shaking it. "Pleased to make your acquaintance."

"We about to sit down to dinner and would be mighty pleased if you would have some with us," Bart said.

"Your wife has kindly offered me a glass of buttermilk," Mr. Hascall said. "And that will be a sufficiency. I have a touch of indigestion from a 'possum some fellers on the railroad roasted in the woods and generously shared with me the other night."

" 'Possum's greasy," Bart agreed. "I don't know what we got today but you're mighty welcome."

The old man did sit down to the table with them and bowed his head when Bart asked the blessing. He passed his plate for some of the rice but refused beef and gravy. Before he put his fork into the fluffy, white mound of rice he straightened up and looked at Bart defiantly.

"I'm a atheist," he said.

"You are!" gasped Della.

"Well, sir, I don't know what your beliefs are but you're entitled to them," began Bart.

"I'll tell you," said the old man, fumbling for a small book he carried in the hip pocket of his overalls. "I got the word right here from Robert Ingersoll himself."

Bart looked at Jincey.

"I'd like mighty well to hear you discuss atheism," he said. "But I'm not sure it's suitable for my little girl. What you say, we wait till after dinner? I ain't in too big of a hurry to get back to the office."

The old man, who said he had been a doffer in a cotton mill in Georgy, until the mill shut down, sat long over his buttermilk and rice, talking about Robert Ingersoll and something he called the Darwin theory. Jincey listened to it from a spot under the window until he started talking about people coming from apes, and she thought that was plumb silly and wandered off to play. Della, too, wearied of the talk and cleared the table and washed the dishes.

Before the day was over Bart found a cot for the old man and set it up in the vacant quarters house next door. And Della had given him a jar of buttermilk and a washpan because he was a clean old fellow and would want to wash himself before he slept.

"What's he gon' live on?" Della asked. "You ain't got any doffers' jobs and I imagine he's got a family back in Georgy he ought to be sending money to."

"I know it," Bart said. "But I got an idea. He's not strong enough for much work. Watching might be something he could do fine. Uncle Bob is talking about getting somebody to watch around the place at night. So much joblessness, so many people on the prowl. He's thinking of putting a watchman down there to keep an eye on the mills and the commissary. Some people may think there's money in the office safe and try something."

"Foot to that," said Della. "He's there himself. Why don't he watch if he wants watching done?"

"He's gone a lot," Bart said.

Della laughed. "I know where. I hear he's taking Miss Reba into the picture shows and talking about gittin' her a car."

Bart turned away. The subject of the Stynchcombs, mother and daughter, still made him uncomfortable. Mrs. Stynchcomb and Della visited some, but he tried not to be around when Mrs. Stynchcomb was there.

Della got back to the watching job.

"If that's work you gon' pay for," she said, "why don't you give it to Fireman or Preacher or somebody already on the place?"

"We need somebody who can carry a pistol or a shotgun," Bart explained. "We never have let the Nigras have firearms."

"Better a friendly Nigra than a strange white man, I say," Della said.

But Bart liked old Mr. Hascall. He walked over to see him after supper a lot, taking him a plate of whatever food Della had left over, and they would sit on the steps of the little house and talk until dark came on and it was time for the old man to pick up his gun and flashlight and make his rounds of the sawmill and cross over the dam to check out the planer and the turpentine still. Sometimes Bart would walk with him and Della

344

couldn't settle down until he was back in the house and safe.

"Keep on!" she raged at him one night when he was especially late getting back. "You fool around with that old coot and some night he's gon' force you to open the safe and then shoot you."

"Ah, no," said Bart. "He's a nice old feller and not too strong. I help him make his rounds and get him to talking so he won't go to sleep on the commissary porch until after Uncle Bob has come in and gone to bed. No use letting him get himself fired for sleeping on duty before he's made a payday."

But the tramps that came after Mr. Hascall didn't get as warm a reception from Della and Bart. There were too many of them, young men and boys with pinched old faces and tired eyes; middle-aged men worrying about folks back in Georgia or over in Mississippi or Florida; sunburned seamen from the boats tied up at the docks in Mobile; dull, sick ones and smart, crafty ones; those who wanted work more than anything in the world and those who didn't care how they got it but wanted food.

Della never failed to give them something—cold biscuits and coffee, if that was all she had left, a plate of dried beans or a jar of milk, a baked sweet potato or a fried egg.

She worked hard with her chickens and cows and garden and made Jincey help her. Jincey sometimes wondered how she could stand to give so much away.

"I can't turn nobody away hungry," she said, sighing. "It's a sin, Jincey. The Lord don't bless them that has and don't share. We'd be hungry ourselves someday if we did that."

But sometimes she wondered how the Weary Willies unerringly found them, coming three miles from the railroad and bypassing the commissary and the boardinghouse to wind up at her back steps.

She asked old Mr. Hascall and he laughed.

"The Knights of the Open Road got their own signs," he said. "I didn't put a mark on your gate, like people will tell you. It's just there, a sign that a kind heart and generous hands dwell within."

Della couldn't help being pleased with that but not for long. She went out to the cowpen to milk earlier than usual one morning and found a strange old woman in ragged overalls and a railroad engineer's cap there before her. She had milked Alice into a gallon lard bucket and was stripping the teats for the cream.

"Lord God Almighty!" cried Della. "Jincey, come a-running and bring me the gun!"

"Is it a snake? You see a snake?" yelled Jincey, running toward her with Uncle Bart's big pistol, held by its barrel at arm's length because she was so afraid of it.

"I'll say a snake!" snorted Della. "The kind that milks cows!"

The woman stood barefoot in the cow lot, backed up against the fence, wanting to run but afraid Della meant to shoot her in the back.

"You're a pretty looking thing!" Della said scathingly. "Sneaking in here and stealing my milk! If you hungry why couldn't you come to the door like an honest person and ask me? I ain't too stingy to give to somebody that's hungry."

"A man maybe," flared the old woman accusingly. "But not a woman. Lots of people help menfolks and run a woman off the place with a gun. They don't like it that there's women have to hobo, too."

"Well, why do you?" asked Della, laying the pistol on the fence post. "Ain't you got a husband or some children to take care of you?"

"I ain't got nobody or nothing," said the old woman. "I ain't et in three days. Gardens ain't much good down thisaway, air they?"

Della glanced over her shoulder at her own garden and gasped. "Well, the Lor-rd! You been at my radishes?"

"They was my supper," said the woman.

Della looked at the dirty, bare feet and the dirty, wrinkled face. It was spring, but the early morning air was chilly and the woman had been coughing.

"Where'd you sleep?" she asked.

"Didn't," said the woman. "Set up all night in one of them vacant nigger shanties. Meant to sleep but the chinches come out of the cracks and went to work. They hungry, too."

Della laughed.

"Well, come on to the house," she said, "and eat some breakfast and rest a while. I got water in the kettle and you can wash up." She grinned at the woman, who was coming slowly toward the lot gate, "I can't give you no milk for your coffee, though."

They never learned the woman's name. Della emptied the kettle in the bathtub and cooled the boiling water down with water from the tap. She put the dirty overalls and shirt in the washpot to boil and brought out one of her own cotton housedresses and some underwear and was surprised to see that the body in her clothes was thinner than it appeared when it was covered with the loose men's clothes. The face, now clean from soap and water, was shriveled and old and the hair, released from the engineer's cap, was white. Della set a plate of grits and eggs and fried meat before the woman and opened a jar of fig preserves and put a pan of biscuits on the edge of the stove, within reach for her.

"Where you from?" she asked sociably once, but the woman, her mouth full, moved her head in the direction of the railroad, and went on chewing. Della meant to ask her name and where she was bound but when she was finished, the woman said off-handedly, "Be all right if I sleep a while before I go on?"

"Well, yes," said Della. "You got to wait till your clothes dry anyhow."

She looked around, trying to think which bed to offer, but the woman beat her to it.

"I ain't gon' sleep in one of your beds," she said. "Hit's warm on your gallery. I'll just bide there."

Della brought her a pillow and an old spread for cover and when she looked out again the woman was snoring loudly. She stirred and coughed occasionally. The late-morning sun beat down on her and Della started to take the old spread off her but she opened her eyes and glared at Della without recognition, pulled the cover closer and went back to sleep.

When Bart came home to dinner the woman slept on, and Della decided against trying to rouse her for more food.

"Who is she?" Bart asked.

Della shrugged. "Just some old traveling woman. She milked my cow and pulled up half my radishes but she didn't tell me nothing."

347

Bart ate and went back to work and Della, going back and forth to the garden, passed the woman two or three times.

"Pore thing," she said to Jincey. "She must be wore out, sleeping like that. But at least she's stopped coughing."

The saw beat for five o'clock and Della hurried to put on supper. The sun was getting low and she thought to check on the sleeping woman but she had the chickens to feed and the eggs to gather and she tiptoed around her without stopping.

Bart came up the path and Jincey ran to meet him.

"That lady," she said, "that traveling lady, is still asleep."

"Oh, surely not till now," Bart said. "Why, that would be eight hours or more."

Instead of going through the front of the house he walked around to the back gallery. The woman was wrapped up in the spread and very still. He reached out a hand to her forehead and said suddenly, "Jincey, go get Aunt Della."

"What is it?" said Della, coming out of the kitchen. "What's wrong?"

"Send Jincey for Ruth and come look," he said. "I think she's dead."

The death of the old traveling woman upset Della more than either Bart or Jincey could understand. Ruth and Matthew came from the quarters and they lifted the old body off the gallery and laid it on boards across the library table in the front room.

"What ailed her?" cried Della. "What made her die?"

Her own body trembled and shook and she couldn't seem to settle down anywhere.

Bart had looked the dead woman over carefully when Ruth undressed her for the ritual after-death bath, which she no longer needed.

"I don't know, sweetheart," he said gently, putting an arm around Della. "She was old and maybe she was hungry and suffering from exposure a long time. Maybe," he added after a moment, "she was just worn out."

"Lord have mercy," whispered Della, leaning against Bart's shoulder. "It's so awful, so awful. The little old thing was stealing milk and I threatened to shoot her!"

"Sugar, these days people be's shot for less than that," said Ruth, trying to comfort her. "You didn't shoot her. You fed her good vittles and give her some of your own clothes to wear and let her rest. Don't take on so, there wasn't nothing you could of done."

"There was something somebody should of done!" cried Della fiercely. "It's not right for an old woman to die like that. We don't even know her ... name!" And she began to sob.

Ruth straightened the thin, brittle little limbs and asked Bart for some coins to place on the eyes. She needed a clean sheet to fold around the little body, she said, and Della searched distractedly for one, taking first one and then another off the shelf and rejecting them because they were torn or stained or rough bleaching which wasn't white enough. Finally she pulled out one of Motherdear's fine old tablecloths, made of soft, gleaming Irish linen and heavy with embroidery.

Bart, who was helping Ruth, saw the cloth and said, "Sweetheart, isn't this cloth too good? Haven't you got something else?"

"No!" said Della shortly. "Let her have the tablecloth. She hasn't had anything else."

Bart shrugged and helped Ruth fold the body into the gentle linen. He and Ruth and Matthew sat up all night. Jincey tried to sit with them, first on the gallery and then in the dining room.

She didn't want to go in the parlor where the body lay, and she was scared of going to sleep. But Bart got her to bed by suggesting that she get in with Della and keep her company. Della had been in the hospital recently and was shaky and upset and Ruth and Bart had refused to let her sit up. She seemed glad to have Jincey crawl under the sheet beside her.

She had been crying, but now she was quiet and she reached for one of Jincey's hands and held it between her two.

"You know what, childee?" she whispered after a moment. "That might of been my mother! She might of come looking for me."

Mrs. Stynchcomb was standing by the roadside when Della drove by to take Jincey and the Bates children to school one rainy morning. She only took them in the car when it was a hard, pouring rain, holding that they were able to walk if the weather was dry, no matter how hot or cold. Only rain, the source of wet feet, made anybody sick, Della contended.

This morning she had the side curtains up on the car and had bundled herself up in Bart's slicker and rainhat. She was struggling with the hand windshield wiper when they came up even with the boardinghouse and she saw somebody by the roadside. She stepped on the brake.

Mrs. Stynchcomb, wet as a draggle-tailed dominecker hen, was limply flapping both her arms.

"Look at her," Della whispered to Jincey. "Looks like a dirty, wringing-wet old dishrag." To Mrs. Stynchcomb she said, "Good morning, you want a ride?"

"Oh, Mrs. McPherson," wailed the little housekeeper. "I want help! Cap'n Barton has decided to dispense with my services!"

"You mean he fired you?" said Della sharply. "Well, git in the car and let's talk about it."

Mrs. Stynchcomb climbed in the back, dripping rain all over the seat and spraying Della and Jincey as she shook drops off her hat and coat. She was wet in the face but from tears.

Della started the car moving and said over her shoulder, "Tell me. When did it happen? And why, for the Lord's sake, is the old buzzard letting you run around in the rain?"

"This morning, this morning when I didn't have his breakfast ready!" wailed Mrs. Stynchcomb. "I had one of my sick headaches and when he come for breakfast and I hadn't even started a fire in the stove, he was very angry."

Della bit her bottom lip and darted a quick, bright look at Jincey.

"Didn't like having no breakfast, huh?"

"He was unreasonable about it!" cried Mrs. Stynchcomb. "He named over all the other times it's happened and told me to pack up my things and he'd take me to the depot in Bayou Bien or to Mobile, whichever I wanted. And Mrs. McPherson, I haven't got any place to go!"

"Didn't he pay you off?"

"He flung, really flung, this twenty-dollar bill down on the table. It's a month's pay, but where will I go to? My brother in Phenix City, where I stayed a while before, him and his wife don't want me there. I couldn't pay railroad fare and rent a place and buy groceries for that. Besides, Mrs. McPherson, I am *not a well woman!*"

The last came out on a high, keening note and Della took one hand from the wheel and leaned back and patted her.

"I know you're not," she said. "I know you're not. What about Reba? Where is she?"

"That's something else," said Mrs. Stynchcomb. "He said he would relieve me of the care of Reba. Do me that favor. In fact, he said if I wanted him to he would adopt Reba and raise her as his daughter and send her to school."

"Ha!" said Della. "I bet he would!"

She pulled up before the path to the Bates's house and opened the back door.

"You come sit up here, Mrs. Stynchcomb, and let the Bates young'uns git in back there."

Instead of getting out through the open door, Mrs. Stynchcomb bunched her bedraggled clothes around her and, like a banty chicken going to roost, she jumped to the back of the front seat, squatted there a second, jumped again and landed on the cushion.

Della's eyes widened and she threw Jincey a look dark with suppressed laughter.

"Well, if that don't be a hog a-flying!" she said under her breath.

Settled on the seat, Mrs. Stynchcomb smoothed her wet clothes around her and started crying again.

"I don't know what to do-o! I don't want to stand in my daughter's way. But what will become of me?"

"Well, don't carry on," said Della. "I'll help you think of something."

Della had the bannisterless bridge ahead of her to worry about and Mrs. Stynchcomb confined herself to sniffling. When they got to the bridge, Della made them all get out and walk and when they got back in the car she said to Mrs. Stynchcomb, "You didn't bring your suitcase, did you?"

"No," said the little woman. "I packed it and set it on the porch but it's so heavy and I couldn't decide where I was going . . ."

"Raining, too," said Della. "But never mind. We'll pick it up as soon as we think what to do."

When Jincey got home from school that afternoon she saw what Della had found to do. She had moved Mrs. Stynchcomb into their house!

The peeling and cracking suitcase was in Motherdear's old room and the little housekeeper, her face powdered and rouged, her thin hair neatly combed, sat and rocked by the dining-room heater.

Uncle Bart was as surprised as Jincey when he came home and found Mrs. Stynchcomb there. He spoke to her politely and passed on to the kitchen where Della busied around the stove.

"What's that?" he said, inclining his head toward the dining room. "What's she doing here?"

"What you mean 'what's that?' " said Della, offering him her cheek to kiss. "That's one of your almighty Uncle Bob's castoff's. He's thrown her out and she's got no place to go."

"Not thrown her out," said Bart, taking off his wet coat and hat and preparing to hang them on the back gallery. "He discharged her, that's all. And he's got a right." He lowered his voice to a whisper. "She's not much of a worker."

"Sand in the sheets, huh?" said Della pertly. "Well, there's something funny about it. Barton keeping the girl and throwing the old lady out."

She noticed Jincey sitting at the kitchen table with a school book she wasn't reading in front of her. "Jincey, go somewhere else. You underfoot here."

Mrs. Stynchcomb stayed—and stayed.

Reba moved into Bart's old room upstairs over the commissary and a new housekeeper, a jolly, fat, loud-voiced woman, who insisted that everybody call her Buster, took over the boarding-house. She wasn't afraid of Cap'n Barton, laughing at him when he turned aggravated with her and scolding him when he pouted. She had boundless energy, sang loudly and impartially called out greetings to anything that moved along the road in front of the house—people or mules or cows or even the angry old gander and two geese Cap'n Barton brought out from town and released by the pond.

It was Buster who told Mrs. Stynchcomb about the man advertising in a Lonely Hearts Club paper for a wife.

She came singing up the road one day after dinner, followed by the geese and a white feist dog she had found abandoned over on the highway at the Front. Her specialty was yodeling and she knew all the Jimmy Rogers songs.

> *"Rather drink muddy water,*
> *Sleep in a holler log!"* she sang.

> *"Than to stay at Barton's Mill*
> *And be treated like a dirty daw-gh!"*

And then her voice climbed into the gymnastics of a yodel.

Mrs. Stynchcomb, who spent most of her days rocking by the front window and crocheting, looked up from what Jincey thought must be the millionth yard of pillowcase edging she had made and whispered, "She's a very coarse woman."

Della nodded. "Common as pig tracks. I like her."

"Y'all geese wait out here," Buster was saying from the gate. "I got bidness in the house—and they don't want your green turds in there!"

Mrs. Stynchcomb winced, but Della laughed and went to greet Buster.

Buster was barefooted and her legs were crisscrossed with briar scratches from her trips around the pasture and to fishing holes in the creek. But she wore a fresh starched and ironed dress and had tied over her big stomach a flour-sack apron which had been boiled till it was snowy white and starched to crackling crispness.

"Allie-Stink!" she called out, waving the newspaper. "I got something you gotta see!"

Mrs. Stynchcomb threw Della a pained look but said politely, "What is it, Buster?"

"Rich old man hossing to make you his bride!"

Mrs. Stynchcomb stopped crocheting and raised her head like a chicken drinking water.

"Aw, go on!" said Della. "There ain't no such animal as a rich man looking. The women find them and snap them up first."

"I don't know about that, Mrs. McPherson," Mrs. Stynchcomb said primly. "What have you got there, Buster?"

Buster read aloud: " 'Widower, seventy, owns good farm worked by tenants. Big lonesome house. Like to meet genteel lady. Object matrimony.' "

Mrs. Stynchcomb dropped her crochet hook and didn't bother to pick it up. "Genteel lady, he said."

"And tenants to do the work," said Della. "That sounds good to me."

"Oh, I don't know," said Mrs. Stynchcomb, suddenly backing off. "I wouldn't know how to answer such a thing as that. I guess I'm too timid for my own good."

"Aw, shit," said Buster cheerfully. "We'll answer it for you. Jincey, run git your mama's pen and ink and paper."

"Aunt," said Della.

"Aw, don't tell me!" said Buster. "You and that young'un alike as two peas! Who you trying to kid?"

"My dead sister's child," said Della.

"Sez you," said Buster.

Mrs. Stynchcomb looked from Della to Jincey, who was coming into the room with paper and pen and ink. She said nothing but she looked thoughtful.

They dispatched the letter to "Widower, seventy, good farm" and within a week Mrs. Stynchcomb had a postcard answer. His name was Samuel Gilstrap and he was going to meet the ladies who had answered his ad at the courthouse in Purvis, Mississippi, the following Friday, weeding them down to one and he would marry her right then and there.

"My!" said Mrs. Stynchcomb breathlessly. "He's a fast mover, ain't he?"

"Man after my own heart!" said Buster. "Now, Allie-Stink, git packed. Me and Della gon' put you on that down train."

"Oh, I don't know . . . I don't know!" wailed Mrs. Stynchcomb, wringing her hands. "I've still got that twenty dollars, but suppose he don't like me. It won't be enough to come home on."

Della raised her eyebrows at Jincey over that word "home."

"I've got five dollars you can have," she said.

"No, you don't!" said Buster. "You got a young'un to see to and there ain't no call for you to fling yore money around like that. Let Cap'n Barton pay."

"Cap'n Barton!" said Della and Mrs. Stynchcomb together.

"Why not?" said Buster. "He's got your girl, ain't he?"

"He says he's doing me a favor to look after her and send her to school," said Mrs. Stynchcomb meekly. "Reba's a big eater and growing so she is almost bursting out of her clothes. That's more expense."

"You right about her busting out of her clothes, especially here," laughed Buster, cupping her hands around her own ample breasts. "But don't tell me about him taking her to raise like his daughter. I'm the one that changes the sheets."

"Jincey, go see about the rice," Della said, frowning at Buster.

When Buster left, Mrs. Stynchcomb walked down the road with her and when she came back she had fifty dollars in U.S. money and word from Cap'n Barton that he would take her to Mobile and put her on the train for Purvis, Mississippi, that very day.

The next week he bought Reba a Model A Ford coupe with a rumble seat to drive to high school in Mobile.

Bart was relieved and happy to have Mrs. Stynchcomb out of the house. If he knew that Cap'n Barton had paid her to go, he never mentioned it.

Once Jincey heard him ask Della why she had decided to invite the fired housekeeper to stay with them. Della had sighed and turned away and said she didn't know, she reckoned she felt sorry for her.

Later Uncle Bart left the house to walk down to the commissary with Mr. Hascall and Della wandered over the yard in the dusk, pulling a weed or two and tucking up a runner from the Dorothy Perkins rose, which was coming into bloom. But Jincey, watching from the window, could tell that she wasn't putting her mind on what she was doing. The sun had set up at the head of the pond, but Della turned her back on the color and leaned against the fence and stared back at the house. Frogs were tuning up down by the branch and a whippoorwill sounded from the grove.

Jincey was supposed to be drying the supper dishes but something about the way Della looked, the droop of her head, the way she leaned against the fence, caused her to drop the dish towel and walk down the path to the gate.

"Aunt Della?" she said anxiously.

Della wiped the back of her hand across her eyes and cleared her throat and said in a cheerful voice, "What? childee. What you want?"

"Nothing," said Jincey, going closer and leaning against her.

Della put an arm around her shoulders and held her for a time, staring out across the field.

"Pore thing," she said. "Pore old thing."

"Who?" asked Jincey. "Not me. I ain't pore."

"I was thinking about that old traveling woman," Della said. "Going here and yonder, no place to lay her head."

"Couldn't you tell if she was your own mama?" Jincey asked. "Don't you know how your own mama looks?"

Della sighed. "I'd a thought I would. But who knows what time and hard living did to her? Or to me?"

The whippoorwill called his lonely questing call and was silent. There was a little break in the song of the frogs and then they tuned up again.

"Aunt Della," Jincey said, "Mrs. Stynchcomb, she wasn't kin to us, was she?"

"Allie-Stink?" said Della, laughing. "I hope not. Did you think I brought her here because she was kinfolks?"

"I didn't know what to think," Jincey said.

"Me, either," admitted Della, half to herself. She turned and started to the house. "I reckon that old traveling woman's dying had something to do with it. I didn't want old Stink but it's a sorry stay-place where they'll turn even a plumb fool out in the rain."

A house in the quarters burned down in the night. Bart smelled smoke and jumped in the car and rushed up there. But it was a one-room batch shack, intended for single men, and it had fallen in by the time he got there. He and some of the men cut pine tops and beat out the fire so it wouldn't spread to the woods and he went home and went back to bed.

The next morning Della saw Cap'n Barton's Reo pass going toward the quarters so fast it lurched from side to side, kicking up the sandy ruts.

"Wonder what meanness Old Scratch is up to now?" Della said to Jincey.

They found out when Ruth came by to help with the washing.

"Whooee, you should'a seen the Cap'n!" she cried. "Come roarin' up there lak a hurricane right out of the Gulf. Jump out of his car and yell, 'You people that's livin' here on my place, gether 'round.'

"Ain't many of 'em in any hurry to gether, so he run from house to house with a slab in his han' and beat on the gallery and yell, 'Come out! Come out! I wants to talk to you!'

"Me and some the other ladies, we steps out the door and say, 'Good mornin', Cap'n,' polite as preachin'. Fireman, he still in the bed, but he come slew-footing out and Clewis and Tad and Percy and Flathead and Jerusha and most of the chill'un. Well, sir, you should'a heahed the piece the Cap'n spoke. All 'bout how it was *his* place we was livin' on and he wanted evvabody that wasn't workin' for him to hit the road!"

"Oh, poor Flathead and Jerusha," said Della. "I reckon they got it."

"Yes'm," said Ruth. "Mist' Flathead and Jerusha so 'shamed for the Cap'n to ketch 'em there after he already tole 'em to git, they didn't say nothin'. They call up they mule and be loadin' the wagon when I lef' to come here."

"Where will they go?" Della asked.

"No tellin'," said Ruth. "Ain't no tellin'."

A week later Della was working in the garden tying up bean runners and had reached the back corner when she heard somebody calling her name. She straightened up and shaded her eyes and looked toward the woods. Something moved back of a swamp myrtle. She walked closer to the fence and called, "Who is it? Who's there?"

A black woman poked her head around the clump of myrtle and said softly, "Me, Miss Della. Jerusha."

"Oh, Jerusha!" said Della, relieved. "What you doing back there? Come on where I can see you."

"Do it be safe?" the woman asked. "Can't let nobody see me and go tell the Cap'n."

"Nobody's gon' tell nothing, Jerusha," said Della. "But if you worried, I'll come over there." She dropped the roll of ragged string she was using to tie the beans into the fence corner, lifted the two strands of barbed wire and ducked under. Jerusha had been sitting back of the myrtle bush for some time, waiting for Della to work her way to that end of the garden, and she had a spot in the weeds worn and smoothed down. Della dropped down beside her.

"Where'd you come from, Jerusha? Where you all living?"

"That long bridge," she said. "Cross little Rainey. We's camping out under it."

"Under a bridge!" cried Della. "Oh, Jerusha, that ain't no place to stay."

"No'm," the Negro woman said. "But it be's better'n no roof at all. Some white folks come and tried to take it away from us but John (you calls him Flathead) act like we Barton hands and had permission to stay there. So they gone now. Stole our mule and wagon and gone."

"Aw, they couldn't take your mule and wagon!" cried Della. "Why didn't you stop them?"

"They be's white," said Jerusha simply: "John say the old mule dying from starvation anyhow."

"Lord have mercy," said Della. "Things have come to some pass when white folks steal colored folks' mules and are scuffling over staying under a bridge!"

"Yes'm, that is the truth," agreed Jerusha. "We heahed they went down to Gunnison and got under it. That a concrete bridge, but they's a heap of water to worry about. Rainey ain't nothing but a little narrow creek."

"Is it snakey?" asked Della, suddenly remembering to look at the lush weeds and stand of ferns around them.

"Yes'm," said Jerusha. "John killed several cottonmouths. We don' sleep down there at night, unless it be raining. They's a sandy bank where it's clearer, not so snakey. But daytimes, when peoples can see us, John say better we stay under the bridge."

"Oh, Jerusha," said Della, standing up and brushing the sand and twigs off her skirt, "I didn't think. You must be hungry. Come on to the house and let me git you something."

"Miss Della, I hate to axe you," said Jerusha, "but if you got rations to spare, I'd druther take 'em to John and Easter. John be's mighty hongry and Easter, she's got the running-off's so bad I know it's from jus' eating nothing but what fish we can ketch and green mayhaws and huckleberries."

Della sighed. "Lord, Lord, there ought to be a better way!"

Jerusha followed her through the garden, crouching to make herself smaller, and waited on the back steps while Della went through the kitchen gathering meal and flour, jars of vegetables and what cooked food she had left from dinner. When she had it packed in a basket she remembered the sick child, Easter, and put in her bottle of peregoric.

"Jerusha, you can't carry all this stuff," she said. "I'm gon' take the car and drive you back there."

"No'm," said Jerusha. "No'm. Cap'n Barton or somebody see me. John ... he didn't want me to come. He didn't want us axing. After the way Cap'n Barton talk, he so *shamed*. He a good man, Miss Della, and ain't no call for him to be so shamed. He work hard all his life and now he starve hisself for us. But Easter sick. I had to come."

Della stood in the middle of the kitchen, trying to decide what to do.

"All right," she said at last. "You take what you can carry and go on back through the woods. As soon as school's out I'll drive over there to git Jincey and I'll leave off the rest of the stuff by the bridge."

"Where? Miss Della. Where you put it so nobody see it?"

Della thought of the trees and bushes around the bridge and she remembered an old and twisted clump of laurel at the edge of the swamp. When he was a little boy, Bart told her, he used to drive the roadcart to Mobile and he always feared that there'd be a bear back of that laurel bush when he came home at dusk. Now he laughed about it, but Jincey had taken to looking carefully at the laurel when they drove by.

"Look back of the mountain laurel on the right side of the bridge," Della said. "I'll hide everything there."

Jerusha took the cooked food and the paregoric and a jar of milk and vanished through the garden. Della, thinking of the sick child, didn't go back to the garden but prowled about the house gathering things to take to her. An old piece of oilcloth would protect her from the damp ground and serve to cover her if it rained. Remembering that Easter was the same size as Jincey, she collected underclothes and a sweater and was folding a pair of pajamas to take when she stopped herself. A child sleeping under a bridge didn't need pajamas. A child had no business sleeping under a bridge! She thought of the baby, Woodrow, who had the same symptoms of diarrhea before he died—of starvation, she knew—and she made up her mind to stop at the commissary and appeal to Bart or, if necessary, to his Uncle Bob, to let the family move back to the quarters.

The office and commissary were quiet and Bart was probably up at the head of the pond and Cap'n Bart was probably in town. Della found the doors shut, and she turned away with some sense of relief. It would have been hard to ask Cap'n Barton for anything.

Except for the blue-tailed skink skittering over the splintery old boards and the light whisper of the coffee-colored creek flowing over white sand, all was quiet at the bridge. Della stopped the car before she reached it and walked to the edge of the bridge calling softly, "Flathead, Jerusha, Easter!" There was no answer.

She knelt down on the bridge and hung her head over the side and peered under it. There was no sign of anybody, only flattened weeds, the worn grass, to show where they had been. She hid her basket back of the laurel bush and got in the car and drove on to Bayou Bien to get Jincey and the Bates children.

That night she meant to talk to Bart about them. She meant to tell him that she wanted to bring Easter to their house and care for her until she was well. But Bart was unusually quiet when he came in from the commissary.

Jincey and Welcome ran to meet him, expecting him to call out to them and stop and scratch Welcome's ears and let Jincey ride the toes of his big work shoes up the hill. Instead, he greeted them quietly and walked slowly on to the house like he was sick.

The day had been hot and Della had said they would have cold leftovers for supper. But now there were no leftovers so she was in the kitchen cooking young mustard greens and chopped green onions in fried meat grease. They were not much more than wilted when she took them out and dropped spoonfuls of meal batter into the hot skillet to make thin, lace-edged corn cakes to eat with the greens.

Bart washed in the bathroom and came to the table with his face and hair still damp. He sat down heavily and faced his plate of young greens and cornbread without interest.

"What's the matter?" asked Della. "Don't you like mustard? This is the first of the year and so tender. Really too tender to pick yet, but I felt like we needed something green."

"Della," Bart said suddenly, pushing back from the table, "I don't want to worry you but it has come to us now."

"What's come?"

"The Depression. Uncle Bob told me today. We rode over to the river in his car and he told me. Things have got so bad, he's cutting my salary in half."

"In half!" cried Della. "Oh, Honey, he can't do that!"

"It's better than cutting me off entirely," Bart said. "There's really not much for me to do with everything shut down. No work to boss, mighty little bookkeeping to do. He's still got lawyers and real estate men looking after property in town, but they're not charging him the full price now. They shouldn't, so many of his houses are vacant and those that are rented, the rent is slow to come in."

Jincey ate steadily through her plate of greens without tasting them. She thought if she stopped chewing she might cry, more from Uncle Bart's worry than because of the money.

Della's face was expressionless. But in a minute she jumped up and went and stood behind Bart's chair and laid her cheek against his hair.

"Don't you worry, hon, don't you worry a minute," she said. "We'll think of something."

"I've thought of everything," Bart said slowly. "At least, I've tried to. I've thought of looking for another job but mills that are still running have all the help they need. I been here so long, I reckon, I wouldn't know where to begin."

"Besides," he said, looking at the new calcimined green walls of the dining room as if he hadn't seen them before, "we got this house—a place to live rent free."

"That's right," said Della. "Lights and water free, and when winter comes, all the wood we need to burn for heat. And our garden, Bart, we gon' have plenty of good vegetables. Milk is scant right now but when Alice comes in fresh we'll have our milk and butter. And this year I want to git two, maybe three hogs. Bart, we gon' be just fine!"

Bart wasn't convinced but he reached for her hand and held it a minute and then started to eat his supper. Jincey had already stopped worrying. They weren't going anywhere and what they had was plenty, plenty.

Bart's salary, even cut in half, was a lot of money—one hundred dollars a month—but it didn't seem to go far. Della bought another Jersey calf at the dairy for five dollars and three little pigs for fifty cents a piece from a Yankee farmer over at the Front, who had lost his land and was moving back up north. She ordered off for 100 Rhode Island Red biddies for five dollars and they came in the mail, cheeping loudly and hungrily.

"I got to have starting mash for them," she told Bart. "I don't care if it is high. When they git to growing and laying, you'll see they're a bargain."

"What, with eggs fifteen cents a dozen?" asked Bart, grinning. But he ordered mash brought out from town for the baby chicks, cracked corn for the old flock and shorts and cottonseed hulls for the cows.

It was all so expensive Della worried about storing it in the side room next to the cowshed and finally brought the chicken feed into the house.

"You not worrying about anybody stealing it, are you?" Bart asked. "You the only person on the place with chicken fever."

"That mash tastes pretty good," Della said. "As many hungry people as passes here, somebody might smell it and help themselves."

Jincey sifted a little into her hand and stuck her tongue to it and decided it did taste good. Not as good as bran they fed the cows, but better than no food at all.

Della continued to leave boxes and bags off behind the laurel bush by the bridge and when she checked back they were always gone but they didn't see Jerusha or Flathead again. Bart gave up smoking Chesterfield cigarettes and took to rolling his own from Bull Durham tobacco, which came in a little drawstring cloth bag and had a small book of thin papers with it. He was clumsy at it. His cigarettes were always misshapen and dark-stained and sometimes fell apart before he had more than started smoking them. Finally he gave it up and stopped smoking altogether.

"I hate that," Della worried. "You don't have many pleasures. Cigarettes make you cough a lot but you do enjoy your smoking."

"I figured it up," Bart said. "Fifteen cents a day is a good sum of money. We got Jincey's schoolbooks to think about buying.

They could run as high as five or ten dollars, and she'll be needing shoes and a coat, won't she?"

Della nodded. "But you git paid enough for that. A hundred dollars a month is a good bit of money."

Bart had been reading the paper and now he folded it and put it down carefully.

"Sweetheart," he said. "It's not a hundred any more. I took another cut—down to seventy-five."

Della shrugged. "Well, that's still more than most gits."

"You forget the twenty dollars a month I been sending the children of that colored woman I killed in the accident."

"Still?" said Della. "Surely, you can quit that now. They must be most grown."

"If they are, they need it worse than ever, the way things are. And I been sending Ma and Mary twenty-five a month."

"Why?" demanded Della. "I thought Motherdear had a bank account! And Mary and Edward, they used to living so high, how can they be calling on you now?"

"Ma's got a little money—a few hundred dollars," Bart said patiently. "But she's scared, Della, scared to death. She thinks if she gets sick we'll send her back to Tuscaloosa, unless she's got money to take care of herself. I tell her better, but she worries—about that and about dying and not having enough to pay for her funeral. She has let them turn off the lights in her house and she's using a kerosene lamp. Mary, too."

He sighed.

"Mary and Edward did live high—too high. But they down to their uppers now. I believe they been going hungry. I saw Edward down by the Van Antwerp building the last time I was in town—all dressed up to job hunt. But he looked thin and white and near about sick."

"Pride goeth before a fall," murmured Della, standing up to go see if her biddies were warm enough. "Well, you do what you have to. We'll manage."

They did manage. They even had luxuries. Alice came in fresh and her milk was so rich and creamy Della made ice cream almost every Sunday, especially if the preacher, Brother Doby Webster, was coming home with them for dinner. She slowly cooked the custard, heavy with cream and eggs, over the wood-stove. (The electric plate was too fast and fractious for this.) And she and Jincey took turns turning the crank to freeze it on the backsteps, leaving it packed in ice and covered with a croker sack to ripen while they were at church.

She divided the clabber which set like snow-jelly in the big yellow bowls in the pantry, churning half of it for butter and buttermilk and turning the other half into a clean salt sack to hang over a bowl to drip on the back porch and make cream cheese.

Mr. Hascall still came by every day for a quart of buttermilk, and at first when he offered to pay Della a dime for it, she turned it down. But after a time he started leaving the money on the table on the back porch and she took it and hid it under a pin tray on her dresser.

One day when the old man stopped by Della had peas and butter beans cooking and a pone of crackling cornbread brown-ing in the skillet.

"Sit down, Mr. Hascall," she invited, "and let me fix you a plate."

He sniffed the air wistfully. "I don't know, ma'am, if I should try it. My stomach gives me trouble. Them's fresh peas and butter beans, ain't they?"

"Fresh out of the garden this morning," said Della proudly.

"I bet you got okra with them?" he said tentatively, peering toward the kitchen.

Della laughed. "Me and you didn't come from Georgy for nothing! 'Course I got okra. Tender little pods I'm steaming on top of the peas. And rice, too. Sit down, Mr. Hascall."

The old man took a chair by the kitchen door. Della got a big plate and served up substantial helpings of the vegetables and cornbread. "How about a sliced tomato?"

"No, much obliged," said the old man regretfully. "The acid don't seem to agree with me."

"How's night-watching going?" Della asked sociably, standing in the door as Mr. Hascall began.

"Ain't nothing much to watch except Miss Reba driving in and out," he said.

"Not at night!" said Della. "She gits in from school early. What's she doing traveling around after dark?"

"I don't know. Cap'n Barton goes to bed and she goes some'ers. Don't say I mentioned it. But she's right young to be on the road like that."

"Does Buster know?" Della asked.

Mr. Hascall laughed. "That Miss Buster, she knows everything."

"Then she'll tell Cap'n Barton," said Della, relieved. "She knows and tells everything."

Buster, showing more diplomacy than Della expected of her, mentioned Reba's travels to the girl herself first.

She told Della about it one afternoon while they were sitting by the millpond watching Jincey swimming. Jincey heard part of it between ducking herself and trying to learn to float on her back.

"What'd she say?" asked Della.

"Said she's got a feller. Some boy over at the Front. They meet over there to spark ever' night or two."

"Well, Buster, did you tell Cap'n Barton?"

Buster giggled.

"Ain't my business to tell him nothing. The girl's young. Got a right to have a beau her age. Let her run out on the old rooster, I say."

"But to meet out at night like that, it's dangerous," said Della. "He ought to let her have company here—maybe over at the house where you can chaperone them."

"You ain't talking to me," said Buster cheerfully, lifting her skirt and swishing her feet around in the water. "I ain't paid enough to chaperone that one!"

Della mentioned Reba's roaming to Bart one night at the supper table and he looked troubled.

"You gon' say anything about it?" Della prodded him.

He sighed. "I don't know. I don't know what to do. She's mighty young and Uncle Bob sure thinks a heap of her."

Della forgot all about Reba when their car broke down and they couldn't go anywhere.

"It's the crankshaft now but it's due for a general overhaul anyhow," Bart said. "I'll get Percy and we'll get started on it in a day or two."

"How long will it take, Uncle Bart?" asked Jincey, looking at greasy parts of the Ford spread out under a tree.

"Week or two," he said, whistling cheerfully. "I don't know what all's wrong with it but Percy will. He's a good mechanic. He's gone to haul a load of lumber to the dock in Mobile. First we've had a order for in some time. It might be we need a part or two and will have to wait for first passing."

"Lord God," muttered Della when Jincey told her. "No church or Sunday school, no going to the post office and seeing people, no Mobile, no coming or going. The Lord owed me a debt and paid me off in loneliness."

Jincey wasn't lonely and she looked at Della thoughtfully. How could she be lonely when there was so much going on?

But Della finished her work early and wandered restlessly around the yard. Jincey was trying to teach a bored and sleepy Welcome to sit up and beg for his food the way Buster had taught her white feist to do but she couldn't settle down to it as long as Della was walking about with the down-yonders.

"How come you say it's lonesome?" she asked.

"Listen," said Della. "What do you hear? Nothing! Who do you see? Nobody! When five o'clock comes you'll hear somebody wham out the time on that old piece of saw and after that . . . nothing! It was this way on East Bay, after you and Woodrow was born. All I could see was sand and water. All I could hear was that lonesome wind! I vow I thought I'd go insane! The devil owed me a debt and paid me off in nothingness!"

Jincey threw Welcome the last piece of bread and hitched her knees up and sat on the step hugging them and listening miserably to the quiet.

They had a postal card from Mrs. Stynchcomb saying she was not the one the Purvis, Mississippi, widower had picked but she had found work in Picayune, Mississippi, staying with a well-to-do widow woman who had both her legs off at the knees.

"You ever see Reba," the letter said, "Tell her howdy from her dear mother."

Della thought about answering it but there was no street address and Bart said Picayune was probably too big a town for Mrs. Stynchcomb to be known to the post office.

Jincey got a letter from Howie, forwarded by Aunt Ina, and he said he was fine and would like mighty well to see her.

"Sorry thing," said Della, lifting the stove lid and putting the letter in the fire. "He could have enclosed a dime or two for postage, looks like. But better write him something before he comes dead-licing up the road. Write it now and I'll send it back to Ina to mail there."

All Jincey could think of was, "Dear Daddy, I am fine and wish you was the same." Della laughed at it but said it would do, to just sign it and put it in a stamped envelope and she would enclose it in her letter to Aunt Ina.

"No use wasting pencil lead on old Sorry Sorelegs," she said.

SUMMER WAS ending. The garden had, as Della said, "done its do." She had canned everything she could get her hands on. She had thought of canning fish and chicken but gave it up when Ruth pointed out that they were to be had fresh from the creek and the yard all winter. She had shelves of jarred vegetables and blackberries and huckleberries and figs, and even a few jars of strawberries from the row in the garden. Her prize, to save for company or Christmas, was the red-gold mayhaw jelly, hard won from the tough and tart little fruits which grew at the edge of the pond.

Jincey was going to pick scuppernongs again and Della walked over to the Bateses with her to see if Virgie and Lula and Zack were ready to start with her.

"No'm," said Miss Eva. "Pa says he don't want the young'uns working theirselves so hard this year."

Della gulped and looked at Jincey. "You don't need the money?"

"No'm, we gittin' along right good now," said Miss Eva, smiling dreamily at something in the house beyond her open front door.

Della turned to see what she was looking at. There on the old iron bedspread, pulled smooth over the thin mattress and touching the scrubbed and splintery floor all around, was a rayon-taffeta bedspread, as pink and puffy as a split lip.

"Why, Miss Eva, you got something brand new!" cried Della. "Can I look at it? It's sure nice, nice as can be."

"Yes'm," said Miss Eva proudly. "My sister, Lena Mae, the one that married the fireman in Prichard, she give it to me. She's a-hep'ing us a right smart now. We thinking about lettin' Lula go yonder and stay with her."

"Well, I sure am glad you're doing so well," Della said. "Maybe your sister will send Lula to high school?"

"No'm," Miss Eva shook her head and smiled proudly. "We don't aim that high. A job'll be good and she could git on at the cotton mill."

"Where's Mr. Bates today?" Della asked as she stood up to go.

"He had some bidness in the woods," said Miss Eva evasively. "I reckon he's gathering light'ard knots for the cook fire. Him and Zack."

The visit had been a disappointment to Jincey. Lula and Virgie hadn't come up with a single game to play but had acted like they were glued to the edge of the front gallery, listening to their mama's talk and admiring the new bedspread. She was glad enough to leave when Della said she was ready.

She picked scuppernongs for a while by herself, but it wasn't any fun and she was reluctant to go back to the arbor until Della and Ruth decided to pick with her.

"We can use the money," said Della, "even if the rich Bateses don't need it."

"Sho' can," said Ruth. "Reckon you know why Mist' Old Pa so rich?"

"I thought it was help from her sister in Prichard," said Della.

"Yes'm, she heping 'em some," said Ruth, laughing. "Tell me she selling the shinny Mist' Old Pa make in Cap'n Barton's woods."

"You don't mean it!" cried Della, teetering on the box she was standing on and pushing her head through the scuppernong vines to stare at Ruth. "Why, that's against the law! They'll be hauling Old Pa off to jail . . . if Cap'n Barton don't run 'em all off the place first."

"Yes'm, sho' will," said Ruth, popping a brown-skinned grape into her mouth and showing her white teeth.

"Aw, you don't know," Della said, after a minute. "How you know?"

Ruth giggled and stepped off her box to tiptoe across the ground, taking big, exaggerated steps and rolling her head from side to side.

"This Mist' Old Pa. Matthew seen him going to his shinny still. Matthew been riding the woods looking for fire like Mist' Bart tell him and he found it, all right! Fire under a big old pot of mash. He hid and watched and heah come Mist' Big Pa tippy-toeing along, peeping into the bushes."

Della couldn't resist Ruth's imitations. She sat down on the wooden box and doubled up with laughter. When she could speak she said, "Did Matthew say anything to him?"

"Nunh—uh! Ain't gon' mess with no white man's bidness! He ain't even told Mist' Bart!"

Della saw Jincey listening.

"Look here, Jincey," she said, "I don't want you to say one word about this! It could git everybody in a heap of trouble. Why, Miss Eva and them young'uns could lose their stay-place."

"Yes'm," said Jincey, eating a grape. "I ain't."

To have Mr. Bates go to jail would be bad—almost as bad as her old fear that Della would be locked up. But to have Miss Eva and Virgie and Lula lose the pink rayon bedspread was too awful to think about.

Dog days came and with them the long rainy season. Uncle Bart and Percy hadn't been able to get the car running and Jincey and Virgie and Zack had to walk to school in the rain. Lula had gone to Prichard to stay with her aunt, and Jincey missed her. She had been the one to think up the good games. She knew the best persimmon trees and how to put violet stems together so they made a bouquet as pretty as if it grew like that in the woods.

Miss Upton had gotten married and the school board wasn't hiring married teachers any more but it wasn't easy to get one to come to Bayou Bien. So, married or not, Mrs. White took the job temporarily. Jincey remembered what she had done to the Boudreaux girls and she didn't like her much but, pushed by

Della, who wanted Mrs. White to think her smart, she studied hard.

Aunt Titter wrote that Aunt Ruby Pearl had fallen down the back steps and broken her hip and Della showed Bart the letter at supper.

"A broken hip," said Uncle Bart. "Sweetheart, I'm sorry. How old is she?"

"Eighty, I reckon," Della said. "She's the oldest of my grandmother's twelve children."

"You want to go?" Bart asked.

"Well, I reckon they could use me. Titter's letter says she's wore out with nursing and the others, Aunt Sweetie and Aunt Jessie, are old themselves. But how would I go? I mean, no car, no money. Jincey's in school and I wouldn't want to take her out."

"You go ahead and plan to take the train," Bart said. "I'll get Ma out here to look after Jincey and me. Plan to go tomorrow if you want to. I can telephone in a telegram to Mobile if you want to send it to your cousin to let her know you're coming."

"Oh, it seems like too much!" sighed Della. "I don't know if we can do it. How would I get to the train in Mobile?"

"I'm gon' get Percy and see about that now," said Bart, going to the back gallery for his slicker.

Bart and Percy had pulled the car under a shed down back of the commissary and they worked on it all night. The next morning when the six o'clock saw was beating, Bart walked up the hill, grease on his face and in his hair, his blue eyes tired but alight with pride.

"We did it," he said. "She runs. Percy is gassing and oiling her up now and I'm gon' clean up and take you to Mobile."

When Jincey came home from school, Motherdear was there and Della was gone.

"Hey-o, old girl!" cried Motherdear. "Come help me fire up this stove. I must put on the rice for my boy's supper."

Jincey was glad to be able to build the fire for her and later she wished she had cooked the rice, too, for Motherdear sure-god made it gummy. But she seemed happy to be there and talked and sang and recited her poetry and Scriptures with fresh verve.

Jincey enjoyed it but she missed Della and followed Ruth around when she came to do the chores Motherdear couldn't do, like milking the cow and feeding the hogs. Ruth wasn't Della but she was the closest to Della of any person, Jincey reckoned.

The three shoats were fat. Jincey took a stick and, from a perch on the hogpen fence, scratched their backs while Ruth fed them. But they didn't seem to be eating. One of them continued to lie on his side, snorting and snoring, even after Ruth had thrown corn in the pen and poured slop in the trough.

"Do, Jesus, I believe Miss Della's pigs is sick," Ruth said. "Jincey, go tell Mist' Bart. He may know something to do."

Jincey didn't want to make the trip to the commissary but Ruth pushed her. "You know Miss Della counting on these pigs for winter meat. Now git off that fence and light a shuck!"

Bart searched his medicine shelf in the commissary and brought home two or three kinds of medicine, including copperas to mix up with warm mash for the pigs. He came in from the hogpen looking worried.

"I don't know if I've helped them any. They sure look funny. I'd hate to lose them, hard as Della's worked to raise them."

"Oh, and that lovely sausage and souse meat! Do save the swine, son, if you can!"

The rain stopped and it turned hot and bright and so dry Jincey never expected to get another ride to school. But one morning Reba stopped and picked up Jincey and the Bates children when they still had a mile to walk. The prospect of riding in Reba's new Model A was electrifying.

"I call the rumble seat!" yelled Zack as they ran toward the car.

"Dibs on the rumble seat!" echoed Virgie.

Jincey was disgusted with herself for not having been quick enough to grab the finest of places to ride in an automobile, the darling rumble seat, and she stomped irritably to the front of the car and opened the door—just as Reba moved a suitcase to the floor.

"Just put your feet on that suitcase, Jincey," she said. "It won't hurt it none."

"Ain't you gon' be late for school?" Jincey asked curiously, as

Reba started the car moving. To get all the way to high school in Mobile Reba had to leave an hour earlier than she did.

"I'm not going to school," Reba said.

"You ain't got a holiday," said Jincey flatly. "I know. I been watching the calendar, hoping one would come up to save me from Mrs. White. How come you ain't going to school?"

"If you must know," said Reba, "I'm running away ... to get married!"

"Married!" gasped Jincey. "You ain't that old!"

"I'm sixteen," Reba said calmly. "This car was my birthday present from Cap'n Barton."

"That's pretty old," agreed Jincey.

"Old enough," said Reba.

They rode along in silence, except for the delighted windy whoops and squeals coming from Virgie and Zack in the rumble seat. Jincey had known Reba was old, but *married?* She was struck dumb by the import of that news.

They turned in the highway by the Whites' store and Reba stopped the car.

"Y'all study hard," she said, flapping her hand as the three of them climbed out of the car and reached the ground. "And Jincey, don't say nothing about you-know-what till you git home tonight. Then you can tell."

"You mean you ain't told them?" gasped Jincey.

"Whatcha think loco." said Reba, letting out the clutch. "I'm running away!"

"Why's she running away?" asked Virgie, as Zack stood, bedazzled, watching the shiny little car kick up gravel in the distance.

"To git married," said Jincey.

Jincey didn't realize until later that she had told you-know-what, contrary to Reba's request, but it was all over the school in no time and, of course, Mrs. White heard it right away. She was in the store during the lunch recess when Cap'n Barton came in for the mail and she told him. He was waiting in his car for Jincey when she came out of school.

"Come on, little Della," he called out. "I'm gon' give you a ride home."

Two rides in one day, Jincey thought happily, and then she turned shy. She didn't want to go without Virgie and Zack and she didn't know how to ask Cap'n Barton if he planned to take them, too.

She hesitated on the steps.

"Ah, I know your name is something else," said Cap'n Barton. "I forget what. But come on, I'll take you home."

"It's Jincey," she told him carefully. "Jincey McPherson."

"Child, I don't care what your name is. Get in the car!" the man said impatiently.

His annoyance sparked the same in Jincey.

"You'll have to wait for Virgie and Zack," she said stubbornly.

Cap'n Barton threw back his head and laughed. "All right, little Jincey-Della-McPherson," he said, "we'll take the Bateses too. But I want to talk to you. Get in."

When she was in the front seat he was no longer laughing. His light blue eyes, very like Uncle Bart's and Motherdear's, were anxious and waiting.

"Where did Reba go?" he asked.

"To get married," said Jincey.

"You know who? And where?"

"No, sir," said Jincey, shaking her head. "She didn't say. Just said she was old enough and going."

The old man gnawed at his thumbnail and looked out across the schoolyard.

"Did she say to tell me anything?"

"No, sir, she just said I could tell it when I got home from school. But I forgot and told Virgie right away."

He sighed heavily. "Yes, I heard." He started up the car. "Here come the Bateses. Call 'em."

Awed by a trip in the Reo, the children were quiet all the way home. Jincey sat up straight and looked out the glass windows, but once she thought she heard Cap'n Barton making a noise like he was crying.

Buster walked up the road to visit Motherdear. When she had taken a chair and sat down Motherdear beamed on her and said sociably, "How is my sweet brother?"

"Well, he ain't sweet, I can tell you that much!" laughed Buster. "He's about as sweet as a sore bear."

Motherdear folded in her pink lips and rocked very fast. It sounded like criticism and criticism was not suitable from a servant. Jincey, listening, knew that much, but Buster didn't care. She considered herself as good as anybody and better than most and she ran her mouth when she wanted to.

Now Buster saw there was going to be a sag in the conversation and she hurried to tuck it up.

"It's that little girl that left," she said. "You know she run away to git married to some little squirt she met over at the Front and the Cap'n is plumb grieving hisself to death. He don't say nothing about it but I can tell. He hardly eats. I even made chicken pie yesterday and he barely touched it. And roam, that's the walkingest man I ever seen! Everywhere on the place walking."

"Walking is a very healthful exercise," put in Motherdear. "Of course, my brother has a nice car. He could ride if he wanted to. But our papa was quite a walker. I recollect that he walked over to the river to check his holdings over there—a distance of eight miles!—and was back before dark. He believed in walking."

"Well'm, I never knowed the Cap'n to walk before," said Buster. "He'd walk to his meals but until Reba left he was everywhere in that Reo. Now looks like he can't bear to git in it."

"Pooh," said Motherdear. "What would my brother care about a child? Daughter of a housekeeper, wasn't she?" she asked pointedly. "Robert Barton is a handsome man, if I do say so myself as shouldn't. He could have his pick of the young women in Mobile. His interest in that child was fatherly, nothing more."

She put her little feet on the floor and stood up. Buster, recognizing it as dismissal, stood up too, winking at Jincey. She got in a last lick as she picked up her sunhat.

"For a father, he sure did a heap of hugging and kissing," she said.

Jincey had trouble getting to sleep some nights. Della had been gone a week and she still had to fight the old fear that she might not come back. The nights were warm but she wrapped up in a gray outing-josie Della had left hanging in the closet, hugging it to her and smelling the Della smell of morning cooking and Mavis talcum powder and Elizabeth Arden night cream around the collar.

One night she huddled in the old robe on her cot, thinking of Della and listening to Motherdear and Bart snore. Bart's snores, coming from one side, were keen, light snores. Motherdear, on the other side, was a gruff, mannish kind of snorer, Jincey decided. You wouldn't think a soft, puddingy old lady could snore so fierce.

She stirred and wrapped the josie closer and prepared to go to sleep when a sharp gun blast sounded near the commissary.

"Uncle Bart!" Jincey called, but his snoring had ended abruptly and he was hitting the floor.

Jincey, still wrapped in Della's robe, was in the doorway as Bart pulled on his pants and grabbed his pistol and flashlight.

"What is it, Uncle Bart? Can I go, too?"

"No, no!" Bart said. "You stay here with Motherdear. If she wakes up, tell her . . . I don't know. I'll be back."

He was gone, a little shaft of light bobbing down the road.

Jincey stood by the window listening and watching a while. She saw the lights go on in the commissary. A whippoorwill sounded back in the woods but there was no other sound, except Motherdear's snoring. Her feet felt cold and she got back in bed to warm them and presently she slept.

When Jincey woke she thought for a minute Della was home and the mill was running again. There was the smell of meat frying in the kitchen and a throbbing, whining sound coming from somewhere. Then she knew it was not the mill but Motherdear crying. Wailing, sobbing, noisy crying.

She got out of bed and hurried into the dining room. Motherdear sat at the table with her head pillowed on her arms and Uncle Bart stood beside her, patting her shoulder, offering her one of his best white Sunday handkerchiefs. Ruth was in the kitchen cooking breakfast.

"What is it, Uncle Bart? What's the matter?"

Bart said gently, "I'll talk to you in a minute, Jincey. Go see Ruth."

Ruth was stirring the grits when she went in the kitchen, but she put down the spoon and sat down and pulled Jincey onto her lap.

"Cap'n Barton's dead, Honey," she said. "Old Mr. Hascall thought he was a robber and blowed his head off. It sho' is bad. Law come out and got the old man and put him in jail."

"Cap'n Barton, where's he?" asked Jincey fearfully, remembering the traveling woman's stiff little body lying in the front room.

"Undertaker's in Mobile. Mist' Bart up all night, telephoning. He got me and Matthew up to hep him. Sho' was a mess. Blood and brains all over the ground."

Jincey began to cry. Not for Cap'n Barton or Mr. Hascall in jail or blood and brains on the ground. She didn't know why she was crying except that Della wasn't there.

"Hush, baby, hush!" crooned Ruth, bumping the straight chair back and forth to make it rock. "Ruth wid you and Miss Della coming home today. Mist' Bart done sent the telegram."

A lot of relatives came out from town and as far away as New Orleans and Richmond, Virginia, for the funeral. Some of them stayed in the rooms over the commissary and Buster fixed for others at the boardinghouse.

Motherdear and Mary stayed with Della and Bart.

"Bartons is swarming," Ruth told Della. "Most of 'em ain't see the Cap'n since they grandpa died, but they heah now!"

"Well, where there's a death . . ." Della started to say.

"Where there's death, there's hope!" said Mary from the doorway. She held a glass in her hand—tea, Jincey thought, although nobody else drank iced tea before breakfast.

"Hope of heaven?" asked Della, without looking up from the onions she was chopping to go in potato salad for later.

"You could say that," giggled Mary. "I was thinking of hope, that all of us, who got deprived by our rights by Uncle Bob, can now start to live a little. I know he promised to leave the bulk of his estate to Bubba—but is that fair? I don't think so and neither do any of the others. Grandpa was an old crazy who believed that only the males in the family should inherit. He left his daughters one hundred dollars a piece and everything else to

Uncle Bob. You can see why there's no love lost between him and his sisters. Some of them will be glad to chip in to pay for that fancy coffin he's in!"

"Motherdear . . ." began Della, for Motherdear had not stopped crying for two days.

"Oh, A.K.," said Mary scornfully. "Annie Katherine hasn't got sense enough to hate him. Her mind quit functioning back when they were children picking pomegranates together."

"Well, with the mill shut down and nothing coming in, I don't reckon there's a lot to fight over," said Della.

Mary hiccoughed gently and, holding the door frame with one hand, carefully turned herself around.

"Only about a million dollars," she said over her shoulder.

Della wouldn't let Jincey go to the funeral. It was no place for a child, she said, and Bart agreed. Ruth said she would stay home with her.

"Matthew going but he be's family," Ruth explained. "Me and Jincey gon' stay home and freeze the cream and ice the cake for after the funeral."

But none of the relatives came back to the mill after the graveside services in the pine grove cemetery over at Bayou Bien.

Even Motherdear and Mary went back to Mobile.

"Reckon they all rushing to see their lawyers," Bart said, smiling wryly at Della as they sat down to supper.

"Is there really a lot of money?" Della asked.

Bart nodded.

"Well, why did he let folks around here go on starvation?" she demanded. "Flathead and Jerusha sleeping under a bridge. You staying up all night to make a old car run when he could have bought you a new one, like he did for that little hussy, Reba! Motherdear and Mary taking money from you when he had plenty. That old woman . . ." her voice broke.

"I reckon he was afraid it wouldn't last," Bart said, standing up. "People got money, they worry about things like that."

"Then if you ask me," said Della, beginning to stack the plates. "Old man Hascall did a good day's work!"

Bart looked shocked and then just tired, gray-faced, weak-tired.

He turned from the table. "I got to go back down there," he said. "I want to telephone the sheriff about Mr. Hascall. What he did was my fault. I persuaded Uncle Bob to give him the watching job. He wanted to run him off the place. The old man couldn't see good and he was bad to drop off to sleep. He wasn't expecting Uncle Bob to come walking through the mill at night. He'd always driven in before. He woke up and was scared and just pulled the trigger, I reckon. It was my fault."

"Tell them that," said Della sarcastically, when he was out of earshot. "And maybe they'll put you in jail instead."

Mr. Hascall did finally come home on Bart's say-so and went back to his house up the road. But he was a different old man now, even Jincey could see. He wouldn't do any more watching, although Bart sort of halfway suggested it as a job for him, and he didn't take pleasure in sitting on the steps reading his Robert Ingersoll book.

He would take buttermilk, if Della sent it to him by Jincey, but he wouldn't come by the house to get it any more. One day Jincey went with the milk and he wasn't there. She looked in the house and his things were gone—the blanket, the coffeepot, the skillet, the bar of soap and the razor.

Bart looked sad when Jincey, breathless from running, rushed in to the commissary to tell him about it.

"Poor old man," he said. "Poor old man."

Later he and Della walked over to the house to see if Mr. Hascall had left a note or any sign to tell them where he had gone. There was nothing but the bare cot, the cold ashes on the hearth and a few brown leaves blowing across the floor.

"You reckon they'll blame you for gittin' him out of jail and letting him run off?" Della asked.

"They could," Bart said. "I reckon they could."

The Barton relatives may have blamed Uncle Bart. They went to court and lawyers and bookkeepers arrived and spent days in the office reading ledgers and papers.

Bart made them welcome and took his rod and reel down off a hook on the wall and spent the afternoon in Jincey's pirogue at the head of the pond fishing.

Buster, with no meals to cook, swept the offices and commissary and the upstairs rooms a lot, trying to find out what the men were up to.

"The way I got it figgered," she told Della, "if they could ketch Mister Bart in something the least bit out of the way, they'd run him off the place and divide everything up between that crowd from Mobile and them other towns off yonder."

"You reckon?" said Della. "They won't find Bart McPherson doing anything out of the way, I can promise you that." She sighed. "But Lord, ain't it a mess?"

One afternoon Buster paused at the steps before she came in and asked, "You got company? I don't want to butt in, if you have."

Della had come around the corner of the house from the hog-pen.

"Company? Why you ask that? I never have company. My shoats is missing. Rooted their way out of the hogpen and gone. Wonder what on earth could of happened to them."

"Cholera," said Buster. "They didn't root out. They died and Mister Bart had 'em took out. All the hogs around here got the cholera. Ain't one alive on the place."

Della sat down hard on the edge of the gallery.

"My pretty pigs," she said. "So fine and fat. What will I do?"

Jincey, recognizing it as real loss, edged closer and sat beside her on the gallery.

"The winter meat," said Della. "All we had."

"Yeah," said Buster sympathetically. "It sure is bad."

They sat on in silence for a time and Della finally pulled herself up and said, "Come on in. I got the coffee hot."

"The company I was speaking about," said Buster, seating herself at the kitchen table, "was your sister-in-law and them friends of your'n from Mobile—you know the policeman and his wife?"

"Tee and Ina. Did they come out here?" asked Della, surprised. "And with Mary? I didn't know that. You sure?"

"Seen 'em over at the commissary, standing talking to Mister Bart," said Buster. "I had to go upstairs and when I come down they was gone. Thought sure they'd come up here."

Della waited uneasily for Bart to come in but he was late getting home and when he had just walked in the door and taken off his hat, Matthew, riding the black horse, Rip, galloped up to the gate.

"Mist' Bart, fire! Fire in the woods!" he shouted. "Traveling toward the turpentine still!"

Bart grabbed his hat and ran out the door.

"I'll take the car and rout out what men are left in the quarters. You go on back and start wetting down anything in its path that you can. Della, Jincey, you can help. Go get on the telephone and get central to call the government fire tower and anybody else that can help us!"

They ran every step of the way to the office and Della made the call, cranking the wall phone and shouting until she was sure the voice answering "Mo-beeuhl!" knew what she was talking about.

Then she grabbed Jincey's hand and they ran across the bridge, through the lumberyards and past the Bates's house toward the still. Mrs. Bates and her children were already in the woods, going to meet the fire that was gnawing its red-tongued way toward them across the pine straw, with green pine tops in their hands, beating out the low, nibbling blaze and whapping at flames. The wind hadn't seemed to be blowing but the fire made its own wind—a blazing, roaring wind that turned pine trees, their catfaces flowing with rosin, into pillars of flame and sucked and growled across the dry earth, consuming everything in its path.

Bart ran from group to group, shouting instructions. Clewis and Matthew were sent to hitch up the mules and plow a fire break between the now-smouldering turpentine still and the lumberyards. Zack was sent to start the ram, a little pump down in the creek that ordinarily filled the planer boiler but was now connected to a hose they were going to turn on the planer shed to wet it down.

"Where's Old Pa, Miss Eva?" Bart asked after he had dispatched Zack.

Miss Eva, her face smoke-blackened, her hair streaming in sooty tendrils, lifted stricken eyes to his.

"I ain't seen him since noon, Mist' Bart," she said, stumbling a little from weariness, and went on beating at the fire. A truckload of men from the Front arrived and went to work with hoes and pine tops. Ashes and bits of burning bark flew through the air and settled on faces and clothes. Jincey smelled her hair burning and she slapped at it with one hand and brushed ashes out of her eyes with the other.

"I think they got it out at the still," Ruth said, stopping to catch her breath.

Della turned to look at the dark shed, which housed the turpentine still and the vats of rosin. Its roof steamed from the water but it seemed to be whole.

Suddenly she let out a scream and Jincey and Ruth jerked around to see the wooden staves of one of the many barrels of rosin falling apart—slowly, gracefully, like a flower opening— and a molten tide of amber-colored gum flowing like a river straight for Bart's feet.

"Bart, look out!" screamed Della. And he turned but the liquid fire pushed and laved at his feet and swept him down like a floating log.

Jincey heard his cry, a piercing, womanish scream of pure agony, and she saw the men running to him.

They carried Uncle Bart to the house and cut his clothes off him as well as they could. Dr. Willis came and looked at him and told Della they couldn't move him again. He wouldn't even try to dig out the chunks of rosin, which had cooled and hardened like brown bottle glass and were embedded in his flesh.

Dr. Willis took off his coat and rolled up his sleeves and went in the kitchen and made gauze poultices and showed Della how to put them on Bart's body, replacing them with new ones as they dried.

He stayed all day and at sunset, when he prepared to go, Della walked to the gallery with him.

"Will he live?" she asked.

He shook his head. "I don't know how long. Maybe a while— weeks, a month, I don't know. With pain like that, it's better ... it would be better ..."

"Will he be conscious again?"

The doctor shifted his bag to his other hand and sighed tiredly.

"I've seen some badly burned people—ship explosions in the bay—that did get better. I couldn't say. You never know. He could."

"Will you git word to his mother?" Della asked.

Ruth and Matthew came and took turns with Della in changing the damp poultices. As the days passed the stench of burnt flesh was heavy in the house. Della walked out into the air when she could. Matthew followed her to the gate one afternoon and said, "You know they find Mist' Old Pa."

"They found him," Della said dully. "I didn't know he was lost."

"Yes'm, night of the fire. Mist' Bart couldn't find him. Miss Eva neither."

"Where was he?" Della asked without much interest.

"Dead. Burned to death in the woods. It was his shinny still caught the woods on fire. Spark from the kettle. He tried to put it out and it got away from him. Trapped him. They found him soon as the woods got cool enough to look."

"Oh, Lord, Lord!" cried Della. "Poor Miss Eva. Poor young'-uns."

"Yes'm," said Matthew. "Funeral's tomorrow."

Della couldn't go but she sent Jincey over with a basket of canned vegetables and fruit from her pantry and five dollars she had been saving.

Mary and Motherdear had arrived and surprisingly decided to stay at the boardinghouse instead of with them.

"We've come to help you if you need us but I think we should stay out of the way until you do," Mary said. But the way she caught her breath and gagged at the smell and hurried outside, Jincey knew she wouldn't spend much time with them.

Motherdear was there a lot, crying and praying and saying Scripture until Della held her ears in pain and urged her to go to the boardinghouse and get some rest.

One night when Della was alone with Bart and Jincey had gone to bed in the next room, Bart moaned and tried to turn and opened his eyes. Jincey tumbled out of bed and ran to the door.

Della was on her feet.

"You awake! You want water?" She had been getting as much in his mouth as she could without strangling him.

He nodded his head painfully.

"Jincey, run!" she said.

Jincey brought the water and Della held up his head to help him sip it. She swabbed his dry and cracked lips with a rag dipped in ice water and mopped his forehead which was raw and peeling from the fire. He smiled at her and closed his eyes.

"You're better," said Della sagging wearily into the rocker. "Bless the Lord, you really are better! Can you eat a little something? Gruel if I make it fast or a little cold milk?"

He shook his head. "Want to talk," he whispered.

Della leaned closer.

"Not legally married," he faltered. "No divorce. Got to get a divorce so . . . you and Jincey . . . taken care of."

"Don't you worry, Hon," Della said, taking his puffy, blistered hand gently. "Don't you worry."

He closed his eyes and seemed to sleep. Della paced the floor the rest of the night, pausing by the bed every few minutes to search his face.

Jincey, hunched up in the rocker in the corner, waited and watched and finally fell asleep and Della half lifted, half dragged her to her bed.

The next morning Ruth and Matthew and Motherdear were all in the kitchen and Della, hollow-eyed from lack of sleep, reached for a cup of coffee and turned to them.

"I think he's better," she said. "He was conscious a few times during the night. He talked to me, asked me to tend to some business for him today. If you all can take care of him till I git back . . . ?"

"You know we will," said Ruth.

"I'll be right here, right beside my baby boy!" cried Motherdear.

"It might take most of the day," Della said. "I'll take Jincey and the car."

In the car, Della explained to Jincey that they were going to take a train when they got to Mobile.

"I'm not sure this old Lizzie will make it beyond Chickasa-bogue swamp, much less to Pensacola," said Della grimly. She had on the brown suit she had made herself the winter before and an old hat she had tried to freshen up by appliquéing velvet poppies on the crown two years before. Jincey wore her Sunday dress.

"Why we going to Pensacola?" Jincey asked.

"Bart told me to," Della said. "To git a divorce."

"From who, Aunt Della, who?" asked Jincey.

"Come to think about it," said Della, turning in the seat to look at her, "maybe from *both* of them! I didn't think. He had so much trouble talking. I thought he meant himself and he must of meant Howie, too. He said we would marry again so it would be legal when the Barton money thing comes up."

She was quiet, concentrating on the road.

"I didn't know Howie didn't git the divorce, although I might have known he wouldn't pay," she said and laughed harshly. "Miss Mary, with the help of Ina and Tee, sure found it out! That's what they come out to tell Bart the day of the fire! Reckon they would of used it against him, too."

Jincey clung to the seat with both hands and took a deep breath.

"Don't divorce Uncle Bart, heah?"

Della smiled at her. "I'll have to ask a lawyer what to do. Bart said go where we're not known. I reckon Pensacola will do."

They found an early train leaving and got off in Pensacola in the late morning.

"Let's walk a little," said Della. "I feel stiff."

They walked up Palafox Street toward the big San Carlos Hotel. Della stopped in front of it and looked in toward the lobby with its big chairs and its palm trees.

"Lord, Lord," she said softly. "The San Carlos. I always thought this must be the finest, most exclusive hotel in the world. I never was in it but now . . ." She turned and looked at Jincey. "I believe I'll buy a cup of coffee here, even if it costs twenty-five cents!"

In the big dining room with a crisp, white tablecloth between them, Della ordered coffee for herself and hot cocoa for Jincey.

While it was coming she said, "You remember my old friend, Bessie Johnson? Madame Zillah, she called herself. I believe I'll call her and ask the name of a lawyer to see."

The coffee and cocoa came and with them a check for fifty cents.

"Highway robbery," muttered Della, but she found two quarters in her worn and peeling brown pocketbook and then fished out a nickel for a tip.

"While I'm here I'll use their telephone, too," she said, heading toward the booth in the lobby. Through the glass door Jincey could tell Della had found Madame Zillah, and in a little while they were on a streetcar on their way to her house.

The barber sign in front of Madame Zillah's house no longer revolved and the big hand advertising palm readings had been knocked catawhankers by the last hurricane. Weeds grew in the narrow plot of front yard and on the porch the old swing hung by one rusty chain.

"Desolate," muttered Della. "Poor Bessie."

Before they could ring the doorbell or knock, the door opened and a thin wraith of a woman in a greasy old bathrobe peered out at them.

"Who is it?" she asked querulously.

"Bessie!" cried Della. "It's Della—and Jincey. Remember?"

"Oh, yes," said the little woman listlessly. "You called. You both want readings? I don't cut hair no more."

"Bessie!" cried Della. "Don't you remember me—Della! You and the ouija board sent me off to Mobile and I found that light-complected man you told me you saw in the cards."

"Yes, well, come on in," Bessie said dully.

The room was hot and the old sofa Madame Zillah motioned them toward smelled of dogs. Jincey looked around, expecting to see the pack of poodles she remembered from her last visit there.

Della brushed hair off a cushion before she sat, rolling her eyes and making a face at Jincey.

"You still have the dogs?" she said to Bessie.

"They're dead," the old woman whimpered. "All dead. My beautiful friends are dead. All dead."

Her eyes brimmed with tears.

"Oh, I'm sorry," Della said hastily. "You do get attached to a dog and they can't live as long as we do, of course. I know you miss them."

She cleared her throat and changed the subject. "Bessie, it's been a while since that day I came here running from Little Howie and you sent me off to Mobile. You remember?"

Bessie reflected, reaching for a deck of cards on a little table by the sofa.

"I get so many customers," she said. "Did you both want readings? It'll be a dollar and a dime apiece."

Della looked at Jincey and shrugged helplessly.

"Just me," she said. "Jincey has plenty of time to worry about her fortune."

Bessie started to shuffle the cards and Della looked at Jincey. "Honey, why don't you go walk around the yard? The air is so fresh and nice outside this time of day."

Gratefully, Jincey pulled herself out of the hairy, smelly old sofa and headed for the door.

"Goodbye, Miss Zillah," she said.

The old lady didn't answer. Her fingers fumbled with the worn cards and she spilled a third of them as she attempted to deal them out on the table. As Jincey opened the door and closed it behind herself she heard the old refrain: "To your house, to your heart, to what's sure to come true . . ."

There was no place to sit on the porch and Jincey was too tired to wander up and down the sidewalk. She stood by the steps and stared at the dead, non-revolving barber sign. Divorce, she thought, and some of the old dread of the word took hold of her. Divorce. Bart thought divorce was a sin but he was asking for one.

To make things legal, Della said. But suppose it didn't work? Jincey shivered in the hot afternoon sun. I could ask Daddy, she suddenly thought. If I begged him, maybe he would go give that lawyer the money and we could go back home and be all right.

In a few minutes Della came out of the house, brushing her suit and taking deep breaths to get the dog stench from her nose and lungs.

"Whoo!" she said. "What a dump. Poor Bessie. Did you ever in your life see anything more pitiful? I wouldn't have spent that 'dollar and dime' with her but I think she needed the money— maybe worse than we do. Jincey, she never did remember who I was!"

"Aunt Della, I could ask him..." Jincey began.

"Wasn't it funny," Della went on, unhearing, "that I was all set to reunion with a old friend? I was going to git advice and help and... well, comfort, I reckon. And it was like she had never seen me before."

Della stumbled over a rough bit of sidewalk and Jincey reached out a hand to her. To her surprise Della had tears in her eyes.

"Guess what my fortune was," she said, laughing shakily and wiping her eyes. "Same as before! I'm gon' meet a light-complected man. A light-complected man who'll love me and be good to me and mine!"

Suddenly she started laughing. She put one arm around Jincey and crossed her stomach with the other one and laughed and laughed as if she'd never stop.

Jincey started to laugh with her and then she stopped, uncertain and uneasy.

"To your house, to your heart...! said Della, choking and sputtering and doubling up with laughter, while tears streamed down her cheeks.

Jincey stood and waited and after a time Della wiped her eyes weakly and strove for sternness. "You set me off, Jincey. You made me make a fool of myself like this."

The streetcar came and they got on and after they had rattled along for several blocks, Jincey tried again. "If you want me to, I could ask Daddy to git the divorce... to pay."

"Lot of good that'll do," said Della absently. "I'll git it myself —both of 'em. Bart said to and I will. It's the only thing he ever asked of me."

"But he don't want one from us," protested Jincey. "He loves us."

Della sighed.

"Love's a word. It means anything you want it to mean. He asked for a divorce and that's what he's gon' git." She looked ahead. "There's the First National Bank building. Let's git off."

But before they went in Della stopped.

"I think I'll call the mill and see if anybody's there and can tell me how he's doing."

Buster answered the telephone and Della came out of the booth looking trembly-tired.

"Worse. The doctor's there. Said come at once."

She took a deep breath and reached for Jincey's hand. "They always say, 'Come at once.' "

There were no more trains to Mobile that day but a bus would be leaving in an hour. Della bought tickets and got some coffee for herself and a cold drink for Jincey and they walked up and down Palafox Street looking in store windows.

Once they passed the park where she had played and Jincey looked at the green iron bench, half expecting to see the man with the ice skates there. Della was silent and Jincey thought she was glad to keep moving until she finally stopped and leaned against a storefront and said, "Childee, I'm so tired. Let's sit somewhere."

They went back to the bus-station waiting room and Della sagged into one of the seats and closed her eyes.

Jincey watched the people line up at the ticket counter and listened to a nasal voice over the loudspeaker announcing the departure of buses for Cantonment and De Funiak Springs. The smell of bus-station hot dogs was strong in the air.

"You hungry?" Della asked once.

Jincey shook her head. "Do you think you would know if he dies before we get there?" Jincey asked after a while.

Della nodded. "I think I would. But I can stand it," she said. "You can stand what you have to. A grown person's dying is natural and to be expected. What you never git over . . . ." She paused and her voice dropped so low she might have been talking to herself . . . "You never git over the death of a baby."

Jincey said nothing. That baby, that long-ago baby she could barely remember, was as fresh and real in Della's mind as the day he died. Della could love him who had never really *been* but she could stand to lose Uncle Bart, who was.

Della's hands on her worn, old pocketbook were red and swollen, the nails broken short. It was the first time she had noticed, Jincey realized. She always thought of Della's hands as being slim and long-fingered and young. Now they were old-looking hands. Her eyes traveled up the homemade brown suit to Della's face and she saw the crushed tissue-paper lines around her eyes for the first time.

"Mama?" Jincey said anxiously.

Della, pulled from whatever she was thinking about, turned toward her impatiently.

"Go git me some coffee, Jincey," she said, handing her a nickel.

Jincey stood up. Her legs tingled, her body was numb from weariness and waiting. She walked around Della to the lunch counter and asked for coffee and stood waiting and watching the buses outside disgorge their loads. Most of the passengers were women and children but one man walked among them, a very tall man in faded overalls with a dark-blue billed cap pulled low over his forehead. There was something familiar about him and Jincey wondered if he was somebody who had worked at the mill. He turned the corner of the building and Jincey picked up the paper cup of coffee and went back to the waiting room.

Della was hunched down in the seat with a newspaper spread before her face, too close for reading. Jincey looked at her and saw she was trembling.

"What's wrong?" Jincey whispered.

"Look," gasped Della. "Look there in the window!"

Jincey looked. The man in the faded-blue overalls stood with his back against the plate glass in front of them. His hands were busy with a pocketknife and a little stick of wood.

"It's Howie," whispered Della. "I don't want him to see us! Is he looking this way? He might try to git on our bus and go back with us. He looks in here at the clock now and then. He might see us!"

"I could go and talk to him," began Jincey.

"No!" whispered Della fiercely. "Have him land up at Barton's Mill? No!" But she lowered the paper and suddenly she started giggling.

"Look in his hip pocket," she said.

Jincey had already seen it, the edge of a black book with gold letters which plainly said, "Holy Bible."

The nasal voice near the ceiling somewhere called the bus to Milton and the man in the window folded his knife and put it in his pocket, threw the stick on the sidewalk and walked toward the loading platform.

"Thank God," breathed Della. "He's going back to where he belongs. Pore-do. I couldn't have taken a minute of his foolishness on top of everything else we've got ahead of us."

"I might of talked to him," Jincey began doggedly, but Della wasn't listening.

"Wouldn't you know, wouldn't you know," she repeated, "the son of a bitch would have a Bible in his pocket?"

Della and Jincey drove into the yard near midnight but all the lights in the house were on and as they stumbled wearily out of the car half a dozen people, who were sitting in chairs around the yard, stood up.

Matthew was the first to reach them.

"Is he dead?" Della asked.

"Yes'm. He gone." said Matthew.

Della reached out a hand and touched his shoulder. "Po' Jack," she said softly.

"Yes'm. Po'Boy," he said and ducked his head to hide his eyes and the way his mouth wobbled.

Ruth was there in a minute, enveloping them in her arms. She led them around the house to the kitchen and helped Della off with her hat and coat and made them sit down."

"But I want to see him," Della said.

"No'm, you don't," said Ruth. "He gone. The undertaker come and it be's best, Honey, bes'. He was so bad off. Dr. Willis was here when he died—'most dark it was—and he have Miss Buster telephone the undertaker to come git him."

Della looked around her. "Where's Motherdear? And Mary?"

"Doctor give Miss Annie Katherine a pill to ease her and Miss Mary 'bout drunk so they gone off to the bo'dinghouse to bed."

"Who's that under the tree?" Della asked.

"Be the hands, all that's left. If it be all right with you, they gon' wake him here, even if his body gone. They gon' stay up all night."

Della stood up. "I should go out and say something to them."

"No'm," said Ruth firmly. "They be here tomorrow, too. For the funeral. You all bes' go to bed now."

Jincey leaned against Della, crying.

"Oh, childee," Della said, sitting down and taking her into her lap. "Poor childee." She turned to Ruth.

"She ought to be in bed. But I don't ... I can't ..."

"Sho' you can," said Ruth. "Me and Lil' Sister and Big Sister, we's cleaned up and aired everything and you and Jincey just go on and crawl in your own bed. Us gon' stay up."

Della and Jincey undressed and climbed into bed and Ruth came and pulled a sheet and a faded thin quilt over them. The room where Bart had lain was neat and straight and free of medicine bottles and pans and poultices. The bed was taut and smooth and cool, fresh air blew in the windows.

Outside the voices of Matthew and Percy and Clewis and Flathead murmured softly.

Jincey slept and when she woke up Motherdear and Mary were in the dining room and Della was serving them grits and eggs and fried meat. Della had washed her hair and pressed the brown suit and put it back on and she had laid out a good dress and clean socks and underwear for Jincey.

Motherdear saw Jincey come out of the bathroom and she stopped eating and started crying.

"My boy, my baby boy, he's gone!" she sobbed, reaching out to Jincey.

"Don't do that!" Della said sharply. "She's been through enough for a young'un! She loves him, too."

"And well she might," drawled Mary. "Did he ever adopt her?"

Della handed Jincey a hot biscuit and passed her pear preserves to go on it.

"It didn't come up," she said, not looking at Mary but staring out the window, the biscuit plate still in her hands. "He would have. He wanted to take care of her."

"If he'd wanted to he could have made her an heiress, you know. She could have inherited everything. Not you, a common-law wife. You'd have trouble."

Della's mouth dropped open.

"A what?"

"You know that's all you are—his common-law wife. You were never divorced so you've been living in what they call sin. Worse. You're a bigamist."

Della set the biscuit plate down carefully and walked around the table and, Jincey watching, saw her hand go out like it was on a spring. There was a flat smack, Mary's head flipped to one side and back again. There were red fingermarks on her cheek.

Della stood looking at her.

Motherdear stopped eating and closed her eyes and started babbling the Twenty-third Psalm to herself.

"You slay me," Mary said, laying a soft, white hand against her cheek. "I could have helped persuade the others to give you some kind of settlement. Say, five thousand dollars. But now if you want to go to court and fight for your rights as my brother's woman, you're on your own. I won't lift a finger to help you."

"You listen to me," said Della, gripping the back of Jincey's chair with both hands. "I respect Barton McPherson's memory too much to go to court and say I was his common-law wife and fight over money. He was good to me and Jincey. He fed us and give us a home. I worked for it but he made it possible. Now I ain't fighting for a dime of that poison Barton money. Far as I can see, it's brought little or no happiness to anybody in this world! It's setting up somewhere letting pore niggers starve and driving a man like Old Pa Bates to kill himself making shinny. You think I want any part of that money? Not on your tintype. I can work for what I git. You buzzards flap on in there and fight over the bones!"

They had a graveside funeral service. Brother Doby Webster got off work at the railroad to conduct it. The undertaker had asked for a list of twelve pallbearers, six active and six honorary.

"You mean white men?" Della asked. She couldn't think of

anybody fit to bear Bart's body to the grave except Matthew and Percy and Flathead and Firemen, but Motherdear finally came up with a list, which included the bookkeepers and lawyers from Mobile and Mr. White, the postmaster at Bayou Bien.

Brother Webster talked a long time but Jincey, standing between Della and Ruth and clinging to their hands, didn't listen or look at the gray coffin, poised over the grave on little boards. A chill wind was stirring around in the tops of the pine trees, making a mournful sound. On the other side of Della, Motherdear whimpered.

The congregation from the church sang "Near the Cross" and Jincey started to sing with them but Della squeezed her hand and she stopped.

Where was Uncle Bart? Gone to glory, Brother Doby Webster said, but where was glory? She couldn't see him liking golden streets when he didn't even like a town. If he was freed from his hurting, breath-starved body he would be walking the pine-needle-covered slope beyond the millpond. Or fishing. She liked to think that he might be fishing.

Brother Webster ended with a prayer and the undertaker's men eased the coffin into the ground and started shoveling dirt on it.

"Oh, my baby boy!" screeched Motherdear, rushing to the hole in the ground.

"For God's sake, grab her!" Mary snapped at one of the pall-bearing lawyers.

People were coming up and speaking to them but Della, holding Jincey by the hand, smiled and nodded and slipped through them to where Ruth and Matthew now stood at the edge of the graveyard.

"Well," she said, standing in front of them. "I reckon that's over. We'll go now."

"Miss, you cold!" said Matthew.

"Sho' is," said Ruth.

"Here, wrap up," said Matthew, taking the too-long overcoat he was wearing and putting it around Della's shoulders. "It was Mist' Bart's. He give it to me. Never would wear a overcoat!"

"No," said Della, smiling. "He wouldn't."

She hugged Ruth. "You take care of the cow and chickens and Jincey's dog. Make 'em give you any of my stuff you want."

She turned, pulling Jincey along with her.

"Take care of yourself. I'll write to you someday and maybe we'll meet again."

Jincey hadn't noticed that Della's trunk was on the backseat. It shifted, bumping the front seat, and she turned and looked at it.

"We gone," she said hopelessly.

"We sure-god are," said Della, leaning into the steering wheel.

"Where?" asked Jincey after a time.

"Why, Aunt Sweetie's, I reckon," said Della. "Where else would we go but to our blood kin? We'll stay awhile and then I reckon I'll think of something."

About the Author

Celestine Sibley, reporter-columnist for the *Atlanta Constitution,* has covered every assignment known to newspapering, including floods, fires, murder trials, presidents, politics, and movie stars.

A native of Holly, Florida, she grew up in Mobile County, Alabama, attending public schools and Spring Hill College. She began work on the *Mobile Press-Register* as a fifteen-year-old high school student and continued there until her marriage to a fellow reporter, James W. Little. Her husband, a copy editor on the *Atlanta Journal,* died in August, 1953.

Ms. Sibley has twice served as a juror for Pulitzer Prize newspaper awards, the most distinguished awards in journalism. She has won many awards, including: the National Christopher Award, two citations from the Georgia Conference on Social Work for her stories, and an unprecedented commendation from the Georgia House of Representatives, which she covered for more than twenty years.

Ms. Sibley is the mother of three children, the grandmother of five, and is a member of the Roswell Presbyterian Church, and the author of ten books, previously published.